Peach Blossom RANCHER

People are talking about *Peach Blossom Rancher*:

"*Peach Blossom Rancher* is a fast paced, attention-grabbing book full of action. A great read!"

—Penny Zeller,
author of the *Montana Skies* historical romance series.

"I want Polly to live near me. Not just for the food, which made my mouth water, but she made my Spirit sing too. I feel my absolute faith a little stronger after living with her and Abe this week."

—Deidre Lockart

Peach Blossom RANCHER

ADA BROWNELL

Elk Lake Publishing, Inc.

Plymouth, Massachusetts

Elk Lake Publishing

Peach Blossom Rancher

Copyright © 2016 by Ada Brownell

Requests for information should be addressed to:

Elk Lake Publishing, Publishing, Inc., 35 Dogwood Dr, Plymouth, MA 02360

ISBN-13 Number: 978-1-944430-20-7 paperback; 978-1-944430-21-4 e-book

All rights reserved. No part of this publication, either text or image may be used for any purpose other than personal use. Therefore, reproduction, modification, storage in a retrieval system or retransmission, in any form or by any means, electronic, mechanical or otherwise, for reasons other than personal use, except for brief quotations in reviews or articles and promotions, is strictly prohibited without prior written permission from the publisher.

Cover: Jeff Gifford, GradientIdea.com

Interior Design: Melinda Martin

Editor: Deidre Lockhart, Deb Haggerty

This is a work of fiction. Names, characters, places, and incidents either are the product of the author's imagination, or are used fictitiously, and any resemblance to actual persons, living or dead, businesses, companies, events, or locales is entirely coincidental.

Unless otherwise indicated, Scripture quotations are from the King James Version. For those from the New King James Version, © 1984 by Thomas Nelson, used by permission.

Quotations from the NIV are from the New International Version published by the Zondervan Corporation, The Holy Bible, New International Version®, NIV® Copyright © 1973, 1978, 1984, 2011 by biblica, inc.™ used by permission. All rights reserved worldwide.

Dedication

An Historical Romance dedicated to my husband,
Lester C. Brownell

Acknowledgments

Special thanks to
Deirdre Lockhart of Brilliant Cut Editing,

Fred St. Laurent of
Book Club Network.com and Book Fun Magazine.com,

and

Deb Haggerty of Elk Lake Publishing, Inc.

ADA BROWNELL

1

March 1, 1909

"Come on, boy. Your hard life is over."

The sleek stallion pulled back, snorted, grunted, yanked his head upward, and tried to whirl away. John Lincoln Parks held the reins tight. "Come on. The judge isn't here. The whip's in your past."

Bringing the animal all the way from Colorado's Eastern Slope after the judge's death hadn't been easy and tiredness hung from him. The judge, John's uncle, murdered near Yucca Blossom, would never return to the horse ranch and acres of peach orchards he expected to inherit from John's father.

"He look like he a good 'un to breed." Sweat glistened on Abe's crinkled chocolate brow. "But an animal abused like 'im usually disobedient or loses his spirit."

John rubbed the stallion's neck and then extended a sugar cube in his hand. "I don't want to give up on him yet. Come on, boy. We're friends. You should be tired and hungry after your train trip."

A long red tongue licked the sugar cube into the toothy mouth.

Abe followed John to the horse barn. "I'll get 'im some oats and fill the water trough. He a right pretty animal except fa the welts the judge left on 'im."

"If I'd stayed with the judge, my back would look like his. But you know more about whippings than I do since you went to work on that plantation after Papa became ill and the owner couldn't get it through his head you're not a slave. I'm so sorry. Where's Polly? I hope she's made chicken and noodles and apple pie."

"That woman so happy to have you back, boy. She grieved for Jenny too when she go. But when I came back and walk into this place, that made up for it. Took me too long. She know you coming and is stirring up chicken and dumplin's. Ya like peach cobbler and ice cream? Soon as I'm through here, I need to start turning the freezer."

John tugged the reins gently and guided the stallion into a sturdy stall with an open window out the other side. The horse's head shot up as he kicked, breaking a board in the stall wall.

"Steady there." John touched the animal whose nostrils flared as he snorted. "Don't break a leg."

He extended another sugar lump. The toothy mouth opened, and the treat disappeared.

"Let him settle down before you feed him," Abe advised as he secured the stall gate. "He probably remembers this barn."

The animal flicked his head, tossing a glorious mane and testing the ground with his hooves. John smiled. "We'll need to make new memories. After tonight, we set him free in the pasture for a week or so. He'll probably get acquainted with the mares."

"Will do, seh."

"Don't call me sir," John said. "We're friends and family."

"Tha's right. Thank you, s … John."

John turned to go to the house. A strange, deep noise trickled from the barn loft. John blinked and listened, lifting his chin.

"Is that a human groan?" Head cocked, he stepped to the ladder.

The moan sounded again, and then a feminine sob assaulted his ears.

When John's eyes were just above the loft floor, he saw a stranger sat nearby, her arms grasped around her knees crinkling a faded dress. Messy red hair circled her head. Tears sprinkled freckled cheeks. Eyes opened almost as wide as the stallion's had been.

With another groan, she flopped over on a pile of hay, hugging her protruding stomach.

"Abe!" he yelled. "There's a young lady up here, and I think she's having a baby."

Long wet lashes fringed her tightly shut eyes as she braced for another pain. "Please let me stay here until it comes." She groaned again.

John's mouth dropped open. He blew out his breath.

She settled, the pain apparently letting up for a minute. Rubbing her belly, she looked hard at him. "Please—"

Another pain contorted her features.

John dropped his feet a rung lower on the ladder. "You need help. I'll get Polly."

This had been a stressful day. First, the hard time controlling the stallion and now a pregnant woman about to give birth? He sprinted to the house and banged open the kitchen door.

Polly stood by the sink cutting stewed chicken into small pieces.

"We need you in the barn." John clutched the cold doorknob. "A girl out there's about to have a baby."

"What?" Polly frowned.

He repeated what he said. "She might let you assist."

"Lawd know the barn be good enough for a calf or a colt, but not a human young'un." She moved the pot on the stove to the side and then wiped her hands on a white dishtowel. "Take me to her." She headed outside.

He followed her run-over, nearly worn-out shoes. "You're not able to go up in the loft. Talk to her through the slats."

"She's comin' ta the house, boy." Polly's dark eyes snapped as she turned to him.

Screams filled the barnyard before Polly reached the door.

The young lady yelled, "Oh, God, have mercy on me. Wash away my sins. Help me forgive the man who took advantage of me! Let the child live."

The deep sob and another scream put pain in John's bones. He wanted to plug his ears, but Polly gave him a look that would wilt a cactus. A prayer bubbled out of his soul in silence, *God, help this girl in her suffering. Who on earth is she? Where did she come from?*

The screams stopped, but muffled noises continued.

"Miss?" John called. He looked up toward the loft. "Polly, our cook, has delivered babies, and she's here to help."

"Yes," Polly said. "You come down where we is, and we'll help you into the house."

"I'll be fine here," a soft voice answered.

"You're not having a baby up there." Polly's voice echoed against the rafters. "I'm no young'un, and if you can't get down here, I'm goin' up."

John stepped on the ladder. "I'll help you. We'll go between pains."

"Don't you touch me!" the redhead yelled, grabbing her belly again.

John shook his head, raised his eyebrows, and rubbed his forehead. The woman's prayer went through his mind again: *Forgive the man who took advantage of me.*

"Will you let Polly's husband help you down?"

"Is he old?"

"You could say so," Abe answered behind John. "I'll be glad to help."

Helping the girl down from the barn loft and into the house strained John's patience as much as his muscles. Abe's strong arms assisted John.

Polly hurried with the energy of a much younger woman, opening drawers, grabbing towels and sheets. Then she turned to go to the back bedroom where the stranger lay.

Polly planted her hands on her ample hips. "Now you men git out of here. Somebody needs to stir the pot on the stove, and one of you go to the porch and turn the ice cream freezer."

John picked the porch. The further he got away from the screams, the better. "Where'd that redhead come from, Abe?"

"No ideer. Never see'd her as I know."

"You think she could be the person who stole things from the house?"

Abe didn't answer.

John dropped into the old blue chair beside the freezer, checked the ice, sprinkled on rock salt and turned the handle.

A horse and carriage clattered up beside where he worked. "Get your new stallion home okay, John?" Edwina Jorgenson greeted. She jumped from the carriage and trotted to the porch, her slim figure moving with poetry. "I can't wait to put him with my black mare. She'll probably be ready in two or three weeks."

"Hello to you, too, Ed," John said, frowning. Now wasn't a good time to talk to this woman. "That horse is pretty wild yet. Been abused too much. We—"

A scream came from the house. A frown pinched Edwina's flawless, suntanned face as she bounded up the porch steps and opened the screen door. "What's happening to Polly? We'd better go see."

He dropped the freezer handle and grasped Ed's arm. "A lady in there is having a baby."

"Who is it?"

"I don't know. We found her in the barn."

"Maybe I can help."

"I think Polly has it under control."

Ed twisted away from his hold, grabbed the doorknob and darted into the house before he could protest.

Well, let her go in and listen to her scream. He wouldn't go inside again with all that racket. But the screams soon stopped, and a baby's cry took their place. Even though his stomach rumbled, he still wasn't going in.

The freezer handle became difficult to turn, and with each additional crank, he confirmed the delicious frozen dessert was ready. He piled gunnysacks on top of the freezer to keep the ice cream from melting. Then he stepped down to go to the barn.

Edwina burst out of the house smiling from ear to ear. "It's a boy! A cute little fellow, and his mama is doing okay. Polly did a great job delivering him."

John motioned, "Let's go out by the fence to talk."

She mashed her cowboy hat on her head, and a silly grin pulled at Edwina's face. John guessed she wanted him to ask her to the church picnic, but when they walked to the barnyard, he said, "Do you know that girl and where she came from?"

"Oh, haven't you seen her around? She worked as a maid for the Davenports. I heard she had an affair with Wellington Davenport, and Mrs. Davenport threw her out. Her name is Roberta Bellea Peabody."

She pointed an index finger at John. "You should remember her. She was in our class at school. I heard she's going by Bellea instead of Roberta now."

The gal moved a little closer to John and looked up in his face.

"She grew up rich, but her parents died of pneumonia or flu—I don't remember which. Seems the person who handled the Peabodys' financial affairs got away with all the property and money since she was too young to inherit." She shook her head, "I sure wouldn't have let them by with that. I'd have created a ruckus they'd never forget."

The young lady rancher flipped her blonde braid over her shoulder. "But I wouldn't keep her around here. She has a temper to match her red hair. Yet, after her parents died, she lost her spunk. Claims Wellington compromised her, but nobody believed it."

John took his knife out of his pocket and began grooming his fingernails. "She was doing a lot of praying when we found her, and she wanted me and Abe to leave her alone. Soon as I understood a baby was on the way, I went for Polly."

Edwina wrinkled her little turned-up nose. "What's that terrible odor?"

John stepped to the fence. "Might be coming from my prize pigs. See the big one over there I call Gertie?"

Gertie trotted close and rubbed her prickly mud-covered back on the hog wire.

"I expect to make big money from pork while I rebuild the horse herd and work in the peach orchards. You ought to try a few pigs. You get a quicker turnover with your money than with horses. Your papa used to raise them. Besides, it's always nice to have smoked ham and bacon available."

Edwina leaned over the fence. The pigs grappled with each other over the slop, snorting and grunting. "I might get some. The little ones are cute. Since my papa is in the wheelchair, I'm running everything. How is the pork market doing?"

"It sounded great to me. It …"

Gertie stuck her snout through the fence and sucked Edwina's lacy pink dress. Edwina jerked the skirt out of the slimy jaws and then, stringy pig saliva slid down her pretty legs.

"Eeeeewwww!" she squealed, holding her dress out away from her. "I didn't know pigs would eat clothing."

Laughter almost escaped John's lips. He pressed his fist over his mouth until his insides quit quaking in case she was mad enough to use the gun strapped on her slim middle. "Gertie probably smelled the cornstarch you used to starch your dress. I'd guess for her it was quite tasty. I'll get you a towel."

"Don't bother." She grabbed a big blue handkerchief from the buggy, wiped at her legs and jumped in the driver's seat. "You probably wanted me to stand over by the fence so that would happen. You are incorrigible, John Parks. Get someone else to go to the church picnic with you!"

As the dust rose from her departure, she almost ran into the mailman.

John meandered to the mailbox. Strange. He hadn't asked her to the picnic. He never intended to.

ADA BROWNELL

2

A letter from Valerie MacDougal rested on top of the mail. Delicate handwriting penned his name as well as her name on the return address. John hurried toward the house, remembering her beauty when he walked her down the aisle at Jenny's wedding nearly a year ago. Perhaps Valerie had recovered from her husband's death.

His cheeks stretched into a smile as he ripped the envelope open.

She was coming for a visit! His heart jerked and pounded at the news. Then it quivered and skipped a beat. One of her father's law partners told Valerie about an outstanding physician being held in the asylum, and he wanted her to help present his case in court.

I'm thinking of going back into practicing law.

He stared at the ground, shoved the letter back into the envelope and pushed it into his pocket. *At least she's coming here. Perhaps I can persuade her to forget that and come back to Colorado.*

As he opened the back door, he saw Wellington Davenport, mounted on his copper-red, bay gelding, galloping off John's property toward the road. John rubbed the scar on his cheek. What had Wellington been doing here? If the twerp came to make trouble, John felt up to the challenge.

The dumplings and ice cream were ready and all the excitement about the baby calmed his spirit. Valerie MacDougal and his sister Jenny were coming to visit him in Peachville. His heart skipped a beat. What would Edwina think?

The baby's cry interrupted his thoughts. What on earth was he going to do with a baby under his roof? *How do people live with these noisy little people? Do they ever sleep?*

The next morning the clock rattled its time-to-get-up ring, and the hands pointed at six a.m. He'd barely shut his eyes. The baby had squalled most of the night.

He threw back the covers, slapped the alarm button, yanked on his pants, shirt, and boots. The mirror reflected the dark bags under his eyes. Who'd notice if he didn't shave? Well, Polly would, so he went to work on his whiskers.

When John walked into the kitchen, Polly didn't look so good herself. "Were you up all night with the baby?"

She blinked and nodded. "He's a sweet fellow. Don' know how much he weigh, but he's tiny. Probably just over five pounds. I don't think his mama been eatin' right, ya know? I hope you don' mind, but I think she doesn't have enough milk so the baby is restless. He's hungry. I'll pour milk, tea, coffee, water, even lemonade down that young lady until she has plenty of milk."

"But she can't stay here." John blew air out of puffed cheeks.

"Fiddlesticks." Polly dropped eggs into a sizzling skillet. "Abe and I live here. Her and the baby will be in the downstairs bedroom where she is now."

"I don't know. Ed said Bellea's parents died from the flu or something, and now she has a baby to take care of."

"But you can't throw her and a baby out into the world. She tol' me she used to work for the Davenports. She cooked and cleaned. I could use the help, especially if you hire more hands like you say you goin' to. She seems a right nice girl. She's seventeen, and I saw her with her family while you lived in Minneapolis. Most of the family were redheads like her. From what I can tell, she worked for room and board. The way she reacted to you men, I don't think she'll be a problem for you. They's one man she's desperately afraid of, but she didn't say who."

Abe banged the back door screen. "The stallion already is settlin' down a little, but I think you should be there when I let him go to ta pasture."

John pulled out a chair. "Good. Wait until I get there." He'd probably have to put up with the baby's squalling for a few more days at least. But now, he needed to discuss the letter.

"Jenny, her husband, and a boy they adopted, plus a friend of hers, are coming to visit. They'll be here Wednesday." He slid two eggs onto his plate, six pieces of bacon, and added toast. "I'd like some peach jam, please."

"John, you didn't pray yet." Polly shook her finger at him like she always did when she expected him to shape up.

"Oh, I wasn't going to eat yet. I wanted a head start."

Abe chuckled. Then he spread his napkin in his lap, sobered and prayed such a wonderful prayer for those at the table and the woman and baby in the bedroom that John had chills. Abe had a way of praying from his heart.

Abe had so much energy this morning, he must have snored through the baby's cries and Polly going back and forth to help.

Polly took a plate of food to the young mother before she sat down. A big sigh escaped her lips. "That girl is really weak, and she disturbed. I think she snitched food here and there and went from barn to barn. She's worrying about where they will go. I'd like you to see the babe. He's a good'n, even if he does cry. He's already looked his mama and me over properly, and he's interested in everything around him. Don't think he will have red hair like his mama. He has a mass o' dark hair."

The black hair on Wellington Davenport's head flashed through John's mind. *Perhaps he is the father.*

John gobbled his food so fast he almost asked Polly for a couple more eggs, but she looked as if she could use a nap.

"How 'bout I wash the dishes for you, and you can go see to the baby and his mother," he suggested. Not that he liked dishwashing, but if Polly could do something to keep the baby quiet, it would be worth soaking his hands in hot water.

"Well, tha's mighty nice of you." Abe nodded. "Polly been up a lot with the li'l feller."

"Least I can do." John took his own dirty dishes to the sink and gathered up the skillets.

As he was putting away the last skillet, Polly brought a tiny blanket-wrapped bundle into the kitchen. "Here. Take a look at him. Isn't he a darlin'?"

John hung the dishtowel on the peg. "Okay. Let me have peek."

The fellow's tiny mouth puckered and worked as if he were sucking. Bitsy fingers, perfect with amazing fingernails, doubled into a fist and then opened and stretched.

John's heart jumped. "He's amazing. How can anyone look at a baby and not believe in God?" He touched the teeny fingers, and the tiny hand grasped and held on. "What did she name him?"

"David Jonathan. She hopes he'll be as strong in spirit as David when he slew the giant. His middle name is Jonathan 'cause Jonathan was David's bes' friend."

The mass of dark hair on David's head stood out as Polly talked. John passed his hand over the silky hair. Through the "soft spot" on top the baby's head, he could feel his heartbeat.

Wellington Davenport was wicked to the core. Instead of going to college or working with his father, Wellington spent his time in saloons, gambling and flirting with the girls. He'd even been in jail several times because of his bar fights. Wellington's father always used his money to pay for damages and buy off judges and sheriffs.

But he'd attacked this girl in his own home.

John followed Polly into the parlor, where she sat in a wooden rocker. She extended the bundle. "Hold him. You're gonna be a father someday, so you might as well learn a few things."

John's head wagged. "No." He stuck his open palm out toward the baby. "I need to get out in the barn and help Abe."

"Let me put 'im in your arms for a minute or two. He's nothin' to be 'fraid of." Polly's white smile gleamed as she extended the bundle again.

How could he fear such a tiny person? John stuck out his hands.

"Now watch his back. Put him up against your chest. He likes to snuggle."

John gently hugged David to him. The baby was so tiny. "How can all that noise come out of someone so small?"

"Oh, God gave him good lungs and the urge to cry fo' loving arms to hold them and fo' food. A baby can't survive without that."

"He's quiet now. Did he get enough to eat?"

"He'll be squalling again before long if I don't get back in there and give his mother something more to drink. I think I'll feed her every hour or so until she is producing enough milk to keep her son alive. I've had a hard time getting her to eat because she feels she'll be indebted to you."

"He's in danger of dying?" A sick feeling swept through him as he looked at the tiny, pink and slightly wrinkled face. "Do I need to get him a bottle?"

Polly took the baby back into her arms. "We could let 'im suck on a towel soaked in milk, but it's not best."

John looked out the window at the horses he needed to get out and care for. "We could get a wet nurse, but it'd cost money." He needed every dime to build up the horse herd and have the peach trees trimmed.

"It won't cost much to feed 'er if you'll hire 'er to work."

"Let me think and pray." He turned his gaze from the horses to Polly's round face. "Now I think about it, Jenny told me her friend who worked for the Davenports was raped. But Edwina said she heard the girl was having an affair with Wellington Davenport. It wouldn't be good to keep a girl who would seduce her employer's son. Especially under the same roof with me, since I have no wife, even if I do sleep upstairs. The gossips in town would have a fine time."

"If'n you pray, God will make a way."

Red hair flashed in the dining room door. "Is the baby okay?" the mother asked in a shaky voice.

"He's fine. Still sleepin'. I suppose I need to put him down."

The freckles on the girl's pale face faded as she stared at John. "Please don't tell anyone in town I'm here. Someone's hunting for me and wants the baby."

"Shouldn't I at least tell the sheriff?"

"No!" Her face blanched whiter, and her knees buckled.

John caught her and carried her back to the bed. She weighed hardly anything. Well, he'd see she had enough food available so she could feed little David.

"Don't worry about us telling it in town, but sometimes we have visitors. Edwina Jorgenson was here when you were giving birth. There's no way to keep your whereabouts a secret when she knows. She's a talker."

"Seems like I remember someone here right after the baby was born, but I was so tired I went to sleep," Bellea said. "It's in God's hands now. But I will die before I give away my baby. He's mine."

When John crawled into the covers that night, he forgot all about the young mother. Would Valerie really try to get someone out of the asylum? She also planned to work closely with one of her father's law partners, and it sounded like the man wasn't married. That couldn't be good.

3

The atmosphere in the asylum hung thick with body odor, foul language, unemptied chamber pots, and patients venting their anger.

Dillon Haskill picked up his dirty metal plate and clanged it against the bars over the window in the thick door.

"Let me out of here!" He banged again and again. "I am not insane or demon-possessed. I am a doctor! I'm Dr. Dillon Haskill."

The young patient behind Dillon held his arm and tugged him from the bars. His upwardly slanted eyes glistened with tears that threatened to dribble down his abnormally flat face and nose. His tongue extended from his mouth, and spit ran down his chin. "Please. Don't make trouble. They'll …"

Other patients stared with vacant eyes as they walked around the room like caged tigers, feet moving and heads turning back and forth, some mouths loudly spitting obscenity.

The kid still tugged. The plate dropped from Dillon's hand. The metal dish banged as it wobbled across the filthy wood floor, but Dillon returned to the barred window.

"What's all the racket about?" a deep voice rumbled. A rugged face appeared in the square of light—the guard who threw him into the pit.

"This place isn't fit for animals, let alone humans!" Dillon scratched his beard as he bellowed. "There are lice in here, bedbugs, rats, and it's filthy. The chamber pot hasn't been emptied, and it's about to run over."

Dillon gagged.

"Better settle down there, mister," the guard grumbled. His big dark eyes stared through the bars. "You'll have another fit, and I will not come in to help you when it happens. You got the devil in you, and you're dangerous."

"I've had one seizure in my life." Dillon massaged his thick, filthy hair and winced as the dust and bugs flew. "A horse bucked me off, and I hit my head on the fence. The seizure happened right afterward, leaving me unconscious for a short while. I've never had another seizure."

"Don't argue with me. You got demons in you!" The guard spat. "You'll never get out of here."

"But people who have seizures aren't demon-possessed." Dillon rubbed his head. "Hippocrates, the father of medicine, believed epilepsy is a physical disease that can be treated through natural methods. And I've only had one seizure. I was twenty-three years old when I hit my head four years ago. I want out of here. Now!"

The guard reached into a cabinet on the wall and removed a white straitjacket. A key rattled in the door.

Dillon had to do it now. With the lack of food, every day he became weaker.

"No!" burst from his dried and peeling lips. He wouldn't give up. God would answer.

4

The next morning at her ranch Edwina Jorgenson pounded steak on the cabinet while her father, Paul Jorgenson, worked peeling potatoes at the table. The aroma of oatmeal raisin cookies drifted from the oven.

"Papa, do you think pigs are a good investment?" She tried to keep him interested in everything about the ranch, but lately, he'd seemed to lose focus. The wheelchair grated on his nerves. He'd been breaking horses to ride and sell most of his life, until a wild mustang tossed him off two years ago. Papa hadn't walked again.

Papa dropped a curly peeling into one pan and set the potato in the other. He looked up at her. " You don't want to raise pigs, do you?"

She laughed. "No, not after the run-in I had with a pig the other day. John Parks is raising pigs, and he says they're a great investment."

"You're going to the church picnic with him, aren't you?" Papa smiled. "I think he'd make a fine catch."

Edwina's heart jerked. "He didn't ask me, and he had a chance to do it too! When I went over there to reserve a time for breeding our black mare with his new stallion, he wanted to show me his pigs. Polly delivered a baby for the gal who used to work for the Davenports, but John hardly paid attention. John's all caught up in swine. How's he going to build up his ranch to what it was?"

"Well, what did you think of the pigs?"

"I hate them. One old sow sucked my dress. I wanted to give John a chance to ask me to the picnic, but when I got pig slobber on me, I came home. All he can think about is that ranch. I'd guess his money is tight."

"Is he building up his horse herd yet?"

"He's only been back a few weeks. He's buying good breeder animals, though. He went over to Yucca Blossom and bought the judge's black stallion. John will slowly build back the herd. He's planning to restore the orchards to their former glory, too. The pigs are his way of making quick cash. But they are disgusting animals."

A big guffaw poured out of Papa's mouth, which sounded good to Edwina's ears.

"I saw a beautiful young woman like you who raised pigs and showed them at the State Fair. She won all sorts of awards and ribbons for her animals. When I saw her, the big sow she had on exhibit had been bathed, brushed, and polished until she could have fooled people into thinking the critter wouldn't think of jumping into a mud puddle or eatin' slop. Her pigs probably grew up on corn instead of slop, but I'd bet if you gave them slop they'd eat it. A pig wallows in mud because he doesn't have sweat glands. Wet mud cools them off, keeps them from getting sunburned and keeps away bugs."

"If I bought pigs, where would we keep them?"

"Far away," Papa mumbled.

"Where did you keep them when you had them?"

"Way out in those pens on the back forty acres next to the big hill. Six or seven huts still stand out there to help pigs get into the shade. Don't you remember the building next to the chicken pen is our smokehouse?"

Papa's blue eyes glistened. "Aren't those cookies done yet?"

Edwina let out a yelp, grabbed a potholder, and opened the oven. "Ah! They're just right. But you're going to have to wait a little until I take them up and put them in the container."

"Well, I want one while they're still warm."

Edwina shook her head. "Roll your chair over and help yourself." She placed a saucer on the counter where he could reach it.

Paul put the pan full of peeled potatoes in his lap and rolled over to the sink and pumped a little water over them, swished it around, dumped the water, and then filled the pan again.

"The potatoes are ready to put on the stove." He wiped his hands on the towel hanging near the sink and rolled over to pick up three cookies.

"Hey! Don't eat them all. You'll be too full for dinner."

He took a big bite from one and then shoved the whole thing in his mouth.

Edwina shook her head at him as she set the pan of potatoes on the stove to cook.

"Those were good days when your mama was here," Paul continued, grief still showing in his eyes. But then he smiled. "We had everything we needed to eat right here and money coming in like there was an endless supply."

His cookies had disappeared and so did his smile. He placed the saucer aside, shook his head and lowered it into his hands. When he looked up at her, Edwina thought she saw a tear.

"I'm so sorry, sweet girl, you feel like you need to resort to pigs. I've looked at the books, and you're doing all right with the horses. Forget pigs."

"But I'd like to hire more help," she argued. "Eli is too old to break the animals. Merriweather keeps trying to put it off. The younger you work with colts, the better in my estimation. Especially if you work to gentle them every day and let them get to know you."

"You're good with the horses, sweetie. Merriweather had been a good cowhand, too. Can't figure out what's going on."

"Well, he has the idea in his head he's going to marry me, own this ranch, and then he expects to become the boss. I used to kind of like him, but he's partially the reason I wear my gun all the time. I think he's about as dangerous as the snakes."

"You've never been timid before, girl. Put him in his place and fire him if he doesn't shape up. I've given you the authority to take responsibility, but I'll lay him off if you don't want to. Did Merriweather ask you to the church picnic?"

Edwina put another sheet of cookie dough into the oven, set the skillet on the stove and added lard. "Sure did. I accepted. He asked me last week while I was mad at John Parks. If John wants to be my beau, he better get to it. But I'm going to beg off going with Merriweather. For pity sake, I'm his boss. How can he court me?"

She rolled the pounded steak piece in salted and peppered flour and slid it into the hot skillet.

Paul raised his eyebrows, yet a little smile played on his cheeks. "Well, he didn't ask my permission to court you. Probably he thinks since I'm in this chair, he can do what he wants without my approval. What do you say? Shall we show him who's boss, or do you want to go to the picnic with him in order to get John Parks' attention?"

Edwina frowned, her blue eyes snapping. "On second thought, I'll probably have to go with him since I accepted. Unless I'm really sick or break a leg, he'll see right through my excuse and be mad as a turkey gobbler without feathers."

 5

As soon as John Parks opened the gate to the north pasture and lifted the new leather bridle off the sleek animal's long quivering neck and nose, the black stallion galloped away, stirring the wind like he'd do on the prairie hills when leading a wild herd. His hooves pounded until the ground trembled under John's feet. The stallion's majestic body, head stretched forward, tail and mane flying, streaked along the morning skyline like the champion he should be.

Pinions scented the cool breeze in the early morning light.

The horse came to the white three-rail fence at the north end of the pasture, pivoted abruptly, and rounded the pasture again at a full run.

Bile filled John's stomach and tongue. Would the formerly abused animal jump the fence?

The mare grazing nearby in the green field tilted her head toward the galloping stallion and neighed.

The regal horse swung toward her.

John and Abe walked a distance away to let them get acquainted.

Weariness seemed to spread in John's young bones as he walked. He felt the weight of caring for the people in his home. How long had it been since he'd had a good laugh and no worries?

He sighed, and Abe turned and looked at him.

"The young mama we found in the barn is lots better now." Abe puffed a little and sounded out of breath as he climbed up the hill. "The babe doesn't cry as much, either. What you gonna do with 'em? Polly said you was a prayin' 'bout it."

John rubbed his cheek. The scar seemed to be shrinking some. "You know I wish God would talk to us out loud. Abe, how do you know what to do when it comes to making hard decisions?"

Abe blinked his dark eyes. The fluttering lashes now had grown white, like most of his curly hair. "Oh, God speak to us all right." He patted the area near his heart. "Sometimes I hear 'im right here. Other times, when I's reading the Bible, his will is loud and clear. Right regularly when the preacher gets wound up on Sundays, he say things straight from God. The main thing is to decide to do God's will even before he shows it to you. Then when things develop a certain way, you know what ya s'pose to do."

"I think I need to do more readin' and prayin'." John trudged toward the house.

After John cleaned up for dinner, his gaze followed Bellea Peabody as she brought the baby to the table and sat down shyly, tipping her face downward, letting the light show freckled skin as pale as a bucket of milk. Her shabby dress clung close to her body, and he guessed her bones filled out the garment.

Abe prayed another powerful prayer for each person around the table, and goose bumps raised over John as he whispered his own prayer before lifting his head. Tears pooled in Bellea's eyes but didn't spill onto her cheeks.

"My daddy used to pray." Soft and shaky, her voice barely broke the stillness. "Thank you for praying for me and helping me. But I must be going. I can't keep eating your food forever."

"You're welcome to stay here until you find a job." John didn't even need to think about it.

"I … I don't know if I can get a job with little David Jonathan to care for."

A horse and carriage rumbled into the yard. Taking another gulp of coffee, John stood. A woman in a fancy black hat and velvet cape hopped down and charged forward like a rooster ready to flog.

Bellea gasped and ran for the bedroom, leaving her plate.

A fist or a foot rattled the door.

"I heard you have a young woman and baby here." The red-faced woman barged through the door. "I'm Mrs. Davenport. I have reason to believe you harbor a girl who used to work for me. The boy she delivered is my grandson. I'm not leaving the child for a trollop to raise. I want the babe."

John stared at the woman until he realized his jaw hung open. He closed his mouth tight.

"She enticed my son, and now she can bear the consequences. Besides, she has no money to care for the boy." Her voice rose to a higher pitch. "Let me see him. Where is Roberta?"

John stared at the woman, knowing a scowl scrunched his face.

The lady's fury intensified, and her threatening frown nearly closed her eyes. "Maybe you know her by Bellea? I think she changed her name so people won't know who she really is. Now, young man, I want that baby, and I want him now."

"Ma'am, this is my home, and the baby and his mother are my guests." He took the woman's arm and turned her toward the door. "You are not welcome to come in here and disturb them. Kindly get in your buggy and leave my property."

The lady's dark brown eyes bulged, and her face blotched even redder. "I will not!" she shouted.

Abe put aside his napkin and approached the lady's other arm. The two men led her out and helped her into the buggy.

"John Parks, I knew your parents, and they'd never sanction you bringing that girl into your house and treating me like this. I'll be back!" she shrieked as she flicked a whip at her horse.

John shook his head to get the conversation out of his mind. He trembled all over.

After a few minutes of quiet, he stretched and then went back in the house. He found Polly in the bedroom with Bellea. He leaned on the door trim and peeked inside. "Are you gals doing all right?"

Bellea beckoned him to come in. "Thank you for getting that woman out of here. I need to leave. As long as she knows where I am, she's going to want my baby."

"May as well come on in here and talk," Polly suggested, her voice unusually soft.

John walked to the foot of the bed and stared at the young mother. "Is he her grandchild?"

A sob burst from Bellea's pale lips. "Y … Yes."

"Will Wellington want the baby too?"

The curly head and body trembled. "Wellington! Don't ever allow him in here. He said if I ever tell anyone what he did, he'd kill me."

John puckered his lips and whistled. "Looks like we have a problem on our hands. You have nowhere to go. You staying in my house doesn't look good, and we could have Wellington pounding on our door any minute."

Bellea gasped for air and wobbled slightly as if she could pass out.

Polly lifted the baby from Bellea's arms. "Here. Put ya head back on these pillows before you land on the floor, girl. That-a-way. Good. Now, John, let's think. We have the attic all full of beds and furniture. They's a couple winders up there to let in light. It will probably take me a week, but then she can stay up there. There might even be an old cradle."

"Polly, you're not going up into the attic. The stairs are too steep. I'll go up and see what I can do."

"There's a light up there," Polly said. "But no curtains. While you're working, I'll get dinner. Then I'll see if I can find something to hang on the winders to keep the light from shining out at night."

"Good idea."

The next morning, John stepped onto the back porch about the same time Billy Joe Garner's horse trotted into the yard and ambled toward the house. Waiting until Billy Joe tied his horse to the hitching post, John took several long breaths to embrace the day. Then he stretched his back and felt ready to talk.

"Hey, B.J. What's goin' on with you?"

"Doin' fine, John. I heard you have several new horses and might want to hire somebody."

"Aha!" John laughed. "I have several top-rate animals out there in the pasture."

B.J. turned toward the white-fenced pasture where several horses grazed. "I noticed a black stallion. Was that the judge's mount? He's a fine animal. I'd enjoy working with him again."

John smiled. "That's him all right. I shipped him in a railroad stock car all the way from Yucca Blossom. But he's still a wild one. The judge rode him over there. My Aunt Gertrude didn't know what to do with the horse after the judge was shot. She'd paid board and room for him since the murder."

"Some old man hung for killing him, didn't he? Well, that's too bad." B.J. hesitated then looked John in the face. "I need a job."

"Finally coming to work for me?" John slapped B.J. on the back. "We could use you. Abe and I need help around here—a good man to break and train horses, clean the barn, prune peach trees, pick peaches, irrigate, put up hay—you name it."

"Well, you know I'm good with horses, and I need work."

John grinned. "How soon can you start?"

"Today, if the pay is right."

John gave him a number.

B.J. squinted and eyed the mountains. "That's not as much as the judge paid before he got rid of the horses."

John threw open his arms in frustration. "It's all I can do."

B.J.'s mouth puckered over to one side. "I'll think about it."

John raised his eyebrows. "You should remember I don't train horses with a whip."

B.J. frowned, and then a fake grin wiggled his full lips. "I'll accept. I'll head to the barn and get to work."

John scanned the house a moment. "I'll be out soon and show you around. The black stallion needs a lot of gentle care."

"I like a challenge." B.J. shrugged. His tobacco-stained teeth turned John's stomach. Cigarettes could be a fire risk.

 6

Wednesday the sun shone, but a biting wind blew.

The wind went through his jacket, his skin, and clear to his bones. Then his new felt western hat flew toward the chicken coop. He took off running after it, but his mind went faster than his feet. Where was he going to put everyone? What would Jenny think of a baby and new mother in his house? Would Valerie think he had some kind of relationship with Bellea?

He snatched up the hat just before it went over the fence.

This was probably his chance to deepen the relationship between him and Valerie—if he could get her away from everybody.

He stopped in his tracks when hooves and buggy wheels clattered up the gravel drive. A hand waved, and a joyful voice called out, "John! We're here!"

His twin sister, Jenny, drove the buggy. Valerie MacDougal sat beside her with her cute little boy on her lap. Jenny's husband, William O'Casey, and their adopted son, Stuart, sat in back. But now wasn't a good time for company.

"Polly!" he yelled. "Jenny's here!" He helped the women out of the carriage.

Jenny caught him with a fierce hug. John bent to kiss her on the cheek and turned to Valerie. Her beautiful blonde hair tucked back into little curls glowed in the bright sun as chubby baby arms wrapped around her neck. John's heart skipped a few beats as his big hand touched Valerie's dainty soft one in greeting. He dipped slightly and kissed the tall, gorgeous widow's cheek.

"Did you have a nice trip?"

Valerie smiled, nodded and opened her pink mouth to speak, but Jenny snatched the moment, her expectant face slightly flushed. "We're dusty and tired, but so happy to get here. I forgot how far it is and how much those train engines smoke."

John twitched his lips as lifted their luggage. Why were they early? He needed more time to prepare. "Ummm. We have unexpected company in the house. I'm planning to clean the attic so the gal and the baby can move up there."

"Well, it's a good thing we're early," William added, hefting bags. "Stu and I can help."

Jenny frowned. "Who's here? Why are you putting them in the old attic?"

John grasped another bag, not meeting their eyes. But they might as well know. His face reddened, "Roberta Bellea Peabody. She's actually going by Bellea now. We found her about to give birth in our barn. We brought her in the house, but we are threatened with trouble for helping her."

"Why?" Valerie's exquisite brow wrinkled. She bent into the buggy to get her reticule.

John shook his head at the wonder of it all. "Mrs. Davenport believes the baby is her grandson and wants him."

William and Stuart set down the luggage and plopped down on the front porch swing out of earshot.

Jenny stopped walking and removed her gloves. "So Wellington admitted compromising Roberta? He should have admitted that months ago. Roberta went to the sheriff, but no one would look at her bruises. Wellington claimed he didn't touch her."

John lifted his hat and scratched his head. "Edwina said the word about town is that Roberta or Bellea, or whatever name she goes by, and Wellington had an affair."

"Well, don't you believe it." Jenny slapped her leather gloves against her leg. The dainty hat perched atop her head wiggled precariously. "Right after it happened, she came to me crying her heart out. I saw the bruises. She left the Davenport house before I hopped on Leather and ran away from the judge."

John stared at the clouds, then back at Jenny. "Edwina said Davenports threw Bellea out."

"Valerie and her father are lawyers," Jenny reminded. "They might be able to help, but now it's 'he said, she said.' But why put Bellea and the baby in the attic? No one has ever stayed up there."

John leaned closer. "Polly and I think maybe Mrs. Davenport will believe Bellea is no longer here."

Jenny glanced at the dingy attic window up in the peak of the house. "Might work, unless Edwina comes over. She'll be over here every moment she can get away from her ranch. She's been in love with you since she was about ten. I'll bet she was ecstatic when she found out you came back and took over."

John's face warmed. He rolled his eyes as he caught Valerie's interested look. "She's already been here."

"Anything Edwina knows or thinks she knows will be broadcast everywhere," Jenny added as she turned the bag she carried getting ready to go in the door.

The screen door squeaked as John pressed the beautiful brass doorknob to allow the women and the child to enter. "Come on in, William and Stu. That's a great swing. Our daddy made it. As soon as we get things under control here, I'll give you a tour of the ranch and let Stu try out a horse."

"I want to say hi to Bellea and check out the new little fellow." Jenny moved toward the bedroom.

"Have any goats?" Stu asked, striding beside William trying to match his swagger.

"Not a goat on the ranch." John chuckled. "You still have that old goat?"

"I love that goat!" Stu's eyes gleamed with enthusiasm. "We bought a nanny goat, and they're Mama and Papa now. But Rocky still has an ornery streak. Probably will teach all his kids to butt people, break out of the fence and eat brambles."

Chuckling, John led them into the parlor. "Probably will. Say, do you like pigs? I'm growing pigs for quick cash. The little ones are really cute."

Stu grimaced, eyes bulging, "Is *that* what I smell? Pigs? How could you mess up a nice ranch with pigs? I wouldn't touch a pig no matter how cute they look. They had a greased pig contest at the fair, and William thought I should enter. I cut out ahead of all the other kids, got the pig by the tail and one foot, and held on. The pig squealed, twisted, and turned. Dragged me into the mud, and first thing I knew, he stuck the other foot in my mouth. I let him go so I could puke."

William smiled and shook his head. "Stu still won the prize because he held on until then. I don't think they got the grease on the tail and that one foot."

"Will, are you still traveling part of the time?" John asked.

"I made three trips with *The Passion of the Christ* moving picture show this winter," William said. "Planting, plowing, and other duties on the farm have kept me busy. But I'm anticipating a change. I inherited the farm in Iowa. My father didn't change his will, and his second wife didn't contest it. She and her baby moved in with her parents because her mother is in ill health. Jenny's going with me to see if we should move there and take over the farm."

Murmurs of women making over Bellea's baby drifted from the bedroom.

"Is Jenny still teaching school?"

William stepped closer, his auburn hair and freckles more prominent to John. "Don't let on that you know, but Jenny and I will be parents come August, and she resigned from her job. She hated to quit, but we need to get to Iowa. Last I heard they haven't found a teacher."

"You're going to become a father. Congratulations." John whacked William on the back.

"I'll have a sister again," Stu said softly. "My other sister died of the cholera that took all my family but me." A tear glistened on the young man's scrubbed face.

"Or maybe a brother?" William asked with a smile. "We'll let the Lord send us the one he wants. I'm sure whoever it is will love you like we do." He stopped and looked at John. "While we're here, Stuart will have his twelfth birthday. I wonder if we could have a party tomorrow."

Polly stepped into the parlor. "A party for Stuart? Sure. Boy, do you like chocolate cake thick with frosting?"

Stu licked his lips. "I'd love to have some now."

Polly's smile lit up the room. "How about peach cobbler today? I took it out of the oven not too long ago. I'll slice ham, and we'll have sandwiches, carrot sticks, pickles, and fried potatoes. Will that do you all until supper?"

Stu tugged at her apron. "Can I help so you'll be fast? I can peel potatoes."

"Me, too," William added.

"We need to get settled in our rooms," Jenny insisted.

With William and Stu the kitchen, John helped Valerie and Jenny get their luggage upstairs to their bedrooms. "We're so glad you came, Valerie." He reached for her hand.

He broke out in a sweat as Edwina's face popped into his mind, and he remembered what Jenny said. He shoved Ed's face away from his thoughts. He was going to get better acquainted with Valerie.

"Have a seat." He pointed to the white wooden rocker in the guest bedroom.

Valerie groaned. "I should stand up after that long trip, but my knees feel like I need to sit."

John watched her every move as she settled in the rocker. She pulled Christian Paul to a comfortable spot on her lap and glanced around the bedroom. The baby babbled a few indistinguishable words.

"This is a nice ranch house." Valerie bounced the tot on her knees a bit. "Christian and I would have loved to have had a home this large on our homestead."

"Thank you." John lowered a bag to a vanity seat. "Our parents worked many years to get the ranch this well-developed. Then Dad came down with consumption, and a buggy accident killed Mom. Dad made a big mistake when he let the judge, my uncle, persuade him to give permission to live here and possibly inherit the ranch if he took care of Jenny and me until we reached age twenty-one. Dad might not have realized what he signed. He died the next week."

"Sad how your uncle was murdered." Valerie rubbed her hand over the light brown hair on her little son's head.

"The only good thing about his death is his mistreatment of horses and people stopped." Anger warmed John's face. "Then, too, someone who actually cares about my parents' property lives here and can take care of it. I can't wait to build up the horse herd and work with the peach trees. Right now is the time to prune those trees. I hired a man to help."

"Won't pruning them cut back on the peach production?" Valerie licked her pink lips as if she tasted peaches already.

"Pruning actually increases crop production." He braced one booted foot against the nearby dresser. "Did you notice in the winter the trees are almost flat topped but dip slightly in the middle? We want the tree wide and spreading like an open vase to allow sunlight through. In Colorado, we prune in late winter or early spring before they bloom. If a young tree is trained correctly, it only needs moderate annual pruning when it reaches bearing age."

Valerie's eyes snapped with interest. "You must have worked closely with your father."

John's heart skipped a beat as he smiled at the beautiful woman. "I started walking on stilts like the trimmers use when I was nine or ten. By the time I was twelve, Dad took me out to help with the trees and paid me as well as the trimmers. Only thing, I was slow so they made lots more money."

Christian Paul had dozed off in Valerie's arms. She nestled him on the bed. "When it's nap time, he conks out."

The newborn's loud cry assaulted John's ears. "You probably need to rest too and I need to get up to the attic. Perhaps I can find something to deaden the sound of Bellea's baby's howls. He sure makes a lot of noise."

"Wait until he decides to cry all night." Valerie flicked a dangling curl away from her face. "Christian kept me from sleeping at night for about two weeks after he was born. It's amazing what you can do when you have to."

John stared at her a moment. This woman was not only beautiful and smart, she had grit. When she got over grieving, she'd make a wonderful wife.

Valerie couldn't take her eyes off the man. He reminded her so much of Christian. Tall, muscled, his dark hair curling toward his sideburns and forehead. Gentle in his heart, but strong in character. He'd been so handsome when he walked her down the aisle at Jenny's wedding, all dressed up, looking down and smiling at her without flirting—a perfect gentleman. He'd make a great husband and father to her little Christian.

Her heart skipped. Warmth flowed through her, and she wished for a moment they could get married now. He hadn't asked her yet, sticking to propriety for her grieving, but he was going to. She knew it. For now, she needed to return to Boston, her parents and see if she could help that young doctor being held in the asylum.

ADA BROWNELL

7

By evening the next day, John, William, and Stuart had the attic cleaned, the beds and other furniture arranged into a comfortable room. Sure enough, he'd even uncovered a cradle there.

John about went into a fit when he saw Valerie out on the roof washing the windows on the outside. "Oh, Valerie! You might fall."

She laughed, her voice floating into the room like music. "I've been crawling through windows and sitting on roofs since I was a little kid. I wasn't working then, mind you. I was playing a joke on my parents or playing hide and seek with a friend. Washing these windows was a great excuse to revert to my childhood."

John shook his head at her humor, but twisted his mouth into disapproval and wagged his finger at her.

Polly found old heavy drapes, cleaned and hung them over the sparkling windows Valerie washed.

"Are we done?" Stuart asked.

"Yep."

He eyed William and then John. "Did you say I can have all this stuff?"

A pile with a homemade slingshot, a BB gun, a sack of marbles, and a Chinese checkerboard lay together on the floor. Also a heavy canvas canteen, small cowboy boots that almost fit Stu, a pair of ice skates, roller skates, a toboggan, and skis.

John touched Stu's shoulder. "You can have it all."

"Wow." Stu's eyes and mouth dropped wide open. "Don't know how I'll get all this stuff home."

"We'll find a way to get it there."

"Well, I …"

A loud pounding rattled the door downstairs. John headed for the steep stairs to the lower floor to answer the knock at the kitchen door. "It might be trouble."

Wellington barged into the door without anyone answering it.

"I came to get the baby."

"The baby?" Polly was smearing thick chocolate frosting on a birthday cake.

"Yes. My mother wants the baby." Wellington Davenport's eyes flashed back and forth between William and John as they stepped in front of Polly. "I know he's here."

"What right do you have to take him away?" Valerie joined the group. "You can't decide you want a child, grab him and take him home. You have to prove in a court of law a lawful reason why you have this right."

"Hogwash." Wellington pushed himself into the room. "What do you know? You're a *woman*."

She looked Wellington straight in the eye. "I have two years of law school, and my father is an attorney."

John clenched the young man's shirt with his fist and yanked it into a wad on his chest. "You think a child is here, but remember your mother already visited. We warned her not to come back. Anyhow, Bellea is in a safe place, but I think we should visit with the sheriff concerning yours and your mother's threats."

"You can't hide the baby behind the sheriff." Wellington clamped his teeth tight and threw his body back and forth until he ripped his shirt from John's grasp.

"Does this mean you want to marry Bellea and live as the child's father now? Or does it mean your mom bribed you with gambling money so she could connect with her grandchild?"

"None of your business."

John and William nudged him toward the door.

"My mother wants the baby." Wellington braced a hand on the trim. "And she always gets what she wants."

John shoved Wellington through the door and the young man nearly stumbled down the steps. But then he tripped and fell.

"Sorry," John grabbed Wellington and helped him up. "But you are not taking Bellea's baby and you'd better quit coming into my house and harassing all of us."

"Or what?" Wellington's chin pointed John's way.

"I pray you won't need to find out," John spat.

8

Things weren't going well at Edwina's house either. A dish crashed to the floor. Mama's favorite cake plate.

Edwina cleaned up the mess, paused and stared at Papa. "You can't make Clyde work with the horses today. How can I run this ranch if you keep usurping my authority? Besides, Old Eli is still puttering around—although he told me this morning he's going to quit next week and live with his daughter."

"I'm sorry, Edwina, but Clyde will not accompany you to the church picnic. I wouldn't mind having him for a son-in-law, but two mares are about to foal, and the west fence needs repair. With Eli leaving, we need to get all the work done we can."

"But, Papa," Edwina presented her sweetest tone as he leaned forward, hands braced on the wheelchair armrests. "Clyde should get acquainted with Christian men. Then maybe he'd go to church and clean himself up. I counted on him escorting me."

Papa chuckled, pushed himself higher in the chair, his dark bushy eyebrows still raised. "You aren't interested in Clyde. You only want to make John Parks jealous because he didn't ask you."

She turned her head so Papa didn't see the flush on her hot cheeks. "Don't be ridiculous. John couldn't go with me. He has his sister and that beautiful widow lady visiting. And I think Polly is still taking care of Bellea, and that gal is quite a looker herself."

Her father's mouth turned down. "Shush. Finish packing your picnic lunch and go have a good time. But don't dally too long.

We're shorthanded for work around here. If I could stand a bossy older woman around here, I'd hire a cook so you wouldn't have to do that too. I'd like to hire a foreman to take all the responsibility. What we need is a dependable, trustworthy fellow like Polly's husband."

"A black man?"

Papa shook his head and grunted in disgust. "I don't care what color he is, but we need someone we can trust who knows horses. Our herd is growing rapidly, and since I can't work, we need more men. You have too much responsibility."

When Edwina arrived for the picnic, she parked in front of the church, but she didn't even want to go. She should have stayed home. *How embarrassing to not have an escort.* She shrugged her shoulders. She hadn't realized she was so tired. Morning chores, plus preparing breakfast, lunch for Papa, and filling the picnic basket wore her out.

Leaving the heavy basket in the buggy, she lifted her dress a little to make walking easier and picked her way around wagons, horses, and buggies, trying to find John. Then he appeared, his arm linked with the widow woman. What was her name? Yes. Valerie MacDougal. Daughter of a rich Boston lawyer. No wonder John had her arm tucked closely to him.

"Hey, John," Edwina yelled. "I need help with my basket and my coconut cake."

John turned toward the lady beside him, said something and strode toward Edwina. "Always ready to help a beautiful lady who has food."

The widow took her son from William O'Casey. Jenny O'Casey smiled and waved at Edwina.

John removed the cake from the buggy and then licked his long finger. "Ah. This will make it easier to bid at the auction. That frosting is scrumptious."

"This is an … an auction? I don't remember that part."

"Sure. The men bid on the baskets, and the highest bidder eats lunch with the woman who made it."

A half hour later, John bid the highest for her picnic basket and soon settled beside her on her colorful quilt. "I've got to have more of your cake," he grinned.

"Didn't the widow bring a basket?"

"Oh, no." He filled the tin plate Edwina gave him. "She's still grieving. Besides, Polly packed a basket for Jenny, and William wasn't going to let it get by him. So he paid a bundle for it to bless the church. Mrs. MacDougal and her little boy will eat with them."

Edwina searched his face. The scar from his Uncle Danforth Schuster's whip only seemed to make him more handsome. It accented the smile lines on his tan, slightly whiskered cheeks. But he only had eyes for the fried chicken, potato salad, macaroni with cheese, and greens. Good thing the pastor prayed for everyone's food beforehand.

She threw a napkin at him. "You might want to wipe your fingers."

"Thanks. The chicken's juicy, the way I like it. Love the crispy outside. Are you sure you cooked this or did you hire a cook?"

Edwina leaned toward him and squinted her blue eyes until they almost closed. "I'll have you know my mother was a great cook and taught me how to handle myself in the kitchen."

"Well, Ed, I'm impressed. Good thing I bid the highest on your basket. Otherwise, all the cowpokes in the valley would be pounding on your pa's door asking permission to court you. But I can keep a secret. I'll let them know more about the rough and tough side of Edwina. Let them know how she can handle a gun, break a horse, and I'll drop a little information about her spitfire side."

He winked; and even with his full mouth, she saw his silly grin.

"Okay. You've done it, John. For that, I'll put the cake back in the buggy and feed it to the chickens."

John nabbed her hand. "Don't do that! I paid good money to eat that cake."

She gritted her teeth and held on to the pewter cake plate. "Let me go!"

"No. I kind of like holding your hand."

"Only because you want cake. Let me go, or I'll scream."

"Maybe I should be the one who screams," he threatened softly. "You're the one who won't let me have the food I bought."

"Go ahead." She forced some extra heat into her glare.

John scrunched his face into a frown and opened his mouth as if he were going to scream. But then he released the grip on her hand and rubbed it gently with his thumb. "I had no idea how much I would enjoy holding your hand."

Their eyes connected and held. Edwina's heart skipped a beat and then thumped. He couldn't be going to kiss her out in public like this, but he looked as if he wanted to. His thumb kept rubbing until she edged her hand away. He probably was trying to make a fool of her. She raised her left eyebrow. "Here's another plate. Have as much cake as you want."

John smirked as he cut the beautiful cake and plopped a huge piece on the dish for himself. Then he cut another for her.

The atmosphere between them was as charged as a tornado cloud filled with lightning as they stuck their forks into the heavenly creation.

9

As usual, gloominess hung inside the asylum. One man sat on his bed, head in his hands weeping, guttural groans ripping out his throat.

Dillon Haskill lifted Jimmy Cook into a new position in his bed, hoping to prevent more bedsores.

"Thank you." The young teacher, paralyzed from the waist down, gasped for breath and then choked, showing symptoms of pneumonia.

Dillon sat him up on the filthy mattress, patted his bony back with his cupped hand in an effort to loosen the congestion and then bent him forward. Breathing came easier in that position.

Wishing for pillows, Dillon snatched his thin mattress off his bunk and rolled it up behind Jimmy. "I'll leave you this way awhile, and perhaps you can breathe better."

"Thank ... thank you." Jimmy's face had flushed, turned bluish, but as the moments passed, a better color seeped into his skin and a smile curved his face.

"You know what I'd do ..." He stopped and breathed deeply a moment. "... if I could walk and work? I'd plant a huge garden and grow everything good ... like tomatoes, carrots, and sweet peas."

The man who been weeping nearby sat up and listened. His crying stopped.

Dillon wondered if Jimmy was through talking, but after he rested a moment, the former teacher began again, haltingly but with a shine in his eyes. "I'd have lots of fruit trees. I'd ride a horse across the green meadows and milk a fat cow. I'd go fishing or hunting every day. My pretty wife and I'd eat like kings. I think she would want me back."

"Sounds like a great dream," Dillon assured.

Curly Hicks in the bed across the way stirred and opened his eyes.

"You've figured out a great way to transport our minds to other places—to beauty, peace, and love," Dillon said. "That's what heaven will be like, Jimmy. You'll be able to walk there. You'll be a guest at the Marriage Supper of the Lamb like all of the redeemed church. I imagine we've never tasted food like that will be."

Jimmy wobbled. Worried he might topple from the bed, Dillon propped him better.

"Makes me hungry to think about it." Jimmy reached out a bony hand toward heaven.

"I have some bread left." Dillon held out the morsel. "I'll share it with you."

"No. No," Jimmy struggled to shake his head. "You eat it." A cough tore from his throat, sounding as if it ripped his insides. "When I get to heaven, I'll peek through the clouds and watch you walk out of here and come back to bless other folks like me."

"Don't give up, Jimmy," Dillon scowled. "You've been a blessing to others here, quoting Scripture and telling stories you remember. You helped teach Pete to read. There's nothing wrong with your mind or your thinking. You're paralyzed, and they didn't know what to do with you. But you're still able to teach. There's a chance we might get you out of here."

"I hope so." Jimmy coughed. His color didn't look good.

Dillon shoved his mattress out of the way and gently dropped the patient back so he was lying flat again. Dillon shook his head. Even a cup of hot tea might help Jimmy's congestion. Breathing in the steam would help, too. But Dillon and the other five patients in the room never received any hot food or drinks. They were lucky to have clean water and the cold swill they called soup.

"Man the lifeboats!" Mississippi Smith shouted from across the room. "The pirates are coming. Get your sword! Fight to the death." He kicked at the bedposts, then at the wall and swung his bony fists in the air. "The blood's gushing now! Die! God, save us. Stop your laughing and your shouts of victory. I'll going to fight to the finish."

Dillon had no idea why Mississippi was initially admitted to the asylum, but he heard he had syphilis. But the formerly husky man had been hearing voices for as long as Dillon had been there. Often Mississippi struck out at other patients, but Dillon remained strong enough to get the tall, bony man back in bed.

"Take that, you animal." Mississippi jabbed into the air. "You'll not take our gold or our women!"

Mississippi ranted while Dillon poured enough clean water for Jimmy to wash down the bread he'd fed him.

Finally, Mississippi sank back on his mattress, groaned and grew quiet. His mouth fell open. His big lips wobbled from the following snore.

Dillon suspected Mississippi was suicidal. He refused to eat in recent days—Dillon lost count of how many. If he could find a little stone, he could keep track of the days. How wonderful it would be to have a pen or pencil and paper! He needed to write down his experiences for a testimony, because God would deliver him from this place.

The quietness in the room seemed strange. Mississippi's snores ceased. Dillon stepped closer. Things didn't seem right. He took the now-thin wrist in hand. Mississippi was dead.

10

The next day at the Peachville Ranch when Polly set dinner on the table, John's taste buds already watered.

Stuart's eyes bugged out at Polly's beautiful chocolate creation when he came in from playing in the barn. He stood there swallowing and licking his lips, his eyes big as she inserted candles and Jenny set the table.

"Oh, wow." Stu almost seemed overcome.

Jenny hugged him, kissed him on the cheek, then stood back and looked at the boy. "Happy birthday! Polly knows how to celebrate. But first, you need to wash up."

He was little too rambunctious for John's taste as Stu's stomping feet rattled the dishes in the kitchen cabinet when he took off running to the bathroom. Within minutes, they rattled again and Stu flew into the dining room huffing. His mouth dropped open as his eyes focused on the table and the people surrounding it.

It hit John how he'd done the same things as a child. Ran, rattled dishes, even came to the table before he washed.

The table hadn't looked so beautiful in years. His mother's blue and white china set off the white tablecloth and serving dishes.

He pulled out a chair for Valerie on one side of the table. He grabbed a seat beside her and turned to capture her beauty in his memory. She smiled and reached out and squeezed his hand.

Soon they were all seated, and John lit the candles.

"Ready for you to blow out the candles, Stu," Polly announced, her dark eyes sparkling and hands tucked in her apron pockets.

Stewart rubbed his hands together, leaned and puckered his mouth into a big O.

"Hey, did you make a wish?" John asked.

Stu stopped. "A wish? Sure. I'd like a talking horse."

"No, no, no. You're not supposed to tell what your wish is."

"Better let him blow, or the wax will be down on the cake," Polly pointed out.

Stu let out a big puff and didn't stop blowing until he'd vanquished the last one. "Hey, I got all twelve of them in one breath."

John grinned. "Good job. But why would you want a talking horse?"

Stu raised his eyebrows and shot John a disgusted look. "Can't you guess? So I'd know what he's thinking."

John nodded and scrunched his lips into a thoughtful pose, "I had a talking horse once. He told me he'd rather be a deer because no one rides a deer."

"I guess that's right," Stu agreed. "No one rides a deer. What'd you tell 'im?"

While he waited for John to complete his story, Stu's eyes reflected the light from the window and a smirk played at his mouth.

"I told him it would be a big mistake to become a deer," John wagged his head sagely.

"Why would it be a mistake?" Stu's eyes didn't leave the cake.

"Because if my horse became a deer, he might become a real buckskin!" John's jolly laugh almost rattled the dishes on the table.

"You're terrible, John." Jenny frowned at him, her head shaking from side to side.

William reached out and rubbed Stu's hair. "John's a big tease. He's been picking on his sister all his life—but now you're his new target. Can't let him put too much over on you."

Stu giggled. "I knew it was a joke. We don't believe in wishes like that coming true."

"Right." A proud smile curved Jenny's face.

Polly removed the cake from the table. "We'll let Stuart open his gifts after we eat."

"Time to ask the blessing on the food," Jenny nudged Stu. If she'd been close enough, his sister probably would have nudged John as well.

When the chatter around the table stopped, John cleared his throat. "Abe, we'd be honored if you would pray for the food and for little Stuart here."

Abe shoved his chair back, stood, and raised his face toward heaven.

"Lord, I thank you for this young'un here ya gave to Jenny and Will. We's sorry his family had to go be wid you, but we're thankful Stu be wid us. Bless him. May he live fa you all his days. Thank you for giv'n Jenny such a wonderful husband. We grateful, Lord, for this bounty and the table of food. In Jesus' name. Amen."

Everyone dug into the mashed potatoes, gravy, roast beef, green beans, and a huge apple, carrot, and raisin salad.

"Have you been eating like this all your life?" William asked Jenny.

"Sure have. Polly lived here when I was born."

William leaned toward his wife and winked. "Can't imagine how you ate like this and stayed so small."

John smiled over the way William glanced at his smiling wife and then looked at each person around the table. "We have an announcement to make. Stu is going to have a brother. Jenny is in a family way. Too bad we can't live closer so our little boy could grow up with extra folks to love him."

"Oh, Jenny," Valerie cried. "I'm so happy for you. When do you expect him?"

Jenny's face pinked, "In about six months. We wanted to surprise you all. But William is wrong. It's a girl."

Everyone laughed.

"Nobody knows whether it's a boy or a girl." Polly dabbed her eyes with the edge of her apron.

"Well, I know for sure it will be a baby." John scooted back his chair, got up, and hugged his sister. "Congratulations! Stuart made me an uncle when he became an important addition to our family, and now I'll be an uncle again!"

Polly pulled Jenny into her big strong arms. "I'm happy you going to have a child. You'll be a good motha'. You mama showed you how."

Congratulations came from around the table, and chatter began at a fevered pitch as forks and knives clattered against the plates.

Most of the food quickly disappeared. Jenny jumped up to help Polly clear the table, and John even pitched in.

A smile niggled on his cheeks over the intensity on Stu's face when Polly cut the cake and placed a big piece with lots of shiny chocolate frosting on top in front of him. He dug in, and soon, frosting smeared his mouth.

"Use your napkin," Jenny said softly.

Stu used it but kept working on his plate until barely a lick of frosting remained.

John got up and returned with a pile of gifts.

"Oh," Stuart said, shaking his head no. "The things you gave me from the attic are enough."

John's lips set into a firm line. "It's your birthday, and we're celebrating."

Jenny giggled. "Aw. Unwrap them and afterward thank everybody."

Stu untied ribbons and ripped paper until a pile of gifts grew on his corner of the table. A penknife. A yo-yo. Another slingshot. A red wooden top to spin. A checkers' game. A new shirt.

Stu blinked away tears and ran and hugged Jenny and then William. Then he turned to everyone else. "Thank you!"

Bellea's baby wailed, and the mother made a quick exit as if glad to disappear to the attic. The child geared up to full volume as she passed. John ran his tongue around his teeth, still savoring the chocolate but hoping Wellington wasn't anywhere in the vicinity. Before he found the child, they needed to find another place for her to live. Perhaps Edwina would hire her to help her in the kitchen. Ed was always tired, and Bellea said she knew how to cook.

Finally, John, William, Jenny, and Valerie had a chance to visit without interruptions. Bellea had settled into the attic. The baby slept better. But John heard the kid yowling the previous night and guessed it lasted almost from sunset to sunrise. The little fellow made his presence known now, squawking so loud the noise carried downstairs.

"Did I cry a lot when I was little?" he asked Polly as she filled everyone's coffee cups.

"You a good baby, but a mite spoiled. Jenny was quieter, but she could scream at a high pitch too." Polly lifted the metal coffeepot with expertise before moving to fill Jenny's cup. "Your father, your mother or I always carried John around. He had the colic for about three months. John, you couldn't take a nap without being rocked and with you two being twins, we had our hands full. Jenny didn't like being held so much. I loved the day John finally discovered beds are for sleeping."

"Bellea shouldn't stay in the attic all the time," Jenny raised her eyebrows at him. "Wellington will be back, and the sound still carries when the baby gets wound up."

"I was thinking the same thing." John stretched his legs out and twisted the coffee mug in his hands. "Sooner or later Wellington could find her here. Maybe Edwina could hire her to help in the kitchen. Ed's pa would be there in the house almost all the time so he could look out for her and the baby when Ed is working with the horses."

Jenny propped her head on her hand, "You'd have to make sure Edwina really wants her and the baby there because Edwina can be unpredictable."

"I'll go over and talk to her in the morning." John took a sip of the coffee. "Ed's pa probably would enjoy another person in the house. I'm sure he gets lonely in his wheelchair. It would be a lot better for Bellea than here at our house. Bellea could probably assist him in getting around as well."

"Sounds like a great idea to me." William poured creamer into his coffee. "You're a Christian. We need to keep tongues from wagging the best we can. We should shun even the very appearance of evil as Scripture advises."

A little niggle tickled John's chest. He believed he was a Christian, but his faith had never been weaker. The last few years since his parents' deaths were difficult, especially with the trouble the judge brought into their lives. Yet he wanted Bellea out of the house. With her red hair, she had an almost magnetic attractiveness. He didn't like the temptation. Valerie was more mature, beautiful, sensible, and lovely inside and out. He didn't want to get sidetracked while she completed her mourning.

Yes, as soon as he had the chores completed, he'd ride over to talk to Ed and her pa.

"Want to see our new kittens?" Abe asked Stuart.

"Yes!"

Valerie took Christian upstairs, and the others sat around the table sipping coffee.

William raised his thick eyebrows and gave John a quizzical look. "John, we're leaving for Iowa the day after tomorrow. What would you think of letting Stu spend the summer with you? I know you need help here, and he's a great little helper. You could teach him how to work with the horses, trim peach trees, and maybe pick them later on. I don't know what to expect for sure when we get to Iowa since my father was murdered and I apprehended the man who killed him. Pa's young widow could be a problem too as well as her baby. The situation is quite sticky. I think you know Valerie and Christian will go home to Boston on the train."

"Letting Stuart spend the summer sounds like a great idea, Will," John said. "He could raise rabbits and keep the profits. We have hutches out there. Lots of people buy rabbits for fur. But I can use him as you mentioned in all sorts of places, and Abe and Polly love kids."

"I have school assignments he needs to complete," Jenny added. "He didn't finish out the year in Yucca Blossom. I'm sure you can help him."

John guzzled the remainder of his coffee and stood. "Is he always this well-behaved?"

William laughed. "Oh, he can be a little sneaky at times like he was when he first started hanging out with Jenny and me. But he's accepted the Lord as his Savior, and his parents must have been good at training him before they died. I haven't seen a real rebellious streak in him yet. But age twelve's when some kids start trying to show their independence."

"But he's already had independence," John noted. "You said he was living on the streets, trying to keep food in his stomach and a place to sleep." He lowered his voice and leaned toward William. "Do you think stealing food in order to live could be a habit that will give him trouble later?"

"Oh, no," William picked up his coffee cup to take to the sink. "He was a gift from God to us. He's brought us incredible joy. I think you'll enjoy having Stu around. But we'll ask him first if he wants to stay."

"Great idea." John headed for the kitchen too.

A loud knock at the door rattled the house. "Hey, John!"

John rushed to the door. Billy Joe stood outside, face flushed and his horse's mouth frothing behind him.

"The fence is down in the north pasture. The stallion and the other horses escaped."

11

John's stomach spasmed and pain shot through his stomach. "Oh, no! That was still a good fence. B.J., see if you can catch up with them horses. We'll go out and see what happened to the fence."

John, William, Jenny, and Abe sprinted toward the barn. John exhaled. All the personal mounts and a few others remained in their stalls.

"Will, you and Jenny can take your pick of horses if you want to go along." He threw a saddle over his buckskin, Dynamite, and tightened the cinch. "We could use the help. We'll need ropes. Abe, take the wagon and what we need to fix the fence. Put oats and hay near enough to the place where they got out so maybe the escapees will come back inside and eat. It's about feedin' time."

"I'll grab some sugar cubes," Jenny yelled, running for the house as soon as her animal was ready.

"I'll pick up a few apples from the cellar," Abe shouted.

"Hope the stallion didn't go berserk and break the fence down." John rubbed his jaw. "The back fence is pretty sturdy, although the horses have chewed on the top a little."

"I'd guess Wellington Davenport broke down a section and released them." Sadness paled Jenny's face. "Daddy bought good lumber when he built the fence and made sure it was sturdy. With his illness coming on, he wasn't able to fix fences all the time."

"We shouldn't accuse anyone until we have evidence," William reminded. "Say, did you forget about the babe? Perhaps you shouldn't be riding."

"I know this ranch like my own face. I'll take it easy and look for tracks."

"Watch where you step," John warned. "We don't want to mess up any evidence. There is uniqueness between footprints and even hoof prints."

John let the others watch for evidence on the way to the pasture. He couldn't afford to waste time while the horses, especially the black stallion the judge abused, were out there. He'd be the most apt to run for the hills. The other horses might come back.

"Any horse thieves around here?" William asked when they reached the opening where the horses found freedom.

"I haven't heard of any." John scowled at the break. "People are pretty honest in Peachville and the surrounding area now the judge is gone. But there are poor cowhands and gamblers who might look for a quick buck. Jenny's probably right. I imagine Wellington Davenport did it trying to get even with us over Bellea's baby."

Most of two fence sections were down, and several boards almost broken into kindling.

John dismounted and picked up a broken fence rail. "Looks like prints from the back side of an ax head pounded the nails out on the end of this one."

"That's what it looks like here, too." William was on the ground now and held what was left of a white board. "This one has a smaller print, like the head of a hatchet."

"Look here." John gestured with his open hand. "Here's a tiny chip of red paint. Could be off somebody's ax."

"Here's a cigarette butt," William drawled, handing it to John.

The wheels bounced over the rutted pastureland as Abe drove the plow horses pulling the wagon toward them.

"Whoa!" He yanked the reins, jumped down, and quickly gathered his tools and lumber to the fence line.

John straightened his back while Abe worked. "Be sure to save all these broken boards. We have evidence here."

John picked a big green leaf off a dandelion, folded it, and tucked the paint chip and the cigarette butt inside. Then he stashed the leaf into a corner of his saddlebag. "B.J. smokes. It might be his cigarette butt, but I'll show it to him and see if he had been working in this area. Let's head on out and see what we can find. Abe, you can go look when you're done here. Make one section of the fence a gate. Wind a temporary wire around the post so we can get it undone quick and get the horses back inside."

The men took off through the open space in the fence and scattered, giving their animals full rein.

Jenny dismounted and scoured the ground with her eyes.

"Don't walk about too much until we get a good look at the footprints around here," she told Abe.

"Sure won't."

Anyone who wanted the horses to escape probably would herd them out, Jenny surmised, so she walked to the area where the horses liked to stand under a large tree. Before she got there, fresh boot prints dipped into the soft pasture grass creating a trail toward the corner. Big prints, probably created by someone who carried quite a bit of weight. Hoof prints followed right behind. Whoever it was led a horse.

Something white caught her eye in the shallow pasture irrigation ditch. She rushed to it. Matches. A half-full pack of cigarettes, partially trampled by horse hooves. A squashed section of pasture grass looked as if someone sat there. Jenny found human footprints and two spent shells near the fence. Other hoof prints went the other direction right through it all toward the broken boards.

If someone shot a gun to send the horses out on the run, everyone should have heard it from the house. But with all the talking and laughter, they didn't.

Would Wellington do such a thing? Or somebody else? Did John trust B.J.? Or did Mrs. Davenport hire a person to give John grief?

Jenny backed up to remount the pinto when everything went black. She hit the ground as strong hands whirled her around and tied something black over her head.

"Keep your dirty hands off her!" Abe yelled from across the pasture. "Almighty God, deliver Jenny and her babe!"

Ignoring the pain, she gasped, trying to breathe through whatever was tied around her.

Jenny awoke to Abe fanning her face and dabbing at it with a wet handkerchief. "Good, little gal. You're awake now. You all right?"

She blinked her eyes, trying to see clearer. An old duster coat wrapped around most of her. She wiggled out of the covering and tossed it aside. "I'm still a little dizzy. Did you get a good look at him?"

"I saw 'im, but I never see'd 'im afore that I know of. But he might have worn a disguise. The mustache was crooked. He came from t'other direction. He must've been hiding in all those trees."

She took a deep breath, "John's got a mess a trouble, and Will and I are heading for Iowa."

"The Lawd know who did this," Abe picked her up and helped her mount. She spread her skirts. "The Word say, 'Be sure your sins will find you out.' So, whoever the culprit is, we'll find 'im."

Jenny rode back to the house.
"You okay?" Abe asked.

"I think I'm fine." Perspiration wet her face and the roots of her hair. "The man scared me. I couldn't breathe. I'll take it easy on the way back, and then I'll lie down a while. He probably realized I'd recognize him, so he covered my eyes."

She touched her still-flat stomach and prayed what happened wouldn't affect the baby.

Abe rode ahead so he could report the incident to the men.

"Who do you think it was?" John asked when Jenny rode into the yard.

"I don't know." Her muscles twitched as shivers shook her chin. "I'd guess one of the judge's men is still around. When I was running, one of them went to Yucca Blossom to help the judge bring me back, and I gave him considerable grief." A shaky giggle burst from her mouth. "Rocky, my goat, helped a little, too, when he tried to butt the man to the next farm. He was a young fellow. William came, tied him to a chair and gave him a sermon. But then William let him go. This guy today was bigger and smelled like a tobacco chimney. I touched his beard."

A deep breath filled her lungs as she prayed again that the baby was all right.

"Oh, look," she said softly. "Horses are reaching over the fence for the apples and the feed you placed near the opening."

Sure enough, six horses stretched their hungry necks over the fence, trying to get to the treats.

As soon as Abe opened the fence so they could pass the horses trotted into the pasture, each munching an apple, but the stallion didn't return.

"Don't pound those nails too tight," John advised. "I'm going after my black stallion."

"I'll go with you," B.J. yelled, dusting off his cowboy hat and slamming it on his head. "He's a wicked animal, but he's coming around. He'll make a good stud."

At roughly two a.m., Jenny heard John come in the house. She grabbed a robe and went to talk to him.

"Did you find the stallion?"

"No!" he exploded. His tired face reddened. "We'll probably never see him again, and B.J. said the cigarettes and the butts were probably his."

12

The next morning, John visited the Peachville sheriff.

As John entered, six-foot-six Sheriff Woody Watson spit his wad of tobacco into the spittoon at the corner of his desk and stood. "Hello, John," he greeted. "So glad to have you back in peach country. How's the ranch doing?"

John gripped the lawman's fat extended hand. "Nice to be home, but we have trouble at the ranch."

The man wiped his mouth on his red plaid sleeve, "Trouble?"

"Someone accosted my sister yesterday afternoon while we searched for evidence of horse thieves. Put an old raincoat over her head real tight and got away. Jenny passed out before Abe got to her to help."

"Not good. I didn't know Jenny was around here."

"She and her husband and adopted son are visiting. They're leaving tomorrow. We prayed, and so far Jenny hasn't had any lasting effects." John stuck his long finger in the air. "But she could have. She's with child."

"Why do you think anyone would want to hurt Jenny?"

"Because the horse thieves left evidence all over the pasture and Jenny helped gather it."

"How many horses they get?"

"All the horses in the north pasture escaped through a place in the fence where a couple of people took a hatchet and the back of an ax to destroy a whole length of board fencing. We found most of the horses, but the black stallion is still out there."

"He's an ornery one." Woody dragged a chair for John and sat at his desk, "Strange. About what time of day did this all happen?"

"We noticed it after dinner. We'd had a birthday party for Stu—he's Jenny's son—and B.J. let us know all the horses except the ones in the barn got out. But I know who did it. Wellington Davenport. His mother is hot to have Wellington's son grow up in her house."

The sheriff pulled on the right side of his handlebar mustache. "The Davenports have a grandchild?"

"It's a mess." John rubbed the side of his face. He'd rather not talk about it, but he was certain Wellington let out the horses. "A young lady, a Roberta Bellea Peabody, and her baby are staying at our house. You probably remember she brought her case against Wellington Davenport to you."

A deep frown creased the already permanent lines between the sheriff's eyebrows. "Well, yes. We found no evidence of an assault."

"Mrs. Davenport charged into my house and demanded the baby be given to her because Bellea has no means of support. A couple days later, Wellington showed up trying to get the child. I think he freed my horses and took the stallion to show me we'd better not mess with him. If his mom doesn't get the child, she might cut off his gambling funds."

"What a fine kettle of fish." The sheriff took out a little bag and got another pinch of tobacco and stuck it in his cheek. "His pa better get himself home and stay awhile for a change. He's been a terrible example for Wellington."

"How long's he been gone?"

"Probably close to a month." The sheriff shot a stream at the spittoon. "He's a professional gambler, so Wellington will be like 'im. Only thing, Wellington seldom wins. Mrs. Davenport seems fairly content so long as her husband keeps money coming in."

John handed the sheriff a small paper-wrapped package. "Here are pieces of the fence, cigarette butts we found nearby, and the chips I think came off a new ax. You could see if Wellington ax is missing any paint. If Wellington keeps messing with my stock, coming into my house and making threats, there will be trouble."

"Wellington doesn't smoke, and unless you saw 'im, you can't be sure it was Wellington." The sheriff removed the pencil he'd lodged on his big left ear and pounded the eraser end on his desk.

"I'm sure." John raked his fingers through his thick curly hair. "But he had a friend with him, the guy who assaulted my sister. Jenny thinks it's a young man who used to work for the judge. She'd recognize him, and since she caught him in the pasture, I think that's why he covered her head."

Sheriff Watson returned to playing with his pencil.

"I suggest you get to work on this and earn your pay," John said forcefully. "Are you going to file this evidence, or shall I take it back home and do your work for you?"

Woody stood, tugged at his mustache, and grinned, "Leave it here, boy."

John set the package on the desk. "If I were you, I'd take note that I am no longer a boy."

He strode to the door and slammed it hard enough to rattle the windows and the jail bars.

At the asylum, Dillon watched a patient he knew only as Harris going about the room and collecting bed bugs and crickets. Each time he caught one, he killed it. But he kept the dead ones in his hand.

Dillon tried to talk to Harris when he first arrived, but the man couldn't make any sense.

Curious about what he would do with the bugs Dillon watched, and then should have turned so he wouldn't see what he knew he was going to do. Harris threw a bug in his mouth and chomped it down like he would a jelly bean. He swallowed and threw another.

Dillon whirled around and went to the window. If he could get his mind on something else perhaps he wouldn't vomit what little lunch he had.

13

Shortly after sunrise, John harnessed the horses and parked the wagon in front of the house to take Jenny and William to the train station.

After they loaded their things, the young couple climbed in beside John. Stuart vaulted into the back, tagging along to tell them goodbye.

"How long you gonna be gone?" he asked for about the tenth time as the horses took off down the road. Stuart's face reminded John of his own young vision of Tom Sawyer: straight hair tumbling down over his forehead, a cowlick sticking up at the crown, and hair slightly curling over his collar.

"We might be back in a week or two." William twisted around to see the boy, "But if we decide to move to Iowa, we might stay until fall to get settled. At least by the time summer is over, we'll come and get you so you can start school there in September. You're our son. We'll never leave you behind."

"Do you want to go with us?" Jenny snuggled her arm around the youth and squeezed him to her bosom. "If you changed your mind about staying, you can come."

Stuart gazed toward John, and his cheeks beamed, "I think I'm going to have fun here, but ..." His eyes brimmed with tears.

John stopped the wagon. "You sure you want to stay—for the whole summer? I had things planned, but if you want to go ..."

"I want to stay, but, but ..." Stuart blinked and his fist swiped his wet cheeks. A sob tore from the depths of his chest, "I'll miss you!"

Jenny hugged him closer. "I know. You already lost one set of parents. I'm so glad you love us like you do." She pushed him back a little to look in his face. "We love you like that, but maybe deeper." She grinned. "Don't you know how you weaseled your way right into our hearts with your antics? My parents died too and left me all alone. Your Papa William's parents also are in heaven and left him. It's one reason we have to go to Iowa. We need to see what's going to happen to the farm. You can be sure if we decide to live there, you'll be with us. If we move, we'll have to go back to Yucca Blossom and get our things and sell the property there. You'll never be left behind."

She kissed him gently on the cheek and held his hand until they arrived at the train depot. She gave Stu her handkerchief to blow his nose on and then had to borrow William's to wipe her own nose and sweep away her tears.

"But you and Papa are going to have a baby of your own!"

William reached for his son and helped him from the wagon. "Our baby will not take your place." He laughed, "No one could ever be like Stuart. You're a one-of-a-kind boy and that's powerful good. We have room to love you, the baby, and even more."

John relaxed when a mischievous smile replaced Stu's frown on his slightly freckled face.

Uneasiness gripped John as he strode away from the depot and the train huffed toward Iowa. He held Stuart's fingers in his big mitt, kicking himself for disobeying his sister and giving the child a big sucker to lick.

He lifted the thin boy into the wagon's front seat and turned to go over to the driver's side.

"Stu, how about scooting over? You can drive a team, can't you?"

"I don't know. Papa William still travels in his big peddler wagon, and I think it's too big for me."

"Well, this wagon isn't even half as heavy. Crawl on over there, and I'll show you how to drive a team."

Stu quickly crunched the sucker into bits and swallowed. John poured water from his canteen so they could get the sticky off his hands.

Shortly Stu was situated in the driver's seat, but he was so short his feet barely hit the floor. John handed him the reins.

"Use them this way to turn left. Pull this one to the right when you want them to turn right. Don't pull on them too much. You'd hurt the horse's mouth. You say, 'Giddy-up' when you want them to go. Jiggle the reins a little and click your tongue a couple of times against your mouth."

John leaned toward Stu's ear so the horses wouldn't hear and showed him how to make the sound.

"Are you sure that's not a quack, quack like a duck? What on earth would they do if we had a bunch of ducks quacking? Go in circles?"

John threw back his head and laughed.

Stu flicked the reins and clicked his tongue a couple of times. The horses took off like a rock out of a slingshot. Stu chuckled while he tried to manage the reins.

"Hey!" John yelled.

"Did I do it right?" Stu took his eyes off the road to look at John.

John gently scooted Stu over far enough so he could take the reins in his big hands. "I wasn't finished telling you how to drive the horses. Good thing the horses know the way to the barn."

The horses already galloped too fast for Stu to control, stirring up a dust cloud. A bump hit one wheel.

"Wow. You got that jackrabbit." Giggles filled the air.

"Whoa! Whoa!" John yanked the reins to his chest.

"It felt like the wagon took the curve with two wheels." More giggles.

"Whoa. Whoa!"

"I don't think they hear you!" The giggles erupted into deeper laughter, but Stu clung to John like a sand burr.

"I forgot about the mare having a colt in the barn," John mumbled.

"Huh?"

"Whoa there, Nellie."

A man and a woman in a buggy approached ahead. John did get the team over to the right long enough for the couple to pass on the left, fear enlarging their eyes.

"Oooohhhh. That was close," Stu sobered.

The team hit the ruts and potholes on the long drive home, bouncing John and Stu off the seat, but they landed before John lost control of the team.

Finally, John's white two-story house rose in the distance.

"One more curve and they'll go in our drive and head for the barn," John explained, Stu still glued to his side. The turn wasn't as tight as the last one, and the animals slowed, the harnesses rattling as their hooves pounded the ground. The wheels squeaked but didn't lift. The horses jerked to a stop in front of the barn door, sides heaving, mouths foaming, heads fighting the bits.

"Praise the Lord," John breathed as he dropped the reins.

"You know, I have a goat almost as ornery as those horses," Stuart shook himself off John. "But love that goat. Did you see him at our house?"

"I sure did," John laughed, visualizing the ornery critter always looking for a chance to put his head to someone's backside.

"Name's Rocky." Stu climbed into John's arms so he could help him down, "We got him a nanny goat, and now we have baby goats. I hope Delbert Duggan takes good care of them while we're gone. If we move, I think Papa will bring Rocky and the nanny with us."

John exhaled when his feet touched the ground.

"Sorry," Stu said. "I don't think I want to drive the team anymore."

John rubbed the boy's head, "Don't worry about it. I should have remembered Nellie has a colt in the barn. Mares don't like to leave their colts. I'll give you another lesson later and show you what to do."

"Not until my legs quit shaking," Stu stomped to the porch and plopped on a nearby rock.

As soon as he removed the harnesses, John brushed the horses down and walked them into the barn. The mama and baby happily greeted each other.

Walking toward the house, he noticed Bellea hanging diapers on the clothesline. Her red hair glistened in the sunlight. Every strand flattered her flawless face. Valerie played with her little son on the lawn.

Hadn't it been more than a year since her husband died? She should be out of mourning by now.

He frowned. Two available women here and he had no wife. Well, he'd be sure to send Valerie away tomorrow on the train with a kiss she wouldn't forget, and he'd get Bellea out of the house before he got ideas about kissing her.

14

Sure enough, the next morning at the railroad station John disregarded Valerie's black mourning dress, pulled her close and pressed his ready lips to her lightly painted ones.

She blinked, and her mouth dropped with surprise. Yet elegance radiated from her whole body.

"We didn't have much time together," he whispered near a small ear that held a diamond earring. A pleasing fragrance filled his nostrils. "I don't want you to forget me when you get to Boston. I'm not much of a writer, but I'll write you if you write me. When your mourning's over, I'll come to Boston so we can see what the future holds."

She glanced at the waiting passengers. A smile pulled her lovely cheeks into roses, already brightened with pink. "Sure. I'll write. I enjoyed our visit and will look forward to seeing you."

John pecked Christian on the cheek and then reached out and drew them both into his arms and gave them a squeeze. "We need much more time together."

Valerie clutched his hand with her dainty fingers and held on until the train whistle blew and the conductor shouted, "All aboard!" Then she pecked his cheek.

"I'm glad I met you at the wedding," she said. "Goodbye for now. Tell John bye-bye," she urged her boy. He waved, a huge smile revealing about a dozen shiny teeth.

All the way home, John's heart beat faster than usual. Stuart had stayed home. Polly was plotting her garden, and soon as spring burst into Peachville, she planned to use his help.

Polly stood when John drove into the yard. She held tiny bags of seeds in her hands she received from her order out of the gardening catalog. "Back already?"

"Yep."

"Did you kiss her goodbye?" Stuart grinned, mischief shining from his eyes.

John winked, nodded and headed for the house. He slammed the door as he was used to doing, and the baby screamed from the cradle beside where Bellea worked in the kitchen. She frowned, dropped the spoon she stirred stew with and fussed over the babe.

John went to the sink to fill his canteen. He mentally thanked God his father dug a well, and the house had clean running water.

"Sorry I woke the boy," he said. "I'm not used to being quiet."

Bellea cuddled the tiny fellow in her arms and shot John a look that would melt candle wax. "I'll never get this kitchen cleaned if you can't learn." The freckles across her nose stood out more with her anger.

Irritation rubbed at his insides. *Tiptoe around my own house? Not on your life.* He stared at the young mother and could feel the warm sparks shooting her way.

"Well, if you will quit complaining and the baby will stop screaming, we need to talk. It's not a good idea for you to live here with me, a young unmarried man."

The child hushed, and John took advantage of the moment. "You know Edwina Jorgenson, don't you? She needs more help on the ranch. She's trying to do the cooking, train horses and take care of the whole caboodle since her father is in a wheelchair. She has help with the ranch, and she's a good cook. But I'll bet she'd give you room and board if you'd help her, especially with clean up. Paul Jorgenson probably could use assistance now and then, too."

"Well, soon as I get a little money, I plan to open a beauty parlor or a beauty school," Bellea tipped her pretty head. "I did Mrs. Davenport's hair when I worked there. Her friends used to come over and have me do their hair, too. I did my mom's and my sisters' before they died. I don't know why I'm alive, but I need a way to support my boy."

"That might take a while. We aren't giving you anything to work here, so you need a paying job. Edwina might pay you in addition to room and board. She might even give you extra to do her hair."

He stepped back and eyed the young woman, "Your hair looks really nice. In fact, it's gorgeous. Maybe you could make Edwina's hair beautiful, too."

"Thank you," Bellea's freckled face bloomed red. "If you're not interested in giving me work, I'll talk to her. She should quit wearing that braid or letting her hair fly."

"I'll mention it to Edwina and if she's willing to hire you, I'll take you and your things over there."

Bellea nestled the baby back in the cradle and rocked it. "I'll probably need the cradle if I go to Edwina's."

"Fine. Good idea," John agreed and walked out, stopping his ready hand from slamming the back door.

A few hours later when John knocked on Edwina's door, she shouted, "Come in. Door's unlocked, and I'm busy."

He twisted the knob and found her up to her elbows in a foaming pan full of dishes. Her blonde hair hung in a disheveled mess. Her face blazed almost as bright as her red apron. Her father sat in his wheelchair nearby drinking coffee at a table filled with more dirty dishes.

"Oh, John!" she sighed—music in her voice now. She dried her hands and tried to tuck the stray hair into the loose braid he could now see hanging from the back of her head. "I didn't expect you. You caught me at a bad moment. I'm way behind on my work."

"I understand, gal." He wanted to hit himself in the head. What was wrong with him? Even with her hair all askew, she'd made his heart sit up and take notice. Circles shadowed her eyes. Weariness hung on her like spider webs. Yet an attractiveness clung to her. His eyes narrowed in on the dimples in her cheeks when her mouth twitched.

Embarrassment flamed from her sparkling blue eyes, and she blinked and shook her head at the dirty room. "I … I …"

"Good morning, Mr. Jorgenson." John walked over and shook the man's hand.

"Good to see you, John." A smile settled on his lips as the pale, thin man returned a fairly good grip. "How are your horses doing?"

"Much better after we found those let out of the pasture—except for the judge's stallion. Couldn't find him."

"He might come back." Jorgenson released his hand. "I've had runaway horses return before."

"I hope so." John stopped and took a good look at Edwina, who was at the sink furiously washing dishes. He drew closer. The pants she wore accented her curves. He imagined she bought them in the men's section of the mercantile. "I came to talk about Bellea."

"Bellea?" Her chin dropped.

He stepped to the sink and elbowed her out of the way. "Scoot. I'll wash, and you dry or clean up the table. My mama and daddy taught me how to work and that included washing dishes."

Edwina stomped her foot, and the impact from the boot rattled the house, "You can't do that!"

"Who sez? While you're standing there with your mouth open, I could have washed half of these in the sink. I'll need those off the table soon. While we work, we can talk."

Ed's papa reached out, put his hands on the big wheels and started for the parlor as his feet helped pull the chair with the clunking of his boots.

John's eyes followed him while his hands scrubbed dishes. "Mr. Jorgenson, I'd like for you to hear what I have to say and see what you think."

Edwina picked up the dirty plates and then set them back down. "Well, first, I want you to know why I'm so far behind."

"Something happen this mornin'?"

"Well, Papa didn't feel well in the night, and I didn't sleep much, so I slept in longer than usual. And then this morning when I was out feeding and watering horses, I saw your black. I heard about your trouble with your fence and that you hadn't found the judge's horse. When I saw him near my property, I tried to get the stallion into my pasture so you could come and fetch him. But he ran off, and I took after him on Bullet. Almost roped him a time or two, but he gyrated too much. He's still got wild in him, but he's been fed enough good horse feed he's probably craving oats and a little sugar."

John grabbed a towel and dried several plates, stacking them on the cabinet. "Where was your hired hand?"

"I couldn't find him until I'd wasted too much time and had to get to the house. As you can see, I had dishes to wash, bread to bake and I need to get supper started."

"Well, thanks for trying. At least the stallion must be hanging around instead of going to the hills." He stuck his hands into the sudsy water and scoured more dirty dishes. "As I said, I need to talk to you about Bellea. She needs a job, and I don't want her in my house."

"Why is she there?" asked Jorgenson.

"She's doesn't have anywhere else to go. She cooked for the Davenports besides cleaning."

John dumped the dirty water and refilled the dishpan from the pump and the teakettle. After adding soap, he went back to washing dishes. "What do you two think? Mr. Jorgenson, it probably would be nice to have her around the house in case you need someone when Ed's out with the horses."

Edwina stuck her tongue over her upper lip, licked her lips, and then her dimples did that thing again. "I don't know. Have Wellington or his mother been back?"

"Together they've been there three times. But with the fire you have in your eyes and the gun on your hip, I don't think he'll try anything here."

Mr. Jorgenson's brows pulled his eyes open wider. "But with having a baby, how much work can the girl do?"

"Well, that might be a downside, but perhaps a little later he'd add a lot of joy to your house. My friend, Valerie MacDougal, was here with her little boy, who's about a year old. He's really cute. Bellea's little one does get wound up with his crying. But he's sleeping more at night, and Bellea is a good mother. Before they died from influenza, Bellea took care of her little brothers and sisters. You probably remember so many people coming down with it."

Jorgenson shook his head, "Probably the same epidemic that took my wife."

"I'm sorry." John dried his hands and touched the man's shoulder. "What do you think about hiring Bellea? We aren't paying her, but she's a good worker. She needs room and board. She's gone too long already without having enough to eat, and she's nursing the baby. Bellea probably hates to leave Polly and loves her for all she's done for her. But I admit the young gal isn't too happy with me. I'm too loud, slamming doors and startling her little one. The big thing, it isn't appropriate for her to live with us. Since you're older, Paul, I think it's acceptable."

Jorgenson wheeled his chair a bit closer. "Ed said Wellington is the father. Why doesn't he marry her instead of harassing you folks?"

John went back to the sink and rinsed the remaining clean dishes and stacked them in the drainer. "Bellea hates him for what he did to her. Mrs. Davenport is mighty vengeful and hopes to have her grandson and leave Bellea to fend for herself. Jenny said Bellea reported Wellington to the sheriff after he attacked her, and Woody didn't even look at her bruises. Assumed it was her fault. Bellea has been roaming around since then, surviving in people's barns and eating what she could find. I think she's basically a good girl. She did lots of praying when she was in labor."

"We'll have to think on it," Edwina turned. "Don't you agree, Papa?"

The older man nodded. "Edwina does need help, but I don't know if we're desperate enough to take a woman and her child in."

John wiped off the table with his dishrag and then dried his hands.

"Bellea is not lazy," he added. "She hasn't been any trouble to us. Well, except for the babe crying and Wellington and his mother wanting to kidnap the boy. I think Bellea would be safe here. We don't need to tell anyone where she went. She's great with women's hair, and I imagine Ed would enjoy taking a break and having her hair fixed once in a while." He winked at her. "Who knows? With all her beauty, she might snag a husband."

Jorgenson chuckled. "Our hired hand already is sweet on her."

Edwina stomped her boot again, "I told you he doesn't like me. He wants to own this ranch, and don't you dare encourage him."

"I better git home," John said. "I'll bring Bellea over in the morning so you can talk, and you can decide if you want her here."

"Thanks for helping." Edwina reached for him, gave him a hug and kissed his cheek. "You were a lifesaver today. Thanks to you, my bread will be ready for supper."

"You're welcome," he mumbled. Jenny had been right. Edwina probably had loved him since grade school. Her heart was in her eyes when she stepped away. Yet John didn't have a thing to worry about. Her hired hand would have her married to him before she knew what happened. A lovesick gal was ripe for picking by about anybody.

As he mounted, the vision in his head of Edwina at the sink with her hair looking like the straw for a scarecrow couldn't compare with Valerie MacDougal's elegance. Although raised in the city by a wealthy attorney, Valerie had enjoyed homesteading with her late husband, and she'd be a perfect fit as John's wife. Jenny said Valerie put love in all the canned fruits and vegetables in her cellar. John never met Christian MacDougal, but William described him as an amazing man. Could John compete with his memory and raise his little boy? Valerie might not come back to Colorado to live on a horse farm after being in Boston again. Might she have former suitors there?

15

Two weeks later in Boston, Archibald Forsythe eyed Valerie MacDougal as she strode into the law office to speak to her father, the lead attorney in the practice of Van Meter, Forsythe, and MacDougal.

Aaron Van Meter, her father, added Valerie's last name to the sign above the office as soon as she moved back to Boston, although she only assisted with cases.

The young man watched the elegant lady he once thought he loved. He stood at the door to his office, shiny shoes stuck to the floor. The lady had been a rosebud sort of woman, but now she had blossomed. Archibald didn't know a word to describe the beauty of the tall, thin, blue-eyed blonde dressed in black.

Montgomery Portsmith clapped Archibald on the back, and he about jumped out of his clothes.

"Sorry. But it's no use to think about her, Archie." Monty grinned like he'd won a jury trial in fifteen minutes. "Her papa says she's almost through the grieving process, but she's corresponding with a farmer she met last year at a friend's wedding in Yucca Blossom, Colorado."

Archibald smoothed the left side of his hair to make sure he looked all right. "I need to talk to her. Valerie says she's ready to participate in challenging projects. I've been doing groundwork on an unusual pro bono case. She's the ideal person to partner with me in that, and she wants to know more about it."

Monty's pushy nature popped into his beady eyes, "Tell me about it."

Archie, already standing firm, stretched taller and looked down at Monty, "Not now. It probably will be the most difficult case I've latched onto."

"Wow." The beady eyes stared. "I haven't heard anything unusual in the news. What is it? You can tell me."

"No, thank you. If we ever get to court, you'll probably hear all you want to know."

Valerie turned and walked toward Archibald. "Hello." Her smile lit up his lonely soul.

"Nice to see you, Valerie. Ready to find out a little more about the case?" It didn't seem long ago when he courted her for several weeks and held her hand. She even kissed him on the cheek, prompting him to think of marriage. Then he heard about her engagement to a farmer she'd known for years, and she'd married him. But the poor bridegroom died.

"We have a conference room open, Val." Should he have addressed her as Mrs. MacDougal? "Do you have a few minutes?"

Valerie hesitated. Her long brown lashes blinked. He sensed her brain whirling, wondering whether she wanted to join him on such an unusual case that probably would have wide media coverage.

She took a deep breath. "If it doesn't take too long."

He led the way to the conference room. She probably thought he wanted to resurrect the romance. But the office wasn't the place.

When they sat across from each other, he smoothed his thin mustache. Excitement pumped through him. Sweat dampened his forehead. His heart beat like a ticking clock.

"I've lived for something like this pro bono case. I don't know what you'll think, but I feel God wants me to do it. I've prayed about it, and I know you are the person I need to work with me."

A frown lined her formerly smooth forehead.

He put up his hands. "Don't say anything until you hear me out. Do you know anyone who has been admitted to the asylum?"

She looked at the ceiling, out the window and then stared at the floor. "I don't remember anybody. But people sweep that sort of thing up and put it in with the ashes, never to be heard about again. Families, especially, don't want people to know."

Wanting her undivided attention, he reached over and lifted her chin so he could communicate better. "I told you this is an unusual and important case. I have a friend there, Dr. Dillon Haskill. Dignitaries sent him to the lunacy asylum after he had a seizure at the State Fair in front of everybody. They said he's demon-possessed and a danger to society. Dillon is a brilliant man, an outstanding physician, and friend. He's been at the asylum four years, but he's still a brilliant man and physician. The conditions in the asylum are terrible, and patients don't get enough to eat."

Valerie's jaw dropped. Her pink lips tempted him to think of romance, but he had to stick to business.

She regained her dignity. "I'm interested. But what do you plan to do?"

"Gather evidence he is wrongfully held there. We'll probably have to sue the state for wrongful imprisonment. I'll also see what I can discover about several other patients, to reveal whether they need to be there. Dillon says quite a few who are perfectly sane are held in the place, and there's no way to get out."

"Terrible. Sounds challenging, but a worthy endeavor if we could succeed." Her flawless face bloomed a bright pink. "You're sure Dillon is sane and I'm the person to help?"

Archibald didn't say a word but nodded.

Her eyes sparkled with interest. "I'd love to get involved, but I don't know if I have enough experience." She leaned toward him. "It's important you have a qualified person to assist. Also, I have other opportunities popping up, but I want to know whether I'd rather practice law. This sounds like a formidable case, but that'll make it interesting. Thanks for thinking of me."

She stood, and all Archibald could think about was the rancher in Colorado who already stepped in to take her first husband's place.

She stuck her well-manicured hand out for him to shake.

16

The rooster only crowed twice before John kicked off the bedcovers, got up and dressed in a shirt and overalls. Then he tromped down the stairs.

B.J. was on the porch. "Come on in and have breakfast."

B.J. let the smoke from the cigarette in his fingers curl upward. He shifted one shoulder up and the other down and looked off in the distance. His slightly whiskered cheek wiggled to one side and then back again. "I'm headin' out. I got a better offer, and I'd like my pay."

John's breath puffed his cheeks. He put a hand to his head. "Where you goin'? I thought you liked it here."

B.J. sucked on his cigarette and then spewed smoke. "Sorry, but I need more money. I'll take my pay and hit the road."

John counted several bills as he took them out of his pocket. "I think that's right. You can check to see if it's correct."

B.J. grabbed it, whirled and headed for his horse.

Eyes blinking against the sun, John unfolded his arms while B.J. went. He rubbed the scar on his cheek and turned back inside.

Coffee aroma and a hint of frying bacon filled his nostrils. Abe sat at the table sipping coffee, and Polly stood at the stove, humming while she cooked.

"B.J. picked up his pay and quit us."

"That so?" Abe mumbled. He put down the Bible in his hand. "How long was he here? Three weeks? Probably God's will. I couldn't see that he's helped much. He allus seem off by his self."

John reached for the filled cup Polly had poured. "Well, he's gone, so we will forget about him. Polly, we need to make sure Bellea is out of bed and ready to go to Edwina's right away. I'd like to get over to her house before she starts work with her horses. Besides, she's in desperate need of help now."

A tousled head of hair appeared beside John. "Can I go with you?"

"Sure, Stu, if you check on those rabbits I bought for you yesterday. Be sure they have food and water. Polly, I'll watch the bacon while you yell at Bellea and see if she's up."

John took the fork. Polly always chose a spot on the wood cook stove where the bacon would not burn if you watched and flipped it a few times to make it crispy.

"Bellea, John will be ready to go before long," Polly shouted at the bottom of the stairs. "If you need help with the baby, one of us can hold him."

Polly walked back into the kitchen, a smile on her face. "I'm going to miss her and the baby. Most of the time, she's a picture of sunshine. She ought to sing in church. She has a beautiful voice. Bellea has done every job I asked her to do and done it well. She's a good mother, too. She's had a hard life since her family died."

He forked bacon onto the warm platter. "I hadn't heard her singing. When did she do that?"

Polly nudged John on the shoulder. "She sings to the baby all the time. If you hadn't been afraid the little tyke would fill your ears with wails, you could've stayed around to hear. I think David's favorite is Oh, My Darlin', cuz he always gets quiet when she sings it. You ought to hear her sing hymns. Bellea knows lots of 'em."

John could think of nothing but getting her out of the house.

"If Bellea keep away from Wellington Davenport, she likely have the Lord's blessing. There's no telling what God will do to make her situation turn into good," Abe said, filling his plate with eggs, bacon, and biscuits. "Already the Lord's given her a healthy little boy who brings her great joy."

Stuart burst into the back door, eyes and mouth wide open. "Hey, everybody! We have baby bunnies. More'n a dozen of them! They almost look like mice."

"Sure they're not mice?" John teased with a grin.

"A rabbit wouldn't birth a mouse, John," Stuart's face screwed up with disgust. "You said you raised rabbits when you were a kid. You should know better."

"Did you pick up the baby and take a good look at 'im?" John continued joking.

"No. The mama rabbit acted like a bulldog when I tried to pick one up. Besides, they might not live if I mess with them. Our nanny goat had babies, and they are much cuter."

"Well, those bunnies will be cute little things before ya know it." Polly reclaimed her position at the stove. "Don't forget and get attached. Tha's a lot of bunnies to feed, so they'll go in the skillet or be sold afore we have rabbits in my garden. The rabbit pens are too small, and you're going to have too many."

"But ... but ... I want to have fun with them."

"The instant one of them ventures into my garden, you might not have any bunnies. I have a few things out there I planted in the fall, like parsnips, carrots, and winter onions."

John rubbed Stuart on the back. "You'll have plenty of time to get acquainted with the little ones before we start getting rid of some. I'm giving them all to you, so have fun with them. In a few days, you can pet them and have a good old time. But yes, one by one, the young ones will be sold. But we'll keep the buck and the does, and in about another month, there'll probably be more little ones. In no time, you'll have money in your pocket."

Stuart shook his head. "I can't believe we'd have so many bunnies. How long does it take for them to grow up?"

"Mama jackrabbits usually kick their babies out of the nest when they're still quite small. They can live on grass and that sort of thing, but they aren't considered adults until they're about six months old. We'll try to sell the little ones that don't need mama in about nine weeks—right close to Easter. Many children like to have them as pets. Be sure the bunnies are healthy, though, so the new owners won't feed them to a snake."

A yelp squeaked from Stu, "No! I won't let them be fed to a snake."

John tousled the hair on the kid's head. "No worries. We won't. Hey. After we get back from Edwina's, how about I make you a pair of stilts? The peach tree trimmers are coming, and you can learn how they walk on stilts."

"You mean it?"

"Sure."

"Wow. If I could find a neighbor kid, we could have a circus."

By ten thirty that morning, John, Stu, a shy Bellea, and the tiny baby arrived at the Jorgenson Ranch.

"Come on in everybody," Ed welcomed, waving her hand while she held the screen door open.

Edwina's blue eyes sparkled. Her dimples puckered and relaxed. "This is a fabulous idea to have you come and help us, Roberta. Pa and I needed someone like you since Mama died."

"Thank you." A tiny smile worked its way onto Bellea's lips. "But would you call me Bellea? It was my middle name and my grandmother's name, and I am using that now."

When they were all seated, Bellea wrapped the blanket a little tighter around the baby. "I'll be able to go to church, won't I? Especially after Wellington quits trying to help his mother get my baby?"

Edwina's smile made her glow. "Yes. I like to go myself. It will be great having a gal my age to go with."

"You probably could get Clyde to go with you," Pa injected into the conversation, rubbing his long nose. As his hand dropped, a mischievous grin swept over his pale face.

Edwina stomped her foot and caused the baby to wail.

She shut her eyes, squeezed her lips together and her dimples looked like permanent fixtures until she relaxed. "Sorry. I guess it's a bad habit. My temper gets the best of me. But, Pa, I'm not going to encourage Clyde anymore. He smokes and cusses, and I can't imagine kissing a mouth that's been used as a chimney. Furthermore, whether you believe it or not, he's after this ranch. He's rude, doesn't want to take orders from a woman, but is all honey and molasses when he's trying to budge his way into my heart."

The four of them had a round of chocolate chip cookies, with Stuart choosing milk instead of coffee, and they sat visiting for about twenty minutes.

Then John cleared his throat. "I have tree trimmers coming before long and need to get home. The tree expert is going to see what kind of condition the orchard is in since the judge neglected everything. I'll bring Bellea and all her things over this evening if you're ready for her to come."

"I'm ready now," Ed said. "Is it okay, Papa?"

"Sure. Bellea, we can use you. But keep in mind if it doesn't go well, we'll have to send you go back to John's."

"I understand." Bellea turned the baby upward in her hands. "Would you like to see my son?"

"Sure." Edwina bent, her eyes bright with interest. "I think he's smiling at me. He's adorable."

Bellea held the baby toward Edwina's pa. The man pulled the blanket further away from the tiny face. "He's a sweetie all right. A real looker. Too bad he's so cute. Wellington's mama probably will keep trying."

"What do you think of working there?" John asked Bellea as soon as they jumped into the wagon ready to go back to John's house.

"I imagine we'll be happy there, but I'll miss Polly. She already taught me all sorts of good things I need to know."

John shook the reins. "The door will be open for you to visit anytime. And if you have trouble for any reason, come back, and we'll find you a place to go."

The tree trimmers stood in the yard when John drove the team in. Hank Grisham strode toward him. "A walk through tells me the trees are in pretty bad shape. But I have a great group of workers, and they can turn an orchard around sometimes. We'll be back early in the mornin.'"

Before he left, Grisham gave John an estimate for the work, and John agreed, gritting his teeth over having to pay out more money while nothing seemed to come in.

After he helped Bellea down from the wagon, they walked over to Stu. John's stomach jiggled with quiet laughter. The boy's face screwed up like a bulldog after a cat. He piled manure from the chicken house into a wheelbarrow, as Polly supervised and chickens squawked and flapped their wings. The feisty rooster threatened to flog. Apparently, Stu already knew what to do and gave the old boy a gentle shove aside.

"After this, we'll plant tomatoes and peppers in the hothouse," Polly said when John and Bellea passed. "And maybe a few flowers."

That evening, John saddled the team and drove to Edwina's ranch again with Bellea, the baby, the cradle, and the rest of their things stuffed in a clean flour sack.

Bellea shifted on the wagon seat, seeming a little uneasy. "Do you think Wellington or Mrs. Davenport will find us there?"

"I don't know. You noticed Edwina is no common girlie."

"She always has been different. In school, the boys didn't dare dip her braid in the ink or tease her. One new kid copied the answers from her paper, and she walked past and shoved his face into his desk so hard he had a bloody nose. He never messed with her again."

"That's Ed for you. Glad it wasn't me. I've always teased her a little, and I think she sort of likes it. But notice she wears a gun on her hip at home. On her ranch, she runs into rattlesnakes, horse thieves, and what have you, and she's a great shot. I imagine Wellington knows better than to mess with Edwina. In the first place, she has a short fuse. In one of her snits without a weapon or working up a sweat, she could probably tie him into knots and toss him on his horse. I'm surprised she hasn't done it to her ranch hand if he crosses her one too many times."

"Oh, she'll probably marry him." Bellea offered one of the few smiles John had seen, and it was beautiful.

He laughed. "I thought so this morning, but I got to thinking. If he's planning to marry her to get her ranch, I'm beginning to think Ed's smarter than that."

The team passed through the arching sign over the road with Jorgenson Horses painted on top. The team's harnesses jingled, and their hooves pounded on the hard dirt as they drove up the long drive and into Edwina's yard.

"She always was smart in school," Bellea agreed.

The cool water refreshed Polly as she washed the grime from her face. She patted her cheeks and dried her hands.

"Y'all need to wash up too, Stuart." Her musical voice dipped to a growl. "Look. You tracked mud all ova my clean floor. Why didn't ya clean ya feet? You might even have chicken droppings on your boots."

Stuart made a face and looked down. "Oops. Sorry." He pulled off his muddy boots and plunked them beside the door, releasing dried crusts from the soles.

Polly snatched up the broom and reached for the dustpan, but the front door opened and slammed, shaking the house. "That you, John?"

He always used the back door.

No answer but heavy footsteps strode toward the entrance to the attic stairs.

A half dozen strides by Polly's long legs and she stood face to face with Wellington Davenport. "Where do you think you're going?"

"I'm getting that baby for my mother." Although Polly towered over him by about six inches and outweighed him by at least forty pounds, he shoved her aside with his elbow and clutched the stair rail.

Polly sung the broom and hit him square on the seat of the pants, and he toppled headfirst into the stairs.

"Hit's about time you git a spankin' and taught right from wrong, young man." Polly held the broom ready for a few more swats. "Haven't you done enough to sweet little Bellea? Now you want to harm her son? Want him to grow up in your mama's house, a worthless gambler, ravager of women, and a lazy good for nothin' like you who doesn't fear God or man? It's men like you that God created hell for."

Wellington twisted around to look at her, a bruise mottling dark blue on his face. He stretched out an arm. "Don't hit me with the broom again. You're black. You have no right to touch me."

Polly stuck out a strong hand and yanked him to his feet and got a whiff of strong drink. "Someone needs to get your attention. Becuz you been raised with money doesn't make you high and mighty. You're a poor excuse for a man. Even though his skin is black, my Abe is worth a hundred men like you who won't take responsibility or treat people with respect. Your kind go around drunk and waste their lives in riotous living. You'll wake up someday ol' and feeble and no one lovin' ya. What ya need is to get down on ya knees and ask God for mercy—now!"

She jabbed the floor with her broom handle, and he jumped so high light shone beneath his boots. He staggered over to a chair and put his head in his hands.

"You're drunk."

"What's going on, Polly?" Stuart walked into the room, still drying his hands, leaving dirty streaks on the clean white towel.

Polly didn't have time to discipline him now. "This fella's after Bellea's baby. Says he's the father."

"But, but …" Stu shook his head, pointing to the attic stairs and motioning, trying to remind her Bellea wasn't here.

Polly touched the top of Stu's head and pointed him toward the back door. "I think you better check on those rabbits John bought ya again. Make sure a hawk's not trying to get the babies."

As soon as the screen door squeaked with Stuart's exit, Polly turned to Wellington. "Whether you want it, or like it or not, I's gonna pray for you. I's gonna pray for God's mercy and his blessings on your soul. He'll forgive ya sins if'n you ask 'im."

Polly put her hands on his already bowed head and in a loud voice quoted Scripture on God's mercy, forgiveness, and love for the sinner. Then she got happy and shouted, sang and danced all over the parlor. Wellington stared, his face twitching. She pulled him to his feet again, his cold hand trembling in hers. He seemed sober now.

He squeezed her hand. "Thank you. But you're right. I'm a low-down useless worm. Keep praying for me."

With that, he was gone, his horse galloping as if the devil himself chased him.

Stu slammed the screen door. "No more babies yet, but I might be feeding them too much. The other doe is mighty fat."

"Don't get too attached," Polly warned, still feeling blessed from head to toe. "In a few weeks, we can have one for dinner."

"For dinner?"

"Sure. That's why we raise chickens, isn't it? For fried chicken. John loves fried chicken. Don't you? That's what we're having tonight. But we also can eat fried rabbit. It's jus' as good."

"Why don't we get cottontails? They ain't purty like my rabbits."

"Well, has William taught you to shoot yet?"

"Naw. Mama, er … Jenny thought about it. William, my pa now, is busy with lots of things. But he'll probably do it. MMa said he's really good with a gun. Shot a rattlesnake one time right through the head and saved her life."

"Since you got a BB gun for your birthday, I imagine John and Abe will let you practice on crows and wild rabbits and then let you use a shotgun. A-course we don't eat crow, but we'll eat jackrabbits and quail and pheasant."

Stuart grinned. Polly stretched out her big long arms and gave him a hug. His skinny body clung to her for a minute. Then he looked up at her and smiled.

She wished Abe would hurry and get back home. Would Mrs. Davenport send Wellington come right back to get the baby? Since she'd relaxed, she needed a hug herself.

17

John found a couple of old two-by-fours in the barn. It took only a few minutes to cut them to Stu's height, He sawed a wood scrap and nailed a wedge for the footrest. Then he attached a strip of rubber across the top to hold his feet.

He handed the stilts to Stu. "Here you are, young man. Guide with your arms and feet. Pull up on the stilt with each foot as you walk."

Eyes wide, Stuart watched John snatch his own stilts from the barn, lean against the woodshed, and balance them in front of him. After his feet were in place, John stood erect and took off walking. The stilts clunked on the hard ground every step he took. "See? Easy."

With that, John's stilts trembled. He squeezed his legs closer together and then regained his balance, but almost embarrassed himself. He was heavier than he'd been when he went everywhere walking on the things.

Stu giggled. "Easy, huh?"

"Sure." John looked away. The feel of the stilts returned after a few more steps, and he trotted all over the yard. Then the right stilt stepped on a small rock, and he tumbled to the ground. He hit hard and groaned.

"Are you hurt?" Stu bent down and touched his arm.

John moved his legs and arms and took his time getting to his feet. "Nothing but my pride, I guess. I'm out of practice. I need to fix that now because I'm going out to the orchard to trim trees this morning."

Stu braced against the woodshed and stood his stilts out in front of him. He took off toward the house as if he'd walked on stilts all of his life. "Hey, Polly. Look at me."

Polly opened the screen door and stood there, a little white scarf tied over her head, amazement on her face. "Lawsie, chile. You an ak-ro-bat. John, you might as well get him out to the orchard to help. Don't forget I'm feeding the tree trimmin' crew. There's a big pot a stew simmering on the stove, fresh bread, and four pies in the oven. Abe'll set up the table under the big tree at the side of the house."

John and Stuart carried their stilts to the orchard along with a big jug of water. "These guys have a different type of stilts," John explained. "Having them tightly attached to their legs frees up their arms to work."

Stu stared.

Hank Grisham clunked toward the two. "We need to talk." He took his hat off and ran his fingers over his balding head. "You're going to lose trees, John. Quite a few are in such bad shape, we'll need to cut them down. You'll need to plant new trees if you want the orchard to produce high yields again."

Hot panic shot through John. His inheritance fund was dwindling. "I knew several trees are in danger, but I hoped they could be saved. You mean I might not have a crop this year? The profit from peaches would help me build up the horse herd."

Grisham laughed, "No, I don't think your crop will be lost unless we have a late frost. We'll save the trees we can. We don't see evidence of peach tree borers, so that's good."

John eyed a fluffy cloud in the blue sky. So many things to worry about.

"The trees at the middle of the orchard are in better shape than those on the edges, probably because they don't get as much wind," Grisham continued. "The whole orchard needs irrigating. You can use a horse and plow to clean the creases and get the water next to the trees. I know you watched your father do those things, but apparently the judge had no interest in peaches in the time he lived here."

"Thanks for reminding me about things I need to do." John put his arm around Stuart, "This young man and I want to trim a few branches so we'll know how. Then we'll get to work picking up the cuttings from your crew and putting them in a pile to burn."

The supervisor pointed. "The area over there at the edge of the orchard where we took out three trees would be a good place for the fire. Lots of open ground around it."

John gave Stuart a little shove. "Get on your stilts so you can see."

He helped Stu mount his stilts. John finally had to lean against a tree to get up on his.

Taking a glance at his crew working nearby, Grisham went back to work. "Prune the branches before the sap runs. Since spring is a few weeks away, this is a good time to do it. When we get done, the mature trees should be only about fifteen feet tall."

Cutting while he talked, he showed how to cut small limbs, twigs, and branches so they slightly sloped inward. "Shaping a tree lower in the center allows sunlight to shine on the fruit on the inside as well as the outside. The slight u-shape also makes spraying for diseases and bugs easier. I think the pruned tree's shape is like a person opening his life to the Lord so the sunshine of God's love can shine into his heart, causing him to bear fruit of the Spirit."

"Fruit of the Spirit?" Stu giggled. "People bear fruit? Does a ghost have a part in it? So that's why some people are scary."

Grisham blinked. He stared at Stu for a moment and then rubbed his chin, "Well, nothing ghostly, but miraculous. Fruit of the Holy Spirit is love, joy, peace, patience, gentleness, goodness, meekness, faithfulness, self-control."

"Stuart was an orphan and had to live on the streets for quite a while," John explained, wobbling on the stilts. "After his family died, he had a hard time surviving until my sister and her husband found him. From what I hear, Stu found and chose them."

The boy giggled. "Sure surprised William when he discovered me out on Jenny's farm making friends with the goat. I stowed away in his peddler wagon."

"I'm so sorry about you losing your parents," Grisham said. "I remember Jenny. Sweet and talented girl. Stuart, if you haven't already given your life to Jesus, it's the best thing you can do."

"I did, and it made me feel so good inside. But it's hard not to remember mean people and bad things."

Grisham clipped at a few branches. "Fruit develops on the new growth in a peach tree. I imagine it's the same way for us. We grow when we pray, read, and learn the Bible—believe and practice obeying what it says. I think you're already growing Spirit fruit by being a helper to John."

Stu looked at John and then almost fell off his stilts.

"True," John smiled so wide his ears moved. "You've been a great helper so far, and every day your fruit will be even greater."

Grisham explained and demonstrated more about trimming, and then added, "I think my crew have the high points almost taken care of on the trees. We'll start cutting lower branches and take the rest of the trees down that need to go. And you and Stuart can cut off the suckers growing next to the tree trunks."

Movement flashed in the north pasture. John raised his eyes. Could it be? Was the stallion trying to find a way to get back inside the fence?

He jumped off the stilts. "Grisham, can you show Stuart how to cut off the suckers? I need to go to the north pasture. I think I see a miracle happening there."

John threw his stilts in the corner of the barn and saddled Dynamite, a buckskin with a white mane and tail. He mounted and jabbed his heels into the animal, urging him into an easy canter to the north pasture, hoping not to alarm the stallion on the other side of the white board fence.

Abe stood nearby, eyes sparkling and wide smile glowing with white teeth, revealing the gap from a missing tooth inside his chocolate cheek.

"He wants back inside the pasture, but still skitterish."

John swung the open gate a little wider and set down the partially empty bag of oats he picked up on his way out of the barn. He put the bag, top rolled down, in the horse's view, but not close enough he could get it without coming inside the fence.

The stallion swung his head back and forth, ran in the opposite direction, but came right back. John extended his hand with three sugar cubes. In a blink, the horse took two or three steps inside the gate, eyeing John's hand. Then he pivoted again and galloped out of sight.

Abe shook his head, disappointment absorbed on every wrinkle on his face.

John's belly twisted. "He's limping. I think he's injured himself."

Abe raised his face toward heaven and took John's hand. "Lawd, you know how valuable this horse is ta John. His money's runnin' low and bills is pilin'. You know, Lawd, this stallion can bring cash for breedin'. In your name, I ask he won't need put down. In your name, help him to come right back in that gate."

John barely opened his eyes when the stallion trotted inside, favoring one leg, eyeing John's hand still extended with sugar cubes. The wet tongue jutted out from between thick yellow teeth. The sugar disappeared, leaving slobbers in its place.

Abe shut the gate.

John held the bag of oats close to the stallion's mouth, and as soon as the black head dipped to eat, John set the bag on the ground. Large eyes circled and blinked, but the stallion continued to eat.

Abe visually inspected the four lean black legs. Then he knelt, the knees of his overalls barely missing a pile the animal had deposited.

"He's missing a shoe! Praise the Lawd! Thank you, Jesus."

The horse's head popped up, his hide twitched and he reared up a little.

John rubbed the stallion's shoulders, his fingers working down into the muscles with a gentle touch, the horsehair rough on John's skin. "Whoa there. You're okay. No one here is going to strike you with a whip."

Abe cooed and then sang softly, "Amazin' grace, how sweet the sound," then mounted his horse and took off toward the barn. In moments, he came back with a smile that almost tore into his shiny ears. A gunnysack John knew was filled with the things Abe needed to replace the horseshoe bounced at his side.

After the black trotted off to join the other horses in the shade, John smirked. "I knew singing to cattle at night quiets them, but I never knew it works on the horses as well."

"Amazin' grace will quiet your spirit, too, John. We needs to get back in church."

"Soon as I catch up with the orchard and the horses."

Abe raised his bushy graying eyebrows and stared straight in John's eyes. "Takin' a day off to rest in the Lawd's Presence will make everything else go better. It's jus' like tithin'. When you gives ya heavenly Father his share, ya money and ya time stretch everywhere ya needin' it."

John reached out and hugged Abe. "Thanks for reminding me." He forced a smile, and when he did, he was surprised how the thankfulness flowed through him. "You and Polly are precious people. You always have been like another mother and father. Now you're all I got to keep me on the straight and narrow. Soon's I get everything squared away—"

"Thanks for your love, John," Abe interrupted. "But I'm gonna pray da Holy Spirit goes way beyond me and calls you to back to his Word and his house."

John blinked, swallowed, and headed for the tree trimmers. How was he going to keep up with everything around here? He jerked the reins and brought his animal to a halt. "Abe!" he shouted. "I'll go to church with you on Sunday if you'll pray the trimmers didn't find too much damage and ask God for a great peach crop."

Abe nodded, and then chuckled. "Already did it, and God's workin' on it."

When he rode up to the orchard, John could tell Stu had thrown himself into his job. He smelled of sweat. His shirt was soaked, and his unruly light brown hair stuck to his head as he pulled a mound of tree cuttings to a big pile in the clearing.

"Gettin' too hot, boy? Did you run out of water?"

"Yeh. But this is the last of the cuttings, and I got all the suckers."

Grisham came out of the trees. "This young man is a great worker, and he follows directions well."

Stu ducked his head, a sheepish smile curving his lips. "That would be my new mama and daddy's trainin'. I didn't do so good when I was on my own after my first papa and mama died."

John smiled as Abe took off toward the house.

"Well, John, I have good news and bad news. Which do you want first?"

"Let's hear the bad news first."

"The bad news is you missed Miss Edwina Jorgenson, and she had a fit. She has a mare ready to breed, and she wants you to bring your stallion over right away."

Phooey! John had neglected to tell Ed what he planned to charge. How did she know the stallion was back? Well, he'd go over after supper, tell her to bring her mare over here, and he'd take what she or her papa agreed to pay. He'd have to hurry before she found another stud.

"Okay, what's the good news?"

Grisham's round face split into a big grin, puffing his grapefruit cheeks even more. "Well, you only need about a dozen new trees. The really good news is your man here, Abe, told me he found a patch of volunteer peach trees over by the cellar. Polly said she threw the peach seeds out there because before Abe came back here, no one was available to take out the garbage the pigs can't eat. She gave the pan of seeds a toss from the back porch and now you probably have a dozen small trees, maybe more. Abe said he'd dig 'em up and plant 'em where you took out the dead ones."

"Wow. I didn't notice."

Grisham's face beamed in the bright Colorado sun. "God provides in mysterious ways."

The trimmers had disappeared around the bend in the lane when Edwina came into view, driving the buggy with another horse tied behind.

"John! John. Velvet is ready."

He took a deep breath, blew it out and waited for her to pull up beside him. Edwina jumped out of the buggy and ran around to John and grabbed his hand. "The stallion did come back, didn't he?"

"He's in the corral. He hung around outside the pasture today. He limped, but he'd thrown a shoe. I think everything is all right. Take Velvet over to the corral, and we'll let Abe take it from there."

Abe stuck his head over the corral fence. "I'll come get 'er."

"Come on in the house and visit with Polly awhile." John looked down at his and Ed's hands still linked. Her gloved fingers tightly entwined in his long slender ones. Thinking she might be getting ideas, he gently worked his hand away, and Ed released his fingers.

Her big blue eyes sparkled, and the long lashes slowly lowered. His eyes roamed over her face, down to her lips before he caught himself. He turned toward the house. "Come on, girl. Polly probably has coffee ready."

John opened the door for her, stood aside, and Ed entered, her blonde braid swaying on her slender back.

"Why, Edwina," Polly exclaimed, turning from the dishpan and wiping her hands on a towel. "So nice to see you. How is your papa?"

Polly's ample arms swallowed Ed in a loving embrace. "How is Bellea working out? Is the baby doing all right?"

"Well …" Edwina's pink cheeks glistened.

"Have a seat at tthe table and have a blueberry muffin with us and tell us everything."

Ed took off her gloves and shifted her gun holster so she could sit on the bench behind the table. "Papa is all right, but he gets depressed now and then. Bellea and the tyke are good for him."

When Polly set the muffins on the table, Edwina reached out for them. "Thanks. I worked hard this morning, and it seems like a long time since breakfast."

She chewed, her dimples flashing occasionally. Her hand reached for a napkin, and she dabbed her pretty lips where a smile brightened her cheeks.

"Pop enjoys watching the baby. He likes to watch how the little fellow stretches his bitsy arms over his head. Pa even chuckles at the sneezes. He laughed and laughed yesterday when the boy kept cooing. But he had a bad case of hiccups and his cooing would be interrupted."

Ed's eyes followed John as he sat.

He cleared his throat. "The babe's squalling doesn't bother him? He howled so much here I was hoping I'd go deaf."

Ed patted John's hand. "You don't mean that." Then her big blue eyes caught his, and he pulled his hand away and put it in his lap. The woman wouldn't give up.

"So how is Bellea working out?" Polly set white coffee cups in front of them. Then she lifted the coffee pot and poured. "She is a big help. I feel pampered and spoiled already. The house is clean. Usually, all the clothes are washed, except she has a problem keeping up with diapers. She's made great things to eat. She has recipes Papa really likes. Every day it's exciting to see what she's going to cook."

John frowned. "How does she get all that done with the baby?" How was it possible the tiny boy wasn't raising Ed's roof like he'd done here?

Edwina took a bite of her muffin, shook her head, and smiled at John. "I think the baby likes to watch Papa, too. Papa makes faces and funny noises, and the kid is mesmerized. Ummmm. Polly, this muffin is delicious. Does Bellea have the recipe?"

"Actually, it's one of hers she wrote out for me. Wish we could grow blueberries here. Abe sez the soil doesn't have enough acid. 'Tis nice they get them at the general store."

The back door slammed. Abe and Stuart walked in. "The deed's done," Abe said.

The pink of a sunburn tinged Stuart's cheeks. "You should see how my rabbits are growing." He reached for a muffin. "I let one of the little ones out, and he sure enjoyed hopping around. He even nibbled on grass."

Polly swatted at his hand. "Not until you wash."

From her pocket, Edwina pulled out an already completed check. "That enough for the stud service?"

John scanned the check. He'd hoped for more. It didn't even begin to replace what he'd paid to the tree trimmers. "Sure. But if Velvet has twins, I want one of them."

Ed's eyebrows shot up. "What?"

John nodded, feeling ornery. He covered her fingers with his, and her warm hand grew soft at his touch.

She crinkled her face, and then those blue eyes beamed. "Okay. I'll do it."

18

John yanked the rusty mailbox open. Probably more bills. Yep. A few more big expenses and he'd be broke. The pigs weren't ready to go to market yet. Polly's selling of the extra eggs helped cut the bill at the mercantile, but to build up the ranch, he needed investment money.

With the stallion back, if he could buy a few more mares, he'd be on his way rebuilding a great herd similar to what Dad had.

When he walked in the house, John dropped the mail on the kitchen table.

"Whatcha lookin' so down in the mouth about?" Polly asked, her strong fingers pinching a pie crust into a circle on a pan and filling it with sliced apples.

"Worrying. I had no idea my dad had so many worries."

Polly's flabby chin tucked into her chest. "What? Your papa wasn't a worrier. He gave all his problems to the Lawd."

"Tha's right." Abe sat in a rocking chair, smiling from ear to ear. "Your papa left you a great example. Sometimes I could hear him praying clear out to the barn. I imagine you heard him too. He prayed for me many a time. But when consumption got his lungs, he run out of breath. These ol' bodies ain't fixed now to last foreva'. But soon we gonna have new bodies that won't neva' get sick, get old, or die. We's gonna have a new un. In the twinkling of an eye. And the dead shall be raised."

Polly let out a whoop. Good thing she'd finished with the pie. "Oh, glory!" she shouted, tears dropping on her glowing cheeks. She danced a little circle and then picked up the pie and stuck it in the oven.

"That reminds me, John." Abe rocked back and forth, his cheeks drawing back like a curtain so his wide smile took center stage. "We's all goin' to church tomorra, so I 'magine we better get up early to do the chores."

The back door slammed. "Why do we have to get up early?" Stuart walked in, his hat scrunched down over a freckled face still showing sunburn. "Don't we always get up early?"

John blinked, rubbed his nose and scar, and looked at Stuart. "We're going to church."

"But how are we going to get the old peach trees burned and the horses, rabbits, and chickens fed? B.J.'s gone."

"Abe says when we give to God first, whether it's our time or our money, it makes everything else go better," John explained. "I guess I believe it even if I wasn't doing it."

Stuart was silent for a minute. "Oh, that must be the ten percent stuff I heard about. Like the time I put a dime in the offering plate, and then dimes dropped into the plate, and it was so heavy it crashed to the floor. Dimes scattered everywhere. Down the cracks in the floor. Into mouse holes and even rolled down the steps outside and into the grates in the boardwalk. Dimes—"

"Stuart!" Polly shouted.

"Whoa!" John yelled. "Where did you get that idea?"

Stu removed his hat and plunked it on a hook by the back door. "Well, I dreamed it. But it sorta did happen. After I dreamed it, I did put a dime I'd found in the alley into the offering plate at church. I didn't have anybody to teach me, but God told me to do it. I put the dime in. And then I carried the judge's suitcase to his hotel, and he gave me a whole dollar. Then I met Jenny and William. William bought me breakfast, and then I went home with him. And then I was theirs. Do you see? Dimes did fall from heaven. Well, somethin' kinda like dimes, but better'n money." His eyes glistened.

Polly pulled Stu into a tight embrace.

"Wow," John said. "I've heard God often works in mysterious ways."

"His wonders to perform," Abe completed.

Polly held Stu's shoulders out at arm's length. Her lips thinned and clamped together as she shook her head and stared at the boy. "God's given ya a great lesson and testimony, Stuart. Always believe God and his Word, and he'll be with ya always."

She hugged him again.

"Now go wash up."

A few minutes later, Polly started setting the table for dinner and picked up the mail John left there and thumbed through it. "John, you didn't even open the letter from Mrs. MacDougal?"

"I didn't see one. Maybe I'd better get to my desk and work on my books. I'll read it then."

He grabbed the mail, looked back at Stu with amazement and went into his office.

The bills' totals piled higher than he expected. He forgot he didn't pay his feed bill last month, and he hadn't paid for the load of hay when it came. Then the baby chicks he'd ordered, now ready to pick up. Plus, he'd bought Stu's rabbits and invested in new saddles and bridles.

Before he had nerve enough to read Valerie's letter, he needed a faith boost. He paged to Hebrews 11 where he read *faith is the substance of things hoped for, the evidence of things not seen.* He read on *By faith we understand the worlds were framed by the word of God, so the things that are seen were not made out of things that are visible.*

Each word he read boosted his faith. He read on. *But without faith it is impossible to please him, for he who comes to God must believe that he is, and that he is a rewarder of those who diligently seek him.*

Chills ran up John's arms. He could talk to the One, who created the universe, who made everything out of the invisible. He fell to his knees and rested his head on his desk chair seat. A Presence filled the room, and he knew the King of Kings and Lord of Lords stood beside him.

"Lord, have mercy on me," he prayed.

He repented for his negligence, his lack of faith and gently asked for help. He started with the spiritual, and then broadened to his finances, and before he finished, tears covered his face, and he'd prayed for almost everyone in his life, beginning with Valerie, then Bellea and the baby, and then Edwina and her father, and Stuart, Polly, Abe, Jenny, and William. Then he began on his aunts. An hour passed, and his legs grew numb. But his insides came alive. Joy twirled like a machine pumping encouragement into every part of him.

He lingered on his knees in silence, listening. *Sell the stallion.*

"But, Lord, I was depending on him to build the herd."

Sell him.

Who would buy him? His newfound joy fizzled like a firework that didn't explode.

When he stood, a letter with elaborate handwriting still waited unread, while an enticing fragrance wafted to his nostrils. He walked away whispering a name he knew was his only source of strength and help, "Jesus."

At the asylum Dillon led his choir of five patients in Amazing Grace. Even Jimmy Cook and Pete belted it out while tears rolled down their faces. Other patients also wept. But across the room Bill Brown's face was red with anger. Bill was one of the patients who'd been admitted because of an addiction to alcohol.

When the song ended and they all bowed their heads in prayer, Dillon quoted John 3:16: For God so loved the world that he gave his only begotten son that whosoever believeth in him should not perish but have everlasting life."

"Stop!" Bill shouted. "I want quiet."

He kicked the door and pounded the walls. "Guard! I don't want to hear the singing and the Bible. I have my rights. Make them stop."

Truth was, they were done for today.

A guard strutted inside the room. Guess you're going to have to quit having church in here."

19

The next morning, when he pulled his tired body out of bed, he wished he'd read the letter. He must have been awake half the night, although he'd taken a hot bath before he crawled in. Now he had to rush out to the barn. Abe already squirted milk into a bucket. Stu threw grain to the chickens and gathered the eggs for Polly.

John trudged to the pigpen and poured the slop over the fence into the trough. The bushel of corn was extra heavy as he pushed it in the wheelbarrow toward the pigs. He felt like ignoring the horses. The ones in the north pasture could pretty much take care themselves. They could drink from the stream, and they had plenty of grass. But he needed to take care of those he kept separate in the south part of the ranch.

"I'll hep with the horses," Abe said, carrying the full milk bucket to the house.

"No. I'll fork them a little hay, be sure the water tank is full, and I'll be in shortly," John yelled. "I might need to turn the windmill into the breeze."

While he tended each chore, he meditated on what occurred when he prayed the night before. The feeling to sell the stallion was mighty confusing. Discouragement and fear twisted in his gut, but his heart pumped faith and assurance everything would be all right.

The closer it came to church time, the more peaceful he felt.

At the breakfast table, Stu eyed John's plate, eyebrow uplifted. "You hungry this mornin'?"

John glanced down. He had a pile of six of Polly's light and delicious flapjacks swimming in butter and maple syrup. Six sausages took up the space around the edges. "Guess I am." He ruffled Stu's hair, "You know, kid, I really enjoy having you around. You're quite a feller. I'm so glad you're part of our family and spending the summer with us. Your parents in heaven are so proud of you, like all of us are."

As soon as he cleaned up and dressed for church, John ripped open the letter. A faint scent of perfume drifted up his nostrils, and his throat tightened.

John,

We had a splendid time at your ranch and enjoyed visiting with all of you. Have you heard from Jenny and William? I kept expecting a letter from you, and then realized I need to write first.

Christian Paul is growing so fast. He has a big appetite, and his grandparents make sure he spoiled and properly fed.

The weather here has been terrible since we arrived back in Boston, but that doesn't keep my parents from trying to keep me on the go. They've hired a nanny I didn't want and insisted I go to all the dinners, dances, and parties for which I receive an invitation. It's maddening.

Speaking of my parents, now my daddy has a husband picked for me. He's one of his attorney associates. They forget how much I enjoyed the wide-open spaces, and I don't plan to live in Boston always. Any chance you could come to visit so they could get acquainted with you? Considering the powerful attraction we seem to have to one another, that would be wonderful.

I hope you're getting resettled on the ranch, things are going well, and the poor little mother has found someone to love and take care of her and the baby.

Affectionately yours,
Valerie

John threw the letter into his underwear drawer. He'd guessed it might contain bad news for him, but surely, by the time he got into church, he'd have peace about it.

But when Abe parked the wagon and team in the church parking lot, Polly beside him and Stu and John in the back, a spasm occurred near his heart. He pointed to the cemetery beside the church. "My parents are buried right over there," he told Stuart.

A stricken expression squeezed Stu's face. "I'm too far away now to visit my family's graves. I used to go there every day."

John squeezed the twelve-year-old in a hug. "I'm so sorry. Maybe we'll take a trip to Yucca Blossom before too long."

"Would you?" Stu's scrubbed face and brown eyes brightened.

"Sure." John waited for Abe to help Polly from the wagon. Then he and Stu stretched their legs toward the side so they could hop down.

"Do you ever cry when you're missin' 'em?" Stu's eyes glistened.

"Yes," John admitted. "Don't you?"

"Yeh." Stu swiped at tears.

A sleek horse and shiny buggy pranced into the parking space beside John's rig. A beautiful blonde lady held the reins. John blinked. A *familiar* lady.

"Hey, John," she greeted. "Glad to see you made time for church today."

"Edwina?"

The lady patted the curls and swirls atop her head, dimples tweaking at the edge of her wide smile. "Do you like the way Bellea did my hair?"

His mouth still hung open. A horsefly buzzed by, and he clamped his lips together. He stared at Ed's big blue eyes under all that hair topped by a dainty white hat. She lifted the skirt of the billowing yellow dress, ready to step out of the buggy.

His polished black boots hit the ground as a rider rode in, his horse creating a cloud of dust. Edwina's cowhand, Clyde Merriweather, clothed like a dandy, took off his top hat and beat John to

Edwina's side. "At your service, ma'am." He grabbed Edwina by the waist, set her feet on the ground and linked arms with her.

Edwina peered back at John over her shoulder as she walked with Clyde.

John's feet stuck to the gravel parking lot while he stared. He took a deep breath and thanked God for Merriweather. Perhaps if he gave his life to Christ, he'd make a good husband.

20

A few tears streaked Stu's cheeks as the headstones in the graveyard seemed to capture him.

Abe stepped toward Stu and John. "Aw, but we grieve not as those who have na hope." The older man gazed toward the cemetery. He nodded. "Folks who know Jesus before they died are not in the grave. Their spirit's alive and livin' wit' him, and soon, they's gonna come back wit' him in the clouds and be joined with their new bodies as they come out of those graves. Bible says 'For the Lawd himself shall descend from heaven wit' a shout, and the voice of the archangel … and the dead in Christ will rise, and we who are alive shall be caught up together with them in the clouds.' So we's will ever be wit' the Lawd."

"Yes, Lawd!" Polly shouted, held her ragged Bible up to the sky with one hand and raised the other toward heaven. Then she danced around in a little circle, praising God.

A few folks heading' toward the church stopped and gawked, including Ed and Merriweather. Most smiled and raised their hands with Polly. Merriweather scowled, pulled Ed's arm and they climbed the church steps together.

Old friends John hadn't seen in a long time greeted him and asked about the ranch. By the time he and Stu entered the church, Polly and Abe sat in the back next to the wall. Mrs. Martin pumped her feet on the organ pedals and moved her fingers across the keyboard, playing a tune that caught John's ear the first time he heard it. He couldn't remember the words.

As he and Stu sat on the end of a bench, with Stu on the outside in case they called him for Sunday school, Pastor Brandt strode to the pulpit and began singing, "He took my sins away! He took my sins away!"

John's spirit responded with the words to the song. For the first time in a couple of years, joy surged from his scalp to the pointy toes of his cowboy boots. He said a few words to the Lord and then struck out singing, his baritone voice strong and clear.

Stu held on to John, trying to see the songbook and sing too.

The Kellners, late, as usual, came in, and John noticed Merriweather and Ed seated on the pew's other end. The Kellners attempted to step in front of Merriweather to sit in the middle, but Edwina rose, walked over and sat next to John. Merriweather's eyes bugged out, and he hightailed it over to sit by Ed. The tardy couple nodded their thanks and sat in their vacated seats.

While the pastor preached an awesome sermon on comfort, John barely noticed how Ed snuggled closer to him and away from Merriweather until their eyes connected. She leaned to his ear. "He stinks. Smells like cigarettes."

John hoped people weren't looking. He and Edwina sat on the second row, so probably a few gossips took in the view.

People sang and prayed enthusiastically after the sermon, but before they were dismissed, a lady in a satiny black dress rose on the other side of the church quietly and then went back a couple of pews and forward to talk to … Wellington Davenport? John twitched his mouth to the side. Wellington stood and followed his mother out.

John hadn't noticed them in attendance. They softly closed the door, ending the disturbance.

Ed once again scooted toward John while Merriweather shot him dirty looks.

After the service, John nodded to Edwina and then Clyde. He walked out and guided Stu toward the wagon and waited for Polly and Abe. John tugged at his string tie, loosened it, and unbuttoned his top button. Stu loosened his shirt collar as well.

Finally, Abe hurried to the wagon and grasped the reins. Polly sat on the front bench beside him and chattered happily about the good service. John added a few uh-huhs.

The horses sensed home and freedom, and the closer they got to the ranch, the faster they went. As Abe guided the wagon toward the house, John noticed a carriage and a horse tied to the hitching post. No one came into view.

"Someone's here," he told the others. "Stu you stay with Polly and Abe until I find out what they're doing here."

John eased open the back door and stepped lightly on the kitchen floor. His eyes moved this way and that, searching for an intruder.

Doors slammed upstairs. Something hit a wall. Could the person who had been stealing after the judge left be back?

Since his holster was in a drawer in the bedroom, John grabbed an umbrella for a weapon as he crept past the front entry.

21

Voices mumbled and then became louder. "That girl and the baby must be around here."

"Mother. We shouldn't even be in John's house. You have no right to Bellea's baby."

"They're hiding them here. Get your gun and show those servants and John Parks they'd better tell us where they are."

"Sorry. In case you don't remember, I'm the little one's father, and I'm not going to threaten him. He's safe, wherever he is. Don't be embarrassed because of what I've done. I'm gettin' out o' here before they get home from church."

John sneaked into the closet under the stairs. Wellington's boots clunked down the steps, across the floor, and out the door. Shortly afterward, Mrs. Davenport's dainty steps trickled down and out the back entrance too.

Moving to the window, John watched the shock on Polly's face as Wellington's horse galloped away. Mrs. Davenport, obviously weeping, slowly climbed into her carriage.

"You haven't heard the last of us," she screamed back to the house. "I will have that baby!"

Abe insisted Sunday should be a day of rest as much as possible, so John challenged Stu to a game of checkers. Evidently William had been playing with him too because the little booger beat John three games to one.

"Want to try chess?" John asked, reaching for the chess pieces in the parlor cabinet.

"Sure!"

Stu was so enthusiastic, John thought perhaps he shouldn't try to plan next week's chores while playing a game. But in his mind, he worked the ground in the orchard, irrigated, advertised the stallion in the newspaper, and wondered who he could get to help him hunt and catch wild mustangs. Since Abe had so much experience, perhaps he could go along to advise them. John sure didn't want the old man lassoing them and trying to bring them in.

When Stu gave another triumphant "checkmate!" John gave up. "I think it's time for me to look at the horses and for you to feed your rabbits again. I'll give you boards and chicken wire tomorrow so you can corral them on the grass and let them get a little exercise."

Stu's brown eyes grew large. "Won't they dig a hole and tunnel out and get away?"

"Could be. But don't leave them out there by themselves too long. Then maybe they won't get into mischief or a hawk come by and have one for lunch."

Stu nodded. "I'll build them a little pen and then watch 'em. No hawk will get by me."

Out in the barn, Abe had the stallion in a stall again, rubbing smelly liniment on one of his legs. He looked up at John. "The horse still favors the leg where he lost the horseshoe. Musta done too much runnin' out there on 'is own."

"I think he's tryin' to soak up more of your pampering and spoilin'. How many apples and sugar cubes did ya give him so he'd stand still?"

Abe's eyes gleamed as he grinned at John. "Enough."

"You believe in God telling you things to do, don't you, Abe?"

"Sure do."

"Well, God told me to sell the stallion. I don't know why. I'm pretty attached to him. But God knows my finances are getting tight, and I probably can get good money for him, especially because everyone knows he was the judge's horse, and the man took great pride in his stallion."

Abe frowned. "Might be picked up by someone who wants to race him. God knows what he's doin', but I like dat horse more than you do. If he hadn't been abused, he would be a champion."

"How much do you think I should ask for 'im?"

Abe shook his head, looked at the horse and then at John. Finally, he named a number.

"That much?"

"I wouldna sell him for any less."

John whistled. "That amount should help me catch up on my bills without digging deeper into my savings. Would you tell me what I need to do to catch a few mustangs?"

Abe laughed. "First, you have to know where they are and then, have a hoss fast enough to catch one. Wild horses aren't as plentiful as they were when your daddy caught and trained a bunch of them. Then, too, it's dangerous work. Lots of men breathe their last breath chasing wild hosses. Frankly, I think I'm too old for it."

"I don't want you trying to catch them, but you could be an adviser. Tell us how to go about it. I'm thinking of trying to find a man to go with me who knows mustangs. If we could catch as many as six in the next month, we each would have three apiece. Three horses with strong bloodlines would be a great addition to the herd."

"This stallion here has a good bloodline. If we worked things right and we can find them, I'd guess there's still a herd of mustangs out there. A few families who homesteaded 'round here and didn't make a go of it released their teams and mounts to fend for themselves when they go back East on ta train. We might be able to herd a few of those mustangs inta your pasture."

"Well, I'll leave it in the Lord's hands. If God wants me to sell, someone will buy the stallion at my price. If I don't get an offer, I'll know I imagined it instead of God talking to me. Later, we'll see if we can find mustangs."

Abe gave the stallion a tender rubdown on his neck, shoulders, and along his spine. "Tha's probably a good test. That's the way God told people to test a prophet. If the prophecy came true, it was of God. If it didn't, the person was pree …"

"Presumptuous?" John asked.

Abe closed the stallion's stall and put the liniment on a nearby shelf. "Anyway, he wasn't a good prophet."

22

Archibald Forsythe stopped his buggy in front of the asylum's administration building where a small caretaker's home had been converted into plush offices.

The attorney stiffened his back and resisted a gnawing feeling producing jitters and spasms in his guts. He could do this. God promised to never forsake him.

The administrators' offices squatted far enough away the desperate cries of those housed in the asylum couldn't be heard. The three-story asylum sprawled behind the administration building on a large piece of acreage.

Archibald's shoes pounded bare polished floors down the corridor past offices of a doctor, the director of nursing, security, and toward the office in the corner where bold black letters marked Superintendent on the varnished wood, six-paneled door.

He knocked.

Heels clicked on the floor inside, and then a sandy-haired girl greeted him. "Do you have an appointment?"

"I do." Archibald took a step toward the superintendent's office.

"You can't go in there." The girl scurried behind him.

"That's why I came. Do you want to tell Mr. Forest Spencer that Archibald Forsythe is here to visit Dillon Haskill?"

The aging superintendent stepped into the doorway. "Come in, Archibald. You've been here before, haven't you?" He offered his hand for a shake.

"Sir, may I come in?"

The man looked at his secretary, around the room, to the outside door, back at Archie and then gestured to a chair. "Come on in."

He shut the door.

Archie's dry mouth needed water, but he swallowed hard. "Mr. Spencer, I am an attorney investigating whether three of your patients deserve to be here. Today, I want to visit the ward housing Dillon Haskill."

The superintendent's brows went up, and a scowl found familiar places to crinkle on his face. "I'll have to deny that."

"Could I visit with him outside of the ward? I'd hate to have to get a court order to see him."

Mr. Spencer's neck jerked and his head jarred back like Archibald had struck him. "You don't know what you're asking. The people in here are insane. This is an asylum."

Archie couldn't control the smile wiggling his lips. "I'm well aware this is an asylum, and I have absolutely no fear of being in a room alone with Dillon. He doesn't belong here."

Spencer's eyebrows shot up. "Are you supposed to be an expert?"

"No, but I've read Dillon Haskill's writings about mental illness, and he probably knows more about insanity than you do. But I'm not here to argue with you. I imagine you've never talked to the man or even seen him. Besides reading his writings, I know Dr. Dillon Haskill. He's a medical doctor, and I insist on seeing him."

Spencer's mocking laugh blasted out of his large mouth. "All right, young man. Go ahead and see him. You'll do it at your own risk. A guard will take you there. Leave your wallet and everything else from your pockets here, and the guard will search you for weapons."

The uniformed guard soon patted Archibald down. Then he led Archie to the asylum and to the third-floor unit for male patients. Climbing two stairways, they finally came to the third floor.

"Help!" a woman's shrill scream split the air and the electricity in the atmosphere about burst Archie's heart. "Help me. Somebody help!" Other female voices groaned, chattered and talked nonsense.

When they neared the men's ward, the noise deepened, mingled with cursing.

Inside the dismal unit, Archibald waited alone in a small room with a dirty window until the guard talked to officials. Then the heavy door creaked open, and a handcuffed man with bushy dark hair and beard stumbled inside.

The man stared. Archibald broke out in a sweat.

There wasn't a stick of furniture in the room and no chair to sit on. Only a dirty light bulb provided a dim yellow glow.

"You have ten minutes." The guard slammed and locked the door.

Archie stuck his hand out to the patient. "Dr. Haskill. I'm your friend, Archibald Forsythe, and if you remember, I'm an attorney. I plan to review your case and see if I can get you released."

Dillon jumped back. "Don't touch me. I have lice." His whiskered chin quivered. He put a hand to his face. "Archie! God … bless you. I'm so weak my eyes didn't adjust to this dim light. Of course, it's you."

Archie circled Dillon with both arms. "We'll forget the vermin. I'm going to hug you." His energetic squeeze held the bony man. A soft prayer shot toward heaven from his mouth, and a Presence filled the room.

"Thank you, Jesus!" Dillon tightened his grip around him and then reached toward heaven.

Archie joined him praising the Lord, and in moments, laughter bubbled in the dingy room.

"God is working!" Dillon waved his hands back and forth above his head. "He answered my prayer."

Archie wiped his eyes on his sleeve. "Tell me about your ward."

"We're jammed together with barely space to walk between bunk beds. Usually five to seven of us. Depends on who is in solitary or restraint. But we've had more."

"How about the food?"

"It's not fit to eat, and there's not enough. Patients are starving. If we get anything edible, the guards often eat it. Several in my ward are ill. Most of those who are sane have lost hope."

The room fell silent as they stared at one another. Then Dillon smiled, "Another patient and I, Jimmy Cook, have tried to bring some joy into the place. Jimmy is a former teacher who is paralyzed from the waist down. But Jimmy's been ill lately."

"What do you two do?"

Dillon rubbed his hands together. "We quote from the Bible and tell the stories from books we've read and poems we memorized. When we started this, I saw the first glimmers of hope and joy among all this sorrow and emotional pain."

"Amazing," Archibald smiled. "How about those who are deranged or demon-possessed?"

"Some are dangerous. One fellow keeps targeting a sweet young boy with Down's syndrome. I'm afraid he might kill him."

A fist pounded the door. Archie jumped.

"Time's up!" the guard yelled.

"Outrageous," Archibald shook his head. "Kids shouldn't be housed with dangerous adults. I'll be back, but I don't know how soon." He hugged Dillon again. "Keep being a blessing until the Lord delivers—and he will deliver you."

23

Saturday afternoon, the Horse Ranchers Association met in the Rusty Wheel Tavern. John was almost late. The only vacant seat he could see when arrived stood out between Clyde Merriweather and Billy Joe Garner. John pulled the chair out and sat in it.

"Hello," John greeted them. "I presume you're representing Edwina at this meeting, Clyde. B.J., where are you working now? Are your bosses interested in raising purebreds? I'm really dying to hear this speaker. I think the future of horses is in purebreds."

"I'm thinking everything we learn is money to people who work with horses," Clyde drawled in his southern twang. The cowhand motioned to the makeup-plastered waitress in a frilly dress. "Whiskey. A drink for my friends here, too."

B.J. whacked John on the back. "Good ta see ya. Thank ya, Clyde, old boy. I've been workin' hard all mornin', and I'm thirsty." As soon as the shot glass filled, B.J. emptied it.

The waitress paused, plopped another drink container in front of John, and lifted her bottle.

John held up his open hand. "Thanks anyway, but I don't drink. Besides, I'm too young."

The girl giggled.

"Go ahead and pour him a drink," Clyde insisted. "It's time John grew up."

John shook his head. "Don't waste Clyde's money."

The barmaid poured the drink anyway. John, not wanting to spend all the time before the meeting with Clyde, spied the afternoon speaker, Theodore Balding. "Excuse me for a minute boys," John said. "Balding's an expert on purebred horses. I want to meet him."

He strode to the other table. "Thank you for coming to Peachville. I'm John Lincoln Parks." The two shook hands. "My late father raised horses most of his life, and I'm running the ranch now. I'm really interested in purebreds."

"Sorry about your pa." Balding resettled in his chair. "I met him and visited the Peach Blossom Ranch a couple of times. He had a great spread and outstanding stock."

"Well, when my uncle took over Papa's ranch, he ravaged it. Only two mares and an old gelding were left when he was murdered. I spent my inheritance buying stock. I bought his horse, too, a great stallion whose spirit he almost broke."

Balding turned his head and squinted his eyes. "I think I remember that horse. Still needed some gentle training."

John nodded and leaned forward. "I figure I might be able to save him or at least his bloodline. That would be great for the herd. But I'd really like to invest in purebreds. A mare and a stallion at first. I'd love to raise Arabians."

"Keep your goal in mind, young man." Balding shoved out his chair, stood, and shook John's hand again. "Glad to meet you. So glad you came. If you have more questions after I speak, feel free to come forward."

"Thank you. I'll do that."

Balding walked over to another of the dozen tables covered with white linen cloths, shook hands with two or three people, then went to the podium, smiling. At least a head shorter than John, but a big man nevertheless, filled with knowledge.

As John reclaimed his chair beside Clyde, B.J. guzzled the dregs of the drink intended for John. "I know you don't drink, John," B.J. grinned from ear to ear. "I couldn't let it go to waste."

John listened intently as Balding told a couple of humorous horse stories and then introduced his subject. John barely noted B.J. becoming ill and Clyde offering to help him get home. Strange. The man seemed totally sober minutes before.

When he got wound up, Balding, who was not bald but possessed a thick head of white hair, spoke in a loud authoritative voice. "Thoroughbreds are best known for being racehorses. But thoroughbred can mean any breed of purebred horse. They are valued for their agility, speed, and spirit.

"Thoroughbreds developed in seventeenth- and eighteenth-century England. Native mares were crossbred with imported Oriental, Arabian Barb, and Turcoman stallions."

The speaker rubbed his large hands together, warming his enthusiasm for his subject. "Arabian horses originated among the Bedouins in the Arabian Peninsula. Bedouins claim their Arab horses date back to 3000 BC. Meticulous ancestral records, in other words 'pedigrees,' have been kept since then."

He explained the Bedouins' mounts, hardy in the harsh desert climate and difficult terrain, served as beasts-of-burden or were used in war. The speaker went on to describe the distinct characteristics of a purebred Arabian: dished face, wide eyes, arching neck, high tail carriage, and floating gaits. Plus, the horses learn quickly.

Balding raised his eyebrows, and a little smile creased his face. "The most unique aspect of Arabians is they have one less vertebra than other breeds. Don't ask me why. I don't know."

Should he believe him? Surely, the man was joking.

The expert expounded about keeping bloodlines pure, and displayed photos and paintings for the audience to investigate after the meeting.

"How much would an Arabian mare and stallion cost?" John asked Balding afterward.

He gave John a couple of figures.

Hours later, John dialed Edwina on their new phone. He waited for the party line to open and then shared what he learned. "You should have been there. I hope to eventually buy a pair of Arabians."

Edwina gasped. "They're probably expensive. You think they're a good investment?"

John laughed. "Even better than pigs, and they don't suck girls' clothes or stink up the whole countryside."

Edwina's giggles floated over the line, although an annoying buzz cluttered the connection. "Sounds like a winner to me."

The next morning, as he did chores, John stumbled over something in the barn. Someone lay face down on the straw-and-manure-littered floor, partially covered. He touched the cold whiskered cheek of a dead man.

"Hey, Abe, come here! There's a body here under the straw."

24

Abe rushed around the corner, mouth and eyes wide. "Who he be?"

"I don't know. He's face down." John wagged his head. "Didn't want to disturb the body. I'm goin' for the sheriff."

"Maybe we's better take a good look around first," Abe warned. "You know how dat sheriff is. I don' think this man was killed here. He been dumped."

"Be careful where you step," John said. "Don't trample these unusual bootprints over here on the dirt." He grabbed a length of twine off the wall. Walking in the straw on the edge of the barn floor, he measured the fresh boot prints. A unique design stamped the heel.

"Whoever walked here had big feet and brand-new boots. I'm going to run to the house and get a pencil and paper. I'll sketch the design on the heel and write down what else seems disturbed."

"Can ya use the telephone to get the sheriff?" Abe asked.

"Naw." John stared at the body again. "Can't seem to find the party line open, and I don't want everybody in the county to know I found a body in our barn."

Heart thumping in his chest, he took off running and returned in minutes. He lit the lantern and held it high to illuminate the body and floor. "Look there. Could that be a little vomit on his lips? Do you see blood anywhere?"

"Hey!" Abe spat. "This is B.J. Somebody done killed him."

John's face went hot. A pain shot through his stomach. "It might be B.J. although I can't see enough of him to tell without turning him over. He's an awful color."

Shaking his head and feeling sick, John turned away. *Why didn't I try to talk to him about the Lord when there was still hope?*

An hour later when John pushed open the dirty, sun-bleached door to the sheriff's office, Woodrow Woody Watson lifted his bushy head of graying hair and spat into the filthy spittoon beside his desk.

"What's going on with you, John?" Tobacco juice lingered on his lips and colored his bushy mustache.

"Well, I planned to cultivate my orchards and irrigate today, but this morning I stumbled over a dead body in my barn."

The sheriff curled the end of his long whitish mustache. The skin around his eyes gathered at the corners. His black pupils bored into John. "You kill him? Who is he?"

John stepped closer. "I left him as I found him. He's on his face, so I'm not sure, but I think it's B.J."

"Billy Joe Garner? Didn't he work for you? You have a spat?"

"Billy Joe quit a while back. Wanted more money."

"Give me a chance to eat my food. Then I'll be out to your ranch, and we'll talk."

When John's horse galloped into the yard, Abe waited expectantly.

"What'd the sheriff say?"

"He should be here any minute. Did Polly keep Stu out of the barn?"

"Between the two of us, we kept 'im occupied."

Stuart came from the house and ran toward John. "Hey. You know the old cat that runs around here? She came over with a couple of her kittens while I had my rabbits out this mornin'. The mama rabbit had a stare-down with the mother cat, and then those kittens started playing hopscotch over and around the little bunnies. They'd sometimes tumble around but always come back. So the ol' bunny rabbit ran toward them, and then stood on her hind legs and tried to look ferocious. Those little kittens hightailed it."

A laugh bubbled out of John. "Good. I'd hate to see those bunnies get scratched." He grabbed Stu's shoulder.

When they sat down inside the house, Stu showed him a rabbit picture he'd drawn.

"Good work," John complimented. "Keep it, and you can use it on your 'For Sale' poster."

Stu giggled. "Yes. Before Polly decides to put them in her cooking pot."

A few minutes later, John called him into the parlor. "Abe and I found a dead man in the barn this morning, and the sheriff is on his way here. We're praying for the man's family, and that finding him on our property won't cause us any trouble. I think it's Billy Joe Garner. Pray with us."

They dropped to their knees. Abe and Polly stormed the gates of heaven in loud voices. John quietly asked God to help things go well with the sheriff. Just thinking about a body in the barn tied his guts in knots. Sheriff Woody might get a cocky idea and decide John killed him. Then John kicked those ideas aside because he knew that wasn't faith. Yet all he could say was "Lord, help us and help Billy Joe's family."

Galloping horse hooves interrupted their prayers. They rose as the sheriff pounded on the front door, his intense face and bushy mustache showing through the door window.

"Come right in, or would you rather go to the barn now?"

"I'll meet you in the barn."

John picked up his jacket and exited the back door. "You stay with Polly and Abe," he yelled to Stuart.

On the way to the barn, the sheriff passed John and opened the door.

"Hold it!" John yelled. "You'll need to look at some boot prints. They're pressed so far into the dirt and manure you can tell they were new boots, and the person was extremely heavy or carrying something. An unusual design marks the boot heel."

"Well, you could have put them there," Woody argued.

John held up his lantern. "I measured them. They're bigger than mine, and I haven't had a new pair of boots since my papa died."

The sheriff walked right over the prints, grabbed the body, and rolled it to reveal B.J.'s open and unseeing eyes.

"What'd ya do to him? Bonk him on the head?" The lawman rubbed B.J.'s hair. "I don't see any blood."

"I didn't touch him except to see if he was alive," John said. "I almost stumbled over him, because he was partly under the straw."

Abe edged closer. "We figger he was killed somewhere else and dumped here. Somebody wants to make it look like John is a killer."

"Who would do such a thing?"

John raised his left eyebrow. "Wellington Davenport might. He's been giving us grief, wanting us to give his mother the baby who was born in our barn."

"Is Roberta Bellea still here?"

"No. She got a job. She doesn't want her whereabouts revealed."

The sheriff eyed the house. "Did Polly have a run-in with B.J. like she did Wellington the other day? I heard she attacked him with a broom and left him bruised all over."

Abe stepped toward the sheriff. "That not true. The cocky squirt come in the house threatenin' people and tried to go upstairs where Bellea stayed. He wouldn't listen to reason, so Polly gave him a swat on the backside. He was so surprised he fell forward and hit his head on the stairs."

John bent over the corpse. "I don't think Polly ever conversed with B.J."

"Hmmm." The sheriff investigated the body, pulled up the long shirtsleeves, went over the back and front looking for bullet holes. Then he ran his fingers through the hair. "I don't see a mark on him. Wonder how he died. Better have Doc check him out."

"See his lips?" John said. "Could be dried vomit on them."

Abe's face puckered into seldom-used worry lines. "Well, maybe he was jus' sick and came here for help like the young gal did."

"I don't think B.J. was having a baby." The sheriff's voice sounded like he'd been eating sauerkraut. He stared at John. "I'll wait until after Doc examines him and talk to a few people, but if I don't get some answers, I'll have to put you in jail. You ran from the judge, and you might run from this."

"Jesus, help me," John whispered. With all he had to do on the ranch, he didn't have time to sit in jail and wait for an incompetent sheriff to decide how B.J. died.

Finally, the sheriff rode off leading a horse he borrowed from John, the blanket-covered body draped over the animal.

The next morning John's head felt like he needed to burrow under the covers for at least another hour, but his racing thoughts about the day before jolted him out of bed.

Stuart had stood back showing his anguish as he watched the sheriff and John carry out the body.

"We don't know why B.J. died," John explained as the sheriff disappeared down the road.

The boy's face paled even more. "Why do people have to die anyway?" A muffled sob escaped his young throat.

"Because of sin in the beginning, I guess. It's a horrid sad thing. But Jesus came to defeat death, and if we know him, we'll never die. Even if our body dies, our spirits—who we really are—will live."

Stu was so pathetic John drew him close. "Don't be embarrassed for feeling sad. Jesus wept when his friend Lazarus died."

"But didn't Jesus raise him from the dead?"

"Sure did. After Lazarus had been dead four days. He raised his friend so we would know God even has power over death. But then he walked out of the grave himself."

The youngster had still clung to him.

John shook off the memories and after chores and breakfast went to town. He stopped by the newspaper office and purchased an ad to sell the stallion. Then he went to the saloon. The swinging doors whacked him on the backside as he stared at the dim interior to find someone he could talk to. Seeing no one he'd trust, he went to the bar.

"John, I don't think you're old enough to drink whiskey," the bartender growled, his wrinkled face twisting into a grin as he cleaned the counter.

John leaned toward him and stared into the muttonchops beside his ears and connecting to his mustache. Then he caught the sunken gray eyes with his. "I don't drink anything but milk, water, and coffee, so you don't need to worry about my age. I'm wondering if you know where B.J. Garner has been working. He quit me for more money."

The bartender poured a drink for another man and then inched back toward John. "Tightwad are ya?"

"I paid a decent wage. Have you heard anything about him?"

"All I know is he must have landed a good job because sudden-like he had money—lots of it."

"Thanks." John walked out. From now on, he would pursue his own investigation.

When he got home instead of going to the peach orchard, he found Stuart at the table. "Say, Stu, how about we go for a ride? I need to talk with Wellington Davenport, and you might as well come along."

Stuart shoved his chair back. "You're not going to get in a fight with him, are you?"

"Not planning on it. Want to ask him some questions. See if he knows where B.J. was working, and what he has to say about B.J.'s body showing up here."

John had been allowing Stuart to ride Ol' Kaiser, the gentlest animal on the ranch and John's horse before the judge gambled him away. It didn't take much to buy him back at the Peachville horse auction.

They got John's horse and Kaiser saddled and ready to go, but hadn't mounted when Abe called from the barn. "I have something you should look at."

Abe pointed when John walked in. An ace of diamonds peeked from the straw where they'd found the body.

"What'd ya think?" Abe asked.

"Well, neither one of us play poker. It could have been Wellington, or might have belonged to B.J." John picked it up and stuck it in his pocket. The card could be significant.

"Get off. Get off. Help. Help!" Stuart yelled outside the barn. He stood beside Old Kaiser. He hit the horse's big belly with his fists. "That hurts! Move!"

"What on earth?" John breathed and started running. Before he got to the child, the boy bent over and grinned.

"What happened?" John panted.

Stu flushed. "Well, Ol' Kaiser stepped on my foot and wouldn't move. It hurt."

"How did you get him to move?"

"I ran my hand down his leg and tugged on the hair behind his hoof, and he lifted his foot like he does for you. Took me a bit to remember that's all I needed to do. He sure didn't pay any attention to my yelling. Acted like he hadn't done anything."

John rubbed Stu's hair. Laughter dislodged some of the tension in his gut. "Great job figuring out what to do. Is your foot okay now?"

"Sure, since the big lug isn't standing on it."

Abe stood near the barn, his body jiggling with his chuckles.

"Tell Polly I'm taking Stu with me," John called. "We're going over to Davenports, and we'll be home for dinner."

The ride over to the elaborate ranch was enjoyable. John hadn't been there for a long time. He couldn't understand why Silas Davenport didn't stay home more. In addition to the horse and cattle ranch, the man was part owner of an ore smelter in Leadville. But Silas spent most of his time traveling about the country gambling.

Rumor claimed Silas was so good at the games or at cheating that he brought in almost as much from gambling as his ranch and his business made. His wife and Wellington enjoyed staying home, spending the man's cash.

When John knocked on the door at the Davenport ranch house, he didn't expect Silas to answer, but he did. The rotund gambler, dressed to show his wealth, wore a dark suit with a gold watch chain dangling over his stomach. The fellow could be a tough old hombre.

"Yeh? What ya want?"

The man had aged some, and his frown settled comfortably on his round tanned face.

John spread his legs and stood tall. "I need to talk to Wellington."

Silas stared at Stuart a moment, glanced back into the house, then glared at John. "He's not here."

John cast a pointed glance at the hitching post and the corral. "I see his horse out there and the buggy. Sure he didn't come in, and you didn't know it?"

"I said he's not here." Silas shoved the door and attempted to close it. It stopped when it collided with John's foot.

John edged his shoulder into the door as well, pulling Stu by the hand. "I need to talk to him. I found the body of Billy Joe Garner in my barn this morning."

A throaty woman's gasp came from the room.

Silas paled. "Why you telling us?"

John barged into the room a little further. "He used to work for me, and we got along fine. But he quit and went to work for someone who could pay higher wages. I heard he had plenty of money to spend. Maybe Wellington knows who he was working for."

"Sorry, he isn't h—"

"Pa, who was at the door?" Wellington sprinted down the stairs.

John pushed the door open wider. "Wellington. It's John Parker. I need to find out who B.J. Garner went to work for. I found his body in my barn this morning."

John stepped into the house. Wellington stood there, his jaw dropped. He stared at John while his mother looked on. "He's dead?"

Mrs. Davenport, who had been observing the conversation, ran from the room, a handkerchief over her mouth.

Silas moved out of the way, and Wellington shuffled toward John. "I can't believe he's dead. He was working for us, training horses and helping Mother with odd jobs. Who shot him?"

He wasn't pretending.

"We don't know who killed him. He might have died of natural causes. Doc is looking the body over."

Wellington's eyes caught his father's. Silas quickly turned away.

"Why would he go to your barn?" Wellington asked.

"His body appears to have been dumped there."

Wellington put his hand to his forehead. "He looked so healthy."

"Well, whoever dumped him on my property probably wanted to make it appear as if I was involved with B.J.'s death. Only the murderer left boot prints showing he wore new boots with an interesting heel imprint. I copied the design."

"Sounds mighty hard to prove." Silas jutted out his jaw.

Wellington said, "I didn't kill 'im. I liked B.J. Mother liked him a lot, too."

The room fell silent. Stuart, eyes wide, stared at the chandeliers, grand piano, red velvet settees, brass lamps, large mirrors, marble columns, and oriental rugs.

"I neglected to introduce you to Stuart, my nephew." John gestured toward the boy. "He's a great helper on our ranch. If you'd like some, he has some cute bunnies for sale."

Wellington opened and shut his mouth, and then he started to speak and shut it again. Finally, he bent to greet Stu. "Hello, Stuart. Glad to meet you."

"I don't think we need any rabbits, Stuart," Silas said. "But thanks for telling us."

Wellington leaned toward John's ear and spoke softly. "I want to apologize for being so rude about Bellea and the baby. Something happened to me when Polly started praying for me. I have been a fool. I'll not try to take my son, but I'm going to get a job and support him. Mother"—his eyes wandered toward his father—"and my pa won't give me money to pay Bellea. Now they even cut off my gambling and drinkin' cash. It's the best thing that's happened to me. I'm going to get a job."

John struggled to keep his jaw from dropping. "Does B.J.'s death have anything to do with this?"

Wellington's white face wrinkled into a frown. "I didn't even know he was dead, but I'm not surprised you think I dumped his body in your barn."

"Who else would do it?"

"Nobody I know." Wellington wagged his head. "But B.J. was a gambler. Maybe he had some unpaid debts."

"For some reason, I believe you. Don't prove me wrong."

John stuck out his hand to shake with Silas. Silas hesitated then extended his fat paw.

"This is not over," Silas spat through his tobacco-stained teeth. "You came here to say my son killed him. You can't accuse my son of murder and get by."

John raised his left eyebrow, leaned forward, and slapped Silas on the back. "I didn't actually say that. Don't worry. The sheriff might not try to find the person who killed B.J., but I will not give up until I find out who killed him and dumped the body. B.J. was my friend, too."

25

"That's some house!" Stuart whistled as John helped him into his old saddle on top Kaiser's back. "But the whole place stinks. Smells like cigar smoke."

John grinned as he mounted Dynamite and pointed the horse toward home. Stuart encouraged Kaiser into a brisk trot and seemed to enjoy the ride.

The cold wind sent chills down John's back, and he expected a spring snow would start soon. *Hopefully, this will be the last cold snap before the peach trees blossom.*

"You cold?"

"Yeh. But this is fun. We're not too far from home, are we?"

"Not too far. Would you like to stop at Edwina's and warm up? We could see her and Bellea and the baby."

"I wouldn't mind sitting by a fire for a while. Maybe Bellea will make hot chocolate or give us cake and milk. But you're not going to argue with Ed like you usually do, are ya? I hate it when people get mad at each other. Reminds me of the old man in the general store in Yucca Blossom. Got really mad at me a bunch of times when I stole food. Like the Yucca Blossom barber, too. When Jenny took me to get a haircut, the barber had a fit. Said all sorts of nasty things. Said I probably had lice."

Stuart was quiet a moment. "God forgave me for stealing apples and things."

"Right. If you asked him, the Lord forgave you. But I can't promise anything with Ed. When I'm around her, arguments happen. It's like stepping into a hole in the dark. I don't see it coming until after I'm already in it."

"Don't you like her?"

"Sure. She's okay."

"But not as much as you like Valerie?"

"Well, Ed can't compare with a beautiful woman like Valerie."

"Edwina was purty, purty, purty at church on Sunday, and I saw her snuggling up to you. She was purty as a bluebird."

"She moved over toward me because her ranch hand smelled like a chimney."

"Well, I don't blame her. But when she looks at you, her blue eyes sparkle."

John changed his position in the saddle. "Blue eyes always sparkle when light shines on them."

Stu giggled. "Do Valerie's do that?"

John thought a moment. He didn't even remember the color of Valerie's eyes. "I don't know."

The horses trotted into Edwina's yard. She carried a bucket out by the barn. She dropped it and ran toward John.

"Well, hello, stranger." Even in the cold, cloudy day, the twinkle warmed her blue eyes.

He couldn't even speak until he inhaled a deep breath. "Hi, Ed. We've been over to Davenports. Thought we'd drop by and see how you and everyone are doing."

"And get warm," Stuart added. "Got any hot chocolate?"

John caught Stu's eye and shook his head.

"Sure." Edwina shoved stray hairs from her braid under her cowboy hat. "Bellea will have it ready in a flash. I imagine you're in somewhat of a hurry because it could snow. Did you sell the stallion?"

John tied the horses to the hitching post and helped Stu off Kaiser's back. "Put an ad in the paper this morning."

"How much you wanting for him?"

"I'm thinking I'll take the best bid. You don't want him, do you?"

"Yes, I want him. But I don't have the cash to outbid Wellington or some of the other rich folks. How about I take him and split the stud fees with you for the first six months?"

"The first year?"

Ed frowned and removed her hat as they entered the house. Her blue eyes sparkled up at him. "Deal?"

John hung his and Stu's hats beside hers hanging from a hook on the wall. "Deal."

John tugged his glove to shake. He couldn't resist caressing her cold fingers before he released her hand.

Edwina grinned and slipped out of her coat. "You two can hang your jackets over there. Bellea? We have three orders for hot chocolate, and the rest of you might as well join us at the table."

Stu plopped his coat over the hook and smiled. Then his eyes grew big, and he blinked. A young girl about his age came toward them. She sighted him and stopped in her tracks. "Who are you?"

Stu lifted his chin. "Who are you?"

Bellea entered the room carrying the baby. "Stuart, this is Annamarie. She's a neighbor, but she lives quite a distance away. She comes over sometimes to visit while her mother is in Philadelphia."

"Mom thinks I need to get experience working around a woman rancher," Annamarie explained. "Then when she found out Edwina has a baby living here, Mom thought it was the greatest thing ever. I am learning to take care of him. She tells me I have a lot to learn before I get married."

"You're getting married?" Stuart's eyebrows shot up.

"Not now, stupid. When I grow up."

Stuart stood there gaping at the girl. Bellea handed the baby to her and began gathering ingredients. "You want hot chocolate, too, Annamarie? And you, Mr. Jorgenson?"

"Hot chocolate all around," Edwina said. "Although coffee's his favorite, Papa loves chocolate."

"How about a quick game of checkers?" Annamarie asked Stuart. "I can play even with David on my lap. He likes to watch."

Stuart followed the girl to the parlor. Then Mr. Jorgenson wheeled into the kitchen, his reading glasses still hanging on the end of his nose. He peered up over them and stuck out his hand to shake. "Nice to see you, John. How's the peach ranch doing?"

"I think we're ready for the trees to blossom." John shook the man's hand and marveled at his soft palm these days. "We've had them trimmed. Took out some dead trees, and Abe disked and even watered. It's starting to look like a well-cared for orchard."

"And the horses?" Jorgenson's shaky fingers took off the glasses and set them aside. A day's growth of whiskers covered the lower part of his face.

John moved next to the man's wheelchair. "I'll have four more colts in a month or so. But I'm selling the stallion. I imagine you heard we finally found him after he got out. Edwina bought him."

The man jolted, his body moving up in the high-backed wheelchair. "How'd she do that?"

Edwina grabbed her papa's arm. "We're going to split the stud fees for a year. I tried for six months, but John wheeled and dealed until I agreed to a year. But I'll have foals from our herd for free. I'll discuss how I need to handle that later, Pa."

"Did you mention it to Clyde before you made the deal?"

"No. If you remember, I'm half owner of the ranch, and Clyde is only a ranch hand."

"But I wanted…"

"I found Billy Joe Garner dead in my barn this morning."

"What?"

Edwina froze where she stood, her eyes wide. "No!"

Her father's jaw flexed with emotion.

"Dumped there. I found unusual boot prints in the dirt and manure. Big new boots with an unusual heel design."

"Where'd the bullet hit 'im?" Paul Jorgenson asked.

John shook his head. "He wasn't shot. There was no blood, and he didn't even have a mark on him. Do you know who he went to work for after he quit me? The Davenports. He was helping with horses and doing odd jobs for Mrs. Davenport since her husband is gone all the time."

"I heard B.J. and Mrs. Davenport got along famously. I saw them together in town a couple of times, and they sat mighty close on the buggy seat."

Jorgenson gave his daughter a dirty look. "I don't think we should spread gossip around."

John nodded. "Silas Davenport is home now. We came from their place. I thought Wellington had something to do with the murder and dumping the body on my property since he and his mother are furious at me. But his feet aren't nearly as big as the prints in my barn, and he acted genuinely shocked and grieved by B.J.'s death."

Edwina shook her head, bouncing the long blonde braid on her shoulder. "Oh, you can't tell anything from the way Wellington acts. He's been a liar and no-good all his life."

"I hate to say it," Paul Jorgenson added, wheeling himself to the table to get his hot chocolate, "But Edwina's right. Wellington isn't worth the dirt he stands on."

John sat down and stirred his steaming chocolate. "For some reason, I believed Wellington. Strange. A week or so ago, Polly gave him a swat on the behind with a broom for demanding we give his mother Bellea's baby. She preached him a fiery sermon and then prayed for him. I think Wellington could have had a touch from the Lord."

"I'd never believe it." Jorgenson slurped his chocolate. "Would be a miracle greater than me standing up and walking."

"Now, Papa." Edwina cleared her throat. "Don't limit God. You still may stand up and walk."

Pale and shaky, Bellea stepped toward the table. "Wellington is a beast. Don't believe a word he says. He might have murdered me if I hadn't took off and hid."

John glanced first at Jorgenson, at Edwina, and then Bellea. "It's hard to look at another person and believe he's capable of murder—or even what he did to you, Bellea. Wellington might be responsible for dumping B.J.'s body in my barn, and he might have killed him somehow that doesn't show. But if we believe God can change the vilest sinner, wouldn't it include Wellington, too?"

Bellea burst into tears and ran from the table.

"Hey, Stuart!" John yelled. "Don't you want your hot chocolate? We need to get home."

"I couldn't go without trying to beat her after she wiped all my men off the board," Stuart complained, clomping into the kitchen.

Annamarie smiled behind him, her blue eyes snapping. "I'd have beat 'im in the second game if we could play a little longer."

"Horse feathers." Stu gave her a look that might singe her hair. "We were tied."

Stuart blew his hot chocolate a moment and gulped it down. "Let's go."

They quickly said their goodbyes and returned to their saddles.

"So you couldn't resist those blue eyes, and they distracted you," John teased as they rode.

"I coulda beat her."

"I'm sure you could." John chuckled. "I should have had blue eyes when I played checkers with you. I've always earned it when I won. You're a good player, and I don't think the girl is that good. Those blue eyes were your problem."

"No, they weren't!" Stuart insisted. "She beat me."

"Uh huh. Don't go teasing me about blue eyes if you can't resist big blue eyes, either. But for your information, I'm going to marry Valerie, even if she doesn't have blue eyes. But she might. I don't remember, but she's an elegant woman."

"What's elegant mean?" Stu made a face. "All I know is she isn't like you, and Edwina is. Valerie is nice, and she's really purty. But she's a city lady. She walks like a strutting bird. Her hats have feathers, too. Can you imagine her in a cowboy hat?"

Before John could answer, Wellington Davenport shot by on a galloping horse. Not even glancing at them, Silas raced a lathered pony, apparently trying to catch his son.

Stu stared at the disappearing riders. "What's the hurry?"

John would go back to see the sheriff tomorrow. Maybe he'd find out.

As they guided their horses toward the barn, big snowflakes whirled to earth and in only minutes whitened the ground.

It was cold day in Boston, too, and Dillon was embarrassed for the man when Bill took off all his clothes and began parading around the room. "I'm going to take a shower," Bill announced. He looked here and there and everywhere in the room looking for a shower. "I know it's here," he said. "I took a shower yesterday."

Some men about the room began chiding the man and made suggestive dirty remarks. Bill appeared cold. He sneezed, shivered but kept insisting he was going to take a shower.

Finally, Dillon led him to a corner of the room, and said, "Here it is."

Bill walked into the corner, made washing motions, and then returned to his bed and put his clothes back on. His face wore a contented smile.

26

When Valerie looked outside the next morning, big snowflakes rushed to the ground in Boston too, like the cloud of locusts that came on the wind and devoured her late husband's corn field.

She didn't want to go out, and she didn't want to leave her little boy. But she had to. Work waited in the law office.

Valerie thrust Christian Paul into the nanny's arms, and Christian reached for his mother and screamed, tears running down his chubby cheeks.

"Poor baby." She held out her arms to take him. "I don't want to leave you."

Fire shot from the nanny's eyes. Valerie couldn't even remember the woman's name. Whenever she saw the woman, all she thought of was "heartless."

"I told you to quit spoiling the child!" the nanny screamed above Christian's shrill cry. "Now go away, and he'll be happy."

The angry woman tried to swat the baby's bottom with one hand while holding him with the other. Christian shoved the nanny's chest and shot out of her grip, landing on the floor. The child's eyes widened. He grew pale as milk, and then his eyes disappeared into his head.

Valerie screamed. She dashed to the stairs. "Help! Mother! Christian's unconscious! Call the doctor. I think he's dying."

"See what you done now?" the nanny shouted.

Valerie knelt beside her son. She could not lose her child. In between sobs she prayed, "Jesus. Jesus. Jesus."

Mrs. Van Meter rushed into the room. "What's going on here?"

The nanny shrugged. "Your daughter made me drop him."

"I should be taking care of him myself." Valerie ran her hands gently over her son, praying for a miracle. The boy blinked. His eyes became normal, but a moan came from his pale little lips.

"King Saul's grandson, Mephibosheth, was crippled by a fall from his nurse's arms." Valerie bowed her head again while tears gushed down her cheeks. "Lord, help little Christian to not be crippled."

The child stirred when the doctor walked into the room. Christian wailed softly but barely moved.

Dr. Cabot knelt and moved his fingers over the tyke's head, neck, arms, torso, hips, and legs. Christian stiffened and screamed when the physician touched the right leg. Still probing and being careful of the leg, the doctor lifted his eyes and stared first at Valerie, then her mother, and finally the nanny.

"He has a broken leg. How did it happen?"

The nanny stepped closer. "His mother made me drop him."

Valerie rose up.

"I did not." She shoved herself high enough to look into her mother's eyes. "She tried to paddle him with one hand and hold him with the other. He shoved and landed on the floor—hard." She gritted her teeth until they hurt. "I want this woman fired and out of this house."

"But, Valerie," her mother said in a wobbly voice. "Don't you remember how hard it is to find a good nanny?"

"Well, I'm his mother, and I'll take care of him. If I have to be out, you can do it. You don't need to go to every tea in town."

"But your father made all these appointments for you, and besides, he wants you to come into the office every day. He wants you to argue an important case and get to know Archibald Forsythe better. I'm sure you know Archibald will make a good father. He is the most promising attorney on Father's staff, and you'll never want for anything if you marry him. No more living in a shack out in Colorado with the snakes and rough men who go around carrying guns and burning houses down."

"John Lincoln Parks does not live in a shack."

"I knew you intended to go back to Colorado and marry another penniless man," Mrs. Van Meter spat.

Valerie faced the doctor. "Surely, you can give my little son some pain medication and set the broken bone."

Dr. Cabot stood to his feet. "He should be in the hospital where we can keep him immobilized. That is absolutely necessary for proper healing. It's so close to his hip he might always have a limp."

Three days later, Valerie had stopped weeping and sat beside Christian's crib in a large, donated house recently converted into a children's wing for the Boston Hospital.

"Private rooms are so nice, and I'm sure you're thankful Christian has one." Archibald Forsythe straightened his pant legs as he sat in a chair opposite her.

The wire-rimmed glasses on his nose enlarged his hazel eyes so much he reminded Valerie of the big horned owl sitting on a telephone pole near the Colorado homestead. Archie had been reading a piece about children healing from broken bones and now removed the spectacles, making him look more like the handsome man he used to be.

"If your father hadn't bought this big house and given it to the hospital, you'd be in a room with at least a half dozen kids and their parents."

"I'm so happy Papa bought it." She smiled at Archibald. "I hated for Christian to suffer pain while being exposed to the kids around him who had croup and pneumonia, screamed and carried on. Pop got a crew in here, and since the house was vacant, it could be cleaned and filled with beds in only one day. With a possible measles outbreak, it's a good thing they completed everything so fast. This will bless many in this region."

The white-haired doctor and a chubby nurse stepped into the room and went to Christian's crib. Valerie rushed to their side. "When do you think he'll be able to go home?"

Silence filled the room. Did the old man have a hearing deficiency? At length, he sighed. "The problem is the break was so close to the hip joint."

He slowly lifted Christian's leg up and down. Christian cried out, jerked away and tried to get up.

"Lie still," the doctor commanded.

The nurse held the boy to the bed while the doctor continued to move the leg.

Doc looked up. "He might have to learn to walk again. How old is he?"

The room grew blurry as panic pumped through Valerie. "He's seventeen months old. He loves to walk and run. Why would he forget how to walk?"

"The leg might be tender and give him pain until it's completely healed. But the muscles might try to atrophy while it's not used. So it would be best if he stays in the hospital awhile. I don't have a lot of experience in broken bones of young children, but I've heard they heal fast. Since the swelling has gone down, we'll take off the splints tomorrow and make a plaster cast around the upper leg. We'll leave the knee so it can bend, and he'll be able to walk easier."

Fear dried Valerie's mouth. "And then?"

"We'll have the nurses work with his legs, moving them back and forth to stimulate the muscles. After another week, we'll take him by his hands and allow him to walk, increasing little by little how far he goes. Then we'll know if he's going to have any trouble with the hip. If he does, he might end up with a limp."

"I'm not going to accept that," Valerie said. "I believe in God, and Christian will be all right."

"I've seen a few miracles." The doctor nodded his sage, white head. "Some things can't be explained by man. So, Mrs. MacDougal, pray for your miracle and believe. This accident was unfortunate. I hope your son is as good as new in a few weeks. The break might heal in as many as three or four weeks. Be patient. For that long this little fellow needs to get lots of rest and not move around too much."

When the doctor left, Valerie faced Archibald. The fellow had been handsome in his college days. Now his facial features sometimes froze in his courtroom face. He'd argued tough court cases. But since spending so many hours in the hospital with her, his features softened some.

He reached over, held her hand, and smiled. "Pray with me."

She sighed, and then closed her eyes. "Oh, God. Please don't let little Christian end up with a limp." A sob ripped out of her throat, and Archibald enfolded her in his arms. Tears wet his cheeks as well. He held her until her crying ceased.

Sleep engulfed Christian once again. Valerie stood. "Maybe I should go for a walk outside."

"Good idea." Archibald studied her. "But I've been away from work for too long. Remember the case I mentioned about the asylum? I asked your father and the committee if you could represent three clients with me on this complicated and intriguing pro bono case. Are you still interested?"

"Maybe when Christian's leg has healed, and he's walking again. Tell me about it again."

Archibald walked to his briefcase and retrieved papers. "I am going to file a suit against the state to have my friend, Dillon Haskill, released from the state asylum for the insane because he is not insane. Yes, he had one seizure, but never another. He is a medical doctor."

Valerie shook her head. "That will be a difficult case to win."

"The asylum has a number of patients afflicted with seizures, and their doctors and some ministers believe a person who has what they call an epileptic fit is either insane or demon-possessed."

"Demon-possessed?" Valerie exclaimed. "Ack."

"Dillon has been in the hospital four years now and is a wonderful Christian. His father is a minister. Dillon and a paralyzed teacher in the ward help patients they're confined with. Dillon even started a little choir, teaching them fun and encouraging songs. He recites poetry, tells stories from the books he's read, quotes Scripture, encourages patients when they're upset or on the border of violence. He'd even keep the chamber pots emptied if they'd let him."

Valerie's jaw dropped. "What a horrible situation." She blinked several times and then finally closed her mouth. "Employees should keep the pots emptied."

"The whole asylum is filthy, dark, and depressing—the worst place I've seen in life. Even jails are in much better condition."

Rubbing her hands together, Valerie stared off into the distance, imagining the scene. "How soon do you need to know if I want in? I would think you do need help, and it's an interesting case."

"I'd like to take you on a tour of his ward. If your mother or someone is here with little Christian, I'd like to do it this week so you can think about how we should present evidence for Dillon's release."

Valerie grabbed a chair and sat. "I'll have to think about it a while. No doubt such a visit would be disturbing. When I studied law, though, I wanted challenging cases. This would be challenging for sure."

27

The snow on Peachville Ranch already was quite deep.

"Hey, Stu! Come help me push this sleigh out of the shed."

Stu forsook his snowman and hustled to John, kicking snow up in his trail of footprints. "We goin' sledding?"

"I'm going into town to see the sheriff. I'll try to get home early so I can give you a sleigh ride when I get back. How does that sound?"

"Fine!" Stu beamed. "Wish the girl over at Edwina's house would come over and help me build a fort. I'd love to have a snowball fight and whack the uppity look off her face."

John edged his winter hat farther down over his ears and wagged his head. "What'd ya think Jesus or Jenny and William would think of that?"

Stu made a face. "Maybe I could stick snow down her neck. Or race her down the hill over there."

"Where did you put your birthday presents? Seems to me you I gave you a toboggan. We put your gifts in a corner of the attic. A toboggan's better in deep snow than a sled. Runners won't work very well in this soft, wet snow. You can try out the toboggan on the hill but be careful. They're hard to steer. I'll help you with it tomorrow."

"Why can't you do it today?

"Getting tired of hanging out with grownups?"

"Aw." Stu dropped his head. "The snow might melt by tomorra."

John kicked the deep snow. "It's not even wise for me to leave home today. But I need to talk to the sheriff, and I should do it today. Go ahead and build the fort. If I have time when I get home, I'll have a snowball battle with you. You might wish I hadn't volunteered. I'm pretty good at it."

"Phooey." Stu giggled. "You probably forgot how, like you did with the stilts. You'll be ducking for cover."

"Go in and get warm once in a while," John advised after he hitched a plow horse to the sleigh and climbed on. "You don't want frostbite."

He'd driven the sleigh only a little way when he met Edwina driving a sleek pinto pulling her big sleigh. When her eyes caught on John, her pink-cheeked smile reminded him of the first husk peel down an ear of corn.

"John!" The word wiggled around on a certain tone from her happy lips. "I gave Annamarie a sleigh ride, and now I want to pick up the stallion."

"I'm sorry. I probably won't be back for a while. It might be better if you wait for a day or two so I can help you take him to your place and get him settled. But you could go ahead and visit with Polly. Stu hoped Annamarie would come over so he could use his snow fort."

Annamarie beamed. "Aha! He's about to get sacked."

Both girls giggled as the horse jerked the sleigh into motion. It whipped back and forth to each side of the slick road while the girls yelped and then drove straight toward John's house.

The sheriff had a good fire going, and John welcomed the heat as he stomped snow off his boots and whacked his pant legs.

The sheriff's feet flew off his desk and thumped to the floor. "What brings you out on a cold day like this, John? Have new evidence, or are you confessing?"

John slipped off his gloves and dragged a battered chair near the desk. "Well, I went to Davenports and talked to Wellington." John eyed the smoky ceiling. He shrugged and shook his head. "I don't think Wellington was involved in B.J.'s death. He acted shocked when I told him Billy Joe is dead."

"So?" Sheriff Woody Watson placed his chin in his hand, propped on his other arm.

John leaned his chair back and let it balance on the back legs. "What did Doc say when he looked at the body?"

"I don't know that I rightly need to tell you. Billy Joe's pa isn't going to bury him until tomorrow, so Doc can study the body longer and they'll have more time to dig the grave in this frozen ground. Doc thinks B.J. was poisoned or smothered."

John frowned. "Who would have access to poison?"

Woody's lips drew up into a wrinkled pucker. "Anybody who buys rat poison."

"Pttthhh!" John spat air at the absurd notion. "And how would they get B.J. to eat it? Did Doc rule out natural causes like choking on meat or some illness? B.J. was sick when he left the saloon the night before I found the body."

The sheriff pulled a tin of chewing tobacco from his back pocket and placed a wad of leaves in his cheek. "Natural causes don't seem likely if we believe someone dumped the body in your barn."

John's reaction came from his belly and landed on his face. First, he frowned, and then his spirit melted, and he almost smiled. "True. I'm fairly sure Wellington had nothing to do with it, though. I don't know who else it would be."

The sheriff's office door rattled as someone stomped on the boardwalk outside, apparently knocking off snow. The doorknob turned, and Wellington burst inside. His nose was the color of a ripe cherry in July. A fur parka, gloves, and a hat protected the rest of him. His dark brown eyes sparkled.

He nodded at each of them. "Hello, Sheriff. Hi, John. I'd guess you're discussing who might have dumped B.J.'s body in your barn. Well, Sheriff, I didn't do it. But I don't have much of an alibi. I was home."

The sheriff wiggled the boot he'd placed on his left knee. "Keep talking, Wellington."

Wellington shrugged his narrow shoulders. "I don't know anything more about what happened to B.J., except my mother hired him to do odd jobs around the house and go with her when she wanted to go out. She always had trouble with the horses and didn't want to risk a runaway. Then all of a sudden, B.J. disappeared."

"What did your father do when he found out she hired Billy Joe?" the sheriff asked.

"Well, he hadn't been home until four or five days ago. He'd been gone almost a month. Hiring B.J. was fine with Papa. He never did anything around the house when he was home, and when B.J. came, we had lots of things needing fixing. When he's home, Papa spends his time in the Peachville pool hall and the saloon enjoying the pretty girls—kind of like I do."

John shivered. How could the Davenports be so rich in wealth and so poor in good sense and real love? He pictured Valerie. That elegant woman would be a fine wife, and he and she would live for God and be a close, loving family.

"Does your papa go to church?" John asked. "I don't remember him being there much."

"He shows up a few times a year. Thinks it's good to keep people aware that he has so much property and owns the smelter."

"I'd forgotten he bought the smelter." Sheriff Woody fiddled with his mustache. "Don't some smelters produce arsenic when they're purifying the metal?"

Wellington's glance swiveled to the door, then back to the sheriff. "I've heard they do, but I don't think Papa ever collected it or sold it. His partners might."

The sheriff raised his bushy eyebrows. "Did you have access to arsenic?"

Wellington's face reddened. "No. What would I want with it?"

"To pass on to B.J.?"

"Absolutely not. B.J. was my friend." He stomped out of the sheriff's office. The door slammed so hard it jiggled the building.

John shook his head again. "I don't doubt they were friends. They're both gamblers. But on the other hand, Mrs. Davenport might have been running low on cash since she was giving a lot of it to Billy Joe. People about town say he had a lot of money recently."

The sheriff got up with a groan and put a fresh pot of coffee on top of the stove. "Yet B.J. wasn't robbed when he was killed. Plus, folks at the saloon said B.J. had won some recently."

John shook his finger. "Whoever dumped the body in the barn was a big person, if we can judge by those boot prints." He glanced out of the window. "That's another reason why I don't think Wellington did it. He's sort of puny. His feet aren't even big. Wish we knew for sure the cause of death."

The sheriff's eyes widened. "Doc investigated the inside of B.J.'s mouth. Looked at his teeth. He'd like to examine the contents of his stomach. But he's not authorized to do an autopsy."

"Were there any blows to the head? After seeing something on B.J.'s lips, I can't help but think poison. But I've got to go. Stuart is expecting me to play fort with him."

"Might be too late to play in the snow," Woody remarked at the window. "It's melting."

John grinned. "I think there'll be plenty left for a few snowballs."

"Remember, John, don't go anywhere out of town. You're still our number one suspect."

John wagged his head. "You have enough evidence to show I wasn't involved. Doesn't make sense how some sheriffs grab the first suspect and pin the crime on him."

"Well, B.J.'s pa is back in town, and his sister. They want the murderer caught."

"Guess I'll have to see what else I can find out about who killed Billy Joe."

John stepped out into the snowy, slushy boardwalk and ambled past the ladies' dress shop. Watching his feet didn't slip, he climbed the steep stairway to the upstairs physician's office with a Walk In sign posted on the door window.

A woman was engaged in a low conversation with the doctor. Doc smiled at John. "Hey there, son. I'd like you to meet Phila, Billy Joe's sister. Phila, this is John Lincoln Parks, an outstanding young man in our community. From what I hear, John's on his way to bringing his parents' ranch back to its former glory."

John grasped the daintily manicured hand. "Nice to meet you, miss. Where you from?"

"Minneapolis. Attended a women's college there, and now I've opened a millinery shop."

"Interesting. I have an aunt in Minneapolis. I lived with her a few months. It's a fine city. All this snow must have made you think of home."

John's eyes caught a moment with her big brown ones. Then he came to his senses. "I came from the sheriff's office. I've been trying to help discover what happened to Billy Joe, and so far, we don't know why his body was dumped in my barn. But you might as well know I'm the sheriff's number one suspect since I found the body."

The twinkle faded from her captivating eyes. Her face blanched to the color of her teeth, and she wobbled as if she might faint.

The doctor gave her smelling salts, and he and John helped the woman to a cot in the back room. "You rest there for a few minutes," Doc advised.

John and the doc walked out of the room. "I didn't mean to upset her. It's best for her to know how things stand."

"She doesn't know you," Doc reminded John. "People here don't believe for one minute you are a killer. She's a go-getter who could make your life miserable if she's convinced you killed her brother. From talking to her, she's tougher than she looks."

"Thanks for the warning." John's lips twisted into a smile. "Anything new on the cause of death?"

"It's anybody's guess, and there probably will be lots of guessing going on."

When John arrived home, an intense war battle filled the yard.

"He's been begging for mercy!" Annamarie shouted.

"And then when she's not looking for it, I let her have it!" Stuart's rosy cheeks held a wide grin. The sun shone warm beams on their backs.

"Maybe it's time for a truce," John suggested.

"Make peace with a girl?" Stuart huffed.

"Sure. Invite her and Edwina for supper and maybe you can have another contest with chess or checkers in the warm house."

The back door slammed. Edwina sprinted to them. "How did things go in town?"

"All right I guess. I'm still the sheriff's number one suspect. Met Billy's beautiful sister. Talked to Doc, but everyone has more questions than answers."

Stuart tapped Ed on the arm. "Say, John said I could invite you and Annamarie to supper."

Edwina's tongue flicked over her lips. "Sounds good. But we can't stay too long. My father will begin to worry, and Bellea will too. Plus, the snow's melting."

John reached down and squished a good-sized snowball together. "I don't think the roads have melted enough to cause trouble with the sleigh."

He continued to work with the snowball.

Edwina kept talking. "Polly has some potato soup and cheese sandwiches about ready. But she also made some apple dumplings I'm dying to taste."

When she turned back to the house, John threw the snowball. It hit her back at the waist where the gun belt went around. She whirled, one eyebrow up, and a beady look in her eyes.

"This is war!" she yelled.

In seconds snowballs flew. They hit John in the chest, his head, his face, and he took a whack on his back. John couldn't make snowballs fast enough to keep up with her, so he took his half-made snowball, came up behind her as she reached for more snow, and dropped a handful down her neck.

Edwina's blue eyes lit as she gasped.

He drew her to his side and put his arm around her shoulders. "I'm sorry. I just couldn't resist."

Giving her a little squeeze seemed so natural as they headed toward the house. His eyes caught hers. "It would be nice to have you eat with us."

Standing close to her felt so comfortable. Then he jerked his head and hoped to clear it. He pulled his arm away and made some distance between them. He would not let Edwina sidetrack him from gaining Valerie as his wife.

28

After Archibald Forsythe checked in with security at the asylum, Valerie followed him to the door he held open for her to enter. She jolted back, slamming into a grimy wall, almost gagging at the odor. Chills ran up her spine.

"Stop the voices!" a male voice demanded. "I don't want to kill."

"Will you shut up!" somebody shouted.

"Stop looking at me!"

Obscenities and cursing rattled the walls. Another deep voice sobbed, and soon others joined him.

"God, have you forsaken us?" an anguished cry rose from someone's throat.

"The medical board of lunacy and physicians are still studying insanity." Archibald took Valerie's hand and led her further into the dark building and started up the stairs. "The asylum housed 439 patients in 1899. Dillon Haskill told me lots of them don't deserve to be here."

"Oh, but aren't you afraid of the patients who are insane?"

"I don't think most of them are dangerous to others. They're often more dangerous to themselves. As for Dillon, he only had one seizure, but important people saw it. He wasn't insane then, and isn't crazy now. Although his mother fought for his release, he's still here."

Confusion pinched lines between her eyes. "You said he had the seizure after he was bucked off a horse. He isn't a rodeo cowboy, is he?"

Archibald grasped her elbow and urged her on down the hallway.

"He grew up riding and hoped to pay the bills he accumulated studying medicine. If he had a winning time for riding the bronc in the rodeo, he could have paid all his bills. In fact, the previous year he got the bronc-riding buckle because he had the best time in the event. But four years ago, he flew in the air, and his head hit the top fence rail. He could have broken his neck."

"So sad." Valerie held her handkerchief over her nose as they reached the top of the second flight of stairs and walked down the third-floor corridor.

Archibald peeked into the small barred windows. "Dillon advised me to ask for the asylum report from the Board of Lunacy Commissioners, and I got it. The highest diagnosis was intemperance. In other words, alcoholism, and thirty-seven people are here because of that."

"Amazing," Valerie murmured behind her handkerchief. "I wouldn't think of them as lunatics. I have a couple of uncles who spend half their time drunk. But they're rich, and nobody thinks anything about it. I'll bet it's the fellow in the gutter they pick up and dump here."

Archie shook his head. "Some alcoholics have delirium tremens where they hear or see things that aren't there. What they see is real to them, but others don't understand why they are so frightened."

A tender smile softened his sometimes-severe face. "Could be why some drunks end up here. There are two morphine addicts, too. But sad to say, there are fourteen patients admitted because of epilepsy. They call the seizures fits and usually attribute them to demons."

He peeked into another dirty, barred window and then blew out his lips. "This is pathetic. These people are nothing but skin and bones. Taxes support this hospital, and they should be feeding them well. But I've heard some of the workers talk. If the kitchen sends anything fit to eat, the workers take it. They don't believe people possessed by the devil should live."

Archibald took her trembling hand in his big ones.

Although his touch comforted her, Valerie pulled away. "Demon possession is really scary. I've heard if you aren't spiritually clean, or if you come close, demons can jump in you. Where is Dillon's room?"

He peered into two more rooms. "I don't believe a Christian can be possessed because the scriptures say greater is he that is in us than he that is in the world. Dillon's room should be coming up. Here it is. I see him pacing."

Archie threw back his head and released another big breath. "I hope you're up to this. You have to overlook his appearance. He hasn't had a shave or a haircut in a long time. He looks kind of wild, but keep in mind, he's a perfectly sane, and a great Christian."

Archie glanced behind them. Valerie hadn't noticed the husky uniformed guard following them and watching their every move.

"Guard," Archie said, motioning with his head. "The patient we want to see is in this room."

Keys rattled on the man's hip as his fingers rummaged through them. "You'll have ten minutes. This is a minimum-security ward. But we still can't chance an escape. You enter at your own risk. Did you sign the release?"

"Yes," they said in unison. Archibald's voice sounded a mite disgusted, and Valerie's came almost like a whisper. The guard's beady eyes made her nervous.

"Yes," she repeated, stronger this time.

She reached for Archibald's hand as the guard inserted the key and opened the squeaky door. Praying for strength, wisdom, and protection, she stepped inside. Her eyes hadn't adjusted to the dimness when the door slammed behind them.

Panic heated her face and chilled her bones. Dizziness seized her, but she wasn't going to give in. When her eyes cleared, three smiling faces stared at her. One pair of eyes belonged to a young man with Down's syndrome. He didn't look over ten or twelve years old, and with him standing there, peering at her with delight, she couldn't help but reach out her hand to him.

"Hello. I'm Valerie."

The kid stuck out his short-fingered hand, and his smile stretched wider. His tongue dripped saliva. "My name is Pete. Do you know you're beautiful?"

His slanted eyes blinked.

"Thank you," Valerie said, nodding her head and smiling.

A man with thick black bushy hair stepped closer. Archibald grasped him in a bear hug and then turned. "Dillon Haskill, this is Valerie MacDougal."

When they released each other and patted backs, Dillon nodded to Valerie. Lights came on in his whiskered face. "Ah. You must be the lawyer ol' Archibald said is a tough cookie. He thinks you're the person who can get me out of here."

Valerie wrinkled her brow and blinked. "I don't know. Truth is, I've never argued a case by myself except in law school. I'm thinking it will probably take a miracle, but God is into miracles."

"Don't let her act so humble," Archibald smiled. "She brought several tough people to tears in her courtroom trials. She's made of pure grit. The smell in here bothers her. But don't let her fool you. She's cleaned out barns and chicken houses and witnessed plenty of innocent people being abused."

"Let me introduce everyone." Dillon swiped his hand toward others in the room. "I think you've met Pete."

"Yes," Valerie smiled at the boy again.

Dillon wagged his head. "Don't get near us. We have lice. Archie here will have to burn his clothes and delouse his hair when he gets home. Again. Sorry."

"I forgot," Archibald muttered, rubbing his hands on his pants and brushing down his sleeves. He looked at Valerie. "This is the first time they put me inside the room."

Valerie cringed, feeling crawly. She forced her lips to smile, and when she did, the good feeling drifted to her heart. "Don't worry about it. I contended with mites in our chicken house, and I guess, if these people can live with lice day and night, we can endure it for a few minutes. Could be a good thing to bring up in court. You never know what valuable information and evidence you might find accidentally."

The lumps covered with blankets on several beds caught Valerie's eye. "For the record, Dillon, who else is in this room, and why are they here?"

"Well, Jeremiah, why don't you tell these people why they put you here?" Dillon walked to the rumpled blanket and jabbed his index finger into the bundle.

Jeremiah threw the blanket off, sat his bony body up, stretched, and then ran his long grubby fingers through his straight, wild hair. "Let's see. I stole food at the general store."

A guttural sob burst from his mouth. His tattered red plaid shirt hung over his shaking shoulders. "My little ones needed food. I stole eggs from a chicken house and milked a cow that wasn't mine. But I made my mistake when I started picking up pretty things. But it was worth it! Did we have Christmas!"

Now the tears turned to laughter. "My wife and kids had pretties for their birthdays. And then, I came here. They said I'm a kleptomaniac. They believe I'm insane because I can't keep from taking things that aren't mine. They say I have sticky fingers. Don't you see? They're not sticky. I stole because I had no money, and the other people didn't need what I stole."

"Thank you, Jeremiah," Dillon said.

"How long you been here, Jerry?" Archibald asked.

Jeremiah looked away and then back at Archibald. "Pert near five years."

"That's a long sentence for petty thievery," Valerie commented.

Jeremiah groaned and started crying again. "I knew better. Mama taught me the Ten Commandments and how to live right.

Soon as they brought me here, although I was angry, I repented. God forgave me. Dillon, have I stolen anything in here?"

"Not even a crust of bread."

Archibald glanced at Valerie, then back at the man. "Well, Jerry, this lady and I are trying to get misdiagnosed people out of here. In the meantime, do lots of praying and what you can to help one another."

Pete touched Valerie's arm. "We did have another friend here, but he died. His name was Mississippi. He was nice, and he saw things. He always was on a ship, and he'd yell at his men. Always fought with invisible pirates. But he's dead. Do you think the pirates killed him?"

Dillon put his arm around the lad. "No," he spoke gently. "The pirates weren't real. Only in Mississippi's mind."

Dillon leaned closer to Archibald's shoulder and spoke in a soft voice. "The fellow snoring in the back bunk is Oscar, but people call him Bubba. He's real quiet and nice some of the time. And then something will set him off, or he'll wake up angry, ranting, and raving. He wants to fight when he's that way. Sometimes they put him in a straitjacket or chain his ankles and hook him to the wall. He's delusional and can be dangerous to us and also to the guards who take control of him. That's showed me why people who have no control of their anger are said to be 'mad.'"

"Don't think I'll be using that term about my feelings anymore." Valerie stood on her tiptoes to see the man better.

Dillon introduced them to Jimmy Cook, a former teacher paralyzed from the waist down, admitted only because of the paralysis.

A short distance from the patients, Dillon told about Curly Hicks, a former truck driver, who had a thought disorder, as well as syphilis, and Bobby Ward, who tried to kill his stepfather.

Archibald grasped Dillon's shoulder. "Is there any way you can contact me, or I can contact you without coming out here?"

Dillon bent toward his ear, but Valerie could hear. "There is one really nice guard. I think he might mail a letter for me."

"We anticipated that." Archibald slid paper, two envelopes, and stamps from underneath his shirt.

Valerie turned her back, reached into her bosom, and brought out two pencils and handed them to Dillon. "Be careful," she whispered. "The wrong person could use these as a weapon."

29

John Lincoln Parks drove the team and wagon through the peach orchard, enjoying the blossoming trees' beauty and wondering how he could prevent the forecast frost from wiping out this year's crop.

He about lost his breath thinking about it. His father used to build fires in the orchard. Then John and his dad stayed up all night tending the fires to ensure they didn't get out of hand.

"You know when you give a problem to the Lawd, he'll work it out," Abe said, looking up into the trees. "The way these blossoms look now, you'll have a great crop. We'll all pray, do what we can, and leave the rest to God."

"Do you think we could haul enough wood in here to start fires in the coldest part of the night?" John asked. "I can't get it out of my head how Saint James said 'faith without works is dead.'"

"Might help." Abe twisted to the big pile of dead trees they hauled out of the orchard and never had time to burn. "We have to stay up if we have fires burning."

"I know. Wish I had some little stoves to build fires in so they'd keep going longer and there wouldn't be danger of spreading."

Abe folded his long fingers together. "I've heard people out Californy way been workin' on something like that, but it burns oil. Calls 'em 'smudge pots.' We'll have to treat the fires like a campfar. We could shovel a little dirt ring around 'em."

"Want to start hauling wood?"

"That's the reason you brought the wagon, ain't it?"

John grinned. "You know me pretty well."

Abe threw back his white head, pulled his mouth into a big smile, and laughed until he shook. "You still a young'un in my mind, John."

John eyed him. Was Abe up to doing without sleep? The twinkle in Abe's eyes certainly signaled he was ready for the challenge.

"Let's get to work, boy," the man said.

As they worked, Abe said, "Your daddy planted the orchard on a north-facing hill, so the trees wouldn't warm up and blossom too early. He only fertilized trees after harvest, which also keeps them from budding too soon in the spring. 'Course we was too busy to apply fertilizer early anyhow."

Abe took his ax and shortened some of the long branches in the pile, then threw them on the wagon.

"I remember Papa mowing the undergrowth around the trees because bare dirt would hold heat. We've done so much work in the orchard there's not much of anything growing except a little grass, and now that I think of it, that's a good thing."

"Plowin' the land and redoing irrigation ditches helped. Ta judge didn't take care o' the trees a' tall." Abe grunted as he threw more wood on to haul.

Abe and John rode in the wagon as it bobbled up and down on the rough ground. They had three more fire pits to go on the last row of trees when a frantic scream drifted on the breeze.

John handed Abe the reins. "Stuart's in trouble." He jumped to the ground and took off running.

The overturned slop bucket lay beside the pigpen. Three little pigs ran in different directions. Stuart pursued one of them. "Here, piggy, piggy…"

Stu must have gone into the pen to slop the pigs and left the gate open. That rascal! John shut the gate to the pen and took off after the closest pig. Taking a deep breath, he let out a pig squeal, a hog snort as loud as he could make it, then dropped into a deep, "Piggy, piggy, piggy" and the "Soueeeeee!" like he'd heard at the State

Fair. He kept it up until Stu stopped in his tracks and all three pigs streaked toward John.

John tried to herd them back toward the pen, but the critters took off three different ways again.

One came close to Stu. He held the animal by a hind leg. The pig squealed, and Stu yelled almost as loud. "Help! Help. I can't hold him."

Before John could reach the kid, the pig pulled away. All three pigs raced for Polly's garden spot where her early lettuce, radishes, and peas peeked through the ground.

Stu and John went for the pigs' curly tails. John started his pig calls again, and Stu laughed so hard he fell on the ground. But the kid caught a tail as it went by, and he held on.

John picked lettuce with both hands and moved it close to the snouts of the nasty grunting animals. Instead of taking the bait, the pigs rolled around in the wet dirt between the rows, then devoured the little pea plants bravely reaching for the sun.

Polly shot out of the house carrying a broom. "Get those pigs out of my garden!"

A piglet slipped through Stu's arms as if he were greased, leaving the mud on the boy's face, in his hair, and all over his clothes.

John snatched another by the belly and wrestled long enough the mud almost became his second skin. The piggy slipped through his arms, leaving a thicker layer of wet grime. Although it started to dry, John could hardly see.

Polly had the critters rounded up in a minute or two with her broom, and the little fellers ran toward Mama Pig. Polly whipped open the gate and swatted the animals on their backsides as they trotted inside.

John collapsed in the garden. He gasped for air, exhausted. Stu lay close by huffing and puffing.

"I don't recommend y'all taking a nap out here," Polly spat as she walked by on her way back to the house. "Looks like I better heat up some water in the washtub. Used all the hot water we had for the dishes."

"Well. What do we have here?" The feminine voice struck terror in John's veins. Not Edwina. Not now.

He rolled over on his stomach, hoping to hide his face.

"Trying to look more handsome for me with that mud pack? You know mud does nothing to beautify your clothes. Never works. But might do something for your tough hide." Melodious laughter echoed and assaulted John's ears.

Too tired to speak, he sighed.

"Okay, John, ignore me. But I'm here to pick up the stallion."

30

When he rolled on his back, to John's horror Edwina not only stared at him, but Clyde Merriweather stood beside her smirking.

Anger surged. John sat up. "This isn't a good time. Abe and I are trying to prevent a killing frost in the orchard, and Stu had a tussle with some piglets. Thanks to Polly, they're back in the pen."

He finally tucked his feet under him and gave Stu a hand. "You go ahead and get in the tub. Polly's heatin' water."

"Well, are you going to send the stallion with us today? I wasn't sure I could handle him, so I brought Clyde."

Clyde stuck his thumbs in his overall bib and smirked, his chest stuck out to indicate he'd won Edwina over.

John gritted his teeth. "Sure. Probably a good idea. That package of horseflesh can be a handful. But I won't send him home with you unless you swear you won't use a whip on him."

Ed started shaking her pretty head negatively. Bellea must have done Ed's hair again. Every time he saw her, beauty seemed to radiate from the lady rancher, softening all the anger and worry lines of the past.

John shifted. He'd seen Clyde train horses with a whip. But John had made a contract with Edwina, and he'd have to abide by it.

Abe drove the team into the barn. The wagon was empty, so he must have completed setting up the fire pits in the orchard.

John ran to the cellar and brought up four apples. He stopped at the windmill long enough to splash the mud off his face in the bone-chilling water. Stu followed, trying to knock dried mud off his clothes and shoes. Then he washed.

"Stu, tell Polly I'll be in for supper before long. Abe is already on his way. I'll help Ed get the stallion."

Soon the magnificent animal wore a halter and Clyde held the reins, leading the stallion behind his horse. John hoped he wasn't making a mistake.

The next morning, John dragged his tired legs to the barn. He might as well have carried a bale of hay on his back the way he felt. In the distance, blossoms from creamy white to pink filled the trees. Praise the Lord, the frost didn't get them. Worth staying up half the night.

But…what were those strange white balls moving under the trees and bushes and huddled on the path. Rabbits!

A huge sigh crawled from the bones in his chest and burst from his mouth. He knew the hutches were too full but didn't have time to do anything about it. Too many things going on.

"Stu! Stu! Stuart! You better get out here and get these rabbits. They're everywhere!"

Polly stuck her head out of the back door. "He still in bed."

"Well, tell him to get out now and start catching these rabbits." John puckered his lips, shook his head, ran to the barn, and drug out a large wooden box. He tried sneaking up on three or four of the littlest critters, but as he came near, they took off running.

One little fellow scooted under the lilac bush on the side of the yard. John grabbed a foot, and a little pasteboard container came out with the animal. He dropped the bunny in the big box and read what he had in his hand. "Rodent Killer" etched in big black letters. Smaller print declared "Contains strychnine" above a skull and crossbones drawing.

Where did this come from? He and his father never bought rodent killer, and surely, Abe didn't either. They left the rodents to the barn cats. *This rodent killer box is fairly new and half full.*

A picture of B.J.'s face flashed before his eyes as the sheriff rolled the man over on the barn floor. Perhaps he'd better talk to Woody again. But first, they had to do something about all the bunnies.

While he waited for Stu to get dressed, John checked the hutches. They still bulged because the rabbits pushed against the chicken wire so much it came loose on the bottom of both hutches.

Abe strode up to the rabbit pens. "Is this what you shoutin' at Stuart about? So sorry, John. We shoulda noticed before."

Polly followed Stuart to the men. "Got 'im out here soon as ah could." Polly put her hand on Stu's shoulder. "What was ya yellin' so much about?"

"Rabbits. Rabbits are everywhere."

"Oh, no! Bad enough pigs wallow on my new little plants. But rabbits are death to a garden, and if I have anything to do with it, we's gonna have rabbit for dinner. Abe! Get a gun and kill these critters."

"No. Don't do that." Stu clutched Abe's arm. Terror twisted his face.

"Forget it, Stu," John grumbled. "We'll only kill three unless we can't catch them."

Abe ran toward the garden with a roll of chicken wire and some posts. "It's time we fence these plants in."

Stu found another wooden box and set it upside down with a stick propping it up for a trap. Still buttoning his shirt, he ran to the house and came back with three carrots. He stuck them in the trap and tied a long rope to the box. He barely set it up when larger rabbits hopped inside. He yanked the rope and caught several. Only thing, when he lifted the box to reach in and get a rabbit, at least one other one escaped.

John busied himself repairing the hutches. Then he found a fishnet and caught a few fugitive rabbits. He put them in the big wooden box and discovered energy he thought drained out during the night. Kneeling on the ground, he reached for another furry little varmint, and then something went up his pant leg.

With a yelp, he stood and danced. "You stupid outfit! Get out. Get out. Get out!"

He straightened his leg and shook it. The bunny crawled higher. He grabbed his upper leg and danced some more. "Stupid critter. Get out of there!"

In exhaustion, he sat on the ground and searched up his pant leg, felt a fuzzy foot, and pulled.

Finally, the little bunny dropped to the ground and scurried away, accompanied by Stuart's giggles.

Stu's eyes bulged with humor. "Hey, John, was that the new dance you're learning so you can take Edwina out?" His giggles escalated into deeper laughter as he pointed, gasped, bent over, his body shaking and heaving as he tried to get his breath. He kept pointing but wasn't able to get a word around his laughter.

Then Abe joined the laughing session. Holding his gut, he added his deep rumbling string of "ha-ha" to Stu's more treble voice, but John had it. "Get your BB and shotgun, Stu, and I'll get my shotgun. You're going to learn how to shoot."

Stuart sobered. He gestured helplessly toward the rabbits running everywhere. A pained expression twisted his face. Then his face lit up. "You mean it?"

"Sure. Be quick about it. Tomorrow we're going into town to sell rabbits." He tapped Stu on the head. "Still got the picture you drew of a rabbit? Make a poster out of it advertising rabbits for sale."

Before long, John had scooped up enough bunnies to fill the wooden box. He stopped and showed Stuart safety precautions, how to load both guns, and how to aim and pull the trigger. They practiced on tin cans for about ten minutes, and Stu got the hang of it. John was in a hurry. "Pick out the big critters and let them have it."

"Now listen," Polly argued. "I'm not going to clean shot out of rabbit meat. You give me three of those big ones you put in the box. Let Stu try to shoot a squirrel out of a tree or a crow off the fence."

Stu was so busy learning to shoot he didn't even notice Abe taking three large bunnies out behind the barn.

An hour later, rabbit meat lay in the icebox ready to sizzle for lunch, three white pelts stretched on the barn wall, and Stu had successfully learned to use both his guns.

Polly, bless her heart, had a batch of fresh biscuits, sausage, gravy, and scrambled eggs on the back of the stove.

After they ate and because of exhaustion from the night before, John sat in the parlor with Abe. "I think I might have found what the killer used on Billy Joe." He explained about the strychnine box being planted under his lilac bush.

"Makes me wonder again about Wellington Davenport. He's the only one with a grudge against me. Well, besides his mother."

"What ya goin' to do 'bout it?"

"Talk to the sheriff. That's all I know how to do."

Abe shook his head, wiggling the flabby skin under his jaw. "Don't know as I trust dat sheriff." Then the clouded look in his eyes vanished. "But I trust God. And he in charge."

31

After a short nap, John reached for the thick letter from Valerie with fresh enthusiasm. Maybe this wasn't such a bad day after all.

Yet the sunshine quickly turned to clouds as he read her beautiful penmanship. Bad news hung on every word like those big worms on Polly's tomato vines in the summer. Little Christian had been injured. But the good news came later. He was recovering miraculously, with the broken bone healed and the boy learning to walk again.

Then she described a court case she and Archibald filed with the courts, hoping to get a young man released from the state asylum. Excitement filled every word she wrote.

John tucked the letter in a bureau drawer. Valerie's mother hoped her daughter would marry Archibald. That lawyer would never drag Valerie off to live on a horse and peach ranch in Colorado.

Valerie had been to law school. John didn't know if she graduated, but she could practice law without the degree. All she needed to do was get a license, and her father could help. For all John knew, she already had the law license.

He shook his head, and his heart quivered with it. Being married to an even-tempered beautiful woman like Valerie would help keep him at peace. Ed's face popped into his mind. He stomped down the stairs, snatched his jacket off the wall, and headed outside. He'd feed and water the horses, check the pigs, load up all the rabbits he could, and go into town.

Abe met him outside the barn. "Ya look like a mountain lion about ready to attack. You upset about somethin'?"

John felt himself change into a bedraggled kitten that escaped a gunnysack and swam the river. "Guess I'm too tired to deal with everything." He swallowed, trying to rid himself of the lump in his throat. Grown men didn't cry.

"You too tired. God know about the murder. He know about the horses and ya bills. He know about the peach crop. He know about pigs and rabbits gettin' out. A heavy load on ya shoulders. We's gonna pray, but first, let's think about things we are thankful about. The peach harvest saved by our work in the night. Lift up your eyes. The weather warmed and will heat the soil, so we probably won't have the danger of another late frost."

John nodded, feeling he'd shaken a little sadness from his fur.

"Your herd of nice horses are grazing in a green pasture. Then you got all those rabbits to sell for Stuart, and that probably will make him and his parents happy. An' next week would be a good time to take some pigs to the auction. You don't need to feed all of 'em any longer. It's time to sell the bigger ones."

A horse pounded up to the barn with a smiling Edwina on its back. "Papa connected with some of his friends, and we have the stallion's stud services lined up for the next month. The telephone gives Pa a chance to do important business."

John's heart did a romp in his chest. "That's good news. The phone comes in handy."

Edwina jumped off the horse and grabbed John's hand and tipped her face sideways, lips pursed serious. "Are you sick? You look like you can barely stand up."

"Abe and I stayed up most of the night keeping our smudge fires going on account of possible frost. We saved the blossoms. Guess I'm tired. Besides the pigs getting out yesterday, Stu's rabbits got out this morning. We killed three. If we killed more, we could sell pelts. But we're going to try to sell of the little bunnies in town."

Ed snuggled close to his side. "You should take a long nap. Then you'll be ready to take the world on again."

John searched out her big blue eyes. Some of her sparkle ignited in his heart. He had a good notion to kiss her. Maybe he ought to give up and quit fighting falling in love with her. Yet compared to living with Valerie, life with Ed would be a wild ride.

They walked together hand in hand, strength from the woman at his side oozing into his heart. Then Ed jerked, wrenched away from him, and screamed. They'd wandered too close to the hog pen again. This time pig slobber dripped from her riding outfit.

"John, you are a lousy, horrible tease who enjoys seeing women suffer." She ran and snagged her horse's reins. John's long legs caught her in no time. Before she could mount, he brought her to him, planting all his feelings into the kiss he laid on her lips.

Ed jolted away, fire and shock pulsing on her face. She stomped her foot. "Well, I never!"

As she threw herself in the saddle, John laughed. "Sorry, but don't be too sure."

The way John's heart thrashed, he'd like to kiss her again.

Stu didn't look too happy when he came out to help load up the rabbits.

"All the little bunnies are going to town from the hutches and the boxes," John explained. "When we catch more, they'll go in the hutches. It's probably good we're selling them now. Your parents should be here soon."

"Where we gonna put the poster up?"

"We'll find somewhere for it."

When they reached town, John headed for the feed store. "This business sells chicks every spring, and maybe they'd be interested in this breed of rabbit too. They're mighty fine for pets or fur."

The faded gray eyes of Ol' Charlie Phillips, who owned the store, bugged out when he saw the how many they had. "You sellin' 'em all?"

"Yep." Stu hands stuck in his pockets.

"Right now, near Easter, it's a good time to sell bunnies." Charlie grabbed a little one and looked him over. "Spring is a good time to sell to kids whose parents allow them to raise rabbits. Say, young man, did you raise all these rabbits?"

Stu's scrawny chest puffed. "Sure did."

"Well, you musta took good care of them. They sure multiplied."

"One doe had fourteen bunnies once, and the others a dozen each. In a month, they did it all over again."

Charlie's smile showed a gap missing two front teeth. "You must have rabbits everywhere."

"You said it," Stu chirped. "Some got loose this mornin', but we caught most of 'em." He held up his poster. "I have a poster in case we need to try to get customers somewhere else."

Charlie shook his head. "I have one customer who buys all the rabbit pelts I can give him, and kids probably will snatch up the little ones. How much you want for 'em?"

John stepped forward. "How much will you give us?"

Stu's eyes bugged when Charlie quoted what he'd pay. John and Stu unloaded the critters, and Stu had his pockets full of money.

"You did a great job with those bunnies," John said as they approached sheriff's office. "It wasn't your fault they got loose."

Stuart's chin went up as he stared at the blue sky. "Thanks. I really liked those bunnies, but I knew I couldn't keep 'em all."

John stole Stu's hat off his head. "You're growin' into a man, boy."

Boots propped on the desk, the sheriff snoozed when Stu and John entered his office. John slammed the door shut again, this time rattling the jail. He had a notion to shout, "Jailbreak!" but controlled himself.

When the door slammed the sheriff almost fell out of his wooden desk chair. The wheels started rolling, and he hit the back wall head on.

The man blinked. Then he blinked again and stared. He touched his skull where it hit the wall. Stuart held his hand over his mouth so his giggles wouldn't escape.

John leaned down to Woody's red face. "Hello."

"You're lucky I didn't shoot you two."

"Guess so." John touched the gun on his hip. "Although I don't think you would've got me until you opened your eyes."

One of Stuart's giggles escaped. Woody frowned at him. Then a smile crept under the huge mustache. "What you two boys need? Come to turn yourself in for the murder of Billy Joe?"

John jerked his head negatively. "Brought something to show ya." He set the box of rat poison on the sheriff's desk.

Woody's feet hit the floor. "Don't you go putting poison on my desk. I eat off it."

"Isn't there somewhere you can put it for evidence?"

Woody bobbed his head back and forth. "Anywhere I put it in here, some mouse or rat would eat it. If it's evidence, maybe I can lock it in a cabinet. Where'd ya get it?"

"I found it under a big lilac bush in the back yard. Nobody at Peach Blossom Ranch ever uses rat poison. We depend on the barn cats. This stuff would kill chickens and Stu's rabbits, and if I got another dog, it would kill him too." John shoved it toward the sheriff. "It's a fairly new box of poison, only half gone, and not weathered much."

"Well, that's mighty interestin'," Woody drawled. "Wellington and his pa came here a few days ago and said they discussed B.J.'s murder with Charlie at the feed store. According to them, he said you'd bought rat poison a few days before Billy was killed."

John threw up his hands in disgust. "I didn't buy rat poison! If Ol' Charlie said that, he's mistaken. You know Wellington was the logical suspect for trying to frame me by dumping the body in my barn."

"But you showed me the measurement for the strange boots, and Wellington doesn't have big feet. I think you're running out of excuses, John."

"I also told you I doubted Wellington did it. But whoever did, wants it to look like I'm the killer. I have no idea who would."

"Mr. Davenport pointed out you'd probably read how most people believed Alexander the Great was poisoned with strychnine in his wine. All you had to do was drop it into Billy Joe's drink—wine, beer, or whiskey. He liked it all."

"Only problem with that is I've never put my mouth to an intoxicating beverage in my life, and I've only been in the saloon a few times. And then only to connect with someone or attend the Horse Ranchers Association meeting."

"Oh, but you made a mistake. You bought a bottle of whiskey at the saloon the day of the Peachville Horse Ranchers' meetin' and shared it with B.J., according to a witness and the bartender."

John shook his head and pumped his fists. "I've never heard such nonsense. Looks like Wellington must have done it, and he's gone to lots of trouble to make it look like I did it. Who is the witness?"

Woody stroked his mustache. "I don't think that's any of your business."

Valerie didn't enjoy John's response to her letter at all. John told about the body in the barn, and now the rat poison.

"The sheriff has only one suspect—me," he wrote. "You'd think a lawman would have enough sense to recognize a setup when he sees one. I've been searching for clues to the murder myself."

He shared the humorous story about the pigs and the rabbits and wrote two more lines before he signed his name.

Valerie stared at the words above his signature, John Lincoln Parks: "I am extremely interested in your desire to practice law and spend time with Archibald Forsythe. Where does this leave us?"

Where did it leave her romance with John?

The next day when she and Archibald entered the asylum, Valerie gasped and backed up, holding her nose.

Archibald touched her back. "We'll never get used to the smell in here, but you can endure it. You've done it before."

The darkness in the wide windowless hall created a spooky atmosphere. She knew murderers were held at the asylum, but didn't know how securely.

She blew out her cheeks as nausea threatened to bring up her breakfast. She shook the feeling off and pinched her nose again. "The state needs a new building for these people. This remodeled house wasn't very secure as a residence. It might make a fine boarding house because of its size, but all this wood, plaster, and porous material absorbs filth and odors."

The man beside her looked up at the ceiling, spotted by brownish-yellow leak tracks and places where plaster dropped out. "It would help if they hadn't boarded up most of the windows. Sunshine sanitizes and also helps our outlook on life. They put bars on the windows they kept, and I think the glass is made out of something that doesn't break easily so they could have let more light in."

Shouting and bad language erupted down the corridor. Valerie stopped and didn't move a muscle until the shouting let up.

When they reached Dillon's room, Bubba held Pete with one beefy arm and pounded him unmercifully with an iron fist. Dillon had an arm around Bubba's bloated middle, pulling and trying to talk him out of his rage.

"You were born with the devil in you!" Bubba shouted as he swung his fist again. "All those who look like you should be put to death."

"You're wrong." Dillon grabbed one of Bubba's arms and then the other, to release Pete before he noticed Valerie and Archibald outside the barred window. "Call a guard, Archie!"

"Guards!" Archibald shouted toward the station where the guard who followed them had retreated. The clunk of boots running toward them brought a sigh of relief to Valerie. The uniformed men unlocked the room, took control of Bubba, and jerked a straitjacket on him. Pete fell to the floor when the brute loosened his grip on the now unconscious boy.

The guards led Bubba to the door and hauled him away. Tears ran down Valerie's cheeks. She couldn't ask if Pete was dead.

She and Dillon rushed to his side. "I'm so sorry." She gently touched Pete's bruised face, and then slid her fingers through his dirty hair. "Jesus, help Pete." Her prayer ripped through her chest. "Help him to be okay. Help him to know you love him. Help Pete know I and others love him. He's different, but he's special, Lord. Bring peace and some answers to this place."

Pete roused, and his crooked smile looked beautiful. He reached for her hand and put a wet, bloody kiss on it.

In turn, she kissed his forehead.

"Young man and young lady, you are not to interact with the insane here!" The voice, loud and demanding with a slight whine, belonged to a skinny sour-faced man dressed like he was headed to his own funeral. "Get out of here."

Dillon stood between the fellow and Pete. "This young man has been beaten to an inch of his life. Bubba should be in solitary confinement when he has one of his episodes."

"Don't tell us how to run our sanitarium," the whiner bellowed. "Who are you to give us advice since you're insane yourself?"

"Sir." Archibald stepped forward. He spoke with a normal voice and gave the man undeserved respect. "You should know this woman and I are practicing attorneys. We intend to go to court to prove Dillon here is not insane. It might take a while, but we're going to prove paralyzed people and people born with Down's syndrome are not insane or demon-possessed, either. They should never be housed with someone like Bubba, who does have a mental problem. From what Dillon tells me, Bubba has something wrong in his brain."

Anger twisted the whiner's red face. "Don't try to sell me such garbage. I'm the medical adviser here, and the whole lot of you are crazier than mad dogs."

"Well," Valerie couldn't resist defending the patients, "perhaps you should go back to medical school. We've been doing research, gaining evidence and testimony, and we'll probably see you in court. Furthermore, if anything happens to little Pete here, we'll see you're charged with accessory to murder for housing dangerous patients like Bubba in the same room with an innocent boy."

Dillon and Archibald applauded. Patients in the room and some down the hall joined in.

The whining doctor stretched himself to stand more erect, one eyebrow raised. "I'll see to it you never enter this place again. Get out of here."

"Sorry, sir." Archibald glanced at his watch. "The superintendent gave us ten minutes, and you took up about half of it, so we will stay another five. If you don't like it, talk to him. He granted us approval to come." He slid his watch back in his vest pocket, before meeting the whiner eye-to-eye. "We'll speak to the superintendent about Pete's injuries."

"What will happen to Bubba?" Valerie asked five minutes later as they exited the ward.

Archie shook his head. "They'll chain him spread eagle in solitary confinement. When he comes out, his arms and legs will be bruised and bloody. Bubba might be strong enough to break a bone trying to escape the chains. It depends how long he fights. Poor fellow. He's pitiful when he drops into depression. He's tried to kill himself."

A lump formed again in the back of Valerie's throat, but she held her tears. She had to walk past guards and officials who mustn't know they planned to fight against this abuse. But was it abuse? Something should be done with people out of control like Bubba, who was a danger to others and perhaps even to himself. Surely, someone could help people whose brains were messed up. Was Bubba demon-possessed?

An undeniable possibility. Her spirit silently cried out to God. "Jesus. If only you were here."

32

The metal jail doors clanged shut after the sheriff shoved John inside the cell.

"No!" John's gut protested, and a pain shot through his belly. "I can't stay here. No one is trying to solve B.J.'s murder but me. Isn't it obvious the body was planted in the barn, and the rat poison stuck there to implicate me? I'm certainly not that dumb, and you know it. Somebody wanted B.J. dead and wanted to get back at me by making it look like I killed him. Stu doesn't even have a way home."

The sheriff grinned. "I'll take Stu home to Polly and Abe. You might as well relax. The judge won't be here until next week."

John reached for the sheriff as he turned the key in the lock. "I have horses to tend to. I planned to get some buyers for my pigs. I'm getting things ready for peach season, and nobody will be looking for the killer."

The sheriff chuckled and lumbered away, rattling the keys. "I've got him."

John held the bars in a death grip, rage shaking his whole body. "What possible motive would I have for killing Billy Joe?"

The sheriff had disappeared.

John faced the miserable-looking cot on one side of the small cell—a dirty mattress, no sheets, and a filthy blanket, nothing more.

The next morning, Edwina stood outside John's cell carrying a plate with two cinnamon rolls, a thick slice of ham, and an orange cut in half.

The gal looked even better than the food.

Smiling, he took the plate. "Thank you. You are a ray of sunshine on my black day." He gave her hand a squeeze. "The Lord must have sent you. Thanks for the food and for coming, but I would like a favor." He released her hand to balance the plate and already missed her warmth. "Would you please send Valerie a telegram and ask her if she knows of any good lawyers around here?"

Ed blinked, her brilliant smile flickering into a quick-lived frown. She struggled to put the smile back on, but it didn't quite make it.

"Uh, sure. Give me her address and what you want to say."

As soon as he gave her the address and the message, she wrote it down and turned to go. His heart skipped a beat. "Don't go yet. Stay here and visit a while. I kept wondering who I could get to help me, and I couldn't think of anyone. I've lost touch with most of my friends. A lot of people in Peachville won't understand why I'm in jail."

She stared at him with those wonderful blue eyes, and her dimples winked. "I'm not sure I understand, either. Most people trust Sheriff Woody, but this is horrible. My father's even all upset. Clyde Merriweather got a good laugh out of it. Bellea cried when I told her."

John couldn't resist reaching through the bars and snagging her hand again. "Edwina Jorgenson, you are an amazing woman and …"

Should he say it? She might explode like a firecracker. She squeezed his hand a little, and the peace he drew from her touch flooded to his toes.

"So, what were you going to say?"

"Don't get mad, but I'm realizing there's a lot more to Edwina Jorgenson than I've been giving her credit for."

A giggle exploded, and those blue eyes sparkled as if she'd lit a lamp behind them. "Maybe I've grown up. Life has a way, and the Lord has ways, of getting our attention. But don't forget my temper is alive and well. You're still not going to get by with teasing and playing dirty tricks on me." Enough warmth infused her smile to fry bacon.

"I know what you mean about life and the Lord dealing with our childish ways. I've matured emotionally, but I have a long way to go. Finding B.J.'s body in the barn aged me a few years so I might be white-haired and wrinkled before this mess is over."

Edwina grinned and touched his whiskered cheek. "We can't have that. How would you find a wife if you looked like that?"

They stood in silence. Finally, Ed spoke. "The stallion is giving Clyde lots of trouble. Bucked him off at least three times. I've had to do most of that horse's care. I rode him and tried to train him to jump, but he won't obey commands."

"That's why all I intended to do with him is use him to stud. As long as he brings in the money, we can't complain. Clyde doesn't need to ride him."

"Clyde said he's never seen a horse he couldn't ride, and he's determined to do it."

"Watch him. I'd guess he's going to try the whip. That will make the horse meaner than he already is and destroy all the work Abe and I did with him."

Edwina backed away. Tears welled in her eyes. "I have to go. I need to send this telegram and get home." She rushed back to the bars and reached for his hand again. "I hate seeing you like this! Anyway, how I can help you? We need to talk to some people with common sense and get you out of here before they hang you."

A sob shook her body.

John brought her hand to his lips. "Don't worry. God is in control. But if you have a little free time, ask everyone you meet if they knew Billy Joe and if they would have any idea who would kill him and try to lay the blame on me."

She nodded, and her pretty blonde curls bobbed up and down like beautiful flowers in the breeze.

He kissed her hand again. "I like what Bellea is doing with your hair. It's very pretty."

She smiled, and the tears vanished down her cheek.

John had another thought. "Notice, too, who has big feet and wears boots with an unusual design on the heel."

The next morning after chores, Ed was back. She shoved the yellow telegram into his waiting fingers.

John ripped open the Western Union envelope. His insides shook with expectancy worse than his hands.

"'Father and I arrive in Peachville tomorrow. Looking into your case. Valerie MacDougal,'" he read it aloud. "What on earth did you tell Valerie?"

Ed's full lips puckered. "I said, 'John Parks arrested. Didn't commit the murder. If want to keep him from hanging, come.'"

"You didn't ask if they know any lawyers here?"

She puckered her lips again. "Nope. Didn't figure it'd get the desired results."

John laughed, and it felt good. "Edwina Jorgenson, you're one-of-a-kind! Thank you. That really makes my day. I need to see Valerie anyhow. We've had an understanding about the future, you know."

Edwina gasped. "You're engaged?"

"Not quite. She hasn't been ready to come out of mourning yet."

Edwina's face went as pale as the paper she held.

John's heart took a flip. Sick inside, he gazed at Ed. She was such a sweet gal when she wasn't angry. "That won't affect you volunteering to help me, will it?"

She lifted her chin and stared back, those blue eyes dull. "Sure. I can try to gather some information to give to Valerie. Bellea is a great help, and Clyde Merriweather is falling all over himself trying to keep me happy so he can own the ranch."

"Maybe he's in love with you."

"No more than you are," she shot back. "He's in love with the ranch and thinks he'll be rich. He smells like a tobacco smokestack, and his speech and manners are even worse. I cringe when he touches me. If Papa didn't think he's a great hand, I'd fire him. But at least until I do fire him, he keeps up enough of the work I can get away now and then. If you ever meet someone who would outwork him, let me know."

Her hands had gripped the bars so tight her knuckles turned white. John kissed them. "Thanks, Ed, for your help and for coming. You're a lifesaver."

Hopefully in more ways than one.

33

Edwina was so upset her sweaty hands trembled as she snatched the reins and plopped in her saddle. The picture of Valerie walking beside John at the picnic stuck in her head.

Valerie MacDougal is a beautiful woman. No wonder he wants her. How can I compete with an elegant lady like Valerie?

She was stunning. Born that way like some people are. Her refined features and carefully styled, shining blonde hair looked better than Ed's collectible bride doll's.

Smart, too. An attorney, no less. When John talked about Valerie one day, he added she loved farming and preserving fruit and vegetables, too. How could one woman do so much, and with a smile and looking beautiful?

Meanwhile, Edwina probably was a mess. She lost some hairpins from her curls with the breeze when she came into town. One advantage of the braid: it could bounce around all day and stay put together. But it loosened if she slept in it, and the braid did nothing for her appearance in the morning, day, or night.

When she passed the church, she yelled, "Whoa!" and reined her mount to a stop. The pastor's horse stood tied out front.

She almost stumbled as she hurried in the double doors. "Pastor Brandt, are you here?"

"In the back. I'm studying in a classroom. That you, Edwina?"

Pastor Brandt sat at a small table on a tiny chair beside his son who held a crayon and colored a picture of David and the sheep.

"Little Adam is my assistant today while I prepare Sunday's sermon. Rose isn't feeling well. How can I help you?"

"I'm worried about John Parks. Did you know he's in jail? Sheriff Woody accused him of murdering Billy Joe Garner. John found the body in his barn, obviously dumped there."

The pastor rubbed the back of the graying dark brown hair circling his bald spot. "No, I didn't know. The preacher sometimes is the last person to hear gossip. John sort of dropped out of church when he returned from Minneapolis. But he's been here lately. How can I help?"

Edwina surveyed the low, humble ceiling and tried to keep from bursting into tears. "Most important, you can pray he won't be hanged before we can prove he's innocent."

"Let's start right now." The pastor dropped to his knees and talked to God as if he stood beside him. Then he prayed for Edwina and her papa.

"Pray for the Davenports too," she asked. "I know they belong to your church, but Mrs. Davenport and Wellington have a grudge against John for not allowing them to take Bellea's child. Someone has gone to lots of trouble to frame John, and Wellington might have killed B.J. and dumped his body. Only thing, the boot prints John found that morning are big. Wellington isn't big."

"Wasn't B.J. working for the Davenports after he left John's ranch? I saw B.J. driving Mrs. Davenport about town a lot. He always carried her packages and guided her across the streets and that sort of thing. They came to a couple of church functions together, but Wellington usually drove her to services."

The pastor looked at his small son and stood. "Adam, I'll be right back. I'll walk you out, Miss Jorgenson, while we finish talking. I need to finish my sermon and get home to check on my wife."

They walked past the sanctuary where the elderly Amos McCutcheon swept and cleaned.

Pastor shook his head. "B.J. wasn't such big a man, either. Don't know if he ever attended a worship service. Working for the judge as he did was a different kind of job if you know what I mean. I would have loved to see him give his heart to Christ."

"Me, too." Edwina nodded. "Could you stop at the jail sometime and see John? He's discouraged." She stared at the ceiling. The lump formed in her throat again and threatened to dissolve into tears.

"Sure. I already thought of that."

Hope trickled into Ed. Blinking the tears away, she shook the pastor's hand. "Thanks. One good thing has happened. John's girlfriend, Valerie MacDougal, and her father are attorneys, and they'll be here on the train tomorrow. Pray they can find something to prove his innocence."

Pastor gripped her hand. "I certainly will, and God hears. I imagine John is grateful for you, Edwina, for standing up for him and helping him in his time of need. You're a true friend."

When Edwina mounted her horse again, she muttered, "Yeh. A friend."

She was tempted to stop at the saloon and talk to girls she knew from school who worked there. They might know something important about B.J. and who would like to frame John. But she'd been gone from home long enough. She had work to do.

Already on the outskirts of town, she nudged her horse into a canter. Headed for the barn, he needed no encouragement to speed up.

If only relationships with people developed as easily as those with horses or dogs.

Wellington's buggy clattered into the yard moments after Ed's gelding halted at the barn. He stopped his horse beside her. "I understand you bought John's stallion. I think he'd make a good mate for my new racehorse. The mare will be ready in about three weeks."

Ed needed some time to think. *Does Wellington know Bellea is here?* "Give me a few minutes to take care of my horse, and then we'll see about setting a time."

She dismounted, took off the saddle, and began currying. "Three weeks. So about the first of next month."

"Yes. About then."

"What time of day do you prefer?"

"Afternoon. A couple of hours after our noon dinner."

Ed couldn't think. How was she going to get him out of here before he found Bellea? Silence hung between them until she finished with the horse and had him in the barn.

"Mind if I take a look at the stallion?" he asked.

"Sure. Come on." She motioned for him to follow. He jumped from his mount and walked beside her.

He gave her a grin. "So are you and Clyde engaged yet?"

"No." She refused to elaborate. "You know anything about who killed B.J.?"

"I have no idea, but whoever did must've had it in for John to dump his body in his barn."

"You know John's in jail, charged with murder."

"Aw, that's wrong. My mama's still mad at him about Bellea's baby, but I think the kid will be better off somewhere besides our house. I love my parents, but things don't go well at home. Daddy's gone most of the time. Mama has great imaginations about doing wonderful things, but most of them are all talk. Her main activity is spending money. Guess that's where I got it. But I'm gonna get me a job and earn a living so I can move out. All the anger is getting to me. Besides, the hired hands do the work on our property."

Edwina doubted Wellington could get a job. "What kind of work you going to do?"

"I hear the sheriff is looking for a deputy. I'm good with a gun, and I'd like to do something worthwhile for a change."

Edwina's heart thumped. *The sheriff is tight with Wellington's dad.*

When they reached the horse-training corral, Clyde had the saddled stallion on a rope leading him in circles, and the sleek black animal fought all the way. Clyde held the rope tight to his chest, stuck his foot in the dangling stirrup, and dropped into the saddle.

In seconds, the animal snorted, kicked up his hooves, and bucked and kept bucking. He twirled, and Clyde flew into the air and came down with a thump. Edwina rushed to drag the man by the foot to the fence, the stallion following—rearing, and tearing at the ground trying to get to Clyde.

"He's still a wild one, Edwina," Wellington shouted above the stallion's ranting. "Does he attack other horses? My mare is a valuable racehorse, and I can't risk an injury."

"He might take on another stallion, but I haven't seen him attack another horse. It's up to you."

Wellington stared while Clyde rolled under the fence, dusted himself off, and limped toward the bunkhouse, saying nothing.

Then Wellington laughed loud and boisterous. "Don't think he knew we watched. Doesn't he have more work to do? He can't go to the barn and pout."

"I'll give him time to nurse his ego," Edwina grinned. "He's determined to ride the stallion no matter what. John said he'll probably start using the whip."

"I imagine so." Wellington nodded. "He's a magnificent animal, but a whip never improves the spirit. I can't imagine why he won't let Clyde ride him when the judge rode him for months."

Edwina leaned against the fence. "Some animals sense things about people. Clyde probably tried to show him who's boss without trying to get acquainted. From what I heard, the stallion did give the judge considerable grief, but the man probably made his men work with the animal a lot and the judge always carried the whip."

"Why did John sell him to you? I'd like to have 'im."

"I think God told John to sell him. I don't know why. I have quite a few stud appointments set up already. My daddy thinks God is going to lead John into cultivating a certain breed of horse, like maybe Arabians. Dad says Arabian horses can't be matched for beauty, athleticism, devotion, and companionship."

The young man thought that over. "I've heard they're great animals. Might take special care. I think you'd need to know your horses to train them properly."

What I need is Wellington off the property. "We had a phone installed. You have one, don't you? Give me a call when your mare is ready."

He took a last look at the stallion. They walked back to the barn where he'd left his horse, and she noticed the handsome gambler staring at her. "Something's different about you. You're beautiful. If you aren't courting Clyde, how about letting me take you out to dinner sometime?"

Is the man out of his mind?

"Thanks for asking, but I'm too busy to bother with men. I'm trying to keep John from hanging, and that's more than I have time for."

"So you and John are an item. I might have guessed. You've had a crush …"

"No. It's not what you think. John is practically engaged to a lawyer named Valerie MacDougal. He's not interested in me."

Wellington smirked and rode away. Edwina hoped he didn't see Bellea's face in the window.

34

The next morning, dewdrops sparkled on new spring leaves, but Edwina hated each step the pony took pulling her and her father to the train station to pick up Valerie and her dad.

Edwina brought her father along, loading the wheelchair in the boot because he hadn't been into town for so long and needed a change of scenery. But also to give her strength.

Imaginary dark clouds hid the sunny sky's beauty from her heart. Why should she encourage John's romance with Valerie?

Her heart skipped a beat. She knew exactly why. She didn't want John to hang. The mangy sheriff probably hoped to bring a judge in right away to hang John before anyone could defend him. Well, help was coming, and Edwina had a part in it.

"Sure is a pretty day," Papa commented. "The temperature is getting warm enough to make people grow as well as plants and animals." He winked at her. "Did you know I'm still growing?"

Edwina busted out laughing. "So you plan on stopping at seven feet tall?"

He chuckled. "Naw, I'm tall enough, but I'm still growin' anyhow. Been good having Bellea in the house. She reads the Bible to me. You gals work together to exercise my legs, cook great meals, and I'm waking up inside."

Edwina's stomach jarred like an anvil landed in it. *Was Papa dying? Is he trying to get ready for heaven?*

He smirked. "Don't look so happy about it."

Ed nodded. "Oh, I'm happy for you."

"Then why did you turn pale as a sheep?"

"You want the truth? I think you're trying to get ready to die."

"Not on your life, girl. I'm gettin' ready to live again." His whole face beamed above his dark gray beard. "I've come to accept my injury, and I'm thankful for my blessings. Bellea is a ray of sunshine herself, and you are a joy, too, sweet girl."

Jorgenson shifted toward her, his face deadly serious. "The baby brings joy too. Brings back memories of you. I feel I'm growing spiritually and emotionally. It's like a new day dawned for me. I'm ready to enjoy life again, even if I can't walk. My mind is as sharp as ever."

"Hmmm." What could this mean?

Edwina and her father waited at the depot hoping the train would hurry up and come. While Paul shook hands with almost everyone who passed, Edwina paced back and forth in front of the station like a dog trying to find a hole in the fence. Why had she committed to connect with Valerie? She should be home at the ranch working with three growing colts that would be full grown if she kept fooling around.

She had a mountain of other work that needed to be done today, too, although Bellea sure had been a blessing in the house.

In the distance down the dirt road on the edge of town, the train's smoke billowed. The engine whistled. For once, it was almost on time.

In a whirl of soot, the train rumbled into the station, the cars swaying back and forth, and then the engine screeched to a halt.

Valerie's face peered out the window, but then she pulled back, fanning her pretty head. An overweight cowboy stepped out of the train with a cranky old woman, who hurried toward the baggage car. "Out of my way," the lady screeched. "I need to get my trunk delivered."

"Give me a minute, and we'll get it, young lady." A huge grin settled on the conductor's weathered face as the old lady strutted along the tracks, holding her head high, still in a huff.

A vision of loveliness filled the train platform as Valerie in an exquisite dress waited for the conductor to help her step to the ground. Her gaze connected with Ed. Edwina sensed stress behind that beautiful face. Probably tired—or worried about John.

The cowboy barged in front of Valerie as she and an older man walked onto the train platform. By the way the cowboy smelled when he tromped by Edwina, the elegant lady probably was happy to put distance between her and him.

As soon as he got out of the way, Valerie came and extended her hand. "You must be John's friend, Edwina. Or are you a relative?"

"A friend." Ed took the silky hand into her rough one, wishing she hadn't removed her riding gloves. "John and I attended school together."

Valerie turned to the handsome older man in a suit with a vest, long coat, tie, and derby. "Edwina, this is my father, Aaron Van Meter."

"'Thank you for coming." Edwina shook his hand, almost as soft as Valerie's. After the handshaking and introducing herself and her father, Valerie said, "Well, I'm sure John appreciates you assisting him with this terrible thing he's accused of. I'd like to introduce you to my papa, Paul Jorgenson."

After their handshaking, she asked, "Do you need to take your things to the hotel, or would you like to go to the jail and see John first?"

"I'll tend to the luggage." Van Meter walked toward the depot where a man wearing a railroad hat pulled a cart into a large open door.

"I'm a mess, but I can clean up later." Valerie scanned the Peachville street, her blue eyes moving back and forth. "Let's go see John now."

"The jail is right over there." Edwina pointed across the street where a couple of men sat in chairs on the boardwalk. Wellington Davenport was one of them, and a silver star reflected the sun's rays from his chest.

So he landed the deputy's job. A chill ran down Ed's back. He looked so cocky she felt like whacking him with her reticule.

Wellington's eyes lit like a streetlight touched by a lamplighter. "Why, the view out here is getting better by the minute. Don't you think so, Charlie?"

Charlie, the town drunk, nodded vigorously. For a change, today he was sober. "Sure is!" He stood, removed his ragged hat, and bowed.

Edwina smiled at the skinny pathetic fellow, whose graying hair stood almost on end. If she would have been a preacher, like one of the ladies who came through Peachville two or three years ago, she'd set her sights on converting Charlie. Surely, God would deliver him from whiskey. Maybe if she had a husband, they could win him to the Lord.

"God bless you, Charlie," she murmured. She faced Wellington, who somehow appeared different dressed as a deputy. "We've come to see John."

Wellington jumped to his feet and worked his way around Charlie. "Excuse me, buddy. I need to take care of these beautiful women."

Charlie beamed and stared while Wellington stood aside and opened the door. "John's right inside. He's not going anywhere."

As soon as they entered the jail, John's voice declared, "Well, praise the Lord!" He pressed his face against the bars. "Aren't you girls a sight for sore eyes?"

Valerie had taken the lead. "Hello, John."

John grasped her hand and placed his lips on it. "Thanks for coming."

His gaze wandered to Edwina. "Good to see you too, girl."

Ed nodded. John's eyes lingered on her. Her heart pounded her ribs. Was it only yesterday when he kissed her fingers? She turned away. *No use mooning for him. He loves another woman.*

Valerie leaned closer. "I'm so sorry you've had this happen. I know by your letters how busy you've been and how hard you worked to make your ranch prosper. Father is here with me, and you're going to be released. Have they had a hearing and set the bail?"

"I haven't heard anything but rumors circulating about me having it in for B.J."

Edwina whirled around. "The sheriff threw him in here, and now he's waiting for the judge to come and hang him."

Wellington stood behind the women. "Now, Edwina, we're doing the best we can to gather evidence."

"Like what?" John scrunched his face closer to the bars.

"I followed up on one rumor." Wellington stuck his thumbs in his pockets. "The bartender said you argued with Billy Joe that night."

"That's a lie!" John's face colored with anger. "I don't drink—you know it, and the sheriff knows it. Furthermore, you and your father helped spread rumors."

Wellington blinked and stepped backward. "Sorry, John, but we have witnesses."

Valerie pointed at Wellington. "Could have been paid by the real killer to create a diversion and blame."

"The killer planned to blame John because he dumped the body in his barn." Edwina raised her left eyebrow and shot Wellington a look singed with lightning. "You're the most likely suspect, even if you wear a star. You threatened and worried Bellea and Polly, trying to get the baby, and except for John you might have succeeded."

"Now, Ed, this is none of your business and not any business of this lady with you."

Van Meter opened the door from the sheriff's office into the jail and strode in, the vision of authority as he took his pocket watch out of a vest pocket and glanced at it. "You're wrong there, deputy," his deep bass voice boomed. "The woman you met is my daughter. She's a lawyer. I'm an attorney, too. We came all the way from Boston to see John gets a fair trial. How many minutes do we have?"

Valerie lifted her chin and stared at Wellington. "We want a hearing, bail set, and to know what evidence you have against John."

Wellington pulled his shoulders up and set his hands on his hips, the right hand above his holstered gun. "We'll have to wait for the sheriff and the judge. The sheriff's out of town. Don't know when the circuit judge'll get here."

Valerie clicked her heels on the rough wood floor as she advanced toward Wellington. She held a pack of papers and a pencil. "When will the sheriff return?"

"Late tonight. He went to pick up a prisoner."

Van Meter moved in front of his daughter. "If he's not here early tomorrow, I'll call the judge myself to arrange a hearing or have John Lincoln Parks released." Authority rang in Van Meter's echoing voice. "John doesn't belong here."

"Who is the prisoner the sheriff went after?" Edwina jumped back into the conversation.

"I don't remember his name." Wellington rubbed his ear. "But the sheriff said he stole offerings from several churches. They're bringing him here for trial."

"I remember that." Edwina nodded. "Did they ever find the money?"

Wellington rattled the keys. "I doubt it. He probably spent it or gambled it. Anyway, visiting time is up."

Valerie stepped over and touched Wellington's sleeve. "What did you give us, five minutes, sir? We need private time to speak to John about his case."

Van Meter gently patted Valerie on the back. "We'll return in a couple of hours. Valerie needs time to freshen up anyway, and then we'll prepare for our interview with John. Anything we need to know, deputy?"

"The body was found in John's barn, and two people in town have told us John was out to get Billy Joe."

Edwina's hands pressed together against her lips as if she were in prayer, and actually, she had been whispering to the Lord. An idea trickled into her mind. "Maybe you need to ask the deputy where he was the day John found the body."

Wellington scowled and stared daggers at Ed. "The body probably was planted on Sunday. I was in church."

Edwina puckered her lips. "Oh, yeh. So was I. Seems I remember you and your mother left early. John was there, too."

"I sure was," John yelled, coming to the closest end of his cell. "And you and your mother walked in my house, uninvited. We found you when we came home from church."

"Is that true?" Valerie gasped and arched a delicate brow.

Wellington looked out the window, back toward the office door, and then faced Van Meter. "I could say he's lying."

The attorney squeezed in closer to the deputy. "Is that what you're saying?"

"Well, nobody was there besides John except those black people, and a court won't take their testimony."

Ed laughed, and Valerie joined her, filling the jail with musical feminine mirth.

"How do you know no one was there?" Ed asked between giggles.

"Anybody with good sense would believe Abe and Polly!" John shouted.

"What gives you the idea their testimony won't be accepted?" Valerie inserted. "Are you an attorney?"

John pressed himself into the bars over his cot so he could be even closer. "Truth is, Wellington, you and your mother threatened me several times. And you'd have to be drunk to think dropping B.J.'s body in my barn would be sufficient evidence that I committed the murder. People around here are not stupid enough to believe I'd think putting him in the barn and covering him with a few handfuls of straw would be a great hiding place. It's evidence I've been framed by the real murderer."

"What's all this shouting about?" The sheriff stood at the jail entry, a gun at the back of a handcuffed man.

"Sure glad you're back." Relief refreshed Wellington's face like a cold water wash. "They've been accusing me of being Billy Joe's killer."

"Hogwash. Glad I got back early." The sheriff shoved his prisoner toward the second cell while the crowd parted. "Edwina, I know you. But who are these people?"

Van Meter waited until the prisoner stood safely inside and his cell door clanged shut. "I'm Aaron Van Meter, and this is my daughter, Valerie MacDougal. We are attorneys from Boston here to ensure John Lincoln Parks is treated with respect. Unless you have compelling evidence that he committed the murder, he should be released from jail."

"Did I hear someone say something about murder?" The prisoner, a dried-up old codger, thin as a frog squished under a horse hoof, rasped out. "Sheriff, please don't put me next to a killer! I don't want to die."

The sheriff gestured toward the visitors. "Everybody outta here. Why, your shoutin' scared ol' Charlie so much he had to go back to the bottle. He's headin' toward the saloon right now."

Van Meter placed one hand on his daughter's back and with the other gestured toward the door. "We'll go. But we will be back. We want a hearing to see if you have enough evidence to hold him and if so, we demand bail. Otherwise, you need to let this young man go while you search for the real killer."

Valerie turned toward John, touched a dainty hand to her lips, and threw him a kiss.

Edwina, mouth open, stared at John, so handsome with his dark curly hair that fell toward his shiny, almost black eyes. His cheeks tightened as he watched the departing attorneys. She stepped to him. "Are you okay? Is there anything you need?"

John gripped her fingers and squeezed. "Thanks, Ed, for everything. You're a real blessing."

Wellington's boots stomped on the floor. "Hey! The sheriff said to get out of here."

Edwina couldn't stop the tears from pooling in her eyes. "Bye."

35

John's gut twisted when Edwina's tears rolled. Her footsteps echoed and died. Well, he couldn't do anything about her crying. She'd been so nice. But she had to accept reality. He was going to marry Valerie.

His brow wrinkled. His eyelids squeezed shut, and Ed's face lingered before him. With Bellea doing Edwina's hair, she was almost as beautiful as Valerie. Actually, Ed's freckles and tanned rosy cheeks enhanced her beauty. But beauty went only skin deep, and Ed didn't have the stuff Valerie had. He and Edwina would be quarreling all the time. A spitfire like her married to him would be like setting fire to dynamite. He'd never been a person to put up with nonsense, and temper fits amounted to nonsense. He'd been fussing with Edwina forever. Well, until recently.

The sheriff's boots clomped, and his spurs rattled toward him. "So the Van Meter fellow will represent you?"

"Yes, sir," John smiled. "He's an attorney and so is his daughter. Valerie used to live in Yucca Blossom. She knows this territory and the people. She lives in Boston now, but she'll be back soon." He grinned, but the urge to smile disappeared with a gnawing realization: he might not live long enough to marry her unless the real murderer surfaced.

"Sheriff, you've been pretty sloppy investigating my case. That will come up in court. For instance, you wouldn't look at the big boot prints left by the person who dropped off the body, and you even stomped all over some of the prints in the dirt. You haven't gone to much trouble to uncover the cause of death and showed no interest in the rat poison planted under my lilac bush. Didn't bother to come look at where it was."

The sheriff leaned against the bars. "That's not real evidence."

"I think it is." John stuck his chin out. "Abe and I preserved some footprints. I measured them, knowing you're not much on getting to the facts. What was it you did before you became sheriff three years ago? Oh, yes. Tended bar."

"Well, bartenders know more about the people in a town than anybody else." The man's voice could reach someone on a farm's back forty acres.

"Ah, maybe." John softened his volume a little. "But only the people who drink, gamble, carouse with women and pick fights with their neighbors. The majority of people who live here never set foot in a bar. They're trying to make ends meet and live for the Lord."

The sheriff tightened his whole face into a frown and shook his flabby double chin. "I've solved a number of murder cases."

"Yes, we had two hangings. Both of those fellows were new to town and couldn't afford a lawyer. I'm no authority on those because I was in Minneapolis. I'm warning you I plan to show how sloppy you've been with my investigation, and my lawyers will help. Edwina has been doing some investigating too, talking to people who knew B.J. She probably has evidence written down for the attorneys."

"You tell that snoopy gal to get her nose out of the law enforcement business. She could be polluting the case."

John huffed. "How could that be? I think most of the folks she talked to haven't heard anything from you. Have you talked to Silas Davenport about the murder? Mrs. Davenport? Asked Wellington if he had anything to do with the killing or if he knows anyone who might have done it? Interesting you hired Wellington. You've been in with the Davenports and their money a long time."

The sheriff swore. "Good thing you're behind bars, boy, or you'd get a fist in the face."

"It's the truth." No need to raise his voice. That was a fact, and the sheriff knew it.

John remembered the months he lived with his uncle, Judge Danforth Schuster. "My uncle, the judge, said you wouldn't do anything about him taking a horsewhip to me because you and Davenport were friends. One day when the judge was drunk, he said you accepted money from Silas Davenport. He paid you so he and Wellington could stay out of jail for cheating at cards."

"That's a lie! You keep that up, and I'll hang you myself." The sheriff's neck burned so red, John worried he might have a heart attack or apoplexy.

John laughed. "It makes better sense to let me out of jail, so I can find the real murderer, and you won't need to have all that aired in court."

Sheriff Woody took a deep breath and turned to go. "Those people might be high-powered lawyers, but even if the judge releases you, unless I find somebody else to pin the murder on, I'll have you back in jail as soon as those attorneys leave town."

36

Gloom hung over the asylum ward

Dillon Haskill could see dark clouds through the dirty window. Thunder rumbled. Lightning flashed and cracked, shaking the now tightly crowded room.

The storm barely made more noise than the four new patients in the bunk beds. One patient snored. A few groaned and mumbled. Dillon shoved his fingers tighter against his ears, hoping for shuteye. Bubba, probably bigger than two of the other patients together, grunted like an animal while he yanked the shackles holding his bleeding wrists to the iron bedstead.

A chill ran down Dillon's back. The cold, damp air breathed into his threadbare clothes. He unplugged his ears and tied his flimsy blanket around his waist. Tying it around him prevented other patients from snatching it. Still, he felt the cold. The administration must have turned off the heat. The guards said spring was here, but that didn't mean it was warm.

He ran a shaky hand over his tangled hair and his stubby beard. He scratched. If he could only have a haircut and shave to decrease the lice.

Bubba mumbled in his sleep and jolted upright. Others in the room stirred, and Pete trundled toward the pot.

"The devil's in here!" Bubba shouted.

Dillon moved in time to see him kick Pete in the belly as he tried to pass. The mentally challenged kid grunted and fell to the floor.

Dillon rushed to the boy, taking a strong kick to his hip before he tugged Pete to safety near the bars. Pete vomited as soon as Dillon knelt over him. When the vomiting subsided, the boy held his stomach. "It hurts!"

"Guards! Nurse!" Dillon picked up the tin cup he'd hidden in a corner and used it to rattle the bars on the small window in the door. "Guards! Nurse! Pete needs you."

Tears trickled down Pete's puckered face. His tongue, streaked with vomit, hung over his lips. His short fingers clutched his midsection. "God, help. Please. Help. Need you." A sob shook his body, and he wept in earnest.

"Come back, you devil," Bubba yelled, adding obscenities. "I'll put an end to you!"

"I'll help you get the demon!" Curly Hicks shouted, leaping toward Bubba.

"Guards! Nurse! We have an injury here." Dillon rattled the cup against the bars.

A shrill scream slammed into his ears. Then almost deafening shouting erupted as the unshackled patients jumped out of bed and started pulling one another's hair, beating each other with fists, biting, scratching at eyes. Curly seized a paranoid man by the throat.

"Guards! Nur—!" Dillon yelled. Pain shot through him as someone collided with him from behind, knocking him off his feet and whooshing all the air from his lungs.

"Guar…"

The room went dark.

Edwina sat in the Davenports' parlor, knowing she smelled of horse, hay, and probably pig as the beautifully dressed lady settled daintily across the room, her hair obviously styled by a talented servant and her face lined by years of anger.

Edwina sipped tea from a gold-edged bone-china cup. "I haven't been over to talk to you lately, and thought a visit might be in order." She lowered the cup to its matching saucer. "Lots of things are going on at our house. As you probably know, I now have Judge Schuster's black stallion, and he's going to bring a lot of good blood into the horse herd, even if he has been abused."

"That beautiful black horse was abused?" The lady's delicate dark brows arched. "I saw the judge riding the animal several times before John got a hold of him. The judge rode so tall and proud in the saddle. Both of them made a sight coming down the road."

"Oh, John's father found the stallion out in the hills, brought him to his ranch, but the consumption prevented him from properly caring for him." Edwina tried to divvy up a smile that wouldn't look fake. "John loved the animal, but when the judge took over the ranch, the judge wanted to train the stallion to race, and he used a whip."

"I've seen trainers do that, and I guess sometimes they have to." Mrs. Davenport shivered. "You said lots of things are going on at your house? What sort of things?"

"Oh, the stallion is one big thing. You knew Wellington plans to mix the stallion's bloodline with your herd. How many cowhands do you have now?" She lifted the cup again, unable to hold it quite as steady as Mrs. Davenport. "Seems like with Wellington taking the deputy job he wouldn't have much time to work with the horses. Didn't Billy Joe work for you? Now he isn't here, either."

"I don't know who would want to kill Billy Joe!" A pained expression twisted Mrs. Davenport's face. "He was an excellent worker. Did everything I told him. Took me here and there since I almost had a buggy accident one day. I had become a little skittish about handling the team. My husband and Wellington didn't like it, but the young man was a pleasure to be around."

Ed stirred her tea, the cup ringing a fine note in the quiet room when the metal spoon hit the side. "Well, John is in jail because he found B.J.'s body in his barn, but he didn't kill him. John liked the man. B.J. quit John because he wanted more money."

Mrs. Davenport lifted her chin, a smug smile on her lips. "I paid him well, and he liked it here. He was so gentle helping me in and out of the buggy. Sometimes when I was alone, he'd eat with me and talk with me. Now if I had my grandchild, I wouldn't be so lonely when my husband is out of town. I'll get that baby if it's the last thing I ever do. Do you have any idea where his mama went? She seemed to disappear, but I have a feeling she's around here somewhere."

"You might be correct." Ed wrinkled her brow in innocence. "But surely Bellea has relatives somewhere, maybe in another state, where she could live. Or somebody around here who would give her and the baby a home."

"Oh, I don't think anyone but John and those black people would keep the little hussy." The woman sat up straighter and looked down her nose. "After all, she's not fit company for good people." Her chin trembled. "That's another reason why Wellington should find that horrible girl and take her baby so I can raise him."

Edwina swallowed the lukewarm tea from her cup and set it aside on the delicate saucer. She bridled her angry tongue to keep from slashing apart the woman's reasoning and reminding her about what her son had done to Bellea. Instead, Ed surveyed the room's beauty and then turned to Mrs. Davenport.

"You said your husband and Wellington didn't like B.J. much. Did they ever have an argument?"

The woman touched her finger to the rim of her teacup and circled the gold, creating a little squeak against the china, her other fingers trembling. "I didn't say they didn't like him, but they did have words about how much I paid Billy Joe and the amount of time he spent in the house." She wagged her head. "But I needed him, and there was nothing they could do about it."

"So there was bad blood between B.J. and them?"

"Oh, I wouldn't say that." She patted her hair with a shaky hand. "If my husband was concerned, he could stay home more." She stood, indicating the visit over. "I enjoyed seeing you. If you hear anything about that girl, please let me know."

Edwina got up. "Thank you for the tea and hospitality."

An unexpected feeling of empathy hit Ed's heart. The woman appeared quite pathetic. Mrs. Davenport's eyes darted this way and that. Ed discerned a restlessness, like a horse that doesn't trust his rider. "You never know, Wellington might get married before long and then have six or eight children." Edwina giggled.

Mrs. Davenport raised her head in her usual dignified manner. Tears gleamed in her eyes, and Edwina's heart grieved for the older woman.

She reached for the lady's hand. "I'm going to pray for you, my friend. God has a way of working in our lives, and when his power comes, we can be filled with unspeakable joy and peace."

The lady's eyes opened wide, and her chin dropped. "Why, thank you! I didn't know you're religious. I go to church, but I've never bothered God much about my problems."

"I'm sure God wants you to talk to him. I'm not good at praying in public. But sometimes the Lord and I get down into all my troubles, and when we get done, I find some of my worries vanished. My father and I had difficult times since his accident, but he told me the other day he's finding reasons to live again. I don't know what it all means, but I sure love to see him smile."

Mrs. Davenport puckered her wrinkled lips while she thought on that. "I intended to ask about him. It's such a tragedy that he'll never walk again."

After she'd prayed, Ed left the house amazed by the joy she'd felt in sharing an encouraging word with a woman who was so prickly almost no one would be around her.

She mounted her horse and turned him toward her ranch. For the first time, she understood perhaps a little of how her neighbor felt when she discovered the magnitude of her son's sin. All Edwina had thought about before was how the woman tossed Bellea out of her home with no money and nowhere to go.

Ed knew the wealthy family was embarrassed, even when the sheriff wouldn't believe Bellea when she told about the attack. The sheriff said there was no case against Wellington. Pa said the Davenports probably paid the sheriff off to keep their son out of jail.

Things could get much worse. Ed's heart pounded. Wellington might be the person who murdered B.J.

Her horse was in a good canter now. She waved to old man Livingston driving his mule team and wagon toward home, but she barely noticed him. She kept seeing that yearning for love in Mrs. Davenport. She wanted Bellea's baby, not so she could love him, but so she could feel his little arms around her neck, and he'd call her Grandma.

Perhaps the yearning to be accepted as a friend was why she was so cordial today.

In the distance, Wellington came toward her, sitting proud in the saddle, the star on his chest reflecting the late-afternoon sun. As he drew near, he pulled on the reins and brought his horse to a stop.

"Whoa."

"Everything okay? Where you been, Ed?" His grin revealed his shiny white smile.

"Fine. Fine. I've been over to visit your mother."

Wellington's shaved face lost its usual cocky expression. His almost handsome face was so thin his ears stood out on both sides of his head like wings on a plucked turkey. "My mom? You're kidding. What did you visit about? Your upcoming wedding to Clyde? I imagine she could help you put on a wedding everyone in this valley would remember."

Ed frowned. "I'm not getting married. We had some girl talk. Woman-to-woman type of thing. What's going on in town? Did John get out of jail yet?"

"Oh, no. I think he'll be there until the judge sentences him."

Edwina shook her head, bobbing the curls Bellea created. "Oh, no. John is going to walk out of jail a free man."

Wellington ran his fingers through his wavy hair. "How do you know?"

"Well, I've been talking to God a lot lately, and you or someone is going to find who really murdered Billy Joe."

Wellington's face paled slightly. "I don't know about that."

"Tell you what," Ed grinned. "You talk to God about the situation and see what he tells you."

Wellington's eyebrows shot up. "I … I guess we'll know sometime soon."

All the rest of the way home, with tears running down her cheeks and onto her neck, Edwina talked to God, amazed that, after all this time her mother had been gone, her teaching about God and his Word became real today.

Bellea had told Ed about the horrible encounters they'd had at John's house with the Davenports. Even though Wellington's mother was rich, she didn't seem happy or content. The woman was better at making enemies than friends. But somewhere inside where she stored all her hate, Edwina noticed a soft spot. She prayed somehow she could lead her to the one who gives joy unspeakable and rivers of living water.

After she brushed down her horse and settled the gelding in the barn, Ed headed to the house with new joy surging in her soul. She'd tasted the living water herself and energy pumped to her head, out her fingers, and through her toes.

Pa sat in the evening sunshine on the front porch, Bellea at his side rocking little David. Ed crossed to the other rocking chair but then noticed a shadow inside. Someone bent over her desk. A big person. No doubt about it, someone was rifling through their desk.

She said nothing, but edged to the screen, opened it carefully, and on her tiptoes padded to Pa's bedroom where they kept the desk.

Clyde Merriweather held the wad of cash she set aside to pay bills. Her budgeting and bookkeeping books haphazardly littered the desktop. A lit cigarette rested in a saucer on the side, almost close enough to set the papers on fire.

"Whatcha think you're doing?"

Clyde jumped. His face flared red. His lips drew together in a stiff line, and then he grinned. "Since you've been so busy, I'm helping with your bookkeeping."

"You have no business in …"

Clyde whirled, and then grabbed her and planted a hard, wet kiss on her mouth.

Ed's hand flew out and slapped his whiskery jaw. "How dare you!"

The man softly laughed. "I'm getting a head start on our future."

"You and I have no future, at least together!" Ed pulled her gun from her holster. "Put that money back where you got it, and I'd better not see you in here again. I'd fire you this minute if I had someone else to help with the horses."

Clyde's smile stretched wider. He touched her cheek with his tobacco-stained fingers. "Sometime, I'm going to catch you in the barn, and we're going to have a good ol' time."

"You lay a hand on me, and I'll use this pistol, not point it at you. There is more than one snake I look out for." She gritted her teeth. "You're fired. Get out of here."

Clyde's face twisted, his eyes ablaze with something almost demonic. "I have needs. You have needs, and your pa has chosen me for your man."

He slammed the cash back on the desk, dropping some of it on the floor and knocking the cash box off with it. Swearing, he turned, crashed through the door, and ran to the corral. In a few minutes, he shot down the drive, riding his horse at a full gallop.

As Edwina picked up the mess and set her desk to order, she wondered at the joy she felt only moments ago, and the anger and frustration that pumped through her now, shaking her to the core.

Softly she repeated the name, "Jesus, Jesus, Jesus." A warm trickle of joy wiggled into her chest. Her happiness didn't depend on other people. The joy of the Lord was her strength.

She stepped out on the porch, a smile on her face. "So what's for supper?"

But then she grabbed her father and sobbed.

37

After the attorneys spoke briefly with the sheriff, Deputy Wellington Davenport led Valerie and Van Meter to the jail cell, rattling the ring of keys while he unlocked the door.

John jumped to his feet and showed them to the cot, now neatly covered with clean blankets, thanks to Polly. As usual, Valerie was a vision of loveliness. She wore a navy suit and white blouse.

John smiled and wondered why Wellington didn't bring in a chair for the visitors, but John didn't mind standing.

Valerie's creamy flawless brow wrinkled with concern as she took a pencil and a pad of paper from her father. "Okay, John, we need to know about the day you found the body."

Van Meter sat beside his daughter, pencil above paper. "This questioning is not because we suspect you, but it's a beginning for your defense, should we end up in court."

John shook his head. "I didn't notice a thing when Abe and I hurried out to the barn to do the chores on Sunday morning. We hadn't been to church for quite a while, and we wanted to make it on time. Before, I thought I was too busy, but a hunger for more of God gnawed at my insides. Stuart took care of his rabbits and fed the chickens, and I don't think he went into the barn."

Valerie's pencil scratched across the paper and then poised mid-air before she pointed it at John as he leaned against the jail's rock wall. "Did you notice anything unusual? Anything out of place?"

John rubbed his scruffy hair, trying to look a little better. He touched the scar on his cheek and shrugged. "I don't know if the body was there that morning. I didn't go into that part of the barn."

Valerie stopped writing and lifted her eyes. "Earlier you said Wellington and his mother left church early on Sunday and entered your house before you got home. What was that all about?"

"Hunting for Bellea again, trying to take the grandson. I have no idea if Wellington did anything else. I told the sheriff I suspected Wellington might have murdered Billy Joe, but you see how far that got. Wellington was hanging around the day Bellea gave birth. But we didn't know he was there until he shot out of the driveway. So he's hung around my ranch."

Van Meter's face puckered in disgust. Valerie shook her head and stared at her notes. "When did you find the body?"

"Monday morning. We went out early for chores. I almost stumbled over the body at the edge of a little haystack toward the back of the barn. We also found strange large boot prints on the barn's dirt floor. I told Sheriff Woody about them, and he ignored what I said."

"Not good. Billy Joe worked for you?"

"He wanted more money. He was hired by the Davenports and took Mrs. Davenport shopping and that sort of thing. I heard she paid him well, and the two of them seemed close companions. I was told he had a lot of money to gamble with."

"Perhaps he'd been winning." Van Meter turned his head to the side, wanting John to consider the possibility.

John moved his head back and forth. "I don't think so. Billy Joe told me himself that he couldn't seem to come out on top in his card games, but he wanted to learn. He never had money when he worked for me and asked for an advance more than once."

Van Meter worked the yellow pencil around in his hand. "Must have been totally honest in his games. There's so much cheating goin' on nowadays."

"I don't know," John admitted. "I don't play poker, but one day Billy Joe asked me if I knew how to cheat at cards and not get caught. Also, Abe found an ace on the floor near where we found the body."

Valerie raised her eyebrows. "Did he drink?"

John recalled the times Billy Joe stumbled in after a night on the town. "Oh, yes, but he usually would be ready to go to work the next morning. Seemed to sleep it off."

He stared at Valerie. "One thing puzzles me. He had something white or gray on his lips after he died. I don't know if Doc examined that or not. I found rat poison stuck under a lilac bush at the ranch. It wasn't there before we found the body. Obviously planted, too, because we don't use rat poison."

Valerie and Van Meter both scribbled that down.

A gasp blew out of John's mouth. "Something came to me now that I hadn't thought of before. On Saturday afternoon, before I found the body on Monday, B.J. got terribly ill at the Horse Ranchers meeting after he had a few drinks."

Wellington's boots stomped on the rough wood floor, his fingers rattling the keys again. "Time's up."

Van Meter stood. "Is the sheriff still here? We want a hearing. John's already been here several days. I don't want you slipping a noose around his neck early one morning without concrete evidence he's guilty. And from what we've heard, he's *not* guilty. You aren't even searching for the real killer."

Valerie moved close to John and leaned on his shoulder. He put an arm around her and gave her a little squeeze. "Thanks for coming," he said softly, enjoying her nearness. He kissed the top of her head.

"I don't know how this is going to work," she whispered closer to his ear. "The most we can stay is three days. We should leave in two days. I need to get back to Christian. Dad has important cases going on, and I must do all I can for those poor people in the asylum who shouldn't be there. Some of their lives could be in danger."

Wellington stepped inside the cell. "You don't have time for sweet talk and kisses. Your time's up."

To irritate Wellington, but also for his own satisfaction, John pulled Valerie back to him and kissed her on the mouth.

The smirk Valerie wore didn't quite fit her sophisticated image. "See you tomorrow." She grabbed her paper and pencil off the cot and hurried after her father.

38

On the floor of the asylum, Dillon Haskill struggled through the darkness and finally reached consciousness. Hot panic exploded through his bones. Did he have a seizure?

He worked his tongue around in his mouth and felt each surface. His tongue wasn't sore or damaged. He wiped his lips, but he apparently didn't have erupting saliva. Fear dissolved. He probably hadn't had a seizure. He had been knocked out. But who attacked him?

Al, one of the new patients, stood over him, confusion pulsing from his eyes and his fists holding somebody's shoes. "I'm s-s-sorry," he said. "Everyone was h-hitting each other, and I thought I'd better g-get a weapon and protect myself. I h-hit you over the head with my shoe h-heel. Then somebody tol' me you're one of the g-good guys. I-I ma-made a mistake."

Dillon sat up and held his head and looked at the shoe, more precisely the rubber-covered wooden heel. No wonder it knocked him out.

"Don't worry about it. I'm okay."

"S-somebody tol' me you're a d-doctor." The young man coughed, and it sounded as if he ripped his lungs. "Could you get me well?" he gasped. "The man who b-brought me here said I need in the asylum because I have La Grippe."

"That's interesting, Al." Dillon shook his head in frustration. Archibald mentioned that diagnosis for a few patients when he read the admissions report to him from the Board of Lunacy Commissioners. "La grippe is what some people call influenza. Did you have a high fever or something? How long have you been ill?"

"As long as I can remember. I–It's the cough." Amos opened his mouth and coughed so hard he bent over, gasped for air, and came up with tears.

"You don't look like you have tuberculosis. I'd say you have allergies, not La Grippe."

Dillon gave him a drink of water, wished for medication, and patted Al on the back of his thin shirt with his cupped hands until the cough let up. "Hang in there, Al. Help may be coming."

The patients in the room settled, but some wept. Others groaned and rubbed the places bruised in the fighting.

"Al, do you know where they took Pete? He's the boy who was kicked in the stomach."

Al coughed again. "The guards took him."

Dillon scratched his scalp. "I sure hope they took him to the doctor. He might have been seriously injured."

As Al walked away, nausea clamped down on Dillon's midsection. When were Archibald and that beautiful lady going to come back? Would they come? Would anyone listen to them? Could they bring the case up in court, so those who were not insane would be released or put somewhere they could be helped and comfortable?

He squeezed between a couple of beds, trying to get to his cot. Eyes of various colors stared at him while he stepped over the filth and garbage on the floor. Bubba kept moving from bed to bed. When he sat, he swung his huge foot back and forth, back and forth. Dillon guessed he wanted to trip him.

Dillon turned around, headed along the outside wall, and arrived at his bed before Bubba figured out where he went.

When Dillon lay on his cot, his head still hurt, but since he had time to think, his heart rejoiced. "Thank you, Lord. I didn't have a seizure."

Another seizure would guarantee he wouldn't get out of here.

In the Peachville jail, Sheriff Woody stomped to John's cell. Wellington stood by the open door.

Woody's face glowed red with anger. "You know those lawyer friends of yours must be creating quite a fuss. I've had three telegrams already this morning. The judge will be here this afternoon or tomorra. He started his wire telling me he went to law school with Aaron Van Meter, who contacted him. The state governor sent me one that said, 'I knew John Parks' father well, and I don't think his son would commit murder. Make sure you have the right man.' The district attorney said he'll set a hearing right away."

John jumped off the bed and ran to the bars. "Did anyone have anything to say about trying to find the killer?"

"No. They believe I know my business."

John raised an eyebrow. "There's a difference between knowing the law and upholding it."

Sheriff Woody's face broke out in sweat. "You have a smart mouth, John. That's the second time since you've been here you deserved a fist in the kisser."

The outside door to the sheriff's office rattled. Shortly, Wellington walked into the attached jail with Valerie MacDougal and Van Meter.

"We need some private time with our client." Van Meter held a thin leather case.

"Good morning, John." Valerie, dressed in navy blue and pink, looked stunning. Was the pink a sign her mourning was over?

Van Meter opened his case and removed paper and pencils. "Let's get down to business. The sheriff doesn't give us much time. How are you going to plea?"

John grunted. "Not guilty. The sheriff knows I'm innocent."

"Good." The whir of the pens writing on the white paper was almost music.

Valerie looked at him, affection in her sparkling eyes. "Do you want to make any kind of formal statement at the hearing?"

"Sure. I'll tell how someone went to a lot of trouble to frame me and make it look like I'm the killer. In the first place, it doesn't make any sense."

Valerie brushed a few stray strands of her curly blonde hair away from her face. "What evidence do you think is the strongest?"

"Number one, the boot prints. And the sheriff wouldn't even look at them."

"Next?"

"Number two, the rat poison under the lilac bush. We never use poison on our ranch. Number three, the body was almost in plain sight in my barn. My barn. Four, I got along well with B.J., but he quit me so he could make more money."

John's knees quaked, and his fingers were like icicles. "I don't know where the rumors came from, but somebody paid the bartender to say I bought whiskey for B.J., and we had a big argument. B.J. and I never had a fight. I just turned twenty years old. Even if I wanted to drink liquor—which I don't—I couldn't buy it. I'm not old enough. Only a couple days ago when I went into the Rusty Wheel to ask about B.J. and where he was working right before he was killed, the barkeep asked what I was doing in there because I'm too young to drink."

"What else can you tell us?" Van Meter's pencil poised over the paper.

"The barmaid at the Rusty Wheel can tell you I even refused a drink Clyde Merriweather, Edwina's cowhand, bought me the night of the Horse Ranchers meeting. Clyde also bought a drink for B.J., and later B.J. drank mine. While the speaker was at the podium, B.J. got terribly sick, and Clyde helped him out of the place."

"What else?"

"Then something really strange. Witnesses supposedly reported I bought rat poison from Charlie at the feed store. I did no such thing. Of course, no one reported that until after I told the sheriff about the rat poison I found."

Valerie and Van Meter had been writing furiously. Van Meter touched his mustache, wrote a little more, and then tapped the other end of the pencil on the paper. He lifted his shaven chin. "Obviously, you're comfortable telling what happened. We're going to talk to the bartender again who said you threatened B.J., and we'll talk to the Davenports and stop in at the feed store."

"You can talk to Wellington Davenport here." John pointed at the door to the sheriff's office.

Wellington turned and vanished.

Valerie stood. "We'll also need to have some subpoenas delivered to the people we want to testify at the hearing."

Van Meter licked his lips, stacked his notes into his case, and grabbed a gold-tipped cane. "We'll let you know when the hearing will take place."

The keys the sheriff held tinkled. "Time's up." Valerie and Van Meter walked out the cell door.

The sheriff clicked the lock and followed them. "You'll see the man who killed B.J. is sitting in that cell, and I'll see he hangs."

39

"Stuart! Where you be?" Polly shouted out the back door at the ranch.

She couldn't see the little feller anywhere. Holding up the mail in her hand, she tried again. "Stuart! I need ya."

Abe appeared quite a distance away in the barn door, and Stuart came around the other side of the house riding Ol' Kaiser at a gentle trot. "Come on, old boy." Stu jabbed his heels in his round sides. "You're a horse, not a turtle."

Laughter burst out of Polly. "You're getting right fine at working with horses since John gone. Good job. Ol' Kaiser be trying to make your ride last longer. He like boys who have a gentle touch like you."

Stuart scrunched his tanned, freckled face. "Whatcha want? I still have lots a work to do."

Polly plopped a hand on her wide hip. "So do I. I need you to give this mail to Abe and then go into town with 'im and give it to John. You go with Abe. You've been workin' so hard since John not here you deserve a break. I have a little money here, and I want you and Abe to treat yo selves to an ice cream cone."

"Wow. I'll get at it."

Stu turned Ol' Kaiser around, flicked the reins, and leaned forward, and the animal took off at an "almost" run. Stu bounced in the saddle, his hair blowing in the breeze, and hung on.

John stared at the letter with the Denver address. Raymond Randolf. Who is he? His fingers trembled as he ripped the envelope.

Dear Mr. Parks,

I read your ad in the Peachville Gazette, and if you haven't sold him yet, I'm interested in your black stallion. I will be in Peachville on the fifteenth of the month.

John took a deep breath and then blew, puffing out his whiskery cheeks. How could he meet the man from jail? Would Ed want to sell? Why hadn't the man contacted him before he made the agreement with Edwina?

Abe watched from the other side of the bars with Stu at his side. Abe's forehead creased between his dark eyes. "Bad news?"

John blew again. "Not exactly. A man from Denver saw my ad about the stallion. He'll be here Friday to look at him. You know Ed and I share ownership. I'd like to sell the horse and get the money out of him now. Both of us will have his bloodline in our next generation, and that makes me happy."

Abe blinked several times the way he did when thoughts whirled in his brain. "I heard Clyde Merriweather can't handle him."

"Yes. Ed told me so and worries he'll use the whip. Clyde used to be one of the judge's men, and the judge didn't believe you could work a horse without a whip."

"The stallion still a good steed." Abe rubbed his curly hair. "He showing good spirit after we worked with him."

John licked his lips. "I hope Clyde didn't break it."

Stuart stepped closer. "You s'pose this Denver man is going to race the stallion?"

"I don't know," John answered. "But racing won't hurt him. If he puts his heart into it, like I've seen him do, no other critter can catch him."

Stuart giggled. "I'd love to see him race and leave the rest in the dust."

John couldn't help but smile at the kid. "Say, Stu, did you grow while I wasn't there to keep an eye on you? You look taller."

Abe patted Stu's head with his long ebony fingers. "He's been workin' like a man, trying to do all your chores and his too. He's a great helper. When your sis comes, Polly and me are going to miss this tyke. He's a great 'un to have around."

John reached his arm through the bars and hugged Stuart. A lump gathered in his throat. Silence hung around the friends while the mumble of voices drifted from the sheriff's office.

"Thank you." John captured his emotions, and then pulled his hairy arm back through the bars. "Stu, your parents will be here soon to pick you up and get the rest of their things. They've been delayed because of circumstances in the family and rain in Iowa."

Stuart grinned. "I been missing them. I can work with my Papa William like I been helpin' Abe."

"That's for sure." John nodded. "I hope you've done all your studies. Still working on those books Jenny gave you?"

"Read them all."

"How about those arithmetic books?"

Stu shook his head. "I got stuck, and I'm too busy."

"Well, soon as I'm out of here, we'll get you unstuck. My sis will wring my neck if I don't keep you caught up."

The door rattled, and Valerie and Van Meter followed the sheriff into the jail. Woody's ruddy face scrunched into a frown, while Valerie and Van Meter beamed. "The hearing is set for tomorrow."

Later, around supper time, Edwina arrived with a brilliant smile and a tray filled with juicy chicken fried steak, mashed potatoes and gravy, green beans, a fluffy roll, and warm peach cobbler.

Wellington puffed out his chest, swayed his gun-toting hips, unlocked the jail cell, and said, "Hey, John. How about trading places?"

John grinned. "I'll think about it while I'm eating and thanking the Lord and this beautiful gal."

"How come you have two beauties coming around to see you?" Wellington stared at Edwina as he opened the door and handed John the food.

John's smile stretched even wider as he set the tray on his bed. "I'll never tell."

After Wellington left, John showed the letter about the stallion to Edwina. "Would you like to sell?"

Ed lifted her shoulders and rolled them around as if her back hurt. "How much do you think we can get for him? We'd have to split it."

He squeezed her fingers as they grasped the bars. "That will be nice."

"It's only fair. He's not paid for yet."

John named the price Abe recommended. Ed's blue eyes popped wide open. "That much?"

"Yes. We've had quite a bit of stud business, and pretty soon, that will run out. I think this fellow wants to make a racehorse out of him, and the horse is still young enough to do it."

Ed grinned. "Let's sell, then. We both could use the money, and the stallion is a worry for me. Clyde insisted on riding him, and the stallion didn't allow it. I worked with the horse, but I was afraid he'd kill Clyde or injure him so he'd end up like Daddy. Yet I can ride him. Don't understand it." She wagged her head and then tipped her face away.

"I fired Clyde," her voice came out low. "He tried to take over the money and my bookkeeping."

"He did?" John let out a low whistle. "He deserved to be fired."

"When I discovered him rummaging in my desk, he kissed me with his filthy mouth, thinking I'd let him romance me. I slapped him, and he made such suggestive remarks I was tempted to shoot him."

John shuddered, his stomach clenching to match his fists. "The bonehead! He probably didn't know how close he came to death."

"No, I think he knew. He jumped on his horse and fled."

John sighed. "So you want to sell the stallion? Shall we contact this Raymond Randolf? Send him a wire?"

Ed nodded, her pretty curls bouncing about her face. "I'll do it."

"Deputy?" The deep voice sounded like Pastor Brandt.

The pastor softly walked back to John's cell, leaned forward, his bald head turned, trying to see who was visiting with John.

"Looks like Preach is back." The fellow in the next cell rattled the bars. "What's the matter with you, Holy Man? Why haven't you prayed us out of jail like the people did for the Apostle Paul?"

"Don't think the Lord's letting you out, man," John shot back. "The Apostle Paul didn't commit a crime. The only thing he was guilty of was preaching the gospel."

"Then why you here?"

John shook the pastor's hand. "Thanks for coming again. I can feel the prayer. Look at the supper Edwina brought! If you'll excuse me a minute, I'm going to thank her and the Lord for the food and gobble it up."

After allowing the two visitors inside, Wellington brought a couple of chairs. "I think we can trust you with these."

"Thanks." John was glad for the excuse to sit on his bed and enjoy his meal from his lap.

His guests dropped into the seats. Pastor beamed. "Go right ahead and eat."

John thanked the Lord for his food, grinned at Ed, and plunged into the steak, which though chilled, still set his mouth salivating.

"The Lord is working in your case," Pastor said, his fingers thumbing through his tattered Bible. "He gave me a Scripture for you. He reminded me of Luke 4:18 when Jesus revealed who he is to the Jews as he read from the book of Isaiah in the synagogue. *'The Spirit of the Lord is upon me because he hath anointed me to preach the gospel to the poor. He has sent me to heal the brokenhearted.'"*

He stopped. "This is the part you will especially enjoy. '*To preach deliverance to the captives.*'" Pastor Brandt's voice echoed on the jail's rock walls. "' *… And recovering of sight to the blind.*'" He drew a deep breath and looked at John again. "'*To set at liberty them that are bruised.*'"

John swallowed. His heart quickened. Faith surged through him.

The pastor closed the book. "Then Jesus said, '*Today this Scripture is fulfilled in your ears.*'"

Edwina laughed, her blue eyes sparkling. "How wonderful. God has given me a Scripture, too. I've been praying and wanting to do more for the Lord. When Daddy was injured, God gave me this Scripture. It's found in Nahum 1:7. *The Lord is good, a stronghold in the day of trouble, and he knows those who trust in him.*"

Sheriff Woody had stood outside the cell, then vanished, but Wellington leaned into the bars. "That's beautiful." The deputy shifted away, swallowed, scrunched his lips, and then turned his eyes toward the prisoner. "John, you probably heard how Polly preached to me and then prayed. It felt like heaven came down because she started dancing around. I haven't …" He became unable to speak. Finally, he had control again. "I haven't been the same since."

John's jaw dropped. "Praise the Lord!"

Edwina's hands clapped together, making soft applause.

"After Polly prayed," Wellington continued, "I went to home to my room and prayed. Joy flowed through me like a river. All of a sudden, I was through gambling. Even before my parents cut off my money, I wanted a job, and that's why I'm here."

Was he serious?

"I'm not perfect yet," he admitted. "I've done so many things I'm ashamed of. The Lord is still working on me. This thing about Bellea's baby and Billy Joe's death is giving me trouble. Yet from being in church I know God does the miraculous."

John raised an eyebrow. "Did you kill B.J. and try to make it look like I did it?"

Wellington paled while his head wagged. "No! But I definitely was rude when Mama tried to get the baby. I suspect someone I know well killed B.J. and dumped the body, so I admit I haven't helped Woody much in the search for the killer. I'm afraid where it will lead." He wagged his head, breathing hard. "I've also created a few untrue diversions at my father's suggestion. Please forgive me."

John held his face in his hands and prayed. When he lifted his head, Wellington's uniformed shoulders sagged at he walked back and forth outside the cell.

John cleared his throat. "I forgive you and God will, too."

Pastor opened his mouth as if he was going to speak, but John barged in, "I'll share one of my favorite Scriptures. It's from First John. *'If we confess our sins, he is faithful and just to forgive us our sins and to cleanse us from all unrighteousness.'"*

Wellington nodded, his shoulders now more erect, and his tanned face lost its despair. "Thanks."

Pastor stood. "This reminds me of the time King Saul wanted to kill David. He sent messengers to take David, and when they arrived and witnessed Samuel and the prophets prophesying, God touched the messengers, and they began glorifying God. Saul found out and sent more men, and the Spirit of God was so heavy they too began praising God. It happened again when Saul sent a third group. Then Saul went himself, and even he fell down and worshiped all day and all night."

He continued, "We all have Scripture or a testimony here today. Let's thank God for all the things he has done, and for what he's going to do in the future."

Their praises echoed until outside voices came toward them. Valerie's hands gestured as she spoke in a high voice to Sheriff Woody and Aaron Van Meter.

"We need to make sure we're ready for the preliminary hearing tomorrow," Valerie said, her fair face pink and beaming.

John ran to the bars. "What does a hearing mean?"

"The judge will be looking to see if there is enough evidence to hold you for the murder of Billy Joe Garner."

40

John sat handcuffed beside Valerie in the small, stuffy courtroom listening and running over the points he would make in his testimony. Sweat trickled down his face and neck. He turned to look at Edwina, who sat behind him, twisting a white handkerchief in her fingers and occasionally wiping tears.

The prosecution had presented Sheriff's Woody's testimony and several other flimsy narratives about John having it in for B.J. Valerie reserved the right to call them back for cross-examination later. Then the bartender Jefferson Kelly sat in the witness seat, a smug pucker on his lips, but uncertainty in his eyes.

Kelly leaned forward, sat back, scowled at the ceiling, put his face in his hands, wiggled and jangled coins in his pocket, waiting while the prosecuting attorney shuffled papers.

Finally, the obvious questions slid from the prosecuting attorney, whose tightly buttoned white shirt and black suit coat made John think of a penguin as he strutted back and forth. When he had the bartender's personal information, he halted in front of the witness.

"Do you know John Lincoln Parks?" His high-pitched squeaky voice demanded an answer.

Kelly rubbed his white beard. "Sure. Everybody knows John."

"Do you know Billy Joe Garner?"

The old man pointed at John. "I did before he killed 'im!"

John wagged head.

The lawyer faced John. "So you've seen this man and Billy Joe in the bar where you work?"

"Sure. Lots of times. And I heard John threaten to kill Billy Joe one night while they played poker."

The judge stared at the witness. "Answer the questions you're asked, Kelly. If we had a jury here, we'd have to strike your last sentence."

John wiped his brow.

The prosecutor grinned at the witness and then said, "Did you ever hear John Parks threaten Billy Joe?"

"Yes!"

Triumph twinkled in the attorney's eyes. "What did John say?"

"You cheated me, and when you're not looking, I'll beat every dime out of your body."

"Was that all he said?"

Kelly thought a moment. "Naw. He told B.J., 'You've played your last game of poker.'"

The prosecutor concluded his questioning, a victorious smile working around on his face.

Valerie stood as the representative for the defense. Kelly's eyes darted back and forth over the crowd.

"So you'd say John Parks beat B.J. to death in a dispute over cheating," Valerie said.

Kelly ran his hand through his white hair and nodded. "Yes!"

"How long you been a bartender Mister Kelly?"

"About eighteen months. I retired from the smelter in Leadville."

Valerie's nicely shaped brows lifted. "That's the smelter partly owned by the Davenports, isn't it?"

"What does that have to do with anything?" Kelly's wrinkled face shrank into a frown.

"Isn't arsenic a byproduct of ore smelters? Did you ever collect any?"

Kelly faced the judge with his open palms waving. "No. No."

"How well do you know John Lincoln Parks?"

The witness bobbed his head. "I know 'im."

"How long have you known him?"

"I'd say eighteen months because that's how long I've lived in Peachville."

Valerie rested her head on her clasped hands, bending over to look eye-to-eye with Kelly. "So John drinks and gambles?"

Kelly scratched his white head. "Didn't you hear me tell the other fellow that John was in the saloon playing poker, drinking, and had a fight with B.J.?"

She continued to stare unblinking at Kelly. "Yes, I heard you. So you've known John Parks for eighteen months when John has only been back to Peachville since February."

Kelly's eyes searched for someone in the audience. "Well, he came in so often I thought he'd been here that long."

"Also, I'd like for you to think about your earlier testimony and answer this question again. Did John Lincoln Parks come into the Rusty Wheel and drink liquor and gamble with B.J. when you tended bar?"

Kelly's lips mashed together with disgust. He put his hands in frustration. "Yes! I done told you he did."

Valerie's left brow shot up. "So you allowed an underage person to buy whiskey and gamble? John Parks is only nineteen years old, coming on twenty. He's never had a drink." She drew her outstretched hand across the spectators. "I imagine these people can verify that."

Kelly's face blushed crimson. "I, uh … uh, didn't ask his age. He looks older, don't ya think? How did I know?"

"How much did the real killer pay you to say John threatened B.J.?"

The witness stood. "The man isn't a killer, or I wouldn't have taken his money."

"Sit down!" The judge pounded his gavel on the desk.

Several people jumped to their feet, yelling and shaking their fists.

The gavel struck again. The judge shouted, "Order in the court!"

When everyone quieted, Valerie faced the witness and smiled. "Who paid you to lie against John Lincoln Parks?"

The bartender grasped his chest and slumped to the floor. The bailiff and another man carried him out.

The judge slammed his gavel again. "This hearing will take a short recess. We will continue in thirty minutes."

When the hearing resumed, Valerie called the barmaid who poured drinks the night of the Horse Ranchers meeting.

"Clyde Merriweather bought John whiskey," the maid reported with a grin.

"Did he drink it?"

"He said he didn't drink, and he left it there. But later, the glass was empty."

A rumble of voices floated through the room.

"I call Clyde Merriweather."

Clyde swaggered to the chair.

"Did you buy John a drink knowing he's underage?"

"How do I know how old he is?"

The judge leaned over. "Answer the question."

"Sure. I bought him a drink."

"Who drank it?"

"It was his."

"Isn't it true that John refused the drink, went to talk to the guest speaker, and when he came back, B.J. had guzzled the whiskey you intended for John?"

"I don't know. All I know is the glass was empty."

Valerie called the sheriff back so she could cross-examine him.

"Did the same man pay you to lie on the stand that paid the bartender?" she asked.

"Who are you, a woman, to ask me, the head of law and order in this town, such a question? I refuse to dignify your question with an answer."

"Better answer the lady, Woody," the judge spoke. "I'd hate to order your new deputy to put you in your own jail for contempt."

Woody shrugged. "Nobody paid me."

"I wonder if we got a court order and opened your safe if you could tell where all the money came from." Valerie walked back and forth in front of the witness. "We might be able to pursue that further because I hear you live pretty high on the forty dollars a month your job pays. But right now, we're interested in John Lincoln Parks. Do you really believe John killed Billy Joe Garner?"

"Yes."

Valerie hesitated, and then whirled. "John will testify later, but Sheriff Watson, why did you not gather evidence from John's barn and property?"

One after another, the questions came from Valerie, who now had fire in eyes and flames on her tongue. Each question she asked, the sheriff muttered a low, "No."

"Did you sketch or measure the large boot prints in his barn? Did you bring them to court with you? Where are they?"

"Did you look at the place where the rat poison was found?"

"Did you ask the doctor who examined the body how you would get the rat poison into a drink so that someone would ingest it without noticing it?"

"Did you consider a murderer usually doesn't stash a body on his own property almost in plain sight and then call the sheriff to look?"

"Did you try to find other witnesses who heard the supposed argument in the bar before you accepted people's accusations against John?"

She continued, "John was in the feed store only a few days before he found the body ordering one hundred little chicks. He was in the feed store four days ago picking up the chicks and selling rabbits. I can call Charlie Phillips from the feed store to the witness stand and have him tell if John has ever bought rat poison there, and you'll find out he didn't. We asked him. That's why Charlie hasn't been among the witnesses."

Sheriff Woody lifted his chin in defiance. "But I know John did it! Who else would have killed B.J.?"

"It's your job to find out," Valerie spat.

"Your honor, I believe the sheriff's testimony completes our defense. We have more witnesses, including John who will testify in his own behalf, but I think what we have is sufficient. I submit a motion now to have charges against John Lincoln Parks dismissed, and an order to release John from jail given to the sheriff."

The judge stroked his gray beard, and the room quieted.

"I will now take some time to consider the testimony and evidence. At one p.m., I'll give you my decision."

He stood, his black robe billowing as he walked toward the exit.

John couldn't eat the pastry provided as he waited in a back room with the bailiff. The thought of food turned his already rioting stomach.

A few minutes before the time was up, he settled in the court room again beside Valerie and Van Meter.

"Relax," Van Meter whispered. "None of those people are good liars, and those who told the truth spoke with certainty."

Valerie took John's sweaty hand. "You'll be out of jail this afternoon."

The judge walked in.

"All rise," the bailiff said.

Everyone in the room stood to honor the judge.

"You may be seated except the accused," the bailiff directed.

John stood, trembling, head down, praying under his breath. Then a Scripture ran through his mind: *The fervent prayer of a righteous availeth much.* Strength surged. He spread his legs, stood firm, and he gazed directly at the judge, who pounded his gavel.

"This hearing is now in session. This preliminary hearing has determined there isn't enough evidence in this case against John Lincoln Parks. He is free to go."

Applause echoed.

"Thank you, Lord," John whispered.

"Congratulations," Aaron Van Meter murmured as he hugged Valerie. He stuck out his hand to John. "You're free, young man. Let's go to the café, and I'll buy all of us lunch."

John faced Valerie and gave her a big hug. "Good work, sweetheart. Thanks."

He stared into her intense blue eyes, still filled with the fire of the battle she'd won.

Edwina stood nearby, tears dribbling down her pink cheeks.

Van Meter noticed her. "Edwina, why don't you join us?"

"Thanks, but I have lots of work waiting for me at home." She clapped her hands. "But I'm so happy."

John took Edwina's hand and squeezed it. "Do come with us. You deserve a good meal on someone else, after feeding me so well."

Ed dabbed the wetness from her cheeks. "I'd love to, but I've been gone too long already."

Valerie moved into the circle of conversation. "Speaking of being away from home, we'll need to pack tonight and get on the train early tomorrow. I have a little boy to love in Boston and work to do. So we need to spend all the time we can together."

Edwina smiled at the female lawyer and the woman who would become John's wife. "We're so glad you came to help, Valerie. Thank you."

Valerie stepped close to John and leaned against his shoulder. "I hope they find B.J.'s killer. He's still running around out there."

ADA BROWNELL

41

The sun went down while they ate and completed errands, so John, Polly, Abe, and Stuart stayed the night at the boarding house, partly because they wanted to see Valerie and her father off.

The next morning's passenger train left Peachville whistling and puffing smoke while Valerie waved from an open window, her pink jacket sleeve proclaiming her mourning was over.

As the train huffed over the horizon into the sunrise and disappeared, John stared after them. He'd seen a different side of Valerie. Uneasiness squirmed in his stomach. In the courtroom, energy flowed from her that probably would be difficult to contain without some outlet to release it.

The talent God gave her made a difference in his life, for sure. He shook his head, remembering the little peck he'd placed on her cheek before she departed. Why didn't he give her another kiss she'd remember?

He breathed deeply, puffed his cheeks, and blew the air away. The sunshine warmed his back and worked its way through to his quivering heart. Joy bubbled clear to his toes.

Coming from behind, he caught Stuart with both hands, twirled him around two or three times, and cried, "I'm free! I'm free! Let's go home and get to work."

Polly and Abe joined the rejoicing, pulling John and Stu into a cinnamon-roll hug. "Praise God!" John shouted.

"Yes! Praise the Lord!" Polly cried, her chocolate face shining and crinkling beside her beaming smile.

"Bless God!" Abe pulled John into a hug all by himself. "We's ready for ya to be home."

John jumped into the wagon. Stu hopped in beside him. As soon as Polly and Abe sat on the bench in back, he took the reins, clicked his tongue, and hollered, "Let's go!"

The words and the tune to a song played around in his head as they stirred up dust. Finally, the group squeezed through pedestrians, buggies, wagons, and saddle horses to the outskirts of town. He opened his mouth and sang, "'There's not a friend like the lowly Jesus, No not one! No not one!'"

Polly joined in the singing about Jesus being a friend through dark nights, being near, and never forsaking. The words and Polly's deep and bold alto sent chills up John's back. Then Polly's feet tapping on the wagon's rough floor began, loud enough to set the rhythm until John wanted to dance and his feet caught the beat.

Abe and Stu turned their feet into instruments, too, leaving no need for a drum. Abe's bass and Stu's higher voice blended almost like a quartet.

Fred Rumberger guided his sleek pony toward Peachville past John's noisy wagon. Rumberger, a salesman, had his oily hair slicked back, and he'd donned a navy blue suit. Mr. Arlington, on his white horse, pranced by them while the man stared at the singers until he'd turned his head so far he almost lost his balance in the saddle.

Around the next curve in the road, Edwina headed toward them, riding the black stallion at a full gallop. "Whoa!" she yelled, and her tanned arms tugged on the reins.

She wore those tantalizing curls again, reminding John this wasn't a youngster he'd tormented, but a beautiful woman. He stopped the team beside her. "Hello. I thought you didn't ride that horse much."

"Well, he acted so friendly today I tried it, and he didn't buck once. He must like me."

"Good to see you. We need to talk."

Ed rubbed her nose with a riding glove. "Oh?"

John half expected her to add, "Is Valerie gone?" But he didn't want to start a fuss. "Raymond Randolf should be coming to look at the stallion. What time did he want to meet you?"

Her blue eyes lit. "I'm heading into town now to meet him. I dropped by your place, and nobody was home, so I'm going by myself."

"Does your daddy think the price is sensible?"

"Yep." She grinned. "Thinks it's a good idea to go ahead and sell him since we already have his bloodline in our herds. Daddy knows Raymond Randolf, and he does train racehorses. Dad said he's gentle and can even win the most rebellious horses over with a little sugar and sweet talk."

"Guess I'd better turn around and go with you."

Abe jumped out of the wagon, his long legs crossing the road in moments. "If you two need to talk more, I'd sure like to ride that animal one more time. It'd give you time to catch up on everything before you meet with the buyer."

Edwina beamed. She dismounted, her stylish riding outfit accenting her slim curves. John jerked his staring eyes away but then took her hand to help her into the wagon.

Stu wore a smirk. "I'll sit in back." He dove into an open spot next to the bulging potato and flour sacks on the wagon bed.

When John lifted the gal into the wagon, and they were face to face, he would've kissed her if hadn't had an audience. After all, he probably needed the practice since he let Valerie go without a good smacker.

"Could you take me home when we're through since I won't have a ride if we sell?"

"Sure." Somehow, John really enjoyed her company lately. When the team worked up a good steam, he let them have their heads. "Any new leads on the killer? Heard anything?"

She squinted her big blue eyes. "I think I told you I fired Clyde. I'd wish we had him back if I wasn't afraid of him. There's too much work to do, and somebody has been peeping into our house. I've found footprints under the windows. It's probably Wellington trying to see if Bellea and the baby live with us. I don't know why he'd be suspicious except he might have caught a glimpse of her through the window when he was doing business about the stallion."

"Are you still afraid of Clyde?"

She nodded. "Here I have a peeper, and Clyde could come back any day and try to give me grief. What's wrong with the world?"

"They need Jesus," he mumbled.

The warmth of her head on his shoulder and her body squeezed close to his side filled him with fuzzy delight, while alarm exploded in his brain. She moved away, and a sizzle of anger burst through him. "Do you think Clyde could be still hanging around?"

Ed's chin shot in the air. "I don't think he expects to marry me now and get the ranch. I burst that ego balloon when I slapped him."

"Don't be too sure." John raised his eyebrows. "We need to make it a priority to get you a good ranch hand   or even two."

"Lawd. You knows all of Edwina's needs." Evidently, Polly could hear enough to know what was going on. "You know how good she is, taking Bellea in her home and keeping her and the baby safe. Now, Lord, we're asking you to give your angels charge over Edwina, her family, and her ranch. Be with John and her in the sale of the stallion. In Jesus' name, I pray, and thank you."

The wagon hit a big rut, and all of them bounced, while Abe rode high beside them in the saddle on the strutting stallion, a wide smile curving his aging face.

"Thank you, Lawd," Polly continued. "Praise God, he's working! He hears! He answers and shows us great and mighty things. Glory! Praise Jesus!"

A powerful Presence settled over John. Edwina sniffled beside him. He yanked a square of cotton from his back pocket, and she buried her face in his red handkerchief.

In only moments, joy descended again. Ed grinned and blew her nose. "Thanks for praying. This is a great day. God is with us."

Her upturned face glowed with peace and beauty—that new look again.

Edwina and Randolf had agreed to meet at the stables. The team pulled up in front, and Abe followed close behind. The tall, thin man and the stallion glided with such perfect rhythm they moved like one creature.

Randolf stood in front of the livery stable, his plump jaw hanging. He let out a soft whistle. "That's some horse. Does he come with the rider?"

Abe beamed as he patted the stallion on the neck and murmured, "Good work, boy." Then he looked at Randolf. "If'n I was thirty years younger, I'd love to take my wife and work with him." He shook his head. "I can't go, but if you treat him right, talk to him a lot, and sneak him a treat now and then, he'll lick your boots and do anything you want. You mistreat him, and he's liable to kill ya."

"He tried to kill my hired hand," Edwina added, while John helped her and Polly from the wagon. "And still the fellow wouldn't quit mistreating him."

"Did you fire him?" Randolf moved to the stallion and touched him, then rubbed the long hairy neck while he spoke into the stallion's big wiggling ears.

"Sure did," Edwina admitted. "But it sure put me in a bind. My father is disabled, and I have way too much work to do, even with help in the house."

Randolf tapped a finger to his face. "Edwina Jorgenson? You're the gal who contacted me. Is your father Paul Jorgenson?"

Ed nodded, smiling.

"Was this animal responsible for your father being in a wheelchair?"

"No, no, no. Daddy was injured beforehand trying to take a wild horse. He mentioned he knows you and believes you're a good man."

John walked up to Randolf, extending his hand. "I'm John Lincoln Parks. Edwina and I own the stallion as partners."

"I knew a Parks, who had a wonderful peach and horse ranch here in Peachville. I did some wheeling and dealing with him several years ago. Then I heard he died, and some judge took over the property and ruined it."

"Yes. You met my father. I'm trying to rebuild. Did a lot of work with the peach orchards this spring, and I'm building up the horse herd."

Randolf's gaze lingered first on John and then swung to Edwina. "Why are you selling the stallion?"

Edwina nodded. "I understand you need to know why. John and I don't have the time we should to work with him, but we've had great results making a little money putting him out to stud."

After slipping cubes of sugar in the stallion's mouth, Randolf carefully examined the animal's mouth, hooves, legs, and body.

"This boy takes lots of attention, or he's not happy," Abe added. "He lives for yo gentle words, the curry brush on his itchin' scars, and takin' you on an adventure ride in the wide open spaces. Takes time and commitment."

"He's been abused," Randolf noted, trailing a fat finger down a large scar.

"Judge Danforth Schuster did that." Ed tipped her chin up. "John has a few scars from that man's hand as well. See the one on his cheek?"

"I did notice a faint scar on your face, John." Randolf continued examining the stallion, his rubbery jowls bouncing as he bent to look at the hooves. "What happened to the judge?"

Abe frowned. "Murdered."

"I was there." Stuart edged close to Randolf. "Judge got into an argument with an old man my mama called Grouch. The men was yelling at each other about who was gonna get somebody's homestead down near Yucca Blossom. The judge was makin' fun of the old guy. Then Grouch up and shot 'im. He fell down dead."

"Such a tragedy." Randolf shook his head over and over.

Edwina shuddered. "Horrible."

Stuart turned his head back and forth, a distant look in his eyes. "I didn't like the judge, but my new mama said, 'He can't be dead! He doesn't know the Lord.' She screamed and cried. Before she ran away, the judge had put a bounty on my mama's head 'cuz he had to take care of her until she was twenty-one or the ranch wasn't his."

John ruffled Stu's hair with his long fingers. "And he didn't get it, either, did he?"

Stu giggled. "Nope. The ranch is John's now. John is my new mama's brother."

"Oh," Randolf responded, sending a gentle smile to the boy. "This fine animal appears quite healthy. He's a little suspicious of me yet, but I think we'll get along fine. You never named him?"

John gave the stallion a gentle pat on the rump. "Thought of names more than once, but nothing stuck. I don't know what the judge called him."

Randolf stroked the stallion. "Well, I expect him to run like lightning, but I want him to have a unique name for the racetrack. Anyway, I want him. Was the price I offered agreeable?"

"What do you say, girl?" John shot her an intense look.

"Daddy thinks the price is agreeable, but since we will lose the stud fees, I'd like to ask a hundred more. I think that's good business. What do you think, John?"

A crowd had gathered watching the buyer check out the horse. A hand shot up, and a voice shouted from the back of the sea of faces. "I got a good horse here I'll sell ya for twenty-five bucks."

John stretched his neck as the man in overalls tried to get Randolf's attention. "I'm in desperate need of money. My wife and two kids died, and during their sickness, I couldn't work. I owed the bank, and they took my propitty. I don't even have enough money to get a room at the boarding house."

Edwina stretched up on her tippy toes and craned to see him. "Have you worked with horses?"

"Sure have. Worked a little as a vet, too."

"Can you break 'em?"

"Been saddle breaking horses since I was twelve."

"Tell you what." She elbowed through the crowd to him. "I'm in desperate need of a ranch hand. I have a nice bunkhouse where you can live, even cook your own meals, and once in a while, eat with us. I don't pay much, but the job might be an answer to your prayers—and to mine, too. My daddy is disabled."

"Well, I could come out and talk to you and look it over."

"Get me three people who will give you a recommendation, and I'll hire you right now. What's your name?"

"Max. Max Mosely. But then I couldn't sell my horse 'cause I'd need him. You'd let me keep him at your place, wouldn't you?"

Max didn't look over thirty years old. "Sure would, but I need those recommendations."

While several men gathered around Max to provide a recommendation, Randolf grabbed a valise. "Let's get this transaction completed. We'll fill out the bill of sale, and then go over to the bank, and you can get your money in either cash or check."

While Abe and John stood beside her, three men offered recommendations for Max.

"I'm Jason Thornbush, and I've seen Max ride broncos." Jason stuck his beefy hands into his patched overalls. "But he also has a gentle hand horses respond to."

So many wrinkles creased the next fellow's face it looked as if it needed ironing. But his clear faded eyes sparkled. "All I know to tell you is Max is a hard worker, and he's honest."

Finally, the third man came forward, his muscled body stretching the seams of his shirt and trousers. "Max horses know, and strong," he said in a foreign accent. "Mine friend. His wife he love. Job needs."

John knew Thornbush and had met Max and the old man. "I think you ought to hire Max. But be careful. Don't be careless."

Edwina leaned toward John, an intense frown wrinkling her brow. "I'll not relax until we catch the peeper or until he disappears."

42

Little Christian Paul squealed with excitement when Valerie walked through the door to his hospital room in Boston. He jumped up from where he sat on the floor playing with a wooden train.

His little legs churned with a slight limp across the red-flowered linoleum. "Mama! Mama!"

When he squeezed her tight around the neck, his tears ran down her neck while hers poured over her face. "Oh, baby. My baby. I missed you so."

She pushed away enough to look into his big blue eyes. "You're walking well! I think we need to take you home. Would you like that?"

Christian wagged his head up and down, his smile stretching toward his ears, showing a wet mouth full of tiny white teeth.

The nurse near the door in a white uniform cleared her throat. A frown cracked her intense, set-in-plaster smile. "You'll need to speak to the doctor."

Valerie hugged Christian close again, but let him down to watch him walk. "I think Doc will agree, but if not, we're taking him home anyway."

Dr. Cabot stalked into the room, his white hair standing on end and the stethoscope around his neck swinging. "I heard that." A gentle smile peeked beneath his mustache. Grunting as his aged joints clicked, he bent eye-to-eye with Christian. Christian grabbed the stethoscope, and Doc removed it from his neck and stuck it in the child's ears. Then he cupped the business end over his heart. Christian's eyes opened wide. He jabbered back at his mother.

The doctor laughed, and then stood. "I think you're right, Missus MacDougal. It's time for this little man to go home."

Joy surged through Valerie. "Thank you." She waved her hands up and down as if cheering. "He's walking great with only a slight limp. Thank you!"

The physician scooped up Christian and squeezed the boy to his chest. "He'll have to come in for exercise treatments for a while, but your son is almost back to normal."

"Will the limp ever go away?"

The doctor let the boy go, crossed his arms, and rested his face on his hand while he looked at Christian, now running around the chair and the bed. "We don't know. I'm thinking since he is recovering so quickly, it will disappear."

"What great news."

When the little boy sped close again, she reached and snatched him up. She stared into his big brown eyes. "Sweetheart, you want to go home?"

Christian squealed, hugged his mother tight, and put a slobbery kiss on her cheek. Then he kicked his legs as a signal he wanted down.

Laughter echoed.

"If the nurse could stay here with him while I pull up the horse and buggy to the entrance, I'll take Christian's things out." She laughed. "I'll surprise folks at home when I walk in with him."

The news wasn't so exciting when Valerie and Archibald Forsythe hurried into the asylum the next day. A guard took their identification. Another gestured and led them into the bowels of the asylum. Screams and raucous giggles from the women's unit pierced Valerie's ears, slicing into her heart.

She halted Archibald. "What on earth is going on in there?"

"There's no telling." The attorney shook his head. "Some of those women are greatly disturbed mentally. Others don't have a thing wrong with their minds but are going mad after being locked up. I'm determined to do something about those with a physical ailment instead of insanity."

"Put one person who's demon-possessed in there with them, and there will be problems."

"So true." Tenderness softened Archibald's eyes as he looked at her. "Walk past their unit as fast as you can and don't even look. Today's not the day to try to take on their problems. But we'll do it eventually."

Valerie quickened her pace, her heels clicking on the ancient wood floor. "You sound as if you believe this is a calling from God."

He nodded, the dark circles under his eyes distracting from his face, today especially showing the wear and tear of the courtroom. "I think I told you it is. It's almost a burning in me. Dillon has won a number of patients to the Lord. I haven't had the opportunity. Many of the doctors don't believe in God, but I've had some great conversations sharing my faith with them."

Valerie's mouth dropped open. The screaming volume forced her to plug her ears, but Archie's words rang louder in her head. Who knew the man had such a deep faith?

She was almost running now. They flew up the two flights of stairs. Dillon's unit appeared on the left. The guard who led them down the hallway took the wad of metal keys, puffing and out of breath while he unlocked the barred door.

Patients' bodies crammed together in front of the opening, their faces jammed against the window behind the bars.

"Move out of the way!" the guard shouted.

Others paced the room's perimeter like lions in a cage. Back and forth. Turning. Then back and forth.

"Move!" he yelled again. With a mighty shove, the guard opened the door.

"I don't know if there's room for us in there." Valerie suppressed a shudder. "Seems it's already overcrowded."

Archibald peered at the room, then at the guard. "Any chance Dillon and Pete can visit us in a meeting room?"

For the first time, a smile worked to the man's lips and stretched into a friendly expression. "Sure."

Archibald and Valerie waited outside the room. More than once, vacant eyes stared through the dirty barred window, and then the patients would turn and follow the crowd pacing, pacing, pacing, mumbling, pacing, groaning, pacing, talking to themselves, pacing, pacing.

"Some of them hear voices in their heads," Archibald explained. "That's why they talk to themselves. But many answer the voices they hear."

"I've heard about that." She shuddered. "One doctor recently called it schizophrenia. Sometimes the voice tries to get patients to harm themselves or somebody else."

"True." He wrinkled his brow. "But the majority of mental patients are not dangerous to other people. Frequently they harm themselves. I've seen arms all cut up by people trying to get evil bled out of them. It's tragic. You'd probably find scars up and down the arms of several people in that room. Too many are plagued by Thought Disorders and believe crazy things."

"Do you think they're demon-possessed?"

"From what I've seen, some could be. A Christian doctor who works with the insane said it's difficult to tell unless the demons manifest themselves as some did in Bible days. He prays for all the patients. Only God knows how insanity starts. More and more experts believe it has something to do with chemicals in the brain. But the science is so new, we can't prove these ideas."

Valerie's eyes narrowed. "Well, you've shown me at least two people who don't belong there—Dillon and Pete."

Archibald leaned toward her and cradled her sweaty hand in his. "I'm so happy to hear you say so. We're in this together. With God's help, we're going to get Dillon out, and perhaps we can get Pete into a place with a warm, homelike atmosphere for young people who have similar mental capacity. I'm hoping to help Jim, the paralyzed teacher, too."

The fire of his commitment burned in hazel eyes sprinkled with gold flecks.

Valerie nodded. "Yes. We need to get them out of here. Pete's already been attacked. Bubba's liable to kill him here."

"Bubba is their biggest problem. Once in a while, they put him in solitary, but they bring him back. They shouldn't keep him in any unit unless they strap a straitjacket on him and chain him to a post. Shock treatments could modify his behavior. It helps some of them."

The guard pushed through the patients and brought Dillon and Pete to the door. The husky guard looked down the hall. His baggy eyes rolled toward the visitors, his pale face worried, and hands trembling. "Follow me."

A few doors down the dark hall, he opened a door. "I'll let you meet in here where you can hear one another. Sorry. Standing room only."

Brooms, mops, pails, and clean chamber pots cluttered the tiny closet. The ceiling light bulb penetrated the darkness with an eerie glow.

"Ten minutes."

Valerie put her handkerchief over her nose a moment, breathed, and grinned, stuffing the lacy cloth in her reticule. "So tell us the news, Dillon. But first, let me tell you, God already answered a big prayer for me. My little Christian is walking and barely limps. He went home with us yesterday."

"Praise the Lord." Dillon's smile split his weary face.

Pete inched toward Valerie, looked up at her, and she held his hand. The boy's eyes twinkled as he mimicked Dillon. "Praise the Lord!"

Archibald nervously nodded. "It's wonderful. Her little son is such a special little tot. Now let's get to it. What's gone on since we visited?"

Dillon slid a wad of papers from under his shirt. "Thanks for giving me paper and pencil, Archie. I hide them under the mattress, and then I crawl under the bed and write. It's quieter there, and Pete likes to crawl under there with me so people will leave him alone."

His fingers quivered as he leafed through the pages. "The people are becoming skin and bones. Nobody gets enough food to satisfy the hunger. It's easy to recognize new patients because they aren't as thin."

Valerie edged toward him. "How about behavior? Has Pete been attacked again?"

"I've been watching Pete more closely." Dillon shook his head. "I think he got a bruised kidney when Bubba kicked him last time. Severely bruised."

Archie scowled. "The man should be put in solitary until they can control his behavior."

Dillon stuck his eye to the crack in the door. "So far, so good. Hope you can read my writing in case we're interrupted." He turned and flipped the page, rustling the paper. "Bubba choked Amos a few days ago. Amos already has trouble breathing. I thought he was dead when the guard and I stopped Bubba. I think Amos is still at the asylum's clinic. He hasn't come back."

Her stomach spasmed. "Not good. Somebody will be killed in here if we don't get action."

"We have a hearing set for ten o'clock next Monday." Archibald boldly drew a deep breath. "We need all the evidence you can give us."

Dillon smiled. "I've listed all the injuries I know occurred here, along with the date and the details I could come up with. I've noted major uprisings, problems with overcrowding, lack of sanitation, lack of privacy, lack of medical care and decent food. The swill we're fed is not fit to eat. We also have lack of supervision in the wards and even some brutality by the guards and nurses."

He shoved the papers into Archibald's hand. Archie flipped them under his shirt when a shout came at the door. "Get out of there!"

Valerie jumped.

Archibald stepped from the closet. "We needed a private meeting. One of the guards gave us permission to use this place. We can't hear or have any privacy in the ward, at least today."

The guard's long fingers gripped the pistol on his hip. "Are you the people taking the administration to court?"

Archibald shrugged. "I guess you could say so."

"Well, listen to this. You get out of here and leave these poor imbeciles alone. They have enough trouble without you disturbing them. Give the poor folks to their insanity. Then they won't have false hopes, and maybe they'll behave themselves."

Archibald pointed a well-manicured finger at the guard. "I could tell you some of these folks don't belong here and give you reasons why they don't. But instead, this lady and I will argue the case next week in court, and if God is with us, some will be released, and a few will go to more comfortable places."

"Ha!" The guard guffawed and waved them out of the closet. He grabbed Dillon and Pete and secured them with handcuffs.

43

Waking up on the ranch in his own bed caused John to raise a hand toward heaven like Polly and shout. "Glory to God!"

John dressed and hurried to the orchard first thing. He reached up and brought a nearby branch down to see it up close.

The peach blossoms completed flowering, and under each bloom rested a tiny nub waiting to turn into fruit. Joy surged through his belly. If these peaches grew, he'd have a great crop. Furthermore, the trees looked green and healthy. Snow and rain helped, but Abe's and Stu's hard work showed everywhere.

John gazed at the fields. Hay greened the land in the acres to the south. Out in the nearby pasture, his prize animals grazed or waited for a treat or a greeting as they stood next to the white fence, their coats shining, bodies looking healthy and well fed. Most mares either had a colt romping nearby, or their swollen bellies showed one was on the way.

"Thank you, Abe, for keeping the place up." He grabbed the old man's bony frame in a tight embrace. "You're like a second father to me. I love you, man!"

When he released him, Abe's eyes sparkled with unshed tears. "And you're like the son that's been away too long."

A groan shook Abe, but then he straightened, lifting his face to the morning sky. "God, take care of my sons wherever they be. Someday I'll see them again."

John nodded. "With you and Polly planting faith and the Word in them when they were little fellers, I'm sure they're all like young Abes, loving God."

"You's right, John."

Stuart romped up to them, grinning. "I have my book work done, and I'm ready to clean the barn."

John picked Stu up and whirled him around by his hands. Stu screamed and laughed until John set him down. "Today's your day off, boy. You and Abe did a great job while I was gone. Now have some fun. Might as well saddle a horse and go for a ride. I'm going over to Ed's house after a while. Want to go?"

"Sure. Sounds fun."

"Abe, first I'd like to discuss how you think we can find the killer."

Abe rubbed his curly graying hair. "I thought about it several nights. I keep coming up with the same answer. Pray. Then pray some more. The Bible says, 'Be sure your sin will find ya out.' The Lawd is gonna show us who it is."

John shoveled out the barn in record time. Working up a sweat felt good, but his stomach growled. Boy, was he hungry. He hurried to the house, washed up. As Abe prayed, John thanked God for the food, family, and friends, and then stabbed his fork into crispy fried potatoes, hotcakes with peach jam, and tender smoked ham. He topped it off with a cool glass of milk. The smell of coffee reminded him of jail.

Worry niggled his brain. If they didn't find the killer, would the sheriff be pounding on his door again?

"Come here." Edwina waved her hand toward where she stood beside her house while John and Stu rode into her yard on their trotting horses. A braid swung back and forth over her narrow shoulders.

John dismounted in a flash and helped Stu down before they sprinted to her side.

"Someone's been peeping at us again. I see his boot prints all around the house." Ed's tanned cheeks reddened while her blue eyes squinted with fear. Why hadn't he noticed her beauty before? Gorgeous, even with a braid and no curls? Perhaps thinking of romance made him an easy target for women. He'd have to rethink his desire for a wife.

"Where are the footprints?" He stared and visually searched the hard ground.

"The best ones are always in the soft dirt near a window. Be careful, or you'll step on them." Ed moved several feet away from the house and pointed. "Over there. Next to the house."

John approached the corner of the white structure. His eyes adjusted to the shade and focused on the peeper's tracks. In the shaded, damp, softer earth on the north side, large boot prints stood out so clear they could have been set in concrete.

His heart thumped, and his forehead broke out in a sweat. "Ed! These prints are like the ones left in my barn by the killer."

44

Sweat ran down John's face, and he wiped his cheek with his sleeve. "The design on the heel and the size give them away."

Edwina's mouth dropped open. "We have a killer hanging around?"

John reached out and touched her arm. "Now don't start getting upset. There probably are lots of boots like this around."

She glanced toward the barn and back again. "But you think they're unique. They could be one-of-a-kind made by a shoemaker. They were left by someone with big feet, probably tall, and most likely wealthy."

John knelt and traced their edges with a light touch.

Stu nudged his way close enough to see. "Or at least a big spender, especially for dressing up."

"These aren't run-of-the-mill boots." Ed leaned closer, resting her right arm on John's back. "I've seen this type of boot print before, but I don't remember where or when."

"I made a drawing of the prints in my barn right after we found the body. Looks like we need to measure and sketch these. Then I'll go home, pick up the other drawings, and go for the sheriff. Don't even let the dog or cat run around while we're gone. They might pick up a strange person's scent and ruin what we see here."

Max Mosely trotted into the yard on his Arabian mare, his battered cowboy hat perched on his head. "I'm ready to go to work today, ma'am."

Edwina smiled, lighting up her blue eyes. "You can put your things in the bunkhouse and your horse in the pasture after you care for her. You'll find plenty of feed and water in the barn and a place for your saddle."

John hoped this man wouldn't be a problem for Ed like Clyde was. But he wanted sometime soon to start an Arabian line himself. Picking up that mare for the price Max wanted would have been a steal.

Edwina patted her chest. "If you remember, I'm Edwina Jorgenson." She motioned toward John and Stuart. "These handsome men are John Lincoln Parks and Stuart O'Casey."

Mosely nodded and stuck out a hand to shake. "Good to see you again, John. You, too, Stuart. You folks look a mite disturbed. Anything wrong?"

John gripped the man's hand and then shook his head. "Someone who wears big boots has been roaming around Ed's property and peeping in windows. The heel prints match those left in my barn the day I found Billy Joe Garner's body."

"These are fresh," Edwina added, looking toward the house. "Someone apparently is peeping at night."

"Please keep a lookout for anything unusual, Max," John suggested. "We need to catch this guy."

"Yeh." Stu bounced on his toes. "Perhaps he dropped somethin'. I'm readin' a story 'bout Sherlock Holmes, and he looks carefully for clues. Maybe you could find the guy who made the boots and see who he sold them to."

"Good idea." Edwina nodded.

John squeezed her hand. "I'll be back, hopefully, with the sheriff. I have another idea, too, and we'll see how it works."

"Ma'am, I'll stow my stuff, and then you let me know what you want me to do first." Mosely headed for the barn.

John waited for the man to move on. "Before we leave," he faced Edwina, "I think we'd better talk with your father and warn Bellea. Could be whoever is hanging around is after her."

Ed touched the pistol on her hip. "I think so too. Bellea doesn't wear a gun or even have one. Most people who know me understand I can protect myself if necessary."

When they entered the farmhouse, Bellea's tiny David Jonathan, a miniature Wellington Davenport, lay in the middle of the kitchen linoleum on a blanket and propped on a pillow.

John laughed. "He's sure growing. He's still a tiny one, although he has a mop of dark hair on his head." He bent to the boy and braced his hands on his knees. "Do you like it being with the Jorgensons, Bellea?"

Bellea's red hair glistened in the light coming in the window. Her freckled cheeks pinked. "Things are going fine. Edwina and her father are a pleasure. I'm feeling at home here."

"That's the way we want you to feel." Edwina gave an emphatic nod. "You're family to us, too. If you don't believe it, ask Daddy."

Mr. Jorgenson wheeled his chair closer. "Yes. Bellea is a great blessing. I don't know what we'd do without her and little David. He's such a wonderful child. He keeps us laughing and having a good time, and Bellea helps us all."

David sucked on his tiny thumb, a contented smile on his round cheeks. John reached down and scooped him off the floor. John groaned, acting as if David weighed a ton. "You're heavy! What they been feeding you? Rocks? Concrete? Golden eggs?"

When the rest of the room burst out laughing, David smiled too, waving his chubby arms and dimpled fingers.

The tot squirmed, and John gave him a departing squeeze. "Keep growing, and I'll be back to give you a horsey ride one of these days."

Mr. Jorgenson's smile hinted at mischief. "Girls, I think this man is hinting for a dinner invitation for him and Stu." He folded his lap robe tighter around his legs.

John rubbed his stomach. "Well, if they invite us, we'll be here. These women are mighty fine cooks."

Stu giggled and rubbed his skinny belly too. "Yeh. I'm ready to come. Maybe we can play games."

"You're invited," Ed said, blue eyes big as she reached for John's hand. "I'm so glad you're home now. Your ranch and orchards are looking great. What night do you want to come? We're having chicken and the whole works tonight."

"Sounds wonderful, but not today," John said, almost getting lost in her eyes. "I have work to do, and I need to contact the sheriff again."

He spun to face Jorgenson. "I don't know if Ed told you, but you've had a Peeping Tom around here. She showed me the boot prints under the windows, and it's worrisome. The prints match the big boot prints left in my barn when I found B.J.'s body."

"How do you know they're a match?" Jorgenson arched a brow.

John sighed. "They're unusually large and have a unique design on the heel."

Jorgenson leaned back in his chair, tapping his fingers on the armrests. "If that's the case, perhaps all of us should carry a gun."

"Might not hurt," John muttered.

Stu and John said their goodbyes and Edwina followed them outside. John grasped her rough hand and edged her close. "Stay safe, and don't do anything foolish," he whispered in her ear.

Edwina puckered up and kissed his whiskery cheek, leaving warmth spreading through him. He smiled and turned to Stu. "Let's go!"

He and Stuart mounted and headed toward town.

45

On Monday, Valerie and Archibald stood in a stuffy echoing courtroom before Judge Karl Dougherty, a stern man with a bulldog face. Beside the two attorneys sat three patients from the asylum, their arms wrapped around their bodies in white straitjackets.

Dillon's leg chains rattled as he shifted. Jimmy Cook, the patient paralyzed from the waist down, rested in a wheelchair, slightly moving his upper body into a more comfortable position. Pete, mouth open, tongue visible and dripping, leaned against Dillon's side as if he were a life preserver.

"First, your honor," Valerie nearly shouted, "get these people out of these chains and straitjackets. None of them have harmed anyone, and they are not insane."

The asylum's superintendent stood. His bulging eyes glowed with rage. "These patients must be kept in restraint. They could have a fit and hurt two or three of you before we could stop them."

A rumble echoed in the courtroom.

"Have they ever had a fit and attacked anyone?" Valerie asked, her back stiff and her index finger pointing.

The aging superintendent raised his wrinkled double chin, the folds unfurling like a ship's sail. "Matter of fact they have."

A clatter of voices wafted over the courtroom. The judge pounded his gavel. "Order in the court. This may be only a hearing, but anyone who makes a disturbance will be taken out."

"Your honor, may I speak?" Dillon asked politely, although he appeared to be a wild man with his thick unwashed, uncut, lice-filled hair. His brown sparkling eyes stood out like beacons on his thin face. "I'll tell you when I almost hurt someone."

Archibald stood. His impeccable dark suit and white shirt contrasted with Dillon's ragged pants. "Let me introduce you to this lady and this witness." He gestured to Valerie. "This qualified attorney is Valerie MacDougal, one of the partners in the law office of Van Meter, MacDougal, and Forsythe. She and I have investigated this case for quite some time."

Several people in the audience leaned over and whispered to the person next to them. Valerie suspected they couldn't believe a woman would be qualified to defend anyone.

Archibald waited until he had their total attention. "This is Dillon Haskill. Dillon, please state your name, address, and how you came to the asylum."

Dillon put his chin down on his shoulder and attempted to get to an itch. A fearful rumble swept through the spectators.

"My name is Dr. Dillon Haskill." Dillon squirmed against the straitjacket. "I am a physician. Before a horse bucked me off in the State Fair Arena and I hit my head on a fencepost, my address was 121 State Street. I lived above my medical office. When I hit my head, the injury caused a seizure. Witnesses believed the seizure showed I am demon-possessed."

Low voices echoed, but Dillon continued.

"Instead of being taken to a doctor for the concussion I most likely received, I was taken to the asylum. I've been in the hospital four years. I've never suffered another seizure—or ever been seen by a physician."

"Tell us why your appearance here might add to people's fears," Valerie suggested.

Dillon's eyes drilled into the judge and then surveyed the spectators. "I haven't had a haircut since I was sent here. Although I've taken my shirt and washed it in the little dab of water they gave us, and I tried to bathe, you can probably smell all of us from where you sit."

"You don't need to get too personal," the judge instructed.

"Well, you should know none of us have had a bath or any sanitation. We have lice, and bedbugs and rats fill the crowded ward. The attendants wait to empty the chamber pots until they're almost running over."

The superintendent jumped to his feet. "Judge, if we gave them haircuts, they'd kill the barber with the scissors. If we brought in a washtub, some idiot would pick it up, water and all, throw it at the guards, and escape. Or they'd pull the handles off and beat the guards with 'em, and maybe kill somebody. One patient nearly killed a guard with a window handle."

The superintendent breathed heavily, prepared to continue.

The judge glared at him. "Sit down, sir."

The superintendent raised his wrinkled chin and stretched taller. "That man over there who says he's a doctor attacked a guard himself."

Dillon dropped his gaze to the floor.

Valerie stepped toward the judge. "Our witness is prepared to answer. Why did you attack a guard, Dr. Haskill?"

"We don't get enough to eat, and I could feel myself getting weaker. A patient, who probably is mentally ill or demon-possessed, kept hurting people, including our little friend here." He turned awkwardly toward Pete. "An inmate from our ward kicked Pete multiple times in the stomach and would have killed him if I hadn't fought him off. He kept yelling, 'He has the devil in him!' and kept trying to kick him. Pete has a birth defect, Down's syndrome, which causes him to look different and reduces his mental capacity, but he's smart."

Dillon cleared his throat and scanned the room again. "I studied mental illness with my medical courses. My father is a minister, and he taught me about real demon possession."

The superintendent sprang to his feet again "This imbecile doesn't know anything. He has demons himself."

Dillon ignored him. "May I finish?"

The judge nodded.

"Jimmy Cook over here has nothing wrong with him except he became paralyzed in a logging accident. A tree fell on him. He worked with a lumber mill during the summers, but he was a schoolteacher. He still can teach from a wheelchair. He is not insane, though he can't walk. I have this longing to not only help the people thrown into asylums for every diagnosis under the sun but also to help those who don't belong there get necessary medical treatment."

The judge arched an interested brow, folded his hands, and leaned forward. "But you attacked one of the guards and tried to escape?"

"Yes." Dillon nodded. "But that's why I assaulted the guard. He threw me in there like I'm a bunch of garbage. He's built like an army tank, but one day I couldn't take the filth, the violence, the disrespect, the misdiagnosis, and the swill we had to eat. I felt I had to get out or die, plus I need to help other patients. I jumped him and slapped him around with my dirty tin plate. Another worker came and saved my life because the guard fought back like a prizefighter. I didn't hurt the guard much. But I probably would've died anyhow if Archibald here hadn't given us hope."

Dillon's voice caught. He dropped into the chair next to Archibald, his shoulders rocking in the tight straitjacket.

"May I speak?" Jimmy Cook looked at Valerie. Since the straitjackets held his hands, she pushed his chair toward the judge.

"Your honor, let me introduce you to James Cook," she said. "He taught at Ambrose Preparatory School for nine years. Because books aren't allowed in the asylum, Jim Cook and Dillon Haskill taught little Pete here, and other patients, how to read and work numbers—using only the words and numbers they wrote on bits of paper or scratched on the wall with their spoons. People like Archibald Forsythe smuggled paper to them. Besides that, Mr. Cook told them stories from famous books, and Dillon Haskill sang hymns with them, shared Scriptures and Bible stories."

The lawyers rattled papers. People coughed.

Valerie faced the judge again. "May Jim Cook tell you his side of all this?"

The robed man nodded, obviously interested. "Go ahead. Give us your full name and address first, Mr. Cook."

Cook did, gave a short history of his education, and then he named awards he'd received in science and forestry.

When Cook completed his testimony, the judge looked around the room. "Any more witnesses?"

"Yes!" The superintendent's voice boomed and echoed against the high walls. "I call Dr. Henry Blackburn."

Valerie wheeled Cook out of the way.

The rotund doctor toddled forward. As he sat facing the crowd, he straightened his white cotton jacket over his bulging belly and then smoothed the pocket with his name boldly embroidered on it. He crossed his legs, his bushy white eyebrows standing up, and his bald head shining like a big ball bearing.

Dr. Blackburn stated his name and address, arched those bushy brows, leaned forward, and growled, "You might as well stop this circus now, judge. When we admit someone to the asylum, we've a reason for it."

He eyed Dillon, Pete, and Cook as if he wanted to peel the skin off their faces. "Have you ever seen a person have a fit like Dillon Haskill did? When people have those fits, they fall down, jerk all over, foam at the mouth, gnaw on their tongue, and some can hurt you even though they don't know what they're doing. I don't believe a little bump on the head can cause such behavior."

"What about this ten-year-old kid called Pete?" the superintendent bellowed.

The doctor puffed up the body that already threatened to blow the buttons off his white jacket. "Ever seen a Mongoloid who could read? These folks are making you a laughingstock, judge."

The judge didn't even acknowledge what he said.

Valerie calmly walked toward the witness. "First, I presume you're an employee of the state, Dr. Blackburn?"

"Yes. I'm chief of the medical staff at the asylum."

"What do you say, Dr. Blackburn, about this paralyzed teacher, Jim Cook? Is he insane?"

The doctor focused on the ceiling a moment. "Conditions like paralysis and much of the other insanity manifestations are caused by humors that upset the mind-body balance. They're the reason he can't walk. Not because a tree fell on him."

Valerie scanned the spectators, then turned her face the witness. "Dr. Blackburn, you gave us your name and address, but you didn't mention anything about your education or past experience other than working in this asylum."

"I attended several prestigious schools." A deflated demeanor took over from his face to his belly. He nodded as if assuring himself. "I studied under the famed physician, Rupert Dominique."

Her heart quickened. "Where does this Rupert Dominique practice?"

The doctor cleared his throat. "London."

"Oh." She nodded. "You're from England?"

The doctor stared at the superintendent, and then the judge as if he needed help.

"Well, no. I visited there."

Valerie raised her brows and frowned. "How long did you study with Dr. Dominique?"

"Oh, a long time. Several years."

"You could do that without living in London?"

Dr. Blackburn squinted at Valerie. "Who are you, woman, to question me like this? What do you know about insanity?"

"Witness," the judge interrupted, "answer the question."

The doctor whirled to face him. "I'm not on trial here. We're here to discuss the sanity of these imbeciles. These people are lying about the boy knowing how to read and count numbers."

Anger warmed Valerie's face. *God, give me control and wisdom.* "Doctor, I know mental health is a new profession, and the asylum has only been open a few years. What I'd like to know now is why the wards are like pigpens, why patients don't have enough to eat. What kind of treatment are you giving them?"

The doctor stood and gestured toward his patients in straitjackets. "One look at these folks and you know there is nothing we can do for them."

The superintendent stepped up and led the upset doctor back to a seat beside him. "I'd like to call Rev. Wolf Underwood to the witness stand."

The tall, skinny minister dressed in a well-worn black suit strode to stand before the judge.

"I'm Rev. Wolf Underwood. I've been a preacher for twenty years at Harbor Community Church. My wife and I live in the parsonage next door to the church."

The superintendent led the questioning. "Reverend, do you have experience with demon possession?"

"Sure do." He tented his long fingers. He worked his lips around and wiped them with a white handkerchief. "I've confronted demons many times. I probably could cast them out of the little boy over there."

"So you believe people with Down's syndrome or with less than normal intelligence and those who are insane have demons?" the superintendent asked.

"That's why the asylum can't do anything for them." Underwood nodded. "If they'd put me on the payroll, I could empty the place." He wiggled in his chair and sat straight up, his body glowing. "Jesus cast out lots of demons, and the people he helped became in their right minds like"—he snapped his thin fingers—"that." Then he grinned at the superintendent. "Oh, but you wouldn't let me. Then you wouldn't have a job."

"I'll ignore that," the superintendent answered, a frown freezing on his face. "Some experts believe people who are dangerous, harming themselves or others, often are demon-possessed and should be kept away from the general public. That's one reason why asylums are here. Tell us about the time you cast out demons."

The preacher smiled. "I actually only did this once. I probably could, though, if you want me to work at the asylum. They brought in this man who was hearing voices. I could barely talk to him because of what was going on in his head. He listened to the voice instead of me unless I said the name of Jesus, and then the demons would cry out, 'Leave us alone.' When I even came near him, he'd start shaking and scream, 'No! Leave us alone.' I'd been fasting and praying for days because I knew God had a work for me to do. I laid hands on him, and said, 'In the name of Jesus, every demon from hell that's in this man—go!'"

Tears streamed down the minister's face. "With a guttural cry, the man fell at my feet. I don't know how long he lay there, but I thought he might be dead. But then he blinked, sat up, weeping, and began praising the Lord. He never had trouble with hearing voices inside his head again. He became completely normal. His name is Webb Jordan, and he works in a Pittsburgh bank."

The courtroom was silent.

The superintendent cleared his throat. "Did you ever see a Mongoloid changed?"

"Actually, I never heard of it, and I'm ashamed the one man I told you about is the only genuine exorcism I've done. I've forgotten how God used me, and why and how he did it back then."

He pulled a white, wadded-up handkerchief from his pocket and blew his nose. "I had been fasting and praying for days when that happened. I need to do some repenting and see if God can use me again like he did when I was young and prayed up. May I be excused?"

The judge nodded. Rev. Jordan rushed for the exit.

The superintendent, now pale, walked to his seat and sat down.

Valerie stood before the judge. "I'd like to call Dillon Haskill, MD, back to the stand to bring some clarity to some of the things discussed here."

She scratched her forehead where she guessed lice swarmed. "Mr. Forsythe, would you like to take it from here? You've known Dillon for years."

Archibald stood, rubbed something off his impeccable suit, and shuddered in frustration. "This is another suit I'll have to burn because of the lice. I suggest people in this room who are close to these three patients remove your clothing as soon as you arrive home. Burn your clothes and take a hot bath with lye soap."

Dillon went forward to the witness seat near the judge.

"You've already been sworn in and gave your personal information." The judge gave Dillon a wary look. "You may proceed."

"Thank you, your honor." Dillon squirmed against the restraining straitjacket. "I think I should warn you, too, since some of you probably will discover you have the pesky critters. Body lice can cause skin infections and carry diseases such as typhus or trench fever. If your doctor doesn't have a treatment, take a bath in oils from the tea tree, which is a camphor oil. You also can use oil from cinnamon leaves, lavender, or eucalyptus. Peppermint oil might work."

A triumphant sparkle lit Archie's eyes. "Judge, does this sound like the imbecile the superintendent described?"

He let that sink in. Valerie scribbled.

"Dillon, as a medical doctor, how do you view insanity and the diagnoses of patients at the asylum?" Archibald asked.

Dillon looked straight at the judge. "Let's start with my problem. Hippocrates, the father of medicine, believed epilepsy is a physical disease and can be treated through natural methods. We know seizures can be caused by a birth defect, a brain injury, but also by a high fever, and if the fever goes too high, it could damage the brain."

"How do you know?" Archibald asked.

"Because a normal child or even a completely intelligent, normal adult who has an extremely high fever for an extended length of time often is mentally disabled afterward, or in the common vernacular, mentally retarded, if he lives. But seizures also result from injuries to the head, as I had, or an abnormality in the brain such as a tumor. But we sometimes don't know what causes the convulsion."

"So what do you believe causes some people to lose their minds and become dangerous to themselves and to other people?"

Dillon squirmed again, wiggled his shoulders, and pain etched his face. "My father was a minister. He had some experiences with people who were filled with the devil. Once a man came into a tent revival and tried to kill Papa. Every time Pop said the name of Jesus, the man started screaming and trying to reach my father's throat. 'Jesus, leave us alone!' the man yelled. Papa touched him and said, 'God loves you, young man, and in the name of Jesus, you demons from hell depart.'"

Dillon coughed. "The man screamed 'No!' and Papa put his hands on the man's head and said, 'In the name of Jesus every demon—go!' The man fell to the floor, and I thought he was dead. But then he stirred, praising God, thanking God and Papa for deliverance. The man became a deacon in our church, perfectly normal."

"What are your personal views of demon possession?" Archibald asked.

"My father had a theory, and I'm sure it's true," Dillon proclaimed. "Demon possession is a spiritual problem. Much of what they call insanity today is a physical problem. It could be caused by variations in the chemicals in the brain, which some doctors call humors. Mental disability might be a birth defect such as Down's syndrome. As I said, trouble with the mind could be caused by an injury or a high fever. I know most people who are paralyzed, those who have seizures, or some of the other patients at the asylum, have a physical problem."

Dillon nodded toward the attorneys. "Give me the list of diagnoses from the patients in the asylum who have apparent physical problems and are not getting help or treatment."

Valerie retrieved the list.

Despite his physical appearance, Dillon appeared the professional, although Valerie held the paper in front of his face for him since he couldn't use his hands. "I think I can read this," Dillon began, squinting at the paper. "They took my glasses away when I was admitted to the asylum."

Silence descended on the courtroom as the wild-looking patient stared. Finally, Dillon spoke. "The list is headed, 'The Eleventh Biennial Report from the Board of Lunacy Commissioners, dated 1899 to 1900.' First, I'll read some diagnoses that might"—he eyed the judge—"I emphasize *might* show insanity. Seven types of mania, affecting seventy-five patients. Forty patients diagnosed with five types of paranoia. Six types of melancholia and sixty-six affected. Nine types of dementia affected fifty-eight."

He took a deep breath, squirmed at the straitjacket, and then started on the list again. "Now for the questionable diagnoses. Thirty-nine patients admitted because of intemperance." He smiled. "I don't think those folks listened to Solomon, who wrote in the Bible, *Wine is a mocker, strong drink is raging, and whoever is deceived thereby is not wise.*"

Snickers drifted over the room, so Dillon paused.

"I know some alcoholics end up having delirium tremens but did these people see things that weren't there, or were they pitiful drunks whose families didn't want them around anymore and let them live on the streets? Then the cops came and brought them here?"

He searched the list again. "Eleven men and three women admitted with syphilis. End stage of this sexually transmitted disease can result in insanity, but are the patients held in an area separate from others to avoid spread of the disease?"

Under Dillon's condemning gaze, the superintendent squirmed.

Dillon tipped his head toward the paper. "Here are only a few of the ones I believe aren't a true diagnosis of lunacy. There are so many I think you wouldn't want to hear them all. But I insist on reading at least a dozen. Religious excitement." Dillon scanned the audience where low murmurs began. "Be sure and don't get excited about meeting Jesus and having your sins forgiven, or you could end up in the loony bin."

People covered their mouths to prevent laughter from exploding.

"Domestic trouble." Dillon cocked his head sideways. "Better be sure the neighbors don't hear arguments with your wife. You might be sent to the asylum." A low giggle swept through the crowd, some eyes grew large, and a few made faces at those nearby.

"Ill health and privation. Better not get sick or hungry."

The superintendent jumped to his feet. "This imbecile is again making a mockery of this court."

The judge faced Archibald. "This is an interesting list. May I see the paper he's reading?"

Archibald gave Valerie a nod, who handed it to the judge.

The hard lines in the judge's bulldog face softened as he studied the shaking paper in his quivering hand. "I'll read some of these to the court myself."

He adjusted the spectacles on his nose. "Jealousy. Sunstroke. Grief. Disappointment. Childbirth. Rheumatism. Injury. Suppression of menses. Excessive use of tobacco. Injury to spine. Loss of money. Christian Science. Cerebral hemorrhage. Hmmm. According to what I've learned, that is a stroke where people often become paralyzed on one side, and it may mess up their speech, but they don't lose their minds. I guess it goes along with 'injury to spine.' Paralysis is what we have here with the teacher, Jim Cook."

He lowered the paper, studied Dillon, Pete, and Jim, and then shook his head, and his eyes bore into the superintendent. "Who makes these diagnoses?"

"We have a team of doctors, and then I approve the ones who are admitted," the superintendent declared, his aged chin jutted forward, defiance blazing from his eyes.

The judge turned to the attorneys. "We'll start with these three patients here. Archibald, what do you suggest we do with them if we let them out of the asylum? Do their families want them?"

Archibald's eyes lit up, and Valerie's heart thumped.

Archibald boldly stepped forward. "Jim Cook has a family and probably can go back to teaching somewhere. Dillon can resume his medical practice. Both still have their homes. But Pete? Unless the asylum has it, we don't even know his last name. But he certainly shouldn't be housed with adult mental patients."

Archie took a deep breath, moved to where he'd left his notes. He picked up the pile, flipped through them, and walked forward with one paper flapping in his hand. "Your honor, we anticipated this. We found a home that cares for Down's syndrome people." Archie scratched his scalp, indicating he probably did have lice. "I knew about it because the house was in my neighborhood when I was growing up. I inquired first. I figured it wasn't normal for one family to have more than one person with Down's living there."

He placed the paper on the judge's desk. "This family has four Down's syndrome patients living under one roof. The father still works a job to keep expenses paid. One of the women living there is the homeowner's daughter, and she has the Down's birth defect, but she functions well. She's about age forty, and she helps her mother prepare meals. All the patients there help, even the ten-year-old boy about Pete's size and age. They wash dishes, work in the garden, and a couple of them know how to milk the cows and feed the chickens. I think the house was a boarding house in the past since it has six bedrooms. Patients keep their own rooms clean. But they're taught not to go into the front yard for fear of the neighbors, who would think they're demon-possessed."

The judge leaned forward. "Did you ask if they have room for another person?"

Archibald rubbed his ear. "I visited the homeowner. They have room, but they would want to meet him first." He walked over to Pete, helped him stand and gain his balance in the straitjacket, and then placed a hand at his back as he urged him toward the judge. "Pete, this is Judge Karl Dougherty."

Pete nodded. "Glad to meet you, your honor." His voice wobbled at a treble pitch.

Archibald handed the judge a paper with writing on it and allowed him to read it. Then he picked it up and held it out toward the boy. "Can you read this, Pete?"

Pete beamed, his almost electric smile lighting up his innocent face as he took the paper. "Sure." His short fingers grasped it. "For … God … so … loved … the world!" He lifted his chin and beamed. "I know the rest of it by heart. 'That he gave his only begotten son that whoever be–lieveth.'" He wiped slobber off his chin onto the shoulder of the straitjacket. " … in him should not perish … but have ever … lasting life!" His smile practically lit up the room.

"Thank you, Pete," Archibald said. "Could you tell us why you like Dillon Haskill?"

Pete's smile stretched between his small ears. "Dillon is like a brother to me. He takes care of me when I'm sick. He protects me from the bad guys." Tears filled his pale gray eyes. "I don't know what I'd do without Dillon."

The judge interrupted, "Would you be happy if you could get out of the asylum ward and live in a regular house and play and work with a child who is like you and about your age?"

Pete's face went blank.

Dillon stood. "Your honor, may I speak to Pete?"

The bulldog face softened. "Go ahead."

"Either Archie or I will go with you at first to see if you like the place and the people," Dillon said. "There will be no one there like Bubba."

Pete blinked, his open mouth wobbling as if trying to find words. "You mean it? A real house without mean people shoving against me, kicking me, eating my food?"

Dillon nodded. "Yes, Pete, and I'll come visit you."

"I'd sure like to try it."

Anxious to get home to her little boy, Valerie started picking up papers, thinking court was about over, but the judge wasn't through.

He shot a firm look at the superintendent. "I am going to contact the governor about things we learned in this court today. I'll send him a copy of the Board of Lunacy Report listing these ridiculous reasons for declaring a person insane."

He pointed his long finger at the superintendent. "I want you to see that these three people are deloused, given haircuts—under security—and hot baths and new clothing. Then I want them released and offered transportation to their place of residence. Little Pete will go to the home that welcomed him, as soon as the state agrees to pay for his care. In the meantime, we'll take him to see the residence and meet the family and allow them to meet him."

The judge turned his gaze toward Dr. Henry Blackburn. "Because of incompetency, I want Dr. Henry Blackburn released from his duties. I would like to see Dr. Dillon Haskill hired as medical director. He has accumulated a massive quantity of knowledge about brain disease and other ailments from his studies, but also from being housed among mental patients. I understand some of the wards, which aren't big enough, have had as many as thirteen patients in one small room.

"Dr. Haskill has four long years of interacting with people who lived there. If he desires, he can apply for the job, and I want to know the results in the future."

The judge blinked, his face flushing. "I forgot one important thing. From now on, I want young patients and those admitted because they are mentally retarded, in better words, mentally disabled, kept separate from others. In fact, you should also house dangerous patients in solitary confinement or at least away from the innocents, just as you do with patients in the forensic unit."

The superintendent, lips white, eyes bulged, jumped to his feet. "Where are we supposed to get the money and space to do all that?" He huffed, shook his head, and added, "Your honor."

The judge didn't even flinch. "Your present building was donated by a generous widow. Start seeking another building or donations to build, but don't forget to send a wire to the governor and tell him you're coming to see him to talk about my court orders. I'm sending the orders to him right away."

He lifted his gavel, but a cry rang out in the back of the room. "Your honor? Your honor? I am Franklin Bertrand Petric—a reporter from the local *Sun-Star*. Are you saying you are setting these three patients from the asylum loose to live free in the community, putting the lives of Boston citizens at risk?"

46

Darkness squeezed around Edwina's ranch, clouds budging themselves in front of the moon.

John tucked his blanket up around his neck. The cool, humid air sent chills crawling all over him. Nearby, Max Mosely snored like he'd slept on the ground all his life.

John flopped over on his other side, hoping a little sleep would come before daylight. He and Max had listened and waited for the peeper until Max collapsed on his bedroll. John thought of going home. But he couldn't put Edwina at risk, and he needed to catch B.J.'s killer.

The sheriff only seemed mildly interested the day before when John trotted in with a drawing of two prints from in front of her window and compared them to the drawing of the prints in his barn.

A high-pitched scream echoed in the night air. It tore through John's flesh clear to his bones, and the shrill screams kept coming.

Max jumped to his feet, one hand on his holstered side and the other on the shotgun.

"You go after whoever it is," John whispered. "I need to see if Edwina and all of those in the house are all right."

The screams continued as John ran. Two women's high voices called out to God, along with the baby's voice at top volume. He almost broke through the locked door. He pounded with his fist, his knuckles protesting in pain.

"It's me. John," he yelled. "What's going on?"

Edwina appeared, the belt of a pink housecoat tied around her slim middle. Tears streamed down her face. "I saw him! I saw him! He had some type of hood over his head and only his eyes visible. He peeked around the edges of the blinds. I didn't know you could see in at the edges. I heard something and opened the blind. When I screamed and kept screaming, he laughed, took off, and ran. I had my pistol out, but I shook so hard I couldn't aim."

Bellea walked in holding the screaming baby, tears sputtering out of her eyes like droplets from a dripping pump. "I saw him, too. When Edwina screamed, I ran in here. He was tall, had a hood on, and I think he had brown eyes. Those horrible eyes stared at us, and both of us only in our nighties. The way he stared made me feel naked."

Bellea wore a nice blue housecoat now, similar to Edwina's.

John took a deep breath and tried to slow his heartbeat. "Well, Max is out there hunting for him. We left our horses saddled, but when you screamed, I thought someone was in here."

Edwina apparently recovered from her fright. Now anger blazed on her face. "I'd have filled him with lead if he came in this house. At least one bullet would have stopped him."

John put his arm around her. "If you're sure you're all right, I'll jump on my horse and see if I can track where he went. Maybe I'll connect with Mosely, and we can bring the peeping scum in."

Edwina blinked, blue eyes red from crying, but now blazing. "Go. Hurry."

His saddle already in position, John jumped over the animal's rump and landed, his feet ready for the stirrups. In seconds, the horse galloped onto the road leading to town. Moonlight barely highlighted the gravel road's edge where the wild grasses, flowers, and sagebrush grew. He searched for a good place to hide, but saw nothing.

A horse appeared across the horizon coming toward him. His heart skipped a beat before he recognized Max on his Arabian mare. "I lost him."

Max shoved the shotgun into his scabbard. "Caught sight of him from behind when I first started out. But he already disappeared over the hill, and I never saw him again."

Frustration shook John down to his bones. "Could you tell what kind of horse the Peeping Tom had?"

Max pulled his horse up to the side of John's. "I couldn't see well. He was too far ahead. But from the distance, it appeared brown and husky like a quarter horse. The man rode tall in the saddle. I think if we had a better start, our mounts could outrun his animal."

The moon peeked between the clouds, ready to slip from the horizon behind the fir trees. John took off his hat and whacked it against his lap in frustration. "We might as well forget him for tonight."

He shoved the hat back on his head, looked around, and stroked his animal's neck.

"I'm going to head on home since I'm halfway there. I'll get a couple of hours of shuteye, do a few chores, and go back and check on the girls. I'll sleep on the ground again if that will help us catch him. Ever seen a boot with a similar heel?"

"I don't think I have, but a great cobbler in Denver makes special boots and puts his trademark on the heel. He might have made those boots."

"If this guy knows his boots have a distinct mark, why does he wear them when he drops a body in my barn or spies on beautiful young women?"

Max wagged his head. "He might have forgotten he wore them. Or maybe he's a nutcase and gets part of his jollies out of leaving a hint about his identity."

John twisted his face. "I've read about people like that, but it was fiction—not reality."

Max tapped his index finger against his whiskery cheek. "I wonder if he wears those boots anywhere else."

"Edwina said she's seen similar prints before, but she couldn't remember where."

John returned to the Jorgenson Ranch nearly four hours later, chores done, and he'd had a time of prayer and eaten a wonderful breakfast with Polly, Abe, and Stuart. As his mount trotted inside the Jorgensons' yard, Wellington Davenport stood on the back porch, dressed in his deputy uniform, talking to Edwina and Bellea. Paul Jorgenson sat in his wheelchair nearby, watching and listening.

John didn't greet Wellington. "What are you doing here?"

Wellington frowned. "Hello to you, too. I'm here investigating a Peeping Tom and examining the boot prints you told the sheriff about yesterday."

"Well." John blew out a frustrating breath. "Nothing like a sheriff who sends the fox out to guard the rabbit hutches."

Wellington skimmed the papers in his hand. "The drawings are about the same size and have the same design. I've been warning the women that we probably are dealing with a killer here."

Was Wellington really standing in the same yard with Bellea after all the time John spent trying to keep him away from her? "So you found Bellea and know the child's inside."

"When I knocked on the door, they thought it was you. After they opened it and let me in, it was too late for them to hide. But I mean them no harm. I'll not tell my mother the baby is here unless I'm sure she won't go berserk."

A fire lit in John's bones. "I'll believe it when I see it. Why don't you show me your boots and let me measure them?"

"Oh, John." Edwina's face flushed. "You know Wellington's feet aren't big."

John eyed Wellington's boots. "I'd like to look at one of them anyway."

Wellington sat, pulled off one, and handed it to John. A wide grin sneaked around on his face. If the young man would hang his tongue out, he'd look like a dog wanting to play fetch.

John took the boot and ran up the porch steps. "Hello, Mr. Jorgenson. Where will I find paper and pencil?"

"Hello, John. Thanks for spending the night trying to catch the Peeping Tom." Jorgenson rubbed his nose. "You'll find paper and pencil in the desk in the back bedroom."

John opened the door, picked up what he wanted, and returned to the boot. He drew a pencil around the sole, examined the worn heel, and then handed the boot to Wellington. "Looks a lot smaller. Exactly what I thought, but it's good to know since you were high up on my suspects' list. What size of boot does your father wear?"

Wellington's face paled, and a storm moved over his eyes. "He has bigger feet than mine. But he's not your man. He might not have liked Billy Joe, but he would never peep at women. He has better sense than that. He's no killer."

"Ever seen that type of boot heel before?"

"Are you the deputy or am I?" Wellington stood up straight and stared at John. "But I will answer. Edwina and I discussed it. We both think we've seen those heel prints before, but can't remember where. Sort of seems like I saw them in the churchyard. Edwina can't recall where she saw them, either."

"She told me that. So what do you know about the search for B.J.'s killer, who probably is the Peeping Tom?"

Wellington grinned, his old cocky expression working on his impeccably shaved face. "Last I heard you were the top suspect. I think Woody still believes you did it, but these boot prints have him stumped. He had no ideas at all yesterday."

Edwina stepped closer, her braid back into its customary place. "Have you gone around to the shoe stores and the boot makers to see if they've sold a boot like that? Or if they know a shoemaker who has such a trademark?"

"Yep." Wellington nodded, obviously pleased with himself. "Went to every store that sells boots and to the shoe man in town. Two of them told me of a boot maker in Denver who uses the trademark. His name is Cecil … Cecil Horvat! That's it. Cecil Horvat."

"Did you get an address so we could write him or wire him?"

Wellington's face flushed. "No. Guess I should have. I'm showing my inexperience. I need to go back. I think it was the cobbler who said that. Maybe I wrote it down."

Edwina shook her head in frustration. "I hope so."

Bellea stood beside her, trembling with fright.

"So, Wellington," John went over and stood next to Bellea, "are you going to leave Bellea alone? If not, I'll go in and talk to the sheriff today."

Wellington stared at Bellea, his face tinged with red, and then back at John. He took off his big brown felt hat and ran his fingers through his dark wavy hair. "I'm not going to bother Bellea. I'd like to give her money to support the child, but I know she won't take it. I'd like to see him provided for and be able to see him once in a while. After all, I know he's my son."

Bellea ran into the house and slammed the door behind her.

"Wellington!" Edwina shrieked. "That baby is being provided for, and Bellea is doing it by herself."

John hoped Ed would stop before she gave Wellington a verbal whipping with her sharp tongue. If the sheriff wasn't going to help, they needed the deputy.

47

When Wellington's sleek horse disappeared down the lane, Edwina inched toward John. "Bellea will be fine in a minute, but she still has lots of fear in her. Now. What new ideas do you have to catch the peeper?"

John wished she wouldn't look up at him that way with those blue, blue eyes. He glanced away a moment and considered Valerie's recent letter. She was somewhat entangled with the attorney she worked with. But she still wrote to John, sending affection, adding the news with sweetness and a trace of perfume. Yet he felt an uncanny attachment to Edwina. She needed him, and he needed to find the killer who peeps at innocent women. That's probably what was wrong with him.

He submitted to temptation and reached out and hugged her. After all, she needed comfort, and a little hug wouldn't hurt anything.

Two lines between her eyes marked her forehead, and her mouth pulled into a frown. "We're going to have to do better than we did last night. How about I make a bed on the ground out here around the corner from where the peeper usually stands?"

He squeezed and then released her. "I don't think I like the idea. Wouldn't be proper for one thing. But it might be good to have Bellea use your bedroom tonight. Leave the shades where he can peep in beside them. Both of you leave your clothes on no matter how late it gets. Then you stay in Bellea's room with your pistol ready. Move the baby somewhere else, maybe the kitchen. Even if you have to break a window to shoot, do it."

She tipped her face up at him again. "Are you sure that's what we should do?"

"If your papa is feeling okay, have him stay in the kitchen with a loaded gun. If I come to the door, I'll knock three times."

"Might be a good idea." A troubled frown crinkled her brow.

John rubbed her forehead to take the frown out. "Let's do some investigating. We need to find out where he kept his horse and made his escape."

Footprints led them to the row of trees and bushes in front of the house. The man had tied his mount where the Jorgenson's lawn ended. The boot prints went back and forth to Edwina's window and continued around the house.

"Ummm." He stared at her. "You've been assuming the fellow was watching Bellea? Apparently not. Most of the prints are by what you told me is your window."

Her eyes opened wide. "That's really strange. Before, he did lots of walking around the house. He must have been searching for my room."

"I need a rake." John scanned the yard. "We need to destroy all the prints from last night, Wellington's prints, and ours. We'll leave it clean so we can follow him next time."

Max curried a horse in front of the barn.

"Hey, Max," Edwina shouted. "Could you bring us a rake?"

In a couple of blinks, Max carried one toward them. "Got any new ideas for tonight?"

John grinned. "Well, I'll tell you one thing. If he slips by us tonight, I think I'll get out my bear traps."

Edwina clamped her hands up to her mouth and stumbled a couple of steps backward. "You wouldn't!"

"I think I will." John nodded. "They're no more dangerous than a bullet. After all, he's a killer, not just a peeper. We know that. Billy Joe didn't deserve to be killed, and his body dumped. I didn't deserve to be accused of murder."

She raised a pretty, well-shaped eyebrow. "Bitterness doesn't become you, John."

He laughed. "Ed, you haven't changed a bit. You still want to argue. Be careful, or I'll pull your pigtail."

"You wouldn't dare."

"No use showing our faults before Max." He took the rake from Max, turned the yard tool upside down, and began smoothing out the tracks. "Max, do you think we could wind some ropes around a few small trees between the house and where the peeper will tie up his horse, so we'd trip him when he starts to run in the dark? I'd rather be able to waylay him here, instead of having to chase him while we're shooting bullets at his horse's behind."

Max's smile curved his dark mustache. "We could dig a hole he'd drop into."

Edwina squared her shoulders and planted her hands on curvy hips. "I have a better idea. If I stay outside, I can sneak around and get rid of his horse."

Lights buzzed in John's head as anger surged. "Edwina, have you figured out that the man is after you and not Bellea? If he caught a glimpse of you, he'd have you in a flash and be gone. He's looking for you. Probably a secret admirer."

She wagged her head. "I think it's somebody we don't even know. I don't know why he'd be after me. I'm not beautiful."

"Apparently you didn't look at yourself recently. You're beautiful, and you know it."

"John, you're flattering me to make sure I don't come out and do what I'm capable of doing. I'm a crack shot, and you might need me out here to stop him."

"I'm not going to argue. If you don't like the plan I wanted to make, I'll go home and sleep in my own bed and leave you to this vulture who wants you."

Max stepped closer. "So you found where he kept his horse. I checked it out this morning and saw he'd tied it right beside the lawn and then hightailed straight to it after he peeped inside and found out we were there. Tell you what. I'll get rid of his horse tonight and tie two or three short ropes across different places, so when he goes for his horse, he'll trip. Or I could pull two or three fallen logs into his way."

John lifted his hands. "Sounds good. Whatever is the quickest and will make the least noise is what you should do. Then be ready when he trips."

"I hope there's no full moon," Edwina said.

That got John's attention. "I suggest you not use the overhead electric light if you have one in your bedroom. Light a kerosene lamp in the kitchen. Let it be the only light in the house. Leave the rest dark, so he can't tell you're watching."

Edwina grabbed the side of her head. "We have to get this guy."

John tapped her on the shoulder. "But we don't want to kill him. We need his confession."

48

The courtroom in Boston buzzed at the newspaper man's intrusion.

The judge leaned over his desk, his eyes filled with fury. "Have you listened to anything in this courtroom, Mr. Petric? When did you arrive? Are you hard of hearing? Well, listen up now, young man." He wiggled his index finger toward Archibald, Valerie, and the three patients.

The patients moved in front of the judge. Archie held the back of the wheelchair and Valerie stood behind them.

"This court hearing declares Dillon Haskill and Jim Cook competent, of sound mind, and free to live in the community. The court finds Pete intelligent, not demon-possessed, and able to live outside of the asylum with some supervision in court-approved housing. He will stay in the asylum tonight and maybe tomorrow night. When the home is approved, he can move there."

He pounded his gavel.

"Court dismissed."

Archibald immediately went to work getting the three out of the straitjackets. They all shook their arms afterward trying to get their circulation going.

Valerie hugged Pete, then bent over and wrapped her arms around Jim, who struggled to keep from crying. Dillon Haskill sobbed as she grabbed him and hugged.

He smiled at her. "Thanks. Sorry about the bugs."

Valerie lifted back her head and laughed. "Bugs are temporary."

Archie took his turn hugging the three.

Before leaving the room, the judge stood and motioned to Valerie and Archibald. "I want to visit the home where the family has invited Pete to live. Archibald, can we go there first thing in the morning? Nine o'clock?"

"Sure. I gave you the address. I'll drop by the family's house on my way home today and tell them we're coming."

When the judge disappeared, Archie spun to Valerie. "We did it!"

Valerie wiped an eye. "Praise the Lord!" She shook her head in amazement. "For a while there, I didn't know how the judge was going to react." Emotion took control, and her lip quivered.

The courtroom emptied. Archie snuggled her into his arms and kissed the top of her head. "I've lived for this day so long, but I know Dillon and Jim almost lost hope of seeing it." He pushed her away for a second and then brought her close. "We're a team!"

Valerie's heart quickened, but she didn't want it to. She tried to take control of herself, but when Archie pressed his lips to hers, her knees almost let her sink against him. She stiffened and drew back, blinking at him.

The courtroom face softened while victory, but also fear, shone in his eyes. "I–I–I hope the kiss was all right with you. It felt like it."

She nodded but wanted to run, get in her buggy, and hurry home. Yet she couldn't move. Archie seemed too vulnerable. She smiled. "I think we better go."

They left, holding hands.

The next morning, Archie and Pete met the judge at the home of Ferdinand Ferguson. "Come in, come in," Ferguson smiled at

Pete and extended his hand to the judge and Archibald. Then he shook hands with Pete.

"We're so glad you're here, young man. I presume they let you take a bath, wash your hair, and get a haircut. You look great. I heard the judge changed things at the asylum."

"The bath was wonderful," Pete grinned. He scratched his scalp. "My head doesn't even itch."

"Wonderful." The judge beamed. "Pete can only stay here if you approve and the state releases funds for his care. We'll leave him here a few hours and see if he'll adjust, and if you want him."

Ferguson leaned toward the judge's ear. "I'll take him even if I'm not paid."

"Wonderful. But we'll try to go through the proper channels first," the judge answered softly. "I could have sent someone else to your house, but I wanted to see it for myself and I'm amazed at how you've blessed these people."

"They tell me you know how to read." Ferguson faced the boy. "Come with me. I want you to meet everybody."

In the kitchen, one woman affected with Down's peeled apples, and another rolled piecrust. They looking quite contented talking with one another. An older woman with the syndrome washed dishes. All three looked up when they came in the room.

The older woman grabbed a towel and wiped her sudsy hands. "You must be Pete. We're so happy you are here." She came over and gave Pete a hug.

The boy's eyes sparkled.

Archibald hoped the asylum deloused him and the other patients as the judge had said.

"We have Anna over here washing the dishes. Betsy is peeling apples for pie. Cathy is making piecrust. These gals are good cooks."

Pete ducked his head and peeked at Archie. "I love pie. I tasted it when you brought some to Dillon."

Ferguson rubbed Pete's head with his big hand. "We have lots of pie here. Let's go into the parlor. I have more folks for you to meet."

In the parlor, a dainty little lady with black hair smoothed into a bun sat beside a boy about Pete's size. Both held colorful primary reading books.

"Pete, meet Joey." Ferguson gestured with his long arm from boy to boy. "And this is my beautiful wife, Bernice. She's helping Joey with his reading. What are you reading today, Joey?"

The child smiled. "*The Adventures of Tom Sawyer.*"

"Wow," Archie gasped. "She must be a good teacher. Pete here can read, but he didn't have a teacher who could have class each day. He also didn't have access to many books."

Mrs. Ferguson smiled at Joey, then at Pete, with kind eyes. "I help with the difficult parts. We'll have you reading *Tom Sawyer* in no time. In the meantime, you can listen to the stories."

Joey turned to Pete. "We can learn to play checkers. We also have Chinese checkers. But we can make up our own games, too. Hide and seek is lots of fun outside."

"I hardly been outside." Pete moved toward the big window and eyed the tree beyond, a mixture of fear and adventure in his eyes.

"I think you two will become great friends." Mrs. Ferguson set the book aside. "Why don't we show Pete where he'll sleep in your room?"

When Archibald and the judge left, Archibald was happy clear to his toenails.

That evening, he sent a dinner invitation to Valerie for Friday evening. When the delivery boy brought her acceptance, he hoped a new day had dawned.

The telephone rang, and Ferguson's shaky voice vibrated through the line. "The state picked up Pete, and by the way the man acted, I'm afraid for the boy."

Archibald rode over to Dillon's home, and in minutes, he and Dillon were on their way to the asylum. When they reached the ward where Dillon had been, two smug guards carried a blanket-wrapped body out of the room and turned toward the property behind the asylum.

"What happened?" Dillon asked.

"Who is it?" Archibald strode forward.

Bubba strutted up to the window, his nose twitching up and down. "I killed that little devil."

Dillon gasped. "You killed Pete? You killed Pete?" He shook the window bars. "I should never have left." A sob ripped out of his throat.

Tears ran down Archibald's face. "We shouldn't have trusted them to take him back." He gritted his teeth. "His blood will fuel our efforts from now on. We'll work until never again will a boy like Pete live in an adult asylum."

"They're burying him in an unmarked grave." Dillon pointed. "Let's go out there and give him a service."

The two of them gave a eulogy about a sweet boy who never hurt anyone and whose big heart loved even those who hurt him.

Dillon tipped his face toward heaven. "Jesus, you know how much he loved you. Now he's with you. But his body will rise again, and he'll be completely normal. No Down's syndrome in heaven. You said, 'I am the Resurrection and the Life. He who believes in me, though he die, he shall live. And whoever lives and believes in me shall never die.' Pete loved you, Lord, and I know you loved him also."

"Don't let him die in vain," Archibald muttered.

As soon as they left the asylum, they went to the newspaper office and straight to the publisher and told him about Pete.

"Will he do anything?" Dillon asked as they returned to the buggy.

"I think he will." Archibald pulled his white handkerchief out of his pocket to blow his nose.

49

Darkness descended rapidly on the Jorgenson Horse Ranch, and Edwina felt evil descend like the cloak of Satan.

But she resisted. "I can do all things through Christ who strengthens me. The steps of a righteous man are ordered of the Lord. He leads me beside still waters. Now, Lord, help us catch the Peeping Tom."

She adjusted the window shades to allow the peeper to see easily around the edges into her room, as John had asked. Bellea would go in there as soon as little David was asleep for the night. Pa cleaned his shotgun and prepared to stay on the porch after supper. Max had joined them.

"We sure appreciate your help, Max." She picked up his dirty pie plate. "You've lost a lot of sleep for me. Would you like more coffee?"

"Sure." He held out his china cup in his washed rough hands where grime still lodged in the swirls and lines on his fingers.

Edwina and Bellea finished putting away the last dishes when John slowly rode in, his horse not making much noise.

His boots barely scraped against the steps when he came up on the porch and tapped three times on the back door.

"Anything new going on?" He stared into her eyes, making her heart race, touched her hand, and then let go. "Now Max and I will set up our posts, stay out of sight, and watch to see where the peeper ties his horse. Max will let the animal go while I creep close enough to the house to catch the guy."

"Be careful." Her eyes caught his again.

"Did you gals trade rooms? Are you ready?"

"Sure are, as soon as the baby is asleep."

Each one took his post. And waited.

Ed stood next to the blind-covered window, peeking out. Occasionally she checked the ticking alarm clock on Bellea's white scarf-covered dresser, and each five-minute segment marked by the clock's brass hands dragged by.

Seventy-five minutes ticked off, one by one, and then motion disturbed the trees next to the graded dirt road. Moonlight shone enough to illuminate a tall man tying a horse to her lilac bush. She shifted, straining to see Max the other direction, mostly hidden among the flowers and low branches. His head drooped to the side. He was asleep.

Edwina ran her hand over her pistol and let herself out the rarely used side porch door.

Should she go after the horse first, or approach the man?

Her arm with the gun stretched in front of her as she crept. The tall man had disappeared. She stopped and squinted into the darkness.

Someone struck her hand, yanked the pistol out of her fingers, twirled her around, and clamped her nose and mouth shut so she couldn't breathe.

She twisted, tried to bite the fingers, stomped her boots, but missed his feet. His strong arms held like a vise. His hand slipped a bit, and she pulled a little air through her nose. She tried to scream, but it surfaced as a soft feminine grunt.

Lifting her to his chest, her captor took the reins, threw her in the saddle, and jumped on behind.

She screamed.

The horse burst into a gallop so fast she leaned back, and the hand clasped her mouth again. They shot down the road, the horse's hooves kicking up gravel. At the curve in the road past

John's ranch, they turned. Then they thundered toward the Weaver farm right into a shed beside the Weavers' plow and farm implements.

The horse huffed, panted, quivered.

One of her captor's hands stayed over her mouth while the other dug in his pocket. His fingers slipped off her face. She opened her mouth to scream, but then a big dirty handkerchief pushed in her mouth. She could taste that he'd used the filthy thing and gagged.

"Don't throw up on me, sweetheart," a familiar voice commanded.

Who is he? I know I've heard his voice before.

If only she could vomit. She concentrated on the filth in her mouth, gagged again, but nothing would come up.

John heard the scream, but where did it come from? It didn't sound like it came from the house. He ran to the back porch to where Paul Jorgenson sat in his wheelchair, holding the shotgun in one hand and stroking his neatly trimmed, gray beard with the other.

"What's happening? Someone made a noise filled with terror."

"I don't know. I heard something, too."

John ran to the other side of the house in time to hear a horse galloping away.

Bellea shot out of the house, screaming. "Edwina must have gone outside, and somebody has her. I peeked behind the blind and saw the man with the mask grab her. I was getting ready to break the window and scream for help when he threw her on his horse and got away."

"Where is Max?"

John ran to the front yard. Max sat on the ground rubbing his head.

"I dozed off, and someone hit me from behind."

"Did you see anything?"

"No. I'm sorry." Max wobbled as he stood. "I came to and wondered what happened."

He appeared to be uninjured.

"Bellea, explain to Paul what happened," John yelled. "If you feel like you can ride, Max, let's get going and see if we can catch this filthy killer."

He jumped in the saddle. Max gripped the saddle horn, slid his foot in the stirrup, and sprang into place.

Max's horse had a clear lead, and when John jabbed his toes into Dynamite's ribs and clucked, he took off, their mounts eating up the road like snakes swallowing mice.

Tonight John carried a fire stick ready to light. If he didn't catch the peeper as they chased him down the road, when the time was right, John intended to use the light and find his tracks, despite the darkness.

50

That evening in Boston a chilling wind blew but Valerie donned her new spring lavender dress anyway. The full flowing skirt let her high-heeled shoes with three bows across the top peek out when she walked.

Surveying her reflection in a full-length mirror, she sighed with satisfaction at her once-again slim waist.

Her curled blonde hair swept into a flattering updo, and she perched a small white hat with bows and one white rose atop her head—at an angle.

"You look beautiful," her mother purred, her cheeks flushed. "You and Archibald are finally getting together after all these years." She clapped her hands. "I know you'll be sooo happy. It was just the right time to end your mourning. You should have quit wearing black six months ago."

"Mother." Valerie swallowed. "He's taking me out to dinner. We're probably going to talk about winning the court case. Furthermore, I wasn't through my grief. I still miss Christian."

"Yes. But you are out of mourning now." Her mother winked. "He'll be proposing soon. He probably already has the ring."

"He had a ring before I married Christian."

Mother's grin widened. "That's how long he's loved you. Mark my words. He's never shown interest in another woman."

Tempted to challenge her mother, but deciding to let it go, Valerie checked her makeup and earrings one more time. Dressing up felt great after eighteen months wearing simple black gowns.

"You still writing to the horse rancher in Colorado?"

"Yes."

"Well, I think …"

"If I marry again, it will be between me, him, and the Lord. That's the way it was with Christian, and that's the way it will be if I decide to remarry."

Her mother drew back. She blinked as if Valerie had slapped her.

Guilt flooded Valerie's stomach, but she couldn't apologize and keep her independence. She threw a warm shawl over her shoulders and hurried downstairs. She'd wait in the kitchen for Archibald's knock.

She had settled into a kitchen chair when the strong knock vibrated the front door. Her parents' butler strode to the door and opened it. Archibald stood there, dressy felt hat in hand, every dark brown hair in place, a charcoal-gray suit perfectly fitted over his brilliant-white, starched shirt and a red tie.

His eyes bugged, and he gasped when he glimpsed her. He clasped her hand. "Valerie. You're so lovely tonight."

"Thank you." She puckered her lips into a little grin. "You don't look so bad yourself."

"I did the best I could." He squeezed her hand. "Makes me sort of feel guilty to remember the rags people in the asylum wear."

They stepped into the warm spring night, toward his buggy. "What was wonderful was getting rid of all those lice." She laughed, and then scratched the edge of her scalp. "Just thinking about lice makes me itch."

Archie shook his head. "You amaze me, girl, hugging those patients. God must have been well pleased. But yes." He shuddered. "Those bugs bother me enough I still get shivers thinking about them."

Chills ran over Valerie. "I think, when we continue trying to help patients out there, we should go to the judge and ask for an order to delouse all the patients. I heard they only bathed, gave haircuts, and deloused the ones in Dillon's ward."

As they settled in the buttoned padded seat, Archibald pulled her close. "Let's concentrate on our victory, God's goodness, and being together, not lice."

The darkness made her wonder if she should pull away, but they needed to talk. "I can't help but grieve for Pete. But we need to rejoice. You did a great work there. Even if Dillon and Jim are the only ones we rescue from the asylum, we can be thankful."

Archibald squeezed her shoulders. "Girl, we're a team!"

His eyes sparkled in the moonlight as she enjoyed the wonder of sitting close to him. Although he had courted her before, he'd never kissed her on the mouth until the other day in the courtroom. Could this usually sober attorney set off the fireworks as Christian had done, and as John came close to doing on the train platform?

She shifted toward him, took a shaky breath, and said, "We are a good team, Archie."

He jiggled the reins and signaled the pony to get a move on. Then he grinned at her. "You called me Archie."

A giggle gurgled from her, starting at her heart and coming out her mouth. "I did, didn't I? Is it all right?"

A hearty laugh burst from him. "Sure! I love it. I've been calling you Val now and then. Is that permissible?"

She shifted back against the seat. "Sure. I like it."

The traffic into the heart of the city increased, and Archibald focused ahead. "I think I can do better than Val. How about sweetie? Beautiful? Darlin'? Maybe Mama like Christian calls you?"

She laughed and rested her head on his shoulder. "Perhaps you need to quit while you're ahead."

He chuckled. "As long as you sit close to me like this, I'll agree to anything … well almost."

They walked into the restaurant together with Valerie linked to his arm and staying close.

They held hands over the table as they studied the menu.

"How about lobster tonight?" Archie suggested. "We need to celebrate."

Valerie's mouth watered. "Sounds good. It's been a long time since I had lobster. It comes with green beans with almonds and truffled potato salad. Must be delicious."

They kept holding hands until Archibald asked the Lord to bless the food. All the while Valerie broke the lobster tails, dipped the pink meat into the warm butter, she took peeks at him. Was he this handsome when he tried to win her heart before? She thought not. The old Archie couldn't compete with Christian, and probably not John. But this mature, handsome gentleman, dedicated to the Lord, kept getting higher on the chart.

She chewed the delicacy and swallowed. "Archie, I didn't really know you when I was young. We saw a lot of each other, what with you working in Dad's law office and us going out a few times. I couldn't get it out of my head you were my daddy's partner."

Archie shifted and pulled at his tie. "And I saw only the daughter of the man who held my future in his hands."

She smiled. "I'm getting to know the real man you are, and I like what I see."

The person across the table from her sat taller, and the candlelight glistened in his dark eyes.

"I have to admit I thought I loved you then, but what I see before me tonight is a woman beautiful inside and out—the kind of woman I want."

They held hands on the way home, but both sat in near silence. What else could they say?

Her dead husband Christian's face popped before her, then John's. She remembered his last letter thanking her for going to Peachville to help him get out of jail. But something wasn't clicking. Was it little Christian having a new father? Archie was so comfortable with the little tyke and had been so attentive and understanding when he was in the hospital. He had a connection with little Christian that John didn't have. Did she let their relationship go on too long and get too serious?

She loved Colorado and the country. But did she really love John?

When she and Archibald said goodnight at her home, he lightly kissed her cheek. Disappointment stung her heart.

51

The clouds blew away and moonlight lit the road as John and Max rode up and down Thirty-Ninth and Fortieth Lanes on Peachville's Mesa. They rode past a half dozen farms and peach ranches and didn't sight the peeper again. Then they hit the highway and rode on, scanning for tracks going off another direction.

Frustration tied John's emotions into a frazzled web. If he could just think. They couldn't disappear without leaving some sort of trace. *They had to be right in this area.*

He took off his hat and whacked his leg with it. "I can't figure this out, but we can't give up."

Max drooped in his saddle. He turned and stared at John. "We're about out of the county. We're almost up to the road to White Water. Surely, he didn't get out this far."

"He's hiding somewhere." John ran his fingers through his hair and mashed his hat back on his head, which pulsed with a headache. "We've been at this for almost two hours, going up and down the road. I've used the light and haven't seen an interesting track going off the road except those heading to the ranches and farms. You have to work tomorrow. Why don't you go back to the Jorgenson's'? If there's still a light in the house, check in with Paul Jorgenson and Bellea. Tell them I'm not giving up until I find Edwina. Do the important chores, and if I'm not back in an hour go into town and ask the sheriff to get a posse to help us search. Then stop by my ranch and tell Abe and Polly where I am. They'll pray."

When Max turned to go, John spurred his horse the opposite direction. Edwina's blue eyes filled his brain, and his heart thumped with concern. His rapid breathing kept rhythm with his heart. Could this be more than worry? Had he been around the gal too much with Valerie hundreds of miles away? He should have proposed to Valerie by now if he intended to marry her. His gut twisted. Valerie changed when she started working on the court case with that attorney.

Archibald! How could a beautiful woman like Valerie fall in love with a man named Archibald? John pictured him resembling a barrel, a gold pocket watch chain hanging on his too-small vest. He'd guess Archibald had a shiny bald head. Maybe a ring of white hair circled the bald spot, and bushy white eyebrows and mustache to match.

He shook his head. He needed to get the vision out of his mind and watch more carefully for tracks. Archibald could be a handsome man and he could be passing by the hiding place.

For another hour, he searched. The sun crept over the hill, little by little illuminating the beautiful valley below the high mountains. The mountains still wore white shawls of snow over their shoulders. Pain twisted his insides. Where should he go next?

Lord, guide me.

He headed for the river and crossed the covered metal bridge connecting the lowlands with the higher mesa he'd searched. The horse's hooves rattled the bridge, making it sway a little. It didn't bother John. He'd been over it too many times to count.

The river flowed low today, probably because water was released recently into the canals.

Where would be a good place to hide?

The image of the Swenson's large packing shed out by itself on the lowlands by the river road flashed into his vision. Little more than a roof held up by four-by-fours, the place always had dozens of wooden boxes and bushel baskets stacked around where a person could hide.

He didn't see a soul working yet among the orchards or fields. Radishes, lettuce, spinach, peas, and other early crops flourished nearby. He pulled Dynamite into a slow walk and approached the shed. Was it his imagination, or did someone move in there?

He slid out of the saddle, tied his horse, and dropped to his stomach, his gun drawn.

Guilt swished around in Valerie's blood while she cuddled her son to her bosom at home in Boston. The child awoke when she checked on him after she came into the house, and it was a perfect excuse to hold him.

Yet the peace she usually felt when she held him wasn't there. How had Archie worked his way into her heart? She didn't like city life. She loved wide-open spaces like the Colorado homestead. She envisioned the house, her flowers, her garden, the barn, all before the fire.

She'd rocked the tyke to sleep, but didn't want to put him down. Finally, peace and joy flowed through her—until she remembered a simple wooden grave marker. Grief nearly overwhelmed her. How could she marry Archibald when her husband's grave rested alone in Colorado, with no one to pull weeds and care for flowers since Jenny and William moved to Iowa?

Well, they hadn't moved everything yet. Seems they had trouble in Iowa getting things settled with the stepmother and her family. So they left Stuart with John.

Strange, but from what John said, they'd be back for him. They loved the kid, but from the way he talked, John was attached to the boy himself.

She winced as she remembered how she held Archie's hand last night and wanted him to kiss her. The two of them connected with their minds, their hearts, and their future. They were committed to help the asylum patients but connected by more. Why the guilt?

Was it for Christian, her husband? *But he's dead. He would want me to make a new life and provide Christian with a godly father.*

She brushed her cheek against her son's then leaned back to view his innocent sleeping face, his long blond lashes resting on his chubby cheeks, his pink puckered mouth so wonderful, and his fingers grasping hers. How she loved him.

Thank you, Lord, he's recovering from the accident and the limp is almost gone. I think Archibald loves him, too, don't you?

Her eyes flooded, but she would not cry. God had been with her so far, and he'd be in her tomorrows. *But how could she tell John Parks she thought she loved him, but now she loved another?*

Finally, she nestled Christian in his bed and gently covered him. He raised his spindly arms, stretched, but didn't open his eyes. She patted his chest, and after a few breaths, he relaxed.

She pulled out the chair to her desk, sat, picked up pen and paper, and wrote, "Dear John."

No other words would come from her ink-filled pen. How men hated Dear John letters! Why did his name have to be John?

She wadded the paper, took a clean, creamy perfumed sheet, and wrote, "Dear John Lincoln Parks."

Her head wagged in disgust. She stood and snatched her nightie from the drawer. Could there be another way to tell him? Besides, Archibald hadn't proposed yet.

But he would. She didn't doubt it one iota.

52

Voices came on the breeze from the peach packing shed. Using his elbows, John crawled closer to hear the people inside.

He stopped and couldn't move another inch. Big boot tracks with a special heel design dented into the muddy earth. The prints matched the ones the murderer scrunched into the dust and manure on his barn floor.

Perhaps the wet irrigated earth beneath him, or the sight of the boot prints caused terrible chills to shake his body. The hand holding the revolver wobbled.

John dropped his head against his arm and whispered, "Lord, help me. The murderer is here. Edwina's life is in his hands."

"Quit struggling, Edwina," a deep male voice crooned. "You're making yourself weak and tired. I want you full of love and energy for our honeymoon."

Who is he? He'd heard the southern twang before.

John stuck the gun into his holster, put his knees into the mud under him, and crawled like a wolf ready to attack. He halted close to the new peach crates along the shed's west edge, hoping whoever it was didn't notice the motion.

After what seemed like forever, he leaned around the boxes. Edwina sat tied to a leg of the conveyor belt.

"I don't dare take away the gag," the man said, still talking in low tones. He dragged a box near where Ed's head was thrown back, resting on the contraption. The man dropped to sit on top a wooden fruit container he'd turned to make it taller. Edwina's cheeks blazed almost as red as the blood trickling from her scalp.

The sun hadn't come up enough to light the shaded section over the man's face. "I had to hit you in the head so I could hold you on the horse. You wouldn't hold still."

Fury belched from John's heart to his head. He pulled the gun and aimed. With one shot, he could rescue Edwina.

Then the man turned toward John. John ducked behind the boxes, and his heart nearly stopped. *So that's who the peeper is! Oh, no. He murdered Billy Joe! How could he?*

He'd never even thought of him. Then he remembered the ace from a card deck Abe found in the barn near the body. Things made sense. John had heard this man spent hours in the Rusty Wheel playing poker. Billy Joe probably cheated him. The ace probably fell from B.J.'s sleeve when the murderer dumped the body.

John listened and gripped his gun, hoping he hadn't been seen.

"If you promise not to scream, I'll take out the gag. If you scream, I'll have to shoot you."

John leaned around again as Edwina nodded and the man took out the gag. She coughed and growled for water.

The man lifted a canteen to her face, screwed on the lid, and set it aside. He patted her back, snuggling close.

Edwina twisted against her bond. "Clyde Merriweather! Are you out of your mind? You've been peeping on Bellea and me! Why?"

"We's gonna have a great marriage, honey. Y'all will wish you loved me earlier. Soon's I get your face all cleaned up, we'll go to Parson Delaney, and he'll marry us. I already went to the courthouse and got the license. My sister went with me and signed your name."

Clyde squeezed in closer to Edwina. "I've loved you since the first day I saw you." He grabbed her face and tipped it toward him, then kissed her full on the mouth.

Edwina spit right at him and gagged.

Clyde's big right hand smacked her across the face, hard. The slap's sound assaulted John as well.

Her head dropped to the side, as if unconscious.

John aimed his weapon, his hand shaking with anger. Did he want to explain another dead body? He contemplated that and asked himself how else he could save Edwina. *I need help, Lord. The Bible says you direct the footsteps of those who love you. Help, Lord!*

Finally, Ed stirred. The brute's hand gently rubbed where he'd hit her face.

Then she lifted her eyes and squinted. "Clyde! You know I'll never marry you. I'm in love with John Lincoln Parks. If you think you can force me to marry you, then go ahead and kill me. Being married to you would be worse than death."

John's heart skipped a beat.

Clyde laughed. "Well, sweetie, I knew a long time ago you ached for John. Right after he moved back on his ranch, I knocked down his fence, and a couple of my friends let all his horses out. I should have taken the ax to him instead of the fence."

Paralysis crept into John's mind and body. Clyde worked against him so long ago? His sister had been in more danger than he knew. Even Edwina.

Movement flickered behind him. Several horses pulled up to the ranch house. The posse!

When Clyde moved the other direction, John lay on his stomach and lifted enough to motion for the posse to come their way. Then he crept back to keep his eyes on Clyde, who now took Edwina's hands, petted them, and kissed them.

She grimaced and stretched, trying to wipe his kiss on her pants.

Out of the corner of his eyes, John saw Sheriff Woody, Deputy Wellington Davenport, and the rest of the posse spread out among the fruit trees. A cherry orchard, apricots, and acres and acres of peach trees flanked the vegetable fields and the packing shed.

Yet how could they rescue Edwina without somebody getting killed? Clyde's revolver rested in the holster within inches of his hand, and a rifle leaned nearby against the peach conveyor belt.

John pointed his gun again, keeping a bead on Clyde's upper body.

Backs turned inward, Sheriff Woody and Wellington stood at the corners of the shed now, guns ready, but kept behind the stacked fruit crates except when they peered inside.

"I knew you were stuck on John Lincoln Parks." Clyde's voice rose louder and angrier. "And you didn't keep it a secret. You acted like a lovesick bird every time he came around. When you squeezed up against him in church instead of sitting by me, I decided to kill him."

Edwina's mouth dropped.

"Don't ya look so all-powered horrified. I bought a little bottle of arsenic from a doctor in Dandelion Corners. I told him I had syphilis, and he sold it to me, 'cause some docs think it cures it. But I also soaked rat poison in water and mixed the strychnine with the arsenic. And I left the left over rat poison under one of the bushes in John's yard for evidence.

"During the Horse Association meeting at the Rusty Wheel, I bought John and a few other guys drinks."

Edwina gasped. "John doesn't drink liquor! You should have known."

"While no one was looking, I poured all the poison into his drink. I thought I could prod him into drinking it by calling him a coward, a sissy, and poking fun at him. But he went over to talk to the speaker about raising purebreds. B.J. guzzled his own drink down and drank all of John's poisoned whiskey before I could stop him. B.J. deserved it anyhow. He'd cheated on me at cards for years. I knew it, but couldn't prove it."

"So that's how Billy Joe died." Edwina shook her head and kept shaking it. She gritted her teeth and jerked at the ropes that held her.

"I almost got even with ol' John by dropping Billy Joe in his barn. I would have, too, if the sheriff weren't soft in the head."

Clyde worked his way closer and began massaging her arms. "Don't worry. I don't want to kill you. But I will if you don't do what I say. Understood?"

She nodded.

He turned and relaxed.

John stayed out of sight, but he stuck his pistol in a gap between boxes, took aim at Clyde, and readied the hammer. "Drop your weapons, or I'll shoot," he shouted. "Don't you hurt her again!"

In moments, Woody and Wellington, also hidden behind boxes, had their guns pointed at the murderer. "We heard it all, Clyde," Woody shouted. "Drop your weapons to the ground. You're under arrest for killing Billy Joe Garner and kidnapping Edwina Jorgenson."

Clyde twirled and leveled his pistol against Edwina's head. "Move an inch, and she's dead."

53

The huge black headline in the Boston Sun-Star glared at Valerie when she picked up the morning newspaper to give to her father.

Asylum Patients Set Free.

The lead sentence under Bertrand Petric's byline stated, "Over the protest of the superintendent and advice of the medical director, three patients were released into the community from the Insane Asylum on Monday."

Heated anger burned Valerie's face. Did she dare read further? Her fingers lingered on the top of the page.

The phone rang. She hurried to the study to pick it up before the person gave up or people on the party line took over the connection. "Hello? Valerie MacDougal here."

"Valerie! So nice to hear your voice. This is Archibald."

Her heart quickened at his deep cello voice. "Oh, Archie! Did you see the newspaper?"

"Sure did. The whole article is negative. Petric didn't even talk to the judge, us, Dillon, or Jimmy Cook. I called the newspaper this morning to complain and connected with the executive editor. We are meeting with the editorial board early tomorrow morning. Anyway, I hope you'll go with me."

Valerie smiled, even though Archie couldn't see her. "I'll be there. We're taking Dillon and Jimmy Cook with us, I hope."

"Planning on it." The line went silent a moment. "You know Pete's dead. Bubba killed him."

"Yes. You called, but so much has been going on, I forgot." Her voice caught. "How could I forget Pete?"

"Valerie, I'd like to take you out to the country with me today. Our cook is already making a picnic lunch. We could stop and talk to Dillon and Jimmy on our way out of town."

A ride into the country? When did Archie decide he liked wide-open spaces instead of the city's skitter-scatter and noise?

"How about bringing Christian with you?" he asked.

A lump formed in her throat. How did he know she hated to leave Christian? She'd already been away from him too much. She listened to her heartbeat, afraid to speak.

"I haven't seen Christian in so long!" The cello voice went on. "I don't want him to forget me."

Valerie's smile burst on her lips again. "He won't. You've made a big impression on him. He loves the outdoors, and I'll be beside myself in the country."

"Pick you up about ten thirty?"

Valerie glanced at her reflection in the mantel mirror and grimaced at her messy hair. "Sure. I think I can be ready by then. Mother already has Christian up and eating breakfast."

Nearly three hours later, they stood in the boardinghouse where Dillon had taken a room. Valerie didn't recognize him at first. His freshly cut hair gleamed and lay in waves flowing back from his clean-shaven face. He looked so handsome, she had wondered who he was.

"Dillon?"

He spread his arms. "This is me." He rubbed his chin. "I feel kind of naked but so clean."

"You look way too thin." Archie frowned. "I hope Gertrude fattens you up."

Dillon came out on the porch, wearing an obviously new, checkered cotton shirt, blue pants, and jacket. His new shoes reflected the sunshine.

"You two get rid of the lice?"

Valerie scratched her head thinking about it. "Wasn't sure I had 'em. But our housekeeper burned my clothes, and I'm deloused."

"I burned my suit myself." Archie gave an emphatic nod. "Should have asked Phoebe, our housekeeper, to delouse and save it so I can use it when I revisit the asylum. But I couldn't bring myself to ask her to do it."

Valerie carried Christian in her arms. "Did you see the newspaper?"

Dillon peered down the street and then back at them. "Yes. I expected something like that. That's one reason I stayed in the boarding house. People probably will be looking for me."

"Will you go with us tomorrow to a meeting with the newspaper's editorial board? We'll pick you up."

Dillon grinned, his dark eyes sparkling. "I'd love to."

When they stopped to see Jimmy Cook and his wife they looked so happy. But they also had seen the article.

"Not a thorough piece of reporting the news," Jimmy said.

"We're meeting with the editorial board in the morning," Archie said.

Jimmy beat his fists on the armrests of his wheelchair. "Sounds fantastic. I wouldn't miss it!"

After briefly discussing the meeting with him, Archie, Valerie, and Christian took off down a dusty road for the country.

Blankets of green covered the fields, the hills, and the forests beside the meandering highway where Archibald's pony pulled the carriage, bouncing over bumps, ridges, and potholes.

Valerie tucked her hand under his arm. "How did you guess how much I love the country?"

He squeezed a smile between his slightly whiskered cheeks. "I know you miss the wide-open spaces you had at your Colorado homestead." He shook his head. "Kind of unusual for an attorney."

She briefly touched his hand holding the reins. "Colorado is a wonderful place. But I enjoy many things about Boston."

Little Christian babbled constantly and pointed a tiny finger at cows, horses, sheep, dogs, and flocks of birds. Excitement intensified when he spotted a train crawling over the horizon like a caterpillar.

"Choo! Choo!" he cried, trying to jump up and down in her lap.

Archie pointed and joined Christian. "Choo! Choo!"

Valerie added her choo whistle to theirs, and they all broke down laughing. Christian giggled until Archie couldn't keep going with the train sounds and silliness and drive the pony.

Coming up on the right sprawled a huge red brick, two-story house trimmed in white, its many windows gleaming, and the manicured grounds gorgeous.

The carriage slowed and then stopped. "Looks like all the amenities of the city would be available in a fancy house like this," Valerie remarked.

"Would you like to live there?" A mischievous smile twitched his cheeks.

"I'd love it! I wonder what it's like inside. I can almost imagine the shiny, curvy banister next to the winding stairway."

Archie gripped her hand. "Would you like to see inside? I know the owner. I even have a key. It's a brand-new house and almost finished."

"Really? That would be great fun!"

Archie took Christian in his arms and then helped Valerie out of the buggy.

"The owners must have children," she commented as they stepped on the long walkway to the house. She pointed. "See the swing hanging in the tree, Christian?"

Archie pointed. "The property has a nice caretaker's house, too, and the caretaker's family moved in already. It's the smaller home nestled next to some outbuildings."

When he opened one of the big double mahogany doors, Valerie gasped. "It's more beautiful than I imagined. There's the staircase I thought would be here. The entry and the rooms are huge."

They wandered through the downstairs, and then went upstairs. Archie paused in front of a blue room. "This is their son's room."

Valerie stepped inside. "Nice. Their son will really like this rocking horse."

He put Christian down. "Would you like to look the horse over?"

His dark brown eyes shining, Christian toddled with barely a limp over to the horse. He patted it on the back, and then rocked it back and forth with his hand, smiling.

Archibald turned toward her and dropped to one knee. "Valerie, would you and Christian marry me?"

Her heartbeat shook her ribs erratically like a snare drum in unusual rhythm. She couldn't speak.

"This is my house. I bought the land before you fell in love and married the first time. It took me awhile to recover when you rejected me then. I doubted I would get married at all, but my faith grew. I knew God would send me a good wife sometime. When your husband died in the fire, I built the house on faith for you or someone else God will send."

Valerie considered that, watching Christian rocking the horse. She walked over, lifted him onto the toy, and held on to him as he rocked back and forth.

"Me do," Christian said. "By myself."

She let him grasp the handles, and he rocked and rocked, smiles crinkling his soft cheeks.

Archie stood and gripped her hand in his sweaty one. "I don't want you to marry me because I built the house. I love you and Christian, and I hope you love me. But it's now or never. It's either me or the other guy—that rancher, John Lincoln Parks."

54

Sweat beaded Edwina's face, the weapon cold against her hot forehead. Pain shot in bursts from her bound wrists, and the prickly ropes burned her stomach through her clothes where Clyde tied her to the leg of the conveyor belt.

She wriggled again. Something loosened!

Sheriff Woody stepped into the peach shed. "See this badge? Drop the gun, Clyde Merriweather."

Clyde's pistol shook a little. "You're gambling with this girl's life, sheriff."

She twisted away from the closeness of the man's stinky body. Gun still drawn, John stood at the edge of the shed next to several stacks of bushel baskets. He looked straight at her, motioned with his head and, taking advantage of Clyde's turned back, took off around the corner, and disappeared.

She needed to create a distraction. "Clyde," she purred as sweetly as she could. "If you're sure it's what we should do, I'll go ahead and marry you. I'll need to clean up some."

Clyde relaxed against her. His gun dropped a few inches and pointed away as he looked down at her instead of Woody.

"That's the girl," Clyde grinned. "I knew you loved me!"

A noise rumbled nearby, and then dozens of wooden peach crates and bushel baskets crashed, tumbled, and rolled toward Clyde.

He ducked to keep one crate from hitting him in the head. When he did, the gun came within Edwina's reach. She raised her tied hands and slammed down hard against the gun. It whirled out his grip and flew among the baskets and boxes.

Within seconds, Woody and Wellington pounced on Clyde, jerked his arms behind him, and clicked handcuffs.

John rushed to Edwina. He holstered his gun and knelt before her, slicing through her bounds with his pocketknife. "Are you all right?"

She couldn't speak. She laughed and cried at the same time as he helped her to her feet and hugged her tight. Her numb arms circled his neck. John began kissing her tears away, down her cheeks, toward her ears, and finally to her lips.

Nearby the posse and the farmer jawed about the confrontation, Clyde argued with Woody, but silently John and Edwina stood together, hearts beating in rhythm.

Reluctantly Edwina released his neck, and his arms relaxed. He held her out a little distance from him. His intense dark eyes hit a responsive chord in her insides.

"You sure you're all right?"

"I … I … think so."

He snuggled her close again and placed his lips tenderly on hers. When he lifted them, he whispered, "I love you, Edwina. I'm so glad you're safe."

Did he actually mean what he said? She smiled and rested her head on his shoulder. "Thank God. I'm so glad you found us."

A chuckle rolled out of Wellington. "I heard what you told Clyde. Does all this smooching mean the wedding with him is off?"

John raised an eyebrow, and his sheepish smile sent a thrill through her. "You bet it does."

Edwina's lips formed an O, and her face heated.

John approached the men settling Clyde on his horse, taking the reins in their hands so Woody could lead him. "Thank you,

Woody, Wellington, and all you in the posse, for coming to help. Keep this fellow locked up for a long time."

Holding her hand, John led Edwina to his horse. "Hope you don't mind riding double. Guess we need to go to your house first."

Edwina stopped and looked up at him and nodded, remembering Clyde bonking her on the head so she'd hold still. "Are you going to hug me, or am I going to hug you?"

John laughed. "This is my chance. You can hug me."

He lifted her behind the saddle, and then boot into the stirrup, slid in front of her.

She leaned her head on his back, wrapped arms around him, and settled for a great ride.

55

Valerie turned to Archibald. "Yes."

His eyes grew huge. "Yes?"

She nodded. "We're a team. We belong together, and I love you for who you are. I enjoy seeing you reach out to hurting people. I know you love Christian, and I saw that in your actions even when he limped and could barely walk. Even more, I feel your love for me, and yet I feel your great respect."

She rubbed her thumb against his large palm. "I've been attracted to John Parks, but what we have, Archie, goes much deeper." She kissed his cheek. "I need to find a way to tell him."

Archibald let out a whoop. "You mean it? After all these years you'll be my wife?" He grabbed her tight and found her lips.

Her heart thumped wildly as he held her close. "How about we plan a simple ceremony unless you want a big blowout? If we go simple, we could get married in a week or two. But I would at least like to have time to connect with John."

Archibald hugged her and planted another kiss on her lips. "Maybe you could tell him on the phone. He has a phone, doesn't he?"

"Yes," Valerie breathed, her heart still thumping. "But he's on a party line, and some of those people talk for hours and listen in on other conversations."

"Call him late at night. Maybe those eavesdroppers will be in bed by then."

Archibald rushed over and lifted Christian from the rocking horse. "Hey, boy, I'm going to be your daddy!" He hugged him tight. "But we have a picnic lunch to eat."

Valerie enjoyed the beautiful countryside as they sat and ate. Christian nibbled at his food on the run between collecting sticks, leaves, rocks, and even a grasshopper. But he ate most of his sandwich and his fruit in between, as Valerie took a washcloth to his hands.

"I still have things to do before we meet with the editorial board." Archie picked up the plates and leftovers from the picnic.

Valerie folded the blanket they sat on. "A list of things is waiting for me at home, too." Before long they headed back to town. Valerie leaned on Archie while Christian snoozed in her arms.

The next morning, they picked Jimmy up at his home. His chubby wife, a bun sitting snuggly at the back of her neck, glowed.

"Thank you for helping God work a miracle for Jimmy and me," Mrs. Cook purred.

"You're welcome," Archie and Valerie said at the same time.

"Getting you out is one of the most satisfying experiences of my life," Archibald added, a well-cared-for, toothy smile glowing on his face. "Just wish we could have saved little Pete."

Archie rolled Jim out to the carriage, settled him in the back seat, and tucked the wheelchair in the boot.

Next, they drove to the boarding house to pick up Dillon Haskill. Again, Valerie barely recognized Dillon, and she mentally lectured herself to keep from itching all over at the sight of him. Oh, how much better he smelled!

When they headed for the city, a question hit her. "Who all is on the editorial board, Archie?"

He winked, and then bent toward her. "Let's see … it will be the bigwigs. The publisher, the general manager, the executive editor, the managing editor, a couple of city editors, and probably a couple of reporters. I heard the mayor invited himself, and the publisher agreed."

Valerie stared into his eyes. "You know my father is coming? He called the publisher for permission."

"Yes. He told me at the office. I imagine he'll be a blessing."

Acid dumped into Valerie's stomach and rose to her throat. Would the editorial board be as hostile as the superintendent and the asylum physician?

The newspaper headline and story ran through her mind. She hoped the reporter, Bertrand Petric, wouldn't be there, but she knew he would be. Could she maintain a professional, Christian attitude with him in the room?

How'd he feel about Pete being killed?

Archie patted her leg as he drove the pony. "Don't fret. We only need to state the facts, as we did in court, but now with Pete gone, we have even more to prove for others like him. Don't forget. The Lord has a plan, and he's been directing our footsteps, as well as those of our friends."

A fire lit in Archie's eyes as he lifted her chin. "God is with us!"

A similar fire ignited in Valerie's chest and warmed her all over. "Yes!"

They'd arrived, and soon a secretary seated the smiling group around a large conference table with padded, tufted burgundy chairs.

"I'm Bertrand Jordan, the executive editor." The dark-haired man shook each of their hands, his bushy mustache shadowing his lips. One by one, the executives introduced themselves, and then sat on the other side of the table and discussed the weather, noting it was the first day of summer.

Petric entered, papers and pen in his hand. He said nothing but frowned at each person across from him. Another reporter, Tony Valdez, walked in with him. He set his pen and papers on the table and reached across to shake hands. "Glad to meet all of you. Archie, you and I go back a long way, and you too, Mr. Van Meter." He brightened. "And you, Valerie! So nice to see you. You're as beautiful as ever."

Valerie's face heated. "Thank you, Tony. Good to see you, too, and to know you're doing well. It's been a long time since our school days."

When the mayor sat, his eyes drifted over the guests. He blinked at the publisher. "Where are the imbeciles?"

Archie glanced at Dillon, who sat calm, his dark hair in place, and nodded. Dillon stood, his new suit flattering his thin body.

"I am Dillon Haskill. Archibald asked me to speak first. I lived at the asylum four years after I had one seizure. The seizure occurred at the State Fair when I was thrown during a bronc-riding event, and my head hit a fence post. The dignitaries there believed I had a demon and insisted I am insane. Mayor, you might have been there."

Dillon turned to Petric. "I think you heard at the hearing that I am a physician. I studied two years at Harvard Medical School and then worked with Dr. Bonaparte Biglio a year before opening my practice as a physician where I worked until the accident."

Dillon expounded on conditions at the asylum and then shared Hippocrates' theory about seizures. Then he answered questions.

Taking a deep breath, he added, "I would have liked for you to meet Pete, a wonderful person who had a lower than normal IQ, but a boy who might have been smarter than we are in some ways. People like that young man often are called Mongoloids, but the term's offensive. The correct definition is Down's syndrome. He could read. Professor Jimmy Cook here"—he gestured to Cook—"and I taught Pete to read words we wrote on the walls or whatever we could find because we weren't allowed books. He knew how to work his numbers, too. After our day in court, Pete was going to stay in a home dedicated to care for his kind, but Pete was sent back to the asylum for the night. As soon as he arrived in the men's ward, one of the violent patients killed him. Choked the boy to death because he thought the devil was in him."

Dillon's voice cracked as he struggled for self-control.

The publisher raised his brow at the executive editor, apparently wondering what he thought.

Dillon exhaled. "A home in town had agreed to take Pete. Ferdinand Ferguson and his wife have a child with Down's living with them who is about Pete's age. They also have an older daughter with Down's and two other Down's syndrome women who live with them and cook and help around the house.

"If Pete were here, he would be thrilled to read for you, but as we said, he was murdered. Hopefully, we can bring another released Down's child to show you some day. Pete could have read you the story of Daniel and the lions."

The publisher reached across the table to Dillon. "I'm so sorry."

"Thanks." Dillon nodded. "We'll never forget Pete. We'll work harder than ever to free people unfairly held in the asylum and get medical care for those who desperately need it."

He motioned to the man in the wheelchair. "This is Jim Cook. I'll let him tell you his story himself."

Jim told about the accident, his injury, and the horrible years at the asylum, and then discussed his teaching career, awards, and the job he might get back.

Valerie stood and reintroduced herself. "You should know Mr. Forsythe and I were infected by body and hair lice each time we ventured to the asylum to help these people. The patients need proper food, proper care, and accurate diagnoses. They live with mice, rats, cockroaches, and bedbugs. Their chamber pots almost run over before anyone empties them."

She took a deep breath to clear the pictures threatening to gag her. "The folks living there are not animals." She raised her voice. "Most patients probably can't get out. As Dr. Haskill said, something is physically wrong with some people's brains, and a few might be demon-possessed."

She faced Dillon. "How did you explain that, Dillon, since you're the son of a preacher?"

Dillon smiled. "Mental illness is a physical disease caused by an upset in brain chemicals, often called humors. Sometimes other factors compound this, too. Demon possession is a spiritual problem. But don't forget, by the list the judge and I read, too many are misdiagnosed. They need help, too."

Archibald placed a stack of papers on the center of the table. "The judge issued some orders, and now I have a few more copies of their list of diagnoses."

Valerie couldn't resist speaking. "If you do another story about the asylum, I suggest you interview the superintendent about Pete's death, and why they bury patients who die there in unmarked graves."

They dismissed, shook hands, and received a few solemn responses, but Valerie could see most in the room eyed the former patients with suspicion.

As they left the newspaper office, Valerie's father put his arm around her as they walked out in the sunshine.

"You and Archibald did a great job there. Marvelous evidence for the patients' release. Good work letting them present their case."

He kissed her cheek. "So sorry Pete was killed."

"We have no idea where it all will end." Valerie and Archie linked hands.

Her father's eyes rested on the hands. "Archibald, why don't you come to our house tonight for supper?"

That night Valerie's pleased mother watched their cook, Hilda, slide the silver platter of pork chops on the Van Meters' linen-covered table with other bowls and platters overflowing with food. Blue and white china glistened beneath the huge chandelier's light.

A maid stood nearby while the group settled in their places. Christian, his plump legs wiggling in the wooden high chair, banged a spoon on his metal plate.

Since his injury, Valerie insisted the boy be at the table and now lay her hand on his dimpled one to stop the racket. Her finger rested against her lips as she smiled. "It's time to pray."

She folded her hands into a praying position. With a giggle on his wet pink lips, Christian squished his hands together like Mom's.

The tyke turned to Archie, on his other side. Archie quickly clutched his hands into a praying position. "Got it. I'm ready."

In a sweet voice, Christian repeated grace after his mother.

Mr. Van Meter cleared his throat. He looked at Christian, and then taking the hand of his wife, he bowed his head again. "Thank you, Lord, for our grandson, Christian. Thank you, God, for the food, for each person around this table. Thank you for our wonderful daughter and this man who defended and helped two desperate people obtain release from the asylum. I pray you'll continue to comfort Dillon's and their hearts as they mourn the loss of Pete. Lord, keep Archibald and Valerie in your loving care and direct their footsteps, as we know you do. Amen."

After dinner, Valerie, Archibald, and her parents gathered in the parlor for coffee.

A smile twitched Mr. Van Meter's face. "Archibald, I think you have something to tell me."

Archibald's jaw dropped. Valerie's stomach convulsed as she realized how close she sat to Archie. He scratched his head and cast a sheepish grin at her father. "Did Valerie tell you?"

Van Meter's smile deepened. "We see it in your eyes. Mother and I know something happened between you two."

"Whoa." Archie's gaze sought refuge on the ceiling. "I intended to first ask to court your daughter, but we've known each other a long time, worked together as a team, and encouraged each other. That's more important than courting."

Valerie let out her breath and leaned toward her father, placing her hand on his knee. "Last night he took me out in the country and showed me his beautiful new house."

Archie laughed a less-than-confident chuckle. "I did." His warm smile enveloped Valerie. "I told her I built the house for her, but if she doesn't want to marry me, I'd look for another godly woman to live there with me."

Valerie pretended to scowl. "He told me I had to choose between him and 'the other guy'—right then."

Archie nodded his head and smiled. "And I was serious."

Valerie took his hand and peered into his face. "I said yes."

Mrs. Van Meter clapped her hands. "Oh, my."

"And that's not all." Archie clasped both Valerie's hands in his. "I'm hoping to get married in two weeks. When the house is completed."

"Wonderful." Van Meter pushed from his seat, walked over, and shook Archie's hand, and then hugged his daughter.

"Two weeks!" Mrs. Van Meter gasped. "Two weeks? We can't even make a reservation at the church in two weeks."

Valerie laughed. "Actually, we have no idea if we can get it done in two weeks, but it sounds fine with me. I think The Palace Gardens would be a good place for a wedding, and we'll schedule on a day and time Pastor is free."

"Yes. Yes. Wonderful setting." Her mother's lips pinched tight, and brow scrunched, eyes alight with plans. "But what will you wear?"

Valerie tipped her head. "I think our dressmaker could make a simple creamy white dress and veil attached to a hat in no time if we'd ask. We could pay her extra for giving it priority."

Her mother glowed. "We'll ask for a luxurious satin, embroidery, and pearl swirls."

"Sounds wonderful."

The woman pranced over and folded her arm around Archie. "I've wanted you as a son for years. I loved Valerie's first husband, too, but you have made us so happy."

"So we'll plan on two weeks?" Van Meter pulled Archibald into his embrace and slapped him on the back, reached for his daughter, and Mrs. Van Meter stepped into the circle.

Van Meter raised his head toward heaven. "Lord, I ask for your blessing on this couple. May your love entwine with theirs and continue to lead and direct their footsteps, as you promised to do for the righteous if they would build their house on the rock Christ Jesus."

The next morning, the front page's banner headline read: "An investigation into the state insane asylum launched by the governor."

The most encouraging section of the following story said the state would no longer house Down's syndrome patients in the general adult psychiatric ward. In addition, the state was in the process of purchasing a section of land where light-security patients could grow their own fresh food.

"Wonderful," Archibald remarked as he plopped the news on Valerie's desk. "But what it really means is that reporter, Franklin Bertrand Petric, will be nipping at our heels all the time."

ADA BROWNELL

56

The sheriff and the posse left, leading a horse with a defiant Clyde handcuffed and in the saddle. John realized Clyde came close to leaving the farm with his body thrown over the animal and covered with a blanket. *Thank God I didn't have to shoot him.*

When they reached her ranch, John tenderly lifted Ed off the horse and kept her in his arms, kissing her again on the forehead. Then he dropped.

Edwina gasped. "Are you all right?"

He gazed up at her, resting on one knee. "Never better. But I'd like to ask you a question. Will you marry me?"

"Yes, but—"

"But what?"

"It's not so easy."

"Why?"

"Well, for one thing, you have a commitment to Valerie Mac-Dougal."

John shut his eyes, rubbed his forehead, and took a deep breath. "No."

"No? What do you mean?"

"I didn't ask her to marry me. We wrote and seemed to have an understanding between us, but truth is, I'm in love with you. I tried not to. I wanted to love Valerie. I knew you loved me, and all of a sudden when ol' Clyde kidnapped you, I discovered I can't do without you. I can do without Valerie. I've been doing it. She's a wonderful woman, but we aren't soul mates. God made the two of us to be together. I'm sure of it."

"But what am I going to do with my daddy? Bellea isn't ready to make her own living yet. Abe and Polly live with you. That's another reason why it won't be easy."

John stood, towering over her petite body, while her face tipped up to him, blue eyes squinting in the sun.

He took her by the shoulders. "If God made us to be together, he'll show us how. I already planned on building Abe and Polly a house, even though as long as they want to do it, Polly will help in my house and Abe will work on the ranch."

Edwina shook her head. "But we have so many responsibilities. If only our ranch land connected."

John leaned down and kissed her again. "Let's go inside. I need to ask your papa about courting you and tell him we're going to get hitched."

Edwina didn't move. "Don't you think you better do something about Valerie first?"

"Nope. Your papa doesn't even know we found you and what happened. We need to tell him, and I suppose I should confess we've been smooching all morning—even in front of the sheriff, Wellington, and the rest of the posse."

Edwina sucked in her breath and covered her mouth with her hand. "Whew. I forgot. I'll bet they're telling all over town how I hung on to you."

A chuckle rumbled out of John. "Who cares? I liked it. Perhaps that's what made me take the leap."

"Leap? Are you saying I initiated—well!" she huffed and stomped off toward the house.

He grinned and chased after her. "After that, I couldn't help myself." He snagged her by the hand. "Come on. Let's go tell everybody."

She stomped her foot. "Not until you say you're sorry for saying I made you do it. Otherwise, ride off in the sunset, and I'll tell them about Clyde Merriweather and not say a word about you."

"Come on, girl. I didn't mean anything by it. The leap was my way of admitting my love." He squinted his eyes. "That was hard for me to do after us being at war with each other so many years. But I think I knew all the time you were my sweetheart."

"Really?" she said.

He gripped her hand and brought her closer. "Really."

They walked in the back door and into the kitchen holding hands. Edwina's father stood up in the middle of the floor, crutches under his arms.

"Papa!" she cried.

He paled and wobbled. Bellea reached to steady him. "Edwina! They found you. You're all right. Praise God!"

Bellea led Paul Jorgenson back to the wheelchair, and he plunked down, hard.

Edwina burst into sobs and fell at his feet. "Oh, Papa," she wept. "I didn't know you can walk with crutches."

He patted her on the back. "That's not important. What's important is you're safe."

John stepped forward. "We found her in the Swensons' packing shed tied to a leg of the conveyor belt."

"It was Clyde Merriweather, Papa. He grabbed me in the yard where he was peeping, hit me on the head, and knocked me out. Then he threw me on his horse and promised to make me marry him."

"Clyde?" Paul's jaw dropped. "Oh, Lord, help us."

John planted his hands on his hips. "Clyde had on the boots we've been trying to find."

Bellea shook her head over and over. "He was the peeper. Horrible." She wiggled her finger at Edwina. "Let me look at your head." She pointed to a kitchen chair. "Sit."

John nudged Edwina on the back.

With nimble fingers, Bellea parted Ed's hair in several places where it was easy to see where her scalp had bled.

"Ow!" Ed yelped.

Bellea frowned, standing on her tiptoes for a better look. "She has a big lump and blood in her hair. After she rests, I'll help her wash her hair and put something healing on the place."

"Wonderful," Paul said. "She should get some rest. She's been through a lot and probably hasn't had any sleep."

Weariness drained the energy out of John, and he stood there forgetting he'd been up all night. But he needed to jump into the conversation. He took Edwina's hand, helped to her feet, and draped his arm around her. "Paul, I suppose I should ask if we could find somewhere to talk privately, but I don't think it will hurt the girls to hear this conversation. We have an announcement to make."

Paul Jorgenson raised his eyebrows. "Yes?"

John swallowed. His tongue felt too thick to form words. "I–I want to court your daughter." Then he dumped all the words at once. "I asked her to marry me, and she said yes!"

Edwina's arm squeezed John. His eyes caught hers, and she nodded furiously. "But, Papa, I don't want to go off and leave you. You can live with us, and I'll still take care of you."

"When you planning on doing this?"

John's knees turned to jelly. "We don't know, sir. But we've been kissing. We smooched a lot in front of Sheriff Woody and Wellington when I finally got your daughter untied and safe in my arms. I thought I might have to shoot Clyde because he didn't give her up easily. People will talk, not about Clyde being arrested for kidnapping and murder, but because…"

Edwina's face pinked. "It wasn't all John's fault. When I was free, and Clyde was in handcuffs, I grabbed this sweet man and never wanted to let him go. We've talked. We're soul mates, and we need each other. I would get married tomorrow if we could."

John blew his breath into his cheeks while he fought dizziness and prayed for wisdom and strength. "I'm thinking at least six months. I need to build Polly and Abe a house first, although my house has four bedrooms. Then we could give you the downstairs bedroom."

Paul Jorgenson chuckled.

Rather strange.

"Tell you what, John." Paul wheeled his chair closer. "I give you permission to court my daughter and marry her whenever you are ready."

He rolled his wheelchair over and took Bellea's hand. "We've been wondering how to tell you we're getting hitched."

Edwina clapped her hands over her face and shut her eyes. "Papa! I knew something was going on, but I can't believe it."

Her father smiled. "I told you I've discovered I have a lot of life yet to live. I'm only forty-two years old. If I can get around on crutches, I can run this ranch, and Bellea will help me do it. I actually walked to the barn the other day."

"Amazing." Edwina stood there in shock.

A pleased expression and slight smile crinkled Bellea's face. "I've been helping him exercise almost since the first day I came here. He asked, and I volunteered. You were away a lot, and over these few months, we've fallen in love."

"I'm in love with both Bellea and David," Paul explained.

Edwina smiled. "I knew you love that fellow. He's such a sweetie. So I'll have a brother."

"Sure," Bellea said, and maturity blossomed on the young woman's face. "Paul plans to refurbish the north side porch, and I'll open a beauty parlor there."

"How perfect." Edwina seemed to accept it all. "It has a private entrance."

"When are you two going to tie the knot?" An idea popped into John's head. "We could build a ramp and a wood sidewalk from here to the corral and to the barn. Then if you needed to use your wheelchair to get around, you could go all the way in your chair. Might be easier to use crutches on, too."

Bellea raised her hand. "Remember how I've been taking Paul into town in the buggy to see the doctor? Dr. Billings believes Paul will be able to walk soon on his own if he keeps up the exercise."

"But," Paul interrupted, "we want to get married the first of next month, a simple ceremony with a few guests and the pastor here at home."

"Wow." That's all John could say as Edwina leaned on him.

Paul reached for Bellea. "Edwina, we need to hire another hand to help around here. Max Mosely's brother needs a job, and he lives near here. Max is becoming the best hand we've ever had."

Disappointment played on Edwina's face. "Does… does … that mean you're taking over the ranch?"

57

John started trying to place a call at five a.m. He waited thirty minutes before he got a call through from Peachville, Colorado, to Boston on the party line.

A woman's voice answered.

"May I speak to Valerie, please?"

"It will be a moment."

While he waited, all jittery, he blew out his breath, sucked it in, and blew it out again. What was he going to say? He should have written something down so he wouldn't make a fool of himself.

"Hello?"

His heart palpitated. Hearing her voice was great despite the circumstances. *Lord, give me the words.*

"Valerie? It's John here. I hope this is a good time to phone you. We have problems here getting through on the party line. But I need to talk to you."

"John! I'm so glad you called. Oh, John, I need to talk to you, too. It's really important."

Her voice caught, hinting at a serious problem.

"Are you all right? Has something happened?" Confusion messed with his brain. After being ready to tell her about Edwina, if someone died or a tragedy had occurred, how could he tell her?

"I tried to write to you." Her words wobbled. "I couldn't do it."

"What's wrong? Is Christian all right?"

"Oh yes!" Excitement crept into her tones now. "He's almost able to walk without a limp."

"Well, praise the Lord." He drew a deep breath. "Valerie, I'm going to have to spit out why I called, and then you can tell me what happened. As much as I am fond of you and appreciate the unique person you are, I've made a commitment. I asked Edwina Jorgenson to marry me. I had no idea I am in love with her from my head to my toes until she was kidnapped yesterday. It's a long story. But I need to get that out before we go any further. I intended to marry you. My feelings for Edwina hid a long time, and I finally acknowledged I'm in love with her."

A feminine sigh flowed through the line from Boston. "Oh, John. You are so sweet! I've been trying to work up my nerve to call and tell you I've accepted a marriage proposal from my father's law partner, Archie Forsythe. We've worked together on a case and discovered we …" She choked up. "We need each other!"

A soft chuckle bubbled out of John's mouth. "I understand. Edwina and I told each other we're soul mates, and we can't live without each other, either."

A musical laugh came over the line. "You know about the Scripture that says the Lord directs our steps? Isn't this amazing? I feared contacting you. I didn't want to hurt you, especially because I like you so much, and the Lord worked in your life at the same time. I wanted to tell you before this, but I couldn't figure out how to do it. I couldn't write a letter to tell you and start it out 'Dear John.'"

He couldn't keep the bellowing laughter from erupting. "That's so funny. I think both of us will tell our children and grandchildren about it. You know, Valerie, you're as amazing as I thought you are, but God didn't make us for each other."

"Thank you. You're right, John. Sometime, you and Edwina should come to Boston and see Archie and me. Can you believe we're going to live in the country?"

"Marvelous. You and Archibald are welcome at our house any time. You know where we live."

"I sure do. I know we'll be back to Colorado because I need to visit Christian's grave now and then."

"When is your wedding date, Valerie?"

"July fifteenth. We're going to be married in The Palace Gardens."

"Nice. We are going to wait six months or a year. I'm going to build Abe and Polly a house, and all the plans aren't quite made yet for the Jorgensons' horse ranch. Congratulations, Valerie."

"Congratulations to you and Edwina, John. Send us a wedding invitation and maybe we can come."

"That's the way we should do it," he added. "We're not saying goodbye."

"No, this is not goodbye. We're still friends."

Valerie shared a little information about the family, and John gave her a snippet summary about Clyde Merriweather's evils. He breathed a sigh of relief when he put the receiver down.

Stuart stood close by listening to John's side of the conversation, a smile twitching on his lips. Polly walked into the room, drying her hands on a tea towel. "What's going on? I heard our names."

Voices in the yard drew John to the window. Abe walked out of the outhouse pulling his overall suspenders over his shoulders, looking at the peddler's wagon parked in the yard with a couple of rocking chairs tied on top.

"My new mama and daddy are back!" Stuart ran for the back door, slamming it hard behind him.

ADA BROWNELL

EPILOGUE

August 25, 1910, arrived with John supervising a crew of peach pickers and packers.

"This is the best crop peach growers have had in recent years," he shared with Paul Jorgenson. "Too many bad years in a row caused a good market. Evidently people everywhere are hungry for peaches."

Paul stood nearby, crutches under his arms. Both hands free, he pulled the peel from a big yellow peach blushed red on the cheeks. He took a bite, and juice dribbled down the edges of his mouth. "Ah. Wonderful."

He yanked a big blue and white handkerchief from his pocket to wipe his face. "Nothing better than a tree-ripened peach."

Bellea walked up behind him, took one crutch, and put an arm around her husband's waist. "You hungry already? You had a big breakfast."

Paul grunted as he chewed. "Aw, wifey. I can eat a ripe peach any time. John, how many Arabian horses do you have now?"

"With that new colt, I only have the three. I hope to have at least twenty for breeding."

"Sounds wonderful. How do Polly and Abe like their new house?"

"They're happy as two crickets on a summer night. You probably heard their son is back and working for us. We're building a house for his family, too."

Paul threw the peach pit toward the fence. Using one crutch, he walked to the nearby well and pumped it. Then he washed and wiped his hands. "Max's brother is really a big help, but I'd hoped to hire Abe's son myself. I heard he knows a lot about horses."

"How can he help it, growing up with a father like Abe?"

Paul scratched the side of his nose. "With Max having vet experience and help from his brother, I'm thinking of expanding more."

John nodded toward the pigpen. "Those pigs sure helped me to get on my feet financially. Selling the stallion helped, too. But these peaches are what's putting money in the bank."

"You shipping out peaches on those refrigerated rail cars?"

"Yes. It was quite a challenge. Did you know they cut ice from lakes in the high country during the winter and bring it to icehouses in larger cities? Then they pack it in refillable bins in the top of ventilated boxcars. As the air cools and becomes heavier, it drops down where food is stored, forcing warmer lighter air out through the ventilators. That keeps the food compartment cold. They've been moving meat by rail for years that way."

"Interesting." Paul walked away from the pump. "Have you regretted selling the black stallion?"

"I think it was a good decision. I gave Stuart one of the stallion's offspring, and he's more handsome than his sire." John patted Paul on the back. "I need to get to work. Too bad Ed had to go into town for another wedding dress fitting. Are you going to walk down the aisle next week without crutches?"

Paul peered into the distance. "I was going to try it, but my wifey says I can't risk falling. I'll be blessed to walk beside Ed and give her away on my crutches."

Bellea hugged Paul's waist, holding a squirming David while she talked. "Paul's almost strong enough to walk without the crutches," she bragged. "By Christmas, I think they'll be a thing of the past."

Paul beamed, bent, and kissed her on the cheek. He turned to John. "We best be going home, Bellea. Maybe John can help you get our three bushels of peaches."

Bellea smiled. "John already put them in the wagon."

Her husband put his crutches in, and then slid his backside onto the wagon bed. He pulled his body up with his hands and perched in the driver's seat. Bellea went around to the other side, plunked David on the bench beside Paul, and climbed in herself. Paul shook his head. "I believe soon I'll be helping Bellea and David into these contraptions."

Bellea and Paul both beamed.

The next Friday evening, John headed for the church in a new buggy. Abe, Polly, Stuart, Jenny, and William followed in the wagon. Jenny held John's handsome new nephew, little Isaac O'Casey.

Jenny and her family had arrived Thursday morning on the train. As happy as he was to see his sister, William, Stuart, and the new baby, John could only think about his bride.

Buggies and wagons with harnessed horses already waited beside the church. Several saddled mounts tethered to hitching posts and nearby trees.

The pastor had instructed John to enter the side door to the church office. Pastor Brandt sat in the desk chair, head bowed. He lifted his head and smiled. "Ready?"

Not one doubt jiggled around in John's head. "Yes! Abe is my best man. My brother-in-law, William O'Casey arrived yesterday, and he's an usher. Stuart is back. He'll stand beside Abe. William will carry the ring."

The pastor smiled. "Wonderful. I think you and Edwina are a great match, but I doubted you'd ever get around to getting hitched."

John chuckled. "She began making eyes at me when I hit the age of hating girls. Scared me to death. One Sunday I sat down on the end of an empty pew, and she sat down on the other end. My mother used to say I shot up out of the pew like I'd sat on a hot stove. I walked around to the far corner and found another place to sit. Mom must be looking down from heaven today laughing."

"With your father joining in."

"Took me a long while to realize I love Edwina. I should have been angry at her when Clyde kidnapped her. I told her to go in the house and stay there. But no. She saw Max snoozing instead of watching and took everything into her own hands."

Pastor patted John's shoulder. "Since the sheriff and Wellington overheard Clyde's murder confession, all things worked together for good for those who love the Lord, as the Bible says."

John nodded. "Yes. Isn't God amazing?"

"You said it, brother."

Thirty minutes later, the men lined up in front of the church, and Edwina's little second cousin, Tessie, dressed in pink lacy frills dropped rose petals down the church aisle. Bellea and Annamarie, Ed's feisty neighbor who Stu had played checkers with, followed. Jenny, John's sister, strolled down the aisle as Edwina's matron of honor.

Polly held Jenny's sleeping baby.

The old organ wheezed, "Here Comes the Bride." Paul Jorgenson walked down the aisle while Edwina hung onto his arm, the crutches almost moving on their own under Paul's armpits.

The closer Edwina came down the aisle, the harder John's heart thumped. Edwina's big blue eyes reflected the seriousness of the moment as she looked up at him.

The two of them had discussed their vows on Wednesday, held hands, and prayed for God's blessings. Although madly in love, they agreed they needed to work on not getting upset when they had a difference of opinion.

When he repeated his vows before God, Edwina, and the congregation, a lump came into his throat. A Scripture the pastor said stuck in his mind: *Husbands ought to love their wives as their own bodies.*

Then spiritual strength surged through John as they knelt for communion.

As soon Pastor Brandt pronounced them husband and wife, he added, "You may kiss the bride."

John squeezed his bride close to him, squishing the elegant gown, and knew the joy he felt jolted into her as well. She pressed on the back of his head so that it came back down, and she kissed him back. They became one! Hearts linked forever.

Guests packed into the church clapped and cheered. John reached for her hand, and they sprinted down the aisle and out the door.

John's home had never been so crowded since he'd owned it, as guests piled gifts on the dining room table and found places to sit.

Darkness crowded in long before the two of them said goodbye to guests, family, and special people like Abe and Polly.

The couple escaped a shivaree, but when they climbed into the buggy to leave John noticed a long string of tin cans tied to the back.

"We'll be back in about five days," John reminded Abe. "We're honeymooning in Glenwood Springs."

He clucked to the horse and pointed the buggy toward their honeymoon cottage, the tin cans following and ringing out the message of joy for all to hear.

The End

About the Author

When Ada Brownell sat down to write *The Peach Blossom Rancher*, she drew from her experiences growing up in Colorado's Peach Country, picking peaches and working in a packing shed.

In addition, she uses some of what she learned about mental illness covering the Colorado Mental Health Institute at Pueblo on her beat as a journalist for *The Pueblo Chieftain*. In her work, she received a list from the Board of Lunacy Commissioners showing supposed cause of insanity of patients admitted in 1899-1900 and 1909-1910. She uses part of that list in this book and used that information in developing some of the characters. However, in this book the mental hospital is in Boston, and everything about the asylum is fiction. The Boston asylum began innovative things with patients there to help in their recovery, treatment and well-being by adding gardening as an activity for some housed there in the early years.

The Colorado Mental Health Institute at Pueblo eventually became one of the best treatment centers in the nation for the mentally ill.

A few of the characters in *Peach Blossom Rancher* appeared in *The Lady Fugitive*, the first novel in the *Peaches and Dreams* historical series. Among these characters are John Lincoln Parks, Jenny's brother, and Stuart O'Casey, an orphan adopted by Jenny and her husband, William.

Ada writes with Stick-to-Your-Soul Encouragement. She is the author of six other books, about 350 stories and articles in Christian publications, and she spent a large chunk of her life as a reporter, mostly for *The Pueblo Chieftain*.

Links:
http://www.amazon.com/dp/1489558284
http://www.amazon.com/-/e/B001KJ2C06

iTunes:
http://ow.ly/TY6uO

Amazon Ada Brownell author page:
https://www.amazon.com/author/adabrownell

Facebook:
https://www.facebook.com/#!/AdaBrownellWritingMinistries

Twitter:
@AdaBrownell

Goodreads:
https://www.goodreads.com/author/show/1654534.Ada_Brownell

Blog:
http://inkfromanearthenvessel.blogspot.com

Barnesandnoble.com
http://ow.ly/PUWHO

To receive her newsletter, contact her at:
galwriter777@gmail.com

The Lady Fugitive
By Ada Brownell

How does a respected elocutionist become a face on a wanted poster?

Jenny Louise Parks escapes from the coal bin, and her abusive uncle offers a handsome reward for her return. Because he is a judge, he will find her, or he won't inherit her parents' ranch.

Determination to remain free grips Jenny, especially after she meets William and there's a hint of romance. But while peddling household goods and showing one of the first Passion of the Christ moving pictures, he discovers his father's brutal murder.

Will Jenny avoid the bounty hunters? Can she forgive the person who turns her in?

2015 Laurel Award Runner-up

#Review: "*The Lady Fugitive.* You'll laugh, bite your nails, wish you had a gun to help."

Available in paperback or for Kindle. http://ow.ly/QzlIP

Peach Blossom Rancher is the sequel to *The Lady Fugitive: Book One* of Ada Brownell's *Peaches and Dreams* series

www.ingramcontent.com/pod-product-compliance
Ingram Content Group UK Ltd.
Pitfield, Milton Keynes, MK11 3LW, UK
UKHW021315180426
11947UKWH00015B/1235